THE HONOURS

Tim Clare is a writer, poet and musician. He won Best Biography/Memoir at the East Anglian Book Awards for his first book, *We Can't All Be Astronauts*, while his fiction debut, *The Honours*, was longlisted for the Desmond Elliott Prize. He has performed his work at festivals and clubs across the world, on TV and radio. Tim has also written for the *Guardian*, *The Times* and the *Big Issue*, and presents the fiction writing podcast *Death Of 1,000 Cuts*. He lives in Norwich.

@timclarepoet | timclarepoet.co.uk

'The comparisons that most readily spring to mind are the wildly eccentric and benevolent imaginations of Neil Gaiman and Terry Pratchett'
Guardian

'Riotously entertaining'
Sunday Express

'A darkly compelling read'
Financial T...

'Irresisti...
Huffington...

'It is rare to find such a riveting, fantastical adventure matched by such poetic flair'
Matt Haig

THE
HONOURS

TIM CLARE

CANONGATE

For Omi

This paperback edition published in Great Britain,
the USA and Canada in 2020 by Canongate Books

First published in 2015 by Canongate Books Ltd,
14 High Street, Edinburgh EH1 1TE

Distributed in the USA by Publishers Group West
and in Canada by Publishers Group Canada

canongate.co.uk

1

British Library Cataloguing-in-Publication Data
A catalogue record for the book is available on
request from the British library

ISBN 978 1 78211 479 6

Typeset in Baskerville MT by Palimpsest Book Production Ltd,
Falkirk, Stirlingshire

Printed and bound in Great Britain by Clays Ltd, Elcograf S.p.A.

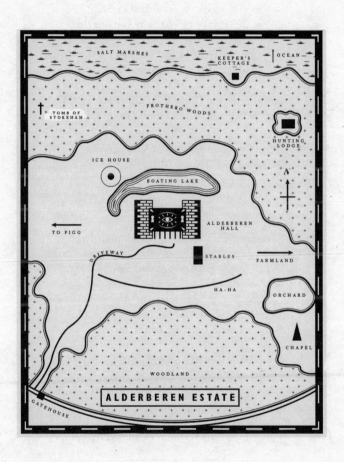

SALT MARSHES

KEEPER'S COTTAGE

OCEAN

TOMB OF STOKEHAM

PROTHERO WOODS

HUNTING LODGE

ICE HOUSE

BOATING LAKE

N

TO PIGG

ALDERBEREN HALL

DRIVEWAY

STABLES

FARMLAND

HA-HA

ORCHARD

CHAPEL

WOODLAND

ALDERBEREN ESTATE

GATEHOUSE

September 12th 1935

The girl with the gun crouched waiting. The dark shape hung over the belt of poplars, then banked, swooping out across the salt marsh. It was coming nearer.

She braced a knee against the wet wall of the trench. The monster pumped its black wings – ragged, impossible. Curls of samphire crunched beneath her elbow as she brought the gun to her cheek. The wind lifted old book smells off the mudflats. Kidney-shaped pools shone copper and gold.

She mouthed the old lesson like a spell, falling into Mr Garforth's quiet, steady rhythm.

To kill a bird, I must first ascertain its speed and trajectory. To do this, I follow it with the muzzle of the shotgun.

She tilted the barrels up and began tracking a spot a yard behind her target. She could hear the thing panting.

When I have ascertained its speed and trajectory, I bring the gun past smoothly.

Any longer and it would see her. Her index finger twitched over the two triggers, dithering between full and half choke. She held her breath and brought the gun up too fast – stopped, waited, let the muzzle fall back in behind her target. She counted to three, tried again. This time, she swung the gun in one clean movement.

If I miss the bird – if I miss – I will miss it in front.

She continued past what instinct told her was the sweet spot.

The gun kicked. A flock of brent geese took off in a rippling blast, their voices like starter motors. Dark bodies and white undertails confettied the air.

Delphine lowered the gun. She thumbed the locking lever and broke the barrel; the breech coughed a spent cartridge into the soft mud at her feet. She pressed her heel on the empty case until it sank. She reloaded.

The sky was red and empty. She hauled herself out of the trench.

On the edge of a small, crescent pool lay a smashed umbrella. As she got closer, it resolved into knuckled wings, cola-black fur, a sharp oval face like a weasel's. The creature was about three feet tall, its huge, shot-shredded wings veined and translucent like the membranes of a leaf. She prodded it with the shotgun. The clump of sedge at its cheek shivered.

She pressed the gun to its ribs and nudged it into the pool. Its huge wings settled across the surface. It floated; in the light of the setting sun, its fur blazed silver. She poked it in the belly; cloudy water puddled through the holes in its wings. The puddles began joining up and, bit by bit, the creature sank: its splayed ears, its closed eyes, the bright ring winking on its clenched finger.

Delphine gazed into the face of death and did not feel afraid. Maybe it was the after-effects of the tranquiliser; maybe it was the thought of her father, and the monsters waiting back at the Hall. The shotgun felt heavy and good.

She was going to kill them all.

Hidden amongst wind-hunched oaks was a cottage. Delphine rapped on the door with the curved iron tip of her crab hook.

'It's me.'

The sound of footsteps, a bolt being drawn. She waited, then pushed at the door.

The ceiling was low and sagged in the middle. Mr Garforth sat testing gin traps by lamplight.

'You're late,' he said. He was struggling to prise open a set of steel jaws. His fingers slipped; the trap cracked shut.

'There was a scout.'

Mr Garforth looked up. 'Were you spotted?'

'I killed him,' she said. 'It.'

He raised his wispy eyebrows. 'What range?'

'Sixty yards.' She caught his frown. 'Fifty. Forty. I hid the body.'

'Good girl.'

She set her gun down by the stove. 'What's for dinner?'

A spider was scuttling across the table. He slammed his palm on it, scooped it up and popped it into his mouth.

'You're not funny.'

He unfurled his fist, revealing the spider, unharmed. Delphine frowned to disguise a smile.

'In you get. While it's still warm.' He nodded at the tin bath by the open hearth. A change of clothes was drying on a chair. 'No sense rushing now. If we do this, we do it proper. I'll rustle up some grub.'

'And then?'

'And then it's time. If you still want to go.'

'I still want to go.'

'Well then.'

Delphine took two steps towards the bath, hesitated. Mr Garforth rolled his eyes. He shunted his chair round until he had his back to the fire.

Delphine lay in the bath with her head tipped back, listening to the water rumble and plop, and pretended she was being boiled alive. Her arms lolled over the sides, fingertips trailing on the cold tiles. Below the waterline, her ankles and buttocks throbbed.

'Excuse me.'

Mr Garforth walked to the fireplace, shielding his eyes. Delphine watched him unhook the cauldron lid and pull out a string bag full of steaming brains. He limped to the table and began slicing them into chunks. When he was done, he set a saucepan on the stove and heated a knob of butter. He added the brains, which sizzled and spat.

'Nearly ready.' He tapped an egg against the rim of the saucepan and cracked it one-handed into the mix, along with some parsley and a splash of milk.

Delphine got out of the bath. A scab on her knee hung open like a dead oyster, blood painting a zigzag down her shin. She put her finger in the blood then licked her finger. It tasted of money.

She took the towel and began with her hair, working outwards from the roots. Her skin prickled in the heat. Above the mantelpiece, a brace of rabbits hung from a nail. One looked like it was whispering a secret into the other's long ear. Beside the rabbits was a wooden cross, and beneath that, a carriage clock. The time was a quarter past seven.

She dried quickly. A salty, fatty aroma wafted from the stove and made her stomach belch. She pulled on her grey knickerbockers, her vest, her long blue woollen socks, then started brushing her smoky hair into some kind of shape. Her hands trembled. Each time the bristles snagged a knot, the tremor passed through damp strands to her scalp.

Mr Garforth set the table for dinner. He laid out knives and forks, a plate heaped with thick doorstops of brown toast, butter in a blue dish, salt and pepper, mugs of tea and, in the centre, the hot saucepan full of scrambled calf's brains. He slapped his hands together.

'Sit. Eat.'

Delphine pulled up a chair and buttered herself two slices of toast. Then she held her plate up while Mr Garforth spooned brains over the top. She waited until he was sitting. He picked up his fork.

'Aren't you going to say grace?' she said.

'Very well.' He bowed his head. Delphine went to close her eyes, but instead she watched him: the freckled nose against fingers pressed in prayer, the flaking, red skin on his scalp, the quiet motion of his lips.

'Dear Lord, we give thanks for the food you have provided for us. May it lend us strength.' The three creases on his forehead darkened. 'Give us help from trouble, for vain is the help of man. Through God we shall do valiantly: for He it is that shall tread down our enemies. Amen.'

He kept his head down, mouthed a silent addendum. His eyes opened.

'Go on, dig in before it gets cold.'

4

He was halfway through his second mouthful when he looked up at Delphine. Her cutlery lay either side of her plate.

'What's the matter?'

She wrinkled her nose. 'It looks like cauliflower.'

'Eat.'

Delphine sighed and began sawing at a corner of toast. Her belly felt tight and cold.

He said: 'We can't do this on an empty stomach.'

'Sorry.'

'There's still time to call it off.'

'No,' she said, then, setting her fists on the table: 'No. I'll kill whoever I have to.'

'Just stick to the plan.'

'I will.'

'Good.' He slurped his tea and reached for another slice of toast. She listened to the slop slop of his dentures as he ate.

'I know the answer to your riddle.'

'It's not a riddle.'

'Nothing,' she said. She watched his eyes for a reaction. 'The answer is: "nothing".'

Mr Garforth sucked his lips. He shook his head.

Delphine threw her hands up. 'Oh come on!'

Mr Garforth shrugged. 'Sorry.'

'Bugger.'

Mr Garforth gave her an odd look. She thought she saw the beginnings of a smile, then he coughed into his sleeve and it was gone.

'Help yourself to seconds,' he said. 'Who knows when we'll get the chance to sit like this again.'

'Not till the next world.'

'Eh?'

'Sorry.' Delphine felt her cheeks colour. 'It's what Daddy used to say. When something was very lovely. "Ah. Not till the next world, eh?"'

'Aha.' His shoulders relaxed, and his head fell into a steady nod. He smiled, and raised his mug. 'Well then. Till the next world.'

'Till the next world,' said Delphine, and gently touched her mug to his.

After they had eaten, Mr Garforth brewed more tea and they sat by the hearth to go over the plan one last time. He made her repeat things. The fire was white and tangerine. The heat made her cheeks glow. She could not concentrate. She had the oddest sensation that she was experiencing the cottage for the first time – that until that night she had never truly seen the pattern on its chipped brown floor tiles, nor smelt the sappy, mellow dampness beneath the woodsmoke. Her mouth was dry, and when she recited his instructions, the voice belonged to a calmer, tougher girl.

Presently, he peered at the clock on the mantelpiece. By flamelight, the loose, spotted skin around his neck looked like scales. He squinted.

'It says it's nearly eight,' said Delphine.

He curled his bottom lip. 'Oh.'

'It's time.'

Mr Garforth took the shotgun and wrapped it in a tea towel. She followed him into his workshop. He set the gun in a bench vice and began winding a handle. Wood shavings lay on the cement floor in stiff blond curls. The handle squeaked with each turn. Vice jaws bit into the towel. Mr Garforth pulled the towel back from the barrels like a barber-surgeon hiking up a patient's trouser leg. He picked up a hacksaw and rested the blade half an inch from the forestock.

'That's too much,' she said.

Mr Garforth started cutting. Steel fell in shining granules. He put a hand on the bench to steady himself. The left barrel dropped, clanging against the cement. The right barrel followed. Mr Garforth unwound the handle a little way. He picked up the shotgun, blew. The sawn barrels gleamed: a bull's snout.

'It's what you need,' he said.

They returned to the front room. She slipped a cloth bandolier diagonally over her shoulder like a sash. Mr Garforth handed her a carton of shells. While he sat wiping down the shotgun barrels with an oily rag, she took each shell from the carton, hefting the paper casing between thumb and forefinger, then slotted it into one of the pouches across her chest, pressing down the flat brass head with her thumb until it was snug. Her crab hook tucked into a long slip pocket on the back.

Mr Garforth looked her up and down, gave a snort of approval. He held out her gun.

'Shall we?'

She took it, held it, testing the new lightness. She nodded.

Mr Garforth picked up the oil lamp. He led her into the backroom, ducking under the lintel with exaggerated caution. They squeezed between packing crates, box traps, poisons, a nested stack of spun aluminium washing-up bowls, three fishing rods and a split cricket bat held together with soiled bandages. Beneath a small window with thick, greasy panes, a brass ring was set into the floor. He hooked it with the end of his stick and, grunting, raised a trapdoor.

The shaft fell away into blackness. The route down was a column of rusted stemples – thick iron bars hammered into rock at two-foot intervals, acting as a ladder. There was a smell like rotting fish.

She turned from the darkness to the old man.

'Well,' she said, 'goodbye.'

'Wait.' Mr Garforth set the lamp down on a crate and left the room. She heard clattering, then he returned with a leather satchel.

'What's in there?'

'Insurance.'

He lifted the heavy brown flap. In the satchel were three condensed milk cans. She took one out. It was surprisingly heavy. From the middle of the lid protruded a five-inch fuse.

'Are these . . . jam tins?'

'Guncotton surrounded by bits of old horseshoe. Mr Wightman supplied those – you can thank him one day.'

'Jesus.'

'Hey.' He jabbed a forefinger at her nose. 'Do *not* use these except as a last resort. That fuse is about five and a half seconds. Call it five to be sure.' The finger hovered. The nail was chipped and yellow, underscored with a sickle of dirt. 'Don't be in the same room when this goes off.'

'I know. I'm not stupid.'

7

He flashed her another look she could not read.

She placed the grenade back in the satchel. Mr Garforth fastened the hasp, then helped her sling the strap over her shoulder.

'Look at you. All grown up.'

'Look at you. All old.'

Mr Garforth half-opened his arms. Delphine looked at him. He let them drop to his sides.

'Remember: nobody has to die.'

'No. We all do.'

He took a deep breath. His shadow was an ogre against the brickwork.

'You sound like a soldier.'

'Thank you.'

'It wasn't a compliment.' He smacked his lips. 'Enough. Let's get this over with.'

Delphine turned her back to the trapdoor and knelt, dangling a leg until her foot found the first rung. The air in the shaft was colder than she remembered; beneath thick socks, her calves stiffened with gooseflesh. She gave Mr Garforth a last nod. Her head felt weight-less.

He narrowed his eyes. 'How long are the fuses?'

'Five and a half seconds. Five to be sure.'

The old gamekeeper nodded. She started her descent.

ACT ONE

December–June

To commence transit the student must fully immerse himself
in the black ocean. The sensation is not unlike drowning
while being burned alive: baptism and cremation.
Remember to remove false teeth.

– *Transportation And Its Practice*, A. Prentice

NINE MONTHS EARLIER

CHAPTER 1

THE FIRE SERMON

December 1934

Condensation streamed down the window of the third-class carriage. Delphine pressed her nose to the glass. Outside, the fields and hedgerows were blinding with snow. Amber fires burned in the eyes of lonely cottages. Her fingers closed round the crisp brown paper parcel in her lap.

Ever since she had seen the set of fine hog brushes in the art shop window, she had known they were the answer. Laid out in a case of polished mahogany, they were elegant and very, very expensive, exactly the kind of grown-up present a sophisticated daughter would give to her artist father. The same night, she had begun saving.

For weeks, she had dropped pennies into the sock that she kept wedged between her mattress and bedsprings, forswearing liquorice, sherbet, lemon bonbons, regarding the tuck shop with the calm, famished humility of Jesus refusing to turn stones to bread. She even sold the brooch her late grandmother had given her – an oval of pink jasper depicting winged cherubs beside a woman playing the harp – to Eleanor Wethercroft for a shilling. A fortnight before the end of term, she tipped out the sock to find a miserable six shillings and thruppence. That night she had lain awake, devastated. The next morning, a letter arrived from Mother. It explained that, instead of getting picked up by car, Delphine was to buy a ticket and catch the train home. With the letter was a postal order for a pound and twelve shillings.

The carriage was cramped and stuffy. On the seat opposite, a big crumpled man puffed at his cigar. He had the persecuted air of one who feels keenly the resentment of his fellow travellers, and resolves, by way of revenge, to justify it. The *Times* crossword lay folded on his knee. He alternated between jotting answers in pencil and breathing slow clouds of pungent yellow smoke. The young lady to his left tutted and sighed, a book* shuddering in her sheepskin-gloved hands.

Delphine pictured Daddy's delight when she stepped through the front door: his sleeves rolled up, his arms spread wide, ready for the crushing hug, the musk of oil paints and perspiration as he pressed her to his hard chest.

'Delphy! Oh, I've missed you. Oh, how I've *missed* you,' he would say, over and over in an ecstasy of love and repentance, and she would wriggle free and eye him with a sudden sternness, and he would look upon her and see, with a start, not the little girl sent tearfully away at the beginning of term, but a noble and self-possessed young adult.

Then she would climb the stairs two at a time, past the photograph of Grandnan and Grandpapa squinting baffled and austere in their thin gilt frame, across the landing to her bedroom. In a wicker basket on top of the toy chest waited Nelson, her teddy bear, and Hannibal, her stuffed elephant. During the long nights of her first term at St Eustace's, if she had pined for them at all, it was only because she knew that seeing them again would reinforce how she had outgrown their downy, threadbare comforts now that she was almost a grown-up, almost complete.

She had never bought Daddy a Christmas gift before. Up until now, he had been the magical provider and she, the dutiful receiving daughter. While a gaggle of aunts – on Mother's side – insisted on

---

* Delphine saw the title, *Murder On The Orient Express*, and realised she had read it in a brief fit of grown-upness two months before. She had powered through three whole chapters before skipping to the end (the novel's primary focus, she had discovered, was not murder, but talking).

bestowing twee, cloche-hatted dolls and Shirley Temple frocks, Daddy always came up trumps with a train set, or a junior woodworking kit, or Meccano, often barrelling in late but bearing a jolly, Christmassy smell, spilling over with festive joie de vivre.

Last year, however, he had not come home at all. Some time after six, Mother had risen from the settee, walked into the dining room and closed the door. Delphine had waited, blowing on the embers of the fire. Two hours later Mother left the kitchen, walking unsteadily, and went to bed.

Delphine realised now that future Christmases were her responsibility. She was a grown-up, and if she wanted magic, she would have to weave it herself.

'Tickets, please.'

The voice loomed close to her ear. She opened her eyes. 'May I see your ticket please, miss?' The conductor's breath was hot and peaty.

Delphine wiped condensation from her cheek and made a show of rummaging in one coat pocket, then the other. The conductor folded his arms. His eyes were grey lozenges converging on a steep, regal nose.

She stood, took off her duffel coat and turned it inside out.

'I'm sorry, I . . . it must . . . '

She clambered onto her seat and groped at the luggage rack, wobbling as the train went over a set of points. Her fingertips brushed the suitcase; she made several half-hearted grasps before the conductor stepped forward and helped her get it down.

She sat. Her thumbs fumbled with the catches; the lid sprung open.

'It's got to be here.' Delphine smeared a palm across her eye, trying to make herself cry – the credibility of her entire performance hinged on it. 'My mother bought it me. I had it. It was *here*.'

She glanced at the conductor. He glowered over flaring nostrils, nasal hair rippling as he exhaled. She rubbed her eyes again.

'I'll need to see it please, miss.'

She stared at the inside of her suitcase, cheeks prickling with heat.

She needed tears. Her eye caught a label inside the lid where Daddy had written her name and address, beginning:

Delphine G. Venner

The Pastures

Something in his familiar, flamboyant penmanship did the trick – her vision blurred. She felt a warm teardrop slide down to her top lip, where it clung. She began burrowing through clumsily folded underthings and small, scrunched packages, pausing to sniff, dab at her eye with a sock.

'Come on, miss – I've a whole train to get through.'

'Ah now leave off the poor girl,' said the big man with the cigar. 'She's going as fast as she can.'

'I'm just doing my job, sir.'

'Well, can't you do it with a bit more chivalry? Look – she's distraught.'

Delphine pushed her face into her hands and heaved out two of her best wretched sobs.

'Every passenger must have a ticket, sir.'

'And she's *told* you her mother bought one.'

'Tickets must be presented for inspection, sir.'

Delphine spread her fingers and peered through the gaps. The cigar-smoking gentleman had set down his newspaper and was puffing fractiously, bathing his head in a little cloud.

'Can't you let her off?'

'I can't change the rules for no one, sir.'

'Don't you "sir" me!'

The conductor took a deep breath and pushed out his lower lip.

The cigar-smoker looked to his carriage-mates for support. The other passengers became pointedly transfixed by a loose thread on a cuff, the view out the window and a novel, respectively.

'Right, fine. How much?'

'I'm sorry, sir?'

'How much?'

'For what, sir?'

'For a ticket, for a bloody ticket, that's what, sir.' He plugged the cigar stub into the corner of his mouth and took out his wallet. 'I am going to pay her fare, and when I get home I am going to commence a letter-writing campaign the pettiness of which you can't imagine. I warn you, I am a very lonely, very bitter bachelor with vast acres of time at his disposal.'

The conductor's eyelid twitched. Sensing a breach in his hitherto bombproof comportment, Delphine flourished a spotted handkerchief and blew her nose.

'That won't be necessary, sir.' The conductor nodded at Delphine's luggage. 'I spotted a ticket amongst the young lady's effects. Good evening, ladies and gentlemen.' And, tweaking the peak of his cap, he left.

The cigar-smoker exhaled through straight white teeth.

'Thank you, sir,' said Delphine.

'Oh, don't you start now.' He reached the end of his cigar, pulled a face and deposited the stub in his jacket pocket. 'What are you looking at? Didn't your mother teach you it's rude to stare? Go on, tidy up that clutter. Stop making a spectacle of yourself.' He unfolded his newspaper with a bang and began to read.

Delphine stuffed her things back into the suitcase, humming quietly to herself.

At the next stop, everybody but the grumpy cigar-smoker disembarked. She realised the low, throaty growl coming from behind the wall of newsprint was snoring. As the train gathered speed, she stretched her legs along the seat and took out a bag of pear drops. She sucked one then held it to the light, where it shone like an opal. Lulled by the rumble of the train, she closed her eyes and fell into a contented doze.

Delphine woke with a start, gripped by the conviction she had missed her stop. The carriage was empty. She swung her feet to the floor and turned to the window. Her groggy face gaped back at her. Beyond the glass, the night was rook-black. Her damp hair stuck to her cheek in strands. She shivered.

Pulling on her duffel coat, she got to her feet and walked around the carriage. It was deathly quiet, aside from a steady *ca-chuck ca-chuck*. Her chest tightened. The train was heading back to the rail yard.

She imagined spending the night on the cold carriage floor, Mother doubled over in tears on a deserted platform, policemen searching the tracks by electric torchlight, digging in snowbanks, the whisper of pencil lead on notebooks, her fellow passengers brought in for questioning, the finger of blame swinging sure as a compass needle towards the large man with the cigar – *well, he was still with her when I left* – the conductor recounting with relish the man's sudden, unprovoked aggression, his wild gesticulations and fiery eyes – *like a fiend he was, sir, like a man possessed* – the newspapers tattooed with lurid headlines: CIGAR-SMOKING CHILD-SNATCHER STILL AT LARGE, and Daddy, ashen, wracked with torment (at this she felt a pang of guilt), before a knock at the front door, and in she would glide to bellows of relief, to tears and a hug as tight and strong as plate armour.

The train began to slow. Delphine looked out the window and saw houses, and a little way ahead, the lights of a station. She yanked her suitcase off the luggage rack and waited at the door as the train shuddered to a stop.

When she stepped onto the platform the full chill of the evening struck her. She set down her case and spent a few moments fastening the toggles on her coat, the engine snorting and steaming behind her. The guard blew his whistle and the train started its long trudge out of the station. A breeze ghosted the nape of her neck. The last carriage filed past and she was alone.

When Delphine turned around, a woman in a cream coat with big black buttons stood farther down the platform. She was soaked in lamplight, her face flat shadow, the crown of her head blazing gold. All around her was ice.

'Delphine? What on earth are you doing there?' She began striding up the platform. Delphine braced for impact. 'Delphine? I've been waiting for you outside first-class. Why are you down here?'

'They said first-class was full.'

'Full? *Full?* On a little branch-line stopper like this?' Her mother drew back and puffed as if recoiling from a hot stove. 'The thing was half empty!'

Delphine hung her head.

'Of all the . . . ' Mother cast about the station, heels scraping the icy platform. 'Where's the stationmaster? I shan't stand for this. I'll wring his – '

'Please, Mother.'

'No.' Mother tugged Delphine's chin sharply upwards and fixed her with keen hazel eyes. 'You paid for a first-class ticket, you should have got a first-class seat. We're not leaving until I receive a refund and a frank and thorough apology.'

'It's fine. I didn't mind. I – '

'Shh! That's quite enough. Honestly Delphine, why didn't you say something? You really must learn to assert yourself.'

Delphine picked up her suitcase and followed Mother in a forced march down the platform to the stationmaster's office, which was closed. Mother rapped on the glass.

'Hello? Hello?'

'Mother, it's closed.' Delphine's fingers ached with cold. Her mittens were deep in her suitcase.

'Your problem is you give up too easily.' Mother switched from her knuckles to the heel of her fist.

'Please, let's just go. I said it's fine.'

'Don't be obstinate.' Mother dealt the door three crashing blows. 'Hello? Ah, it's no use. There's no one there.' She turned and sighed. 'Well? Are you coming? Philip is waiting with the engine running. It'll never restart in this weather so unless you intend to walk home . . . '

Delphine hurried towards the exit.

'Delphine! Don't run!'

Delphine sat next to Mother in the back of the car, listening to the motor strain as it climbed the gears. Road poured through the headlamps, pocked and bright between tall, dark hedgerows. Snow had fallen lightly; every so often the wheels slithered in a patch of slush.

'When we get in you're not to bother your father.'

Delphine bit back her disappointment.

'Yes, Mother.' She glanced out the passenger window. 'I'll say goodnight to him then go straight to bed.'

'What did I just tell you?' Mother grabbed Delphine's wrist. 'Delphine. Look at me. You are not to bother your father, is that clear?'

'You're hurting me.'

'Is that clear?'

Delphine was breathing heavily. 'But I only want to say goodnight.'

'He's been working very hard and he is very, very tired. Dr Eliot,' she flashed a glance at the back of Philip's head, lowered her voice, 'Dr Eliot said he needs rest. You can speak to him tomorrow.'

'He'll be happy to see me.'

Mother closed her eyes and exhaled. 'Of course he will. Look, you can speak to him first thing. Let's you and I keep to the sitting room tonight. I'll have Julia make cocoa and you can tell me what you've been up to at school.'

'I'll just poke my head round the door of his studio.'

'The matter is closed.'

'But – '

'Delphine! If you say another word I'll have Philip turn this car around and you can spend Christmas at your Aunt Lily's.'

Delphine bunched her fists and glared into her lap. She knew Mother might make good on the threat if pushed. Over the past year, Mother had made it clear she did not want Delphine around the house. It would be just like her to seize upon one small outburst as justification for keeping Daddy to herself.

Philip swung the car round a sharp bend. Delphine had to grip the seat to stop her head settling on Mother's shoulder. She leant her hot brow against the cool glass as the car descended towards the village, and home.

When Philip pulled up in the drive the night was tangy with woodsmoke. He opened the door and Delphine's mother stepped out, tugging her coat about her with a flourish.

'What sort of idiot has a bonfire in this weather?' she said.

Delphine thought that this was the *perfect* weather for a bonfire. She followed a few paces behind as Mother walked up the garden path, paused, sniffed the air, then continued up the steps. The little

Pan fountain had frozen over. The lawn was powdered glass. Delphine exhaled, lips spilling mist.

Philip killed the engine. In the quiet that followed, Delphine thought she heard a noise like hail, or the slow winding of a winch. Mother pounded the door knocker.

'Philip, would you come and let us in please?'

Philip whipped off his driving gloves and tugged a bunch of keys from his pocket. Mother stepped aside as he stooped for the lock.

'I can't imagine where Julia's got to,' she said, worrying at her coat cuff. 'She can't have gone home. I gave her clear instructions to wait till we had returned. Philip? What's wrong? She hasn't drawn the bolt, has she?'

'Just a bit stiff with the cold,' he said. He grunted, twisting the handle. The door gave. 'There.' He waited on the doorstep while Mother and Delphine stepped inside.

As soon as Delphine crossed the threshold she knew something was wrong. It took her a moment to realise the hatstand was missing. And the little table Mother liked to set flowers on. And the hall mirror.

Mother looked around with a slight rolling of the shoulders. Hanging thickly in the air was a smell like motor oil and toast.

Mother said: 'Where is he?'

A bang came from the landing. Daddy appeared at the top of the stairs, dragging the longcase clock that Mother's late Uncle Shipton had brought back from Denmark.* He was barefoot and stripped to the waist. His back was covered in red marks.

'Gideon,' said Mother, her voice strangely measured, 'what are you doing?'

Daddy went on dragging the clock down the stairs. As he drew

---

* Great Uncle Shipton had claimed he got the clock after agreeing to referee a swimming contest between four sailors – usually a Dutchman, a Swede, a Norwegian and a Finn. The race was to be run from Aalborghus Castle, across the Limfjord, and back again. The first man to touch the castle wall would win an antique clock. On the morning of the contest, Shipton and a crowd of spectators watched the sailors plunge into the freezing waters. Four heads bobbed as they crossed the narrow channel. Presently, there were three. Then two. Then one. Then none. Some time after midday, the organiser turned to Shipton and asked if he wanted to declare it a draw. Shipton agreed, and received the clock in recognition of his good sportsmanship.

closer, Delphine could hear him muttering to himself.

'Gideon,' said Mother. 'Where's Julia?'

Daddy grumbled something incomprehensible.

'Giddy? Where's Julia?'

'I said I sent her home.' It sounded like Daddy was breathing through gritted teeth. He pulled the clock down another step and the door on the front fell open.

'Please let's sit down, dear. It's terribly late to be rearranging things. Where's the hatstand?'

He muttered into his fist.

'What?'

'It's hooks.'

He widened his stance. With each fall, the clock jangled queasily.

'Hooks? Giddy, darling, what on earth are you talking about? Where's the hatstand?'

'It's too heavy. It's all hooks.' He spat as he spoke. 'I can't . . . I can't . . . '

Mother came to the edge of the stairs. 'What's heavy? I don't understand. Where have all our things gone?' She reached for his elbow.

'Don't touch me!' Daddy lunged over the bannister and swung at her with a wild backhand. Mother stepped back in a practised reflex, turning her face so his knuckles only grazed her cheek. Uncle Shipton's clock rattled down the last few stairs and hit the floor with a crunch of bust workings. Daddy clutched for her throat but she dodged and his fingers closed round the collar of her cream coat. She twisted out of it and lifted her forearm just in time to shield her head as he used the coat to lash at her.

Daddy lost interest. He bundled up the coat and strode down the last few stairs. As he stepped over the clock, Delphine tried to catch his gaze. His eyes were like chips of glass.

'Daddy?' She would snap him out of it. She stretched a smile across her face, took a breath and stepped towards him. 'Daddy, I'm home for Christm – '

'Delphine! No!' Mother threw up an arm.

Daddy rounded on her.

'It's killing me! It's killing me!' He drilled at his temple with two fingers, gasping. 'Man's not supposed to live like this! It goes! It goes! It all goes in!'

Mother slammed against the wall, withering. Delphine looked to Philip, who stood dumbly in the doorway. Philip blinked, took a step forward.

'Mr Venner, I . . . '

Daddy shut his eyes. He ran a hand through his slick silvered hair, whispering.

'It's almost gone now,' he murmured. He stepped over Mother as he had stepped over the clock, carrying her coat down the corridor to the kitchen. When he opened the door Delphine heard the hail noise again, but louder; the oily smell grew stronger. Mother was on her feet, scrambling after Daddy, pleading, shrieking operatically. She grabbed at his back; he bore her like a rucksack as he walked out of sight.

Delphine felt a cold weight in her belly. She walked to the stairs. Her legs felt gluey and she had to grip the bannister. Philip was saying something but it was far away and muffled. The picture of Grandnan and Grandpapa was gone, leaving a dark rectangle of wallpaper. She staggered towards her room. The door was open. Perhaps she had made a mistake. Perhaps everything would be fine.

A shifting, aquatic glow lit the space. The room felt bigger than she remembered. Her bed was gone. There were splinters on the floor. Her books were gone. Her model castle was gone. In the carpet were four dents left by the legs of the toy chest. There was no basket. There was no Hannibal. There was no Nelson.

She stumbled to the window. The fields around the village were blue and still. Down in the back garden was a huge bonfire. She saw the outlines of mattress springs, picture frames, a bike wheel. All around, the snow had melted and where the grass had not been scorched away it shone a lustrous bottle green. Smoke formed a solid, curling pillar. Daddy slung Mother's cream coat into the flames, where it shrivelled. He dropped to his knees and gripped his head, shuddering.

No. He was laughing.

Delphine turned away, dazed and sickened. Her body felt light as a seedpod. She walked out of her room and down the stairs and picked up her suitcase. She walked out of the house to the car, opened the back door and climbed inside. She took out the brushes in their brown paper parcel. She lay down on the back seat and hugged them to her chest.

CHAPTER 2

O QUEEN OF AIR AND DARKNESS

March 1935

Nothing lifted Delphine's mood, not even the monster. Brawny shanks, conch ears, wings like a ripped corset, lips drawn in an endless howl – everything she wanted in a Hell fiend, except life. In its granite throat was a robin's nest. As the car rolled through the wrought-iron gates of Alderberen Hall, the little bird watched from behind a row of lichen-freckled fangs.

Delphine scraped an index finger round her nostril then wiped it on the seam of the leather seat. She sat hunched, her jaw tight. Mother had made her wear a bonnet with a bright green ribbon; she could feel it balanced on her head, conspicuous as antlers.

Beyond the car, the estate spread dew-soaked, teeming. Tall Scots pines twisted out of a flat expanse. In the glassy morning light, she could almost believe she was on the savannah. Chickweed strafed the thickening grass in great creamy splashes. The road swung through a blackthorn thicket spattered with white blooms. They entered the woods.

Through Philip's open window she smelt the sour sweat of nettles. Ferns lashed at the running board. A branch clattered against the windscreen. She caught a flash of dark red behind a rotten log. When she looked again, it was gone.

The woods thinned. Beeches lined the road, their branches hacked back to ugly stumps. Bracken gave way to grass. The driveway began a gentle curving descent.

She saw a boating lake with a little hill beside it. On top of the hill sat a dome of black brick rather like an igloo. Huge shadows rolled across the lawns. All at once she was looking at Alderberen Hall – vast, brilliant – sunlight blazing off the golden stonework of its east and west wings.

A fawn lifted its head at the rumble of the motor. It bounded away, beech trees chopping its movement into a zoetrope flicker. Delphine lined up a shot with her imaginary hunting rifle, picturing a second, invisible head in front of the first, aiming for the eyeball, holding her breath. Pinching.

'Pow,' she whispered. The fawn kept running, oblivious.

Mother shook a pill into her palm from a brown glass bottle. She put her hand over her mouth, as if receiving bad news.

Ahead, Alderberen Hall fattened, gaining detail. Heavy mullioned windows were set in walls of faded golden stone. Six classical columns stood over the entrance. The Hall was symmetrical, its east and west wings reaching forward like the paws of the Sphinx.

Philip switched off the engine and let the car coast the final few yards. Wheels crackled on gravel and stopped. Delphine got out. She waited, hands clasped over her tummy.

Mother took Philip aside. She stood close and spoke quietly. Delphine realised she was being excluded and edged closer, indignant.

'We'll send for you when we need you,' Mother was saying. 'Philip, I . . . the family appreciates your loyalty and discretion over these past few months.'

'Of course, Mrs Venner – '

She took his hand in both of hers. 'I know we can trust you.' When she let go, he glanced down.

'Oh, I . . . ' He took a sharp breath. '*Thank you*, Mrs Venner.'

'Take your aunt on a daytrip somewhere nice. Borrow the car, if you like.'

'Yes, Mrs Venner. Thank you, Mrs Venner.' Philip seemed unable to lift his head. His cheeks were pink. 'Uh . . . uh, so . . . '

'What is it?'

He kneaded his hands, his voice tailing off. 'I was just . . . I mean, so I know . . . to be ready, like . . . for, uh . . . Will . . . *when* will you be wanting me to pick up, uh . . . Mr Venner?'

Mother turned away.

'We will send for you when we need you.'

'Yes, Mrs Venner.' He began backing towards the car.

'Philip? Our cases, please.'

'Oh, sorry, Mrs Venner.'

As he unlocked the boot, Delphine wandered along the front of the house. Between the blocky east and west wings ran a long façade of smutted mustard-yellow brickwork. Up close, its palatial grandeur congealed into the grubby functionality of a sanatorium. A row of black-barred windows filled most of the – she fancied fatal – drop between the two storeys. Ivy clung to the brick in sickly clusters, too brittle to climb down.

'Delphine!' Mother's voice was sing-song but her eyes flashed with warning. 'Let's not keep our hosts waiting, dear.'

A maid stood in the doorway, one elbow propped against the frame. She was young and slight with white-gold hair. Mother turned to wave off Philip. The maid eyed the two suitcases out on the gravel. She trudged over and grasped the handles.

'Where's the rest?'

Mother's smile tightened. 'We have all our luggage.'

'I see.' The maid straightened up, baring her teeth. She was stronger than she looked. 'This way, please.'

Mother turned to Delphine and mouthed 'Come *on!*' before following the maid through the double doors.

Delphine hung back, scraping surly arcs in the gravel. When *was* Daddy going to come? Why hadn't they waited till he was ready? It was horrible how Mother wouldn't let her see him. Delphine spat into the white dust. Mother was a beast.

Above the entrance, stout columns rose towards an architrave crusted in bird mess. As she craned her neck to follow them, she felt a surge of vertigo. She turned away.

'Delphine!' Her name echoed from the corridor.

Lawns spread ripe and unbounded. The distant treeline hung like an unresolved chord. She could run.

'Delphine!'

Then she saw him.

A figure was crossing the lawn – an old man with white side-whiskers and high, knotty shoulders. She couldn't understand how she had missed him. His jacket was clay green against the sun-blanched green of the grass, the blood-dark green of the woods. In his right hand swung a shotgun; in his left, mole carcasses on a string.

He stopped. The dead moles swayed and came to rest, nuzzling his filthy boots. He coughed into splayed fingers, examined them distastefully. The hand dropped away; he glanced about with a sudden wary vigour.

Delphine held her breath. The man looked towards the Hall.

She stepped backwards across the threshold.

'Lord Alderberen is in bed, owing to his dyspepsia,' the maid was saying, her little voice resonating as the corridor opened out around her. 'Wait here in the Great Hall and I'll see who's about.'

'Oh.' Mother stood in the middle of a chequered marble floor, like the last piece in a chess game. 'Are you sure he's well enough to be receiving guests?'

'Oh yes, ma'am.' The maid shot a wistful look towards the domed ceiling. 'It comes and goes. Always seems to flare up when he's got visitors. He's a martyr to his dyspepsia.'

'Can't they do anything for it?'

'You'd have to ask Dr Lansley about that,' the maid called, retreating through a side door with their cases. 'He knows everything that goes on here.'

A slam boomed through the Great Hall.

Mildly buoyed by Mother's irritation, Delphine looked around at portraits of dull ancestors, the grand staircase and the crimson carpet that flowed like lava from the landing above. At the top of the stairs was a painting of a wan young lady with sad eyes and buttery hair. Above the painting, an alabaster frieze showed bulls trampling a phalanx of spear-wielding hoplites on giant ostriches. Electric lights glared in brass fittings. The whole place smelt of polish and hospitals.

'Don't wander off again.' Even with her voice lowered, Mother's rebuke rang off the walls. 'Come here. And don't look at me like that. You're still in disgrace.'

Delphine began walking to Mother across the chessboard tiles. She stopped. In the light from the tall portico windows, Mother looked angular and old. She had lost a lot of weight. Her head looked like muslin stretched over a pine-cone.

'Come here *now*.'

Delphine lifted her right foot. She held it over the boundary between one square and the next. She looked at Mother.

'Please, Delphine.'

Delphine did not move.

'Now!' The word resounded emptily, a thunderclap.

Delphine thought of Mother crumpled on the floor, of how Daddy had stepped over her, and felt a sickly, creeping scorn. She withdrew her foot like a knife. Mother blinked. Delphine turned away.

Her chest was pounding. She stared at the oak-panelled wall and waited for the tide to come crashing back in. Seconds passed. The expected slap to the back of the head did not come. Mother was not going to correct her.

Fear gave way to a numb, terrifying freedom.

'Mrs Venner?'

Delphine turned and saw him: a tall man in hunting tweeds, around Daddy's age, with oily black hair and a narrow moustache. He began descending the stairs, smoothing a gloved hand along the polished bannister. His slicked-back hair, receding at the temples, gave the impression he was moving at speed.

Mother's jaw worked dumbly. At last, she nodded.

The man stopped two steps from the bottom. He held out his palm. A wire ran from his ear to a large battery hanging from his belt. Plugged into the top of the battery was a microphone the size of a digestive biscuit. Mother crossed the floor and placed her hand in his. The man bowed.

'Dr Lansley, Lord Alderberen's personal physician,' he said, almost shouting. 'Pleased to make your acquaintance.'

Mother smiled. Delphine folded her arms.

'Very nice to meet you,' said Mother.

Dr Lansley kept hold of her palm. Her wedding ring caught the light and sparked.

'I hear the Earl is unwell,' Mother said.

'What?'

'The maid said his dyspepsia – '

'Yes, yes. Alice gets overexcited, silly thing.' Dr Lansley placed two fingers in the small of Mother's back and began guiding her away from the stairs. 'Nothing to worry about – some boiled milk and a good night's sleep and he'll be quite restored, I'm sure. Now, would you care to take the guided tour?'

'That's very kind of you, Doctor, ah – '

'Please, call me Titus.'

'We've only just arrived. Delphine needs to unpack her things. She has private study to be getting on with.' She turned to Delphine. 'Don't you, dear?'

Delphine scowled.

Dr Lansley faced Delphine, as if noticing her for the first time. His head had a slight rightward kink, weighed down by the deaf aid, but he was not old – his eyes were ravenous, alert, and beneath his slick dark hair his posture shivered with the concentrated tension of a mousetrap. He looked her up and down.

'Hello,' he said.

'Hello,' said Delphine.

He held her gaze a moment longer, then turned back to Mother.

'Well, we've got a lot to get through but since we're on the subject of families I suppose this is as good a place to start as any.' He took Mother's hand and led her across the Great Hall, their footsteps sarcastic applause. Delphine watched them go. Mother shot a look over her shoulder. 'Now this fellow is Sir Robert Stokeham – good chum of Pitt the Elder, apparently.'

Dr Lansley stopped before a gilt-framed portrait the size of a billboard, lit on either side by electric lamps. As he continued talking,

Delphine edged towards a doorway. 'Look how they've composed the scene around him: the matchlock, the faithful gundogs, the quill and documents lying oh-so-conveniently in the background. You can just imagine, can't you? "Yes, do come in, I'm just cleaning my hunting rifle and – oh look, what's this on the desk? A frightfully important letter from King George the Third? How scatterbrained I am!"'

The Doctor's whinnying laughter faded as she entered a long corridor lined with south-facing windows. She walked in and out of the light, enjoying the cool lakes of darkness.

Why had Daddy insisted they come to this stuffy old place? Surely, if he wanted to get better, the best place for him was home. She stopped beside a door, tried the handle. It was locked.

Pinned to a corkboard beside the door was a typewritten timetable:

S.P.I.M. ACTIVITIES
Monday:
9 a.m. – morning orientation
10 a.m. – breakfast
11 a.m. – true work (M) / hidden steps (F)
12 a.m. – luncheon
1 p.m. – archery
2 p.m. – true work (M) / hidden steps (F)
4 p.m. – wakefulness drills
5 p.m. – dinner
6 p.m. – private study time
9 p.m. – discussion
11 p.m. – supper

There were similar lists for Tuesday to Friday, with minor variations: 'surgery' on a Wednesday afternoon, 'fencing' instead of 'archery' on Tuesday and Thursday, and a 6 a.m. slot on Friday called 'dawnbath'.

Delphine followed the corridor until it opened onto a spacious music room. Her sandals slapped against worn, waxed boards. Sunlight from four windows converged on a dusty harpsichord. On a stand above the harpsichord's double keyboard sat some handwritten sheet music: *The Shadowed Way – Sequence 15*. The corner of the page was initialled: *I.P.*

Mother had forced Delphine to take piano lessons. Just thinking about the *tak-tak-tak* of the metronome made her throat tighten. She rested an index finger on middle C. The key colours were reversed: the majors ebony, the sharps and flats ivory. The key sank; a nasal, spidery twang died beneath the lid.

She entered a wider, longer corridor. As far as she could tell, she was in the west wing, heading north. On her left were tall windows, on her right, white statues of men in laurel wreaths and togas, pottery fragments, a bull's head in alabaster. She came to some double doors. She listened at the keyhole. Nothing. She tried the door knob. The door opened.

The room was thick with the sweet, rank stench of dead flowers. Huge drapes smothered the windows. As her eyes adjusted she saw a billiard table, a leather sofa and a globe the colour of autumn. She could taste the dust in the air. She approached the fireplace. A deep rug swallowed her footsteps.

She wondered if Mother had missed her yet, if she was pacing the hallways, calling. Delphine looked at the oil painting over the fireplace: a Venetian plague doctor in leather overcoat, wide-brimmed hat and white beakmask, gazing down upon a sea of corpses. She did not know much about art,* but something in the mask's dark sockets made the hairs at the top of her spine rise.

On the mantelpiece sat a glazed earthenware jug. It was shaped like a puffy, leering face, the eyes rolled back, the skull hanging wretchedly open. Beside it, bracketed to the wall, was a gun.

Delphine walked over for a closer look. It was a duelling pistol – a flintlock, with a rounded walnut grip, a cleaning rod slotted

---

* Daddy's latest work was a triptych entitled *Trial Of The Profligate*. The three panes showed, respectively, a manacled angel taunted by centurions, a club-footed beggar woman admiring her (male) reflection in a full-length mirror, and an empty bird cage. Though, at first, Daddy's canvases, with their thick, childish lines and botched perspectives, had left Delphine baffled, guilt had hardened into a keen aesthetic eye, and she now recognised them as masterpieces. He stored his works at the studio in London where he painted and often slept. They had been some of the only family possessions to escape the fire.

under the barrel. Duelling pistols usually came in pairs, and she glanced round for another, but it seemed to be the only one. The manufacturer's name was incised on the iron plate beneath the hammer: *Dellapeste*.

In her belly, she felt the flint fall, the flash of black powder, the musket ball thudding into the heart of her arch foe. She lined up candidates and shot each in turn: Mrs Leddington (through the left bosom), Eleanor Wethercroft (headshot). Then, though she was not sure why, she shot Dr Lansley (kneecap, making him bow) before reloading and shooting him again (headshot, point-blank).

Delphine reached for the gun. Her elbow nudged the jug. Its face turned away and, as she grasped for it, the whole thing pirouetted off the edge of the mantelpiece, struck the hearth and broke apart with a chime.

She looked at the brown chunks. Amongst them was a key.

Tingles spread from the nape of her neck down her spine and up to her scalp. She stooped and picked up the key. The head was club-shaped. She glanced around for a locked cupboard or chest. A lacquered Chinese cabinet stood behind the billiard table. She tried the key, but it was too big. She was wondering whether to return and try the locked doors in the corridors, when she heard footsteps.

They were heading north, coming up through the statue gallery. She recognised the loud, reedy voice.

'These two are Minerva and, uh, Bacchus,' Dr Lansley was saying, 'which reminds me, your throat must be dry as a, ah yes. We'll take cocktails in the orangery shortly. The light this time of day – ah!'

'I'm not sure I – '

'Now at the end of the west gallery is the smoking room . . . '

Delphine scurried to the ashy hearth and began sweeping the shards of broken jug into her bonnet. The footsteps drew nearer. As she reached for the last thick sliver, she noticed a slit in the patterned wallpaper. It ran from the floor to just above head height, forming a rectangular outline. She walked up to it and pressed. It gave slightly. She pressed harder. It was a door.

And it was locked.

She ran a hand down the pink embossed fleur-de-lis wallpaper. Her fingertip snagged a keyhole. Mother and Dr Lansley were at the double doors.

'The Society holds a symposium on the last Saturday of every month. You mustn't feel obliged to attend.' The door knob began to twist. Delphine slotted the key into the hole and tried it. It would not turn. Of course it wouldn't. 'Please understand – I admire Lord Alderberen's forbearance immensely. *Immensely*. But we live in a country full of those willing to take advantage of a generous nature.' The doors started to open.

'He's been very kind to us, yes,' said Mother.

The door stopped. 'Oh, I . . . I didn't mean to imply . . . Not *you*, of course.'

Delphine jerked the key the other way. A tumbler clucked and a hinged section of wall swung out.

Dr Lansley stepped into the smoking room, facing Mother. 'I'm talking about a lot of the . . . *creative* types who've arrived since Lord Alderberen opened his home to the Society.'

'Yes. Gideon and I were honoured that Mr Propp thought to invite us.'

'Gideon?'

Clutching her bonnet full of broken earthenware, Delphine stepped through the doorway.

'My husband.'

'Ah.'

She plucked the key from the lock then tugged the lip of the door. She pulled her hand clear just in time. The door shut with a click.

'What was that?' said Mother.

Delphine stood in the darkness, her back to the wall. The air was warm and thick with dust.

'I said "Oh, I see",' said Lansley. 'And is . . . your husband coming to stay also?'

'I thought I heard a noise.'

Delphine held her breath.

'Oh, you will do. Alice, I expect, or Mrs Hagstrom, our house-keeper. We get by on a skeleton staff – Lord Alderberen is rather

'. . . particular when it comes to domestics. Now, this also serves as the card room. What's your game? Bridge? Oh Hell? No, don't tell me – let me guess.'

Her eyes began to adjust. A faint thread of light picked out the door frame. To her right was a narrow passage. It continued for the length of the wall, curving round the fireplace, fading to black.

The tingle spread down the back of her neck again, stronger. She felt like a ghost. She set down her bonnet, closed her fist around the cold brass key.

Behind the chimney breast, the passage waspnecked. Delphine exhaled and squeezed through. Mother and Dr Lansley's conversation faded with the last of the light.

The passage smelt of dry rot and the acrid smack of rat urine. Rough beams scraped her shoulders; something yanked at her cardigan and she gasped. When she reached into the darkness behind her, her hand closed round a three-inch splinter, talon-sharp. She took a step back, unsnagged the loop of wool, continued.

A pipe near her head gurgled and clanged. She tore through a sheet of cobwebs, finding a dead-end. She felt the wall. Wooden rungs like pick-axe handles poked out at two-foot intervals. They formed a ladder leading up. Delphine lifted her head and strained her eyes at the flat and fathomless black.

'Pow,' she said. The word rang slightly, as if there was an opening. 'Pow!' she said, louder. The way it echoed suggested a hollow space above. She tucked the key into her sock, gripped the first rung and began to climb.

The going was easy, with a wall to lean back on if she got tired. She climbed one-handed, keeping the other over her head, flinching with each rung, convinced she was about to dash her brains out against the ceiling.

The ceiling never arrived. Soon, she could hear she had emerged into a second enclosed space. Gripping the ladder, she leaned out, dangling a toe in the air. Her stomach clenched, but her chest surged with warmth. She imagined stepping into a void, falling, breaking her neck, her mangled body lying undiscovered for decades. 'The Venner Vanishing' would become one of the world's great unsolved mysteries – competing theories would abound: kidnapped and sold into slavery in Yemen to settle the Earl's gambling debts; dragged by vengeful spectres into one of the Hall's many ghastly paintings, where she can still be seen, selling matches in a Spanish marketplace; slain by the infamous 'cursed jug' of the Stokehams, which also disappeared on that fateful, terrible day. Then, in the year 2000, a citizen of some queer, barely human future would poke around the ruins of this ancient house, whirring and puttering with his electronic devices. A needle on his chromium instrument panel would swing towards the wall. He would locate the hidden doorway, spring the lock with a special magnetic ray, and there, crumpled in the dusty cavity, the bones of a little girl.

She felt pleasantly giddy. Her sweaty palm slipped from the rung and she fell.

She hit the floor and stumbled forward, grabbing at the walls. She pulled herself upright. From farther up the passage, she thought she heard scuttling – in her shock, she nearly stepped backwards into the hole. Her legs shook and her brow pounded with heat. She had fallen all of two inches. She was alive. And she could hear voices.

She followed the noise along the new passageway, which felt smaller and stuffier. She could not make out words, just muffled rhythms and inflections. A question. A rapid follow-up question from the same person. A short answer. A loud retort. Somebody was very angry.

The passage turned ninety degrees to the left. Either her eyes were adjusting, or it was getting lighter. She wiggled her fingers in front of her face and saw movement.

Another dead end. The voices were close. She could almost hear the words. To her left, dark red light leaked from behind a wooden slat. She prodded the slat. It moved. She poked it again. It slid easily between two runners. She pushed it all the way to the right; light streamed through a hole the size of a shilling. She stood on tiptoes and looked through.

She was peering into a windowless box room. In a bed lay a very old lady.

An electric nightlight threw tortoiseshell shadows across the walls. The old lady was almost completely bald, save for a fine white cowlick that trailed across the pillow. Her eyes were closed. Blue veins forked across her scalp.

Delphine felt a cold thrill. She was looking at a corpse.

The corpse inhaled – a sudden, hungry action with one, two, three catches, like the snagging of ratchet teeth.

Delphine slapped the slat back into place, her heart thudding. She could still hear the rhythms of an argument. Squinting against the gloom, she found a second slat on the opposite wall. She drew it back and pressed her eye to the hole. Nothing. She inserted a finger. Something rough. She tapped gently: wood, hollow. The back of a wardrobe, perhaps.

She felt cheated. Wardrobes and old ladies were dull, dull, dull – they were practically the same thing, if you went by smell. What was the point in building a secret passage if all it led to was furniture and death? She was about to retreat in disgust when she noticed a glow at shin-level.

Delphine lay on her side and nudged open a third slat. She saw the backs of two blue-stockinged feet in low-heeled slippers. The right slipper tapped the carpet.

'If I may s – '

'No, you may not. Please, just shut up.'

Both voices were male. Her view was framed by the legs and underside of a leather club chair. The springs creaked as the occupant shifted his weight. She could see the manufacturer's label and a dropped matchbook behind one of the legs. On the far side of the room, grey pinstripe trousers terminated in a pair of black patent-leather shoes. The shoes plodded in and out of sight, pacing the floor.

The man in the chair sighed – a pained, faintly bovine sound that ended in a rattle.

'Christ's sweet tree. The whole thing's a bloody mess.' His diction was crisp and deep.

The black shoes stopped at the opposite end of the room. They pivoted to face the chair.

'War comes.' The second male voice was slow and purring. Her forearms prickled. She could not place the accent – to her ear, the owner of the black shoes sounded vaguely Russian.

'You are willing it to come,' said the man in the chair.

'It is inevitable.'

'No!' The slippers stamped in unison and Delphine flinched. 'War is never inevitable! That is an excuse, and you, you of *all* people . . . God! They were willing to talk.'

'Talk?' said the black shoes. 'Of course. Negotiate? No.'

Delphine's head was swimming.

'What are we going to do?' said the man in the chair. 'Ivan? I said what are we going to do? We can't fight an entire people. When they find out what you've done we're finished.'

'So you *do* think they plan invasion?'

'I do *now*, yes! Of course I do *now*. You've given her the perfect *casus belli*. They'll have no choice.'

The patent-leather shoes covered the distance to the chair in three strides. Delphine almost cried out – for a mad instant, she thought they would crash through the wall. She bit her lip.

The foreigner's voice was hushed, urgent: 'This. This is your flaw. Innocence. You think family will save you. You think justice will save you. No. Justice is shield of glass. We must have wisdom.'

The slippered feet splayed. She heard the man in the chair take three grating breaths.

'But how can I go on if I trust no one?'

Creases appeared in the foreigner's polished toecaps as his heels rose from the floor. The club chair creaked with extra weight.

'My dear friend.' He spoke in a whisper, but impossibly loud, as if his lips were at her ear. She felt chill and limp; all she wanted to do was surrender. 'You may trust me.'

He stayed on his toes a moment longer, then sank. He began walking away.

'What about Lansley?' said the man in the chair. 'He's going to have kittens.'

'We must not tell him.'

The man in the chair laughed. 'Oh no, I quite agree. *We're* not going to tell him anything. *You're* going to explain to the Doctor exactly what *you've* done and how you propose to keep our heads from rotting on the bloody tips of ten-foot pikes.'

The shoes stopped, side-on. 'We continue visits. We say nothing.'

'Nothing.'

'Nothing. We behave normal, we smile so nicely. If they mention child, we offer to help with search.'

'And when they find out we've got the girl right here, under our bloody roof?'

Delphine felt a horrible electric thrill.

'They must not.'

'You're riding a tiger,' said the man in the chair. 'Easy to start, damned hard to stop. The longer we wait, the worse it is. No, look, you'll just have to go cap in hand and tell them you made a mistake. You were mad. You were drunk – your youthful body couldn't handle the nectar. You're terribly, terribly sorry. Here she is, and no harm done.'

One black shoe tapped the floor. 'It is too late.'

'It's not too late if you act now.'

'I will not give them child.'

'It's not your choice to make!'

'And yet,' said the foreigner, 'I choose.'

'I'll take her. I'll choose for you. What do you think of that?'

'No. I do not think you will.'

'But we have so much to teach each other. You *heard* the things they said. They still respect England. They respect us. We can stop this war before it starts.'

'Lazarus. They are monsters.'

The chair creaked. 'Was my father a monster?'

Silence. Delphine blinked. It was as if time in the room had stopped.

'Your father is dead,' said the foreigner. 'God rest his soul.'

Delphine heard a rustling above the chair, the sound of a match being struck. Seconds later, she smelt the soft aroma of pipesmoke. The blue stockings slid out of the slippers.

'What about the new Britannia? What about everything the

Society was created to achieve? Is that just all . . . what? We just give it up, do we?'

'No. We give up nothing. We go on as planned. They do not suspect us.'

The man in the chair grunted. 'Let me send the child away, then.'

'No. I must keep her in my sight.'

'Why? We could . . . ah!' The pipe clattered on the carpet and bounced underneath the chair, spilling tobacco. Delphine gripped the slat, ready to close it. Springs groaned; the man above grunted; four pale fingertips appeared, grasping impotently. 'Oh, hang it all.' The fingers withdrew. 'Look at me. I can't pick something up when it falls at my feet. It might as well be in China.' He took a breath, and Delphine heard the catch in his throat. 'When we're out there, I feel like anything is possible. I feel hope. But each time we return home I sink deeper into decrepitude. The journey's too much. This body is dying. I can't afford the luxury of brinkmanship.'

The patent-leather shoes stepped into view, close and huge. Before Delphine had time to pull away, pinstripe-trousered knees were touching the carpet and a big tanned hand was reaching for her. Behind thumb and forefinger appeared a face: white moustache, plump cheeks and huge grey eyes.

She was paralysed.

The hand swallowed the pipe and withdrew like a sea monster. The man stood.

'No,' he said. 'Luxury you cannot afford is cowardice.'

Delphine snapped the slat shut, stumbled to her feet and began hurrying back along the passageway. The walls amplified her breathing till the very house seemed to be gasping for oxygen. The blackness was total. Something round and smooth brushed her calf – she choked down a yell. She groped at the void ahead until her fingers found the top rung.

She had to get out. She had to find Mother.

Midday sun flowed through the orangery's domed glass ceiling, trapping everything in a net of shadows. Mother and Dr Lansley were sitting on black lacquered chairs, sipping dark green cocktails. A bronze cherub had its bow aimed at Lansley's temple. About its shoulders, a climbing plant hung leathery and dead.

Delphine marched up to the little wicker table.

'I need to talk to you.'

Dark bars split Mother's face into segments. She looked Delphine from crown to toe.

'You're filthy.'

Delphine glanced down. Her blouse and skirt were caked with dust. Thick clumps clung like fur. She began slapping it off.

Mother wrinkled her nose. 'Oh. Don't do that here.' She flapped a hand. 'Whatever happened? Did you fall?'

'I need to talk to you.'

Dr Lansley grasped the thin stem of his glass between gloved thumb and forefinger. He lifted the drink to his lips, tinting his keen features a queasy, corpse-bloat green. He sipped. His jaw muscles tightened.

'*Mother.*'

'Yes, yes, yes.' She sat back in her chair. 'Well. Go on, then.'

'I mean in private.'

'In that case, you'll have to exercise a little patience. Perhaps if you ask the Doctor politely he'll have the maid show you to your room. I'll come and speak with you when the three of us are done.'

'This is a matter of – wait, what?'

Mother placed her glass on the table with the confident finality of a grandmaster capturing a rook with a pawn.

'You heard me perfectly well.' She flashed Dr Lansley a smile. 'I'll talk when the three of us have finished. Mr Propp has been telling me about his dances.'

A shadow at the window turned. Delphine jolted the table with her thigh, sloshing green liquid into the wickerwork.

Mr Propp was a short, tanned, round man. A silk robe parted about his paunch like theatre curtains, fob watch glinting in the pocket of his waistcoat. Delphine's gaze followed grey pinstripes down to polished black patent-leather shoes. He took a few steps

39

forward, walking with a rocking motion, until his bald head came into the light. He smiled, lifting the tips of a vanilla-white walrus moustache.

'Hello,' he said, in a purring, vaguely Russian accent.

And there were the eyes: huge, grey, unreadable.

CHAPTER 3

METAMORPHOSIS

March 1935

Delphine caught the bullet square in the chest. Its imagined impact carried her back one step, then two. She clutched at her breastbone; warm arterial blood oozed between her fingers. She tried to take a breath. The grey sky descended. She collapsed.

The fall knocked the air out of her lungs. She had expected the bracken thicket to cushion her.

The year was 1916. It was mid-July, and she was an infantryman separated from her battalion in woods outside Longueval. The twig stabbing her buttock was an old bayonet wound. The dead lay everywhere.

She listened, brown fiddleheads of dead bracken tickling her ears. Elms gasped and shushed. Men barked orders. Machine guns called to each other like strange crows. Taking a near-final breath, she smelt earth and the salty-sour aroma of burnt trees.

This, then, was dying. It did not feel so dreadful – just a gradual detachment, a rowing boat easing away from a riverbank. She rested a palm against her chest, focused on the diminishing sink and swell.

A wood pigeon cooed. Somebody screamed for their mother.

She'd heard many tales from the Great War, some in story papers or on the wireless, the juicier ones traded like aniseed balls amongst hunched, furtive peers in the playground: how you could tell if a storm was on its way depending on whether the Boche corpse in the flooded shell crater floated or sank, donkeys drowning in a quagmire, soldiers strolling about bayoneting prone bodies like park keepers collecting leaves. She'd heard the stories of bullets stopped by a breast-pocket bible/hip flask/gypsy's golden tooth, of the captain who kept a bunker full of Turk skulls, lined up in rows, who polished them like trophies and gave them names, who finally lost what remained of his reason after a botched advance, barricaded himself inside the bunker and put a bullet through his brain as the skulls looked on.[*]

She could not stand to be in the house. Oh, how Mr Propp had smiled, plump and squat and harmless, turning up the waxed tips of his white moustache, bowing his bald head, ingratiating – *yes, so charmed, so pleased to meet* – but she had seen the hatred in those hard, grey eyes. Now, whenever she walked one of the long, dark corridors alone, whenever a door cawed open of its own accord, she felt Mr Propp's gaze upon her. She was not afraid of him, but when she lay in her stark new bedroom, the cold silk quilt pulled up to her chin, listening to laughter made strange and mournful by its passage through the lead pipes beneath the floor, to urgent scritching somewhere behind her head, to thuds and creaks and the gasp of a guest lowering himself into a mustard bath, to the lapping of the ivy against the brickwork and to her own rapid breaths, she felt an alertness that made it very hard to sleep. If she slept, she dreamt murky, suffocating dreams that ended in jolts. And so, though she could not accept that she feared Mr Propp, she chose to keep her distance.

Sprawled in the dirt, Delphine the wounded soldier let her head drop to one side. Bracken hung in brittle heaps. Up close, she could see smooth white threads of club fungus sprouting from each stem. A beetle ratcheted its mandibles; its antennae dabbed at the cool air. It looked big as a dog.

She pictured bulldog-sized beetles burrowing up through the mortar-churned earth. Bullets zinged off chitinous thoraxes. Beetles

<hr>

[*] The story went that, as two privates tried to break down the door, they could hear him haranguing each of the skulls in turn for 'bad advice'.

stormed the Boche line, dragging barbed wire in nightmare tangles. Trench walls collapsed. Officers discharged pistols in vain before black antlers gored their stomachs. The Germans routed. They scrambled and fled across pitted, smoking ground, stumbling on severed torsos, but the beetles ran them down. Complicated mouth-parts sprung apart. Heads crunched like coconuts.

And Delphine was there, leading the charge, transformed. She marvelled at her serrated forelegs and shiny interlocking armour. Flares lit the battlefield a glorious victory red.

Daddy would be coming soon. Mother had tried to keep the news from her but Delphine moved through the house like a phantom. Hidden passages honeycombed the west wing. The club-headed key opened them all. Most were dead ends, no more than a couple of yards long, that terminated abruptly to make way for door arches. They were choked with cobwebs, as if nobody had walked them for years.

She had not the faintest idea why someone would go to all the trouble of constructing secret passageways only to make such a bad job of it – they were too narrow for a servant to carry a tea tray – but when she sat between walls she felt quiet and calm and nobody bothered her.

Around her the estate spread ripe and anonymous. South of Alderberen Hall were lawns, then patchy woodland all the way to the gatehouse in the southwest. Bending round the west and north-west of the house was the boating lake, and beyond that, to the far west, was the village of Pigg. To the north was the thick dark mass of Prothero Wood, a mile or so of salt marshes then the sea. To the east, where she lay now, Prothero Wood gave way to farm-land.

She knew Daddy was coming because she had heard Mother asking Alice the maid to place a telephone call. When Daddy reached the Hall, Delphine would tell him what she'd overheard. Mr Propp was a warmongering foreign spy, negotiating with England's enemies (Bolsheviks? Germans?), preparing for a surprise invasion across the channel. There was no sense telling Mother – she had already fallen for Mr Propp's unassuming charms.

All Delphine had to do was speak to Daddy alone, and the whole rotten plot would be unearthed. He would praise her ingenuity, her Great British pluck. Certainly, the reclusive Lord Alderberen – whom she had yet to meet – would be most grateful that she had rooted out two conspirators lurking under his own roof.

Back in her imagination, she stomped across the French battlefield towards the ruins of a bombed-out chapel. Dead horses lay beside craters half-flooded with brown water. The chapel reminded her of the dinner hall at St Eustace's. In the few remaining windows, stained-glass saints gazed down upon shattered pews, spent ammunition cases, mud.

Delphine entered through a low, stone archway – slow, implacable, kicking aside tables, empty bully tins. She sniffed for her quarry.

From the depths of her throat, Delphine emitted a gleeful clicking. She turned to face the figure cowering beneath the altar.

The crunch of a twig. She opened her eyes and found herself staring into the twin barrels of a shotgun.

'Keep still.' The muzzle bobbed inches from her nose. 'Twitch and I'll blast you so full of shot they'll have to hunt for bits of you with a magnet.'

Delphine ran her tongue over the backs of her incisors.

'Um, lead isn't magnetic,' she said, frowning.

She looked up the length of the gun, to a crimson-faced old man. Tussocks of chalky hair capped plate-fungus ears. His green waxed jacket was jigsawed with dry mud.

'Since breakfast I've returned fifteen creatures to the Lord's eternal custody. No odds to Him if I make it sixteen.' The old man took a couple of steps back, lowering the gun to waist height but keeping it trained on her head. 'Sit up.'

Delphine made a show of hoisting herself onto one elbow, then the other. Moss fell from her hair as she dog-shook it.

'I've got spies all over these woods.' Fleshy pouches hung beneath his eyes. 'But your lot never learn, do you? Think you can come crashing through here doing whatever you like, and I won't notice.'

He jabbed the gun at her. 'Well, I do notice. If there's so much as a leaf out of place, I notice.'

Delphine took a shaky breath.

'I don't know who you are,' she said, 'but you're messing with the wrong person.'

He laughed. He actually laughed.

'Go on. Get up.' He gestured with the gun barrel.

She stood. The elm copse was bordered on one side by a hedgerow and, beyond that, a field. She was damp from lying down; the wind whipped round her legs and she shivered.

'You and your friends pleased with yourselves?' he said.

Delphine raised her chin proudly. 'I don't have any friends.'

From the other side of the hedge came a noise like someone shaking out a bathmat. They both turned to look. A pheasant throbbed into the air. At twenty feet its head snapped back and it dropped.

Delphine blinked.

'Look at you,' said the old man. 'Butter wouldn't melt.' He herded her to a gap in the hedge.

Through a frame of jagged twigs, she saw the pheasant thrashing amongst lush green wheat. It rolled onto its belly and stood, shaking dirt from its cream and brown-dappled wings. It accelerated to a dash and took off. A blur of flapping. Its neck lurched back and it fell.

The pheasant attempted a third take-off and the same thing happened. She squinted up at the spot where the bird kept stopping.

'Go on,' he said, 'through you go. What's wrong? Not so eager now you've been caught in the act?'

Her fear was levelling off into curiosity.

'Why can't it fly?'

His eyes widened. 'Magic.'

Delphine tried to look disdainful. 'There's no such thing.'

'That's odd coming from a gypsy.'

'Oh! I am *not* a gypsy.'

'Just a common poacher, then.'

She glanced down at her spread palms, speechless – and, she realised, rather flattered. She inhaled, balled her fists.

'Let me go.'

The old man leaned back. 'No.'

'You can't keep me here. You've got no right, you – '

'Shut up.' He thrust the shotgun at her face.

'This isn't fair! I haven't – '

'I'm carrying the gun. *I* decide what's fair.' He snorted, spat a gobbet of snot into the dirt. 'Torturing my birds – that's not fair.'

The flames were rising again. She shut her eyes, tried to slow her breathing. Pink and green stars fizzed in the darkness.

'Hey!' said the old man. 'Look at me when I'm talking to you!'

Her cheeks prickled with heat. She heard the *whumph* of the pheasant pounding its wings, the squawk as it fell. This was how it always went. They wanted you to get angry. They knew you hadn't done anything wrong so they'd taunt you and taunt you until your head went bad and you really did do something wrong, and then they'd round on you, triumphant: *Look! It runs in the family!*

She opened her eyes.

'Please,' she said.

'Maybe your father's too soft to give you a – ' His sentence cut off as she struck him across the temple. She was not strong but the backhand came as a surprise to them both; she twisted with the blow, shoving the shotgun aside with her other hand. He let go, her heel slid and she pirouetted. She planted her foot. Her mouth tasted of copper. She was facing him. She was holding the gun.

The old man glanced from the shotgun to Delphine. With his hair ruffled on one side, he looked like a sleepwalker. The barrels were pointing at his chest.

'Easy now,' he said.

The shotgun was heavier than she had expected. Little fluorescent worms writhed at the edges of her vision. She felt groggy and outside of herself. Holding the gun did not feel like she had expected. She did not feel powerful. She wanted to give it back.

'Brace it against the soft bit next to your armpit,' he said. He patted the spot on his coat and mud fell away in flakes. 'Keep your arms relaxed. If you hold it tight it'll buck up and your shot'll go high.'

She hesitated, adjusted her posture.

'Not against your collarbone. The fleshy part. Start like this,' he stood with an invisible gun tucked between his elbow and flank, 'and imagine you're pushing a billiard cue. Step forward and push towards your target.'

Cautiously, she lowered the gun to her side, then stepped forward, pointing it just as he'd shown her; sure enough, the butt settled into the nook beneath her shoulder.

'Good. You don't need to be squinting down the sights at this range, either. Just point and shoot.' He was not smiling. 'Get caught up in half an inch this way or that way and you won't be able to react if the bird breaks unexpectedly.'

Delphine felt her left arm – the arm supporting the barrel – beginning to tremble.

'Marksmanship is all about footwork. If your posture's right, the rest is easy.' He mimed holding a shotgun, pivoting at the waist as if tracking a hare over open ground. 'Anticipate its path then step where you want the bird to die.' He demonstrated by placing his left foot forward.

Delphine took a step back. Her forefinger found the coarse metal of the trigger.

'Stay where you are,' she said. 'Uh, please.'

'Of course if your target's right there in front of you, best to take your shot while you've got the chance.' He took another step towards her.

She stepped back again. 'Stop it.'

'Can't think what you're waiting for.'

She let the shotgun dip. 'It's not loaded, is it?'

He reached out and gripped the barrels. 'First rule of game shooting: *never* point a gun at a human being, loaded or unloaded.

You may hit or you may miss,

But for ever think of this:

47

All the pheasants ever bred
Don't make up for one man d – '

Delphine flung her end of the shotgun downwards. The heavy stock hit his foot. He creased, his face twisting shut. She ran.

She followed the hedgerow, soles skidding in leaf mulch. A low bough swung for her head – she ducked, accelerated. When she glanced back he was puffing, red, limping. He had aged twenty years – she saw him now for what he was: a blustering old fool, a pathetic codger versus a spry twelve-year-old, and she laughed at the idiot she was leaving behind and the world tipped and she headbutted the dirt.

She spat mud. Her leg was trapped, her leg was broken – no, she'd just tripped in an old badger sett. She contorted, pulled free. He was nearly on her. She rolled onto her hands and knees and scrambled into the hedge.

Branches clawed and snapped. A bramble snagged her cheek; she batted it away. A hand caught the neck of her cardigan; she tried to double-back and shrug out of it and another hand clutched her shoulder.

'Now I've got you, you devil.'

She wriggled and hissed. He began dragging her out.

He was a lot stronger than she'd expected, his arms like oak roots. She kicked and felt it connect. He cursed, then again as she bicycled her legs, dragging him into the hedge with her. He did not let go.

'Get off!'

'Shh!' he said. He was so close she smelt his sour tobacco breath over the fragrant undergrowth. Warm spittle spritzed the nape of her neck.

'Let go! Let me – '

'*Shut up!*' He clamped a greasy palm over her mouth. She bucked and swatted. 'Damn child! Just shut up for one damn second . . . and *look.*'

Delphine lifted her head. A few thin branches hung between her and the field.

A red-haired lad of maybe seventeen strolled through the young green wheat with his hands in his pockets, puffing on a cigarette and kicking up dirt with his galoshes. He walked to a spot close to the pheasant, which had just righted itself again. He took a final drag on his cigarette, tossed it into the mud. After glancing around the field, he crouched and pulled a wooden peg out of the ground. He began barrelling his fists. The pheasant toppled like a drunk. Wheat parted around the bird as it skidded towards him. She heard it slap its wings against the dirt, making throttled protests. It stopped at his feet. He took it and held it to his chest. The pheasant looked around making small, soft noises. He ran a hand over its plumage as if smoothing the creases out of a favourite dressing gown. With the slight grimace of someone opening a jam jar, he wrung its neck.

She flinched, despite herself. The old man made a noise through his clenched teeth.

The boy eased a fishhook from the pheasant's beak. He fed the bird into a canvas bag, along with the spooled fishing line. He collected some stray feathers, lit another cigarette and walked off, whistling.

The old man took his hand from her mouth.

'Well, I'll be,' he whispered. 'I only hired him three weeks ago, the cheeky . . . ' He glanced around at the hedge. He began shuffling backwards. Grunting, he lifted himself onto one knee, placed both palms against his thigh and hoisted his other leg up. He took a moment to catch his breath, then waited for Delphine to stand.

They brushed themselves down. He picked wet leaves from the wispy remnants of his hair. She found something grey-green and foul-smelling on her skirt. A gust of wind made the elms purr.

He dragged a sleeve across his nose, snorted.

'Even?'

'I'm sorry?'

He extended a palm.

'Henry Garforth,' he said. 'Head Keeper of the Alderberen Estate.'

Delphine eyed his hand. It was a knot of contradictions: huge and callused, bony and quivering. The liver-spotted webbing between his fingers hung like dust sheets over a defunct exhibit. A thick white scar ran from his wrist to the pad of his thumb.

She held out her hand; his swallowed it. His skin was pumice-rough.

'Delphine Venner,' she said as he pumped her arm.

'Right,' he said, letting go, 'and now the formalities are out the way, you can bugger off back to Pigg.'

'I'm not from the village.'

'No?'

'I live at the Hall.'

A grot of black mud clung to his eyebrow. It dipped as he frowned. 'Don't be silly.'

'I live with my mother in the east wing, in the room with the butterfly paintings.' She started walking back and forth along an invisible tightrope. 'We've been here two weeks, well, a week and six days actually. My father is coming on Saturday. He's a famous painter. He killed five men. Germans.'

'You should be in school.'

'Don't go to school.'

'Why ever not?'

'They said I tried to start a fire but I didn't, and they said I tied up Eleanor Wethercroft in the boiler room and left her there over-night, which I did,' she said, without looking up.

'Ah,' said Mr Garforth. He stooped and picked up his shotgun.

'What are you going to do about that man?' she said.

'You mean young Mr Gillow?'

Delphine wobbled, her hands out for balance. 'The one who fished the pheasant.'

'Well . . . ' he kneaded his chin with thumb and forefinger, 'I suppose I'll give him a chance to mention it when I see him tomorrow. Perhaps he stumbled across someone else's mischief, decided to put the bird out its misery. If he doesn't mention it, that's poaching. He'll be out on his ear.' Whipping a handkerchief from his pocket, he started rubbing down the shotgun. 'Now come on, off with you.'

She stepped off the imaginary tightrope and watched him clean. He glanced up. 'That's a ripe-looking bruise you're going to have on your forehead,' he said. 'Best tell your parents you fell out a tree.'

'I will,' said Delphine, 'on one condition.'

'Condition?' said Mr Garforth. He tried to hide his smile by rubbing his chin. 'Go on, then. What's this condition?'

She folded her arms.

'Teach me to shoot.'

CHAPTER 4

ORDEAL BY FIRE

March 1935

Delphine hurried through the corridor. She was hungry. She thought about the Siege of Antioch where the crusaders were starving to death and plundering villages for food and deserting, and some of them began hallucinating from hunger and having visions of God, and as she rounded the corner she crashed into Mr Propp.

'Oh!' Delphine dropped her Mars bar.

Propp took a step back, rubbing his paunch. In the empty corridor, they stared at one another. His big grey eyes did not blink. His mouth was half-disguised behind his drooping white moustache.

'Sorry,' said Delphine.

With a grunt, he began to sink. His smooth scalp tilted towards her and one pinstriped leg bent until his knee was almost touching the floor.

'Ivan?' Dr Lansley was coming up the corridor. He wore a checked cravat tucked haphazardly into his jacket. 'What on earth are you bowing for?'

Propp rose. He looked at his palm. The Mars bar sat in his thick tanned fingers. He turned the black wrapper so the name faced up, red letters on a white stripe.

Lansley appeared at his shoulder. Side by side, the two men were stark opposites: Dr Lansley a tall, skinny wraith of middling years with pale cheeks, oily black hair, black deaf aid and a coal-smudge moustache above a thin frowning mouth, Mr Propp a plump, short figure, old but hearty, round-faced with a shaven head, a brownish complexion and a lush, bone-coloured moustache that framed a full-lipped smile.

In Lansley's severe, haughty demeanour Delphine saw an unbroken lineage all the way back to the Norman conquerors, but Propp contained a little of everything – Egyptian skin, a broad Siberian nose, and eyes tinged with dry, Asiatic glamour. In his patient, canny composure he could have been Jew or Norseman or ancient Tibetan hermit. Lansley was old England, but Propp was the world.

Propp uncurled his fingers. He held out the Mars bar.

She reached for it, half-expecting his hand to snap shut.

'God of war,' he said. The creases around his eyes deepened. He watched her hand withdraw with the chocolate.

Delphine tried not to flinch. The Mars bar felt hot in her trembling grip.

Lansley cleared his throat. 'Well, what do you say?'

'Oh,' she said. 'Thank you.'

'I should think so, too. Now, you are between me and my lunch – move.' He shoved past, wiping his glove on his lapel after he had touched her.

Propp brushed imaginary dust off his knee. He followed at a plod.

She watched him go. What had he meant by that comment? Did he know she was onto him? Was he threatening her?

As she turned away, she spotted something on the floor where he had bent down. It must have fallen from his pocket.

She crouched and picked it up.

It was dull and tarnished, attached to a triangular fob of cracked brown leather.

It was a room key.

Propp's study lay at the end of a gloomy corridor lined with artwork on the east wing's ground floor.

Delphine crept towards a huge panelled door. The walls were lined with increasingly weird and ugly paintings: a drab landscape of scrub, rubble and skulls, a distorted watercolour parody of what she guessed was meant to be a dodo, and several inferior studies of the young blond lady whose portrait hung in the Great Hall, identified by brass nameplates as Lady Anwen Stokeham. In each portrait she towered in a black silk mourning gown, her yellow-white hair swept back from her brow, her face set in an expression of defiant martial beauty. One depicted her on the deck of a storm-lashed galleon, another standing in a forest, a host of savage beasts lying supine at her elaborately side-buttoned black shoes. The final painting appeared to show her in Hell, surrounded by winged fiends, horned, cloven-hooved demons and giant red scarabs.

Delphine remembered how Dr Lansley had mocked the obsequious portrait of the 1st Earl. Whoever had commissioned these paintings had wanted to present Lady Stokeham as a striking, almost mythical figure.

No wonder Lord Alderberen had chosen to hang them here, away from impressionable guests.

The door to Propp's room stood between a pair of small black tapestries – on the left, an eight-pointed star, on the right, a rosy cross within a pentagram within a circle. Delphine glanced back over her shoulder. She listened for footsteps. The paintings looked like windows in a carriage. For an instant, she had the oddest sensation she was on a train.

She knocked on the door. Sturdy wood swallowed the sound. If anyone answered, she would say she was returning the key.

Delphine waited. She checked the corridor.

They were all taking lunch. It was barely past noon, and the Society loved long, chatty meals rounded off with drinks and cigars in the smoking room. The coast would be clear for almost an hour.

She slid the key into the keyhole. She was just checking it fitted, she told herself. Perhaps it did not belong to Propp at all.

The key turned smoothly. The bolt slid aside with a *chuck*.

Somewhere in the Hall a door slammed. Delphine froze, listening. Her chest felt tight. Was this a mistake? She had stumbled across two keys now. Could it really be an accident? She had seen the look in Propp's eyes. What if he had dropped it on purpose?

What if this was a trap?

She looked back up the corridor a third time. One of the wall-mounted light fixtures dimmed then flared back to full brightness. She was alone.

Her collision with Propp had been pure chance. He could not have known she was coming. Had he really, in those few seconds, decided to lure her back to his study? How could he know that she would take the bait, that she would even recognise a dropped key *as* bait?

The security of the Empire might be at stake. The evidence she was hunting for might be feet away. She ran her fingertips down the grooved door and thought of trench periscopes, mortar blasts, Vickers guns strafing larch spinneys through fog. Her breath rose and fell.

She closed her fist around the cold green glass of the rose-cut door knob.

She stepped into the room.

In the centre of the table, rounds of boiled gammon steamed and glistened. There were devilled eggs on a silver platter and potato salad and steamed spinach in glass bowls, garnished with croutons. There was a dish of prunes stuffed with walnuts, and beside it clay pots of mayonnaise and mustard.

Gideon Venner did not feel hungry.

The car journey had been long, sticky and nauseating. Something had been wrong with the air. Twice he had asked Philip to stop so he could stand by the side of the road and breathe. For the last part of the trip he had stripped down to his vest, and if not for Philip's constant critical glances in the rear-view mirror he would have taken that off too.

Now the maid had left him here alone. Where was everyone?

Coming to Alderberen Hall had been a mistake. He could feel its history pressing down on him, a wet heat. There were too many memories.

Too many ghosts.

'Ah! Our new guest.'

A short, bald, thickset man had entered the banqueting hall.

He looked Greek or Turkish or perhaps Arabic. Surely this couldn't . . .

Gideon used his napkin to wipe the sweat from his throat. He rose.

'Gideon Venner.' He extended a damp hand. 'It is a true honour to meet you at last, Mr Propp.'

Mr Propp smiled. 'We do not speak of honour, my dear brother.' He crossed the room with a strange elegance. 'We speak only . . . of *will*.' At this final word his hand engulfed Gideon's, pumping furiously.

Gideon stared into the old foreigner's wide grey eyes. For an instant, he thought he felt a freezing current flowing up his arm.

Mr Propp let go.

Gideon blinked. He flexed his fingers. The tension in his forehead had dissolved to almost nothing.

'You.' Mr Propp pointed. 'You are artist.'

'How do you know?' Gideon looked at his hand. 'Did you . . . '

'No, no.' The old man laughed. 'Your wife tells me. Come.' He beckoned. 'Quick, before we eat. I show you something. In my study.'

Delphine told herself not to rush. She had plenty of time.

Propp's study had no windows. One wall was taken up with glass-fronted bookshelves that rose to the ceiling. There was an armchair, a wardrobe, a wicker basket heaped with logs, a mahogany escritoire writing desk with its lid rolled down, and a wide fireplace. In the middle of the rug was a tea trolley. Several saucers, a knife, a plate covered in crumbs, an empty bottle of calvados and two crystal tumblers jankled as she pushed it aside to get to the desk.

The room stank of pipesmoke and brandy. It was surprisingly cold – the skin on her neck and forearms had pricked up. She tugged at the desk lid.

It was locked.

She cast around for a key. What if she forced it?

But then Propp would know he had been found out. He might flee, or hunt her down.

She was about to turn her back when she noticed a tiny white triangle poking from beneath the closed lid. She knelt. It was the corner of a piece of paper.

Delphine licked her thumb and forefinger and tugged. The paper resisted. She tried again. It started to slide out through the crack.

She almost had it out when the paper snagged on something. She pulled. The top of the sheet tore sickeningly.

She examined the damage. The rip went right along the top of the page. She felt as if she were choking. She tried holding it back together. Was it still noticeable? Yes, very.

There was nothing to be done. She just had to hope that Propp would not notice. She spread the page flat on the desk lid. It was handwritten in blue ink on smooth rag paper with crisp edges. The text was annotated in several spots by a second author – the marginal notes were not in English; they were peppered with exclamation marks. These additions, she assumed, had been made by Propp.

She read:

> *believe we were sent as punishment for their sins. They had grown idle – so the second book teaches – foregoing the hunt and strength and the extermination of fear, and adopting the sedentary life of the farmer. They had forgotten Hem, Makash, Requen, Dar, Matesh and Ko, cultivated grain alcohol and opened their minds to foreign ideas. They had mixed with the vesperi.* And when we came – so the third book teaches – their warriors were slow with drink and they had lost the tongue of the horned pantheon and so could not call to Hem, Makash, Requen, Dar, Matesh nor Ko (who would not have heeded their petitions in any case), and thus they were brought low, and made serfs in the land they once ruled. Whether atonement (if possible at all) is best reached through self-abnegation and acceptance of this divine punishment or by exacting vengeance upon their subjugators is a tense point of doctrinal*

And the page ended there.

It sounded like something from the Bible. Delphine did not recog-

---

* Propp had underlined this word three times in red ink. The third stroke ended in a blot, as if his pen had lingered while he contemplated adding a fourth.

nise any of the names. She wrinkled her nose. Maybe it was a red herring.

She slipped the paper back under the lid, taking care not to tear it any further, and turned to the bookshelves. As she crossed the room, she noticed four deep dents in the rug, left by the trolley's casters. She would have to remember to return it to its original position before she left.

She tried to open the shelves' glass doors. They were locked too. She peered at the tomes inside – tobacco- and scab-coloured spines, with crumbling gold-leaf titles in French and Latin and languages she didn't know.

A clatter made her spin round. She held her breath, listening.

There. A scuffling, like a rat.

The sound had come from behind the green armchair. The armchair squealed and growled as she heaved it aside.

She had revealed a large object covered with dust sheets. She knelt. She felt dizzy. The sound had stopped.

The dust sheets were grey and slightly clammy beneath her fingers. She bit her lip. She lifted a corner. She squinted. Wires? Her head was blocking the light from the room's single bulb. She leant to the right.

Voices.

She dropped the sheet and leapt up. The words were muffled but the easy, baritone lilt was unmistakable.

Propp was coming.

She felt the walls closing in. What was he doing back so soon?

Delphine threw her hands up, clutched at her hair. She caught her panicked reflection in the bookshelves' glass doors and stopped.

Mother had taught her to plant her feet firmly on the floor and take a deep breath whenever she felt overwhelmed. Delphine forced herself to hold still for a single inhalation. She breathed out.

She could lock herself in.

She ran to the door. The keyhole was empty. She must have left the key in the other side of the door.

Propp's voice was getting nearer. She heard him chuckle.

There were no windows, no exits except back the way she came.

She ran to the wardrobe. The doors creaked as she eased them open. She gritted her teeth. Propp's voice in the corridor continued.

The wardrobe was full. The bottom was heaped with packing cases. The hangers were thick with clothes – one side full of Mr Propp's usual pinstripe suits and neatly pressed trousers, the other packed with plus-fours and little jackets and lots of male garments many, many sizes too small for him. She shut the doors.

Propp was just outside the room.

The fireplace! The hearth was spacious (Delphine had heard Dr Lansley loudly complain that the Hall's ancient flues were too wide and lacked suction), the iron grate replenished with fresh kindling and logs. She could hide herself inside until he had gone. She was about to scramble in when she remembered she had moved the armchair. She grabbed it and began dragging it back into position.

She heard Propp's voice rise in surprise. He turned the key. The door locked. He rattled the door knob.

Delphine ran to the fireplace and ducked under the lintel. She heard the bolt unlock. The chimney was broad and cool. Hidden behind the lintel, a raised brick platform curved out at chin height to form the base of the flue. She threw an arm up onto it. Her palm skidded in hard, crumbly dust. Ash rushed about her ears as the study door swung open. With a hop, she dragged herself up onto the smoke shelf.

Pulling her legs up behind her, she remembered the tea trolley, shoved into a corner so she could reach the desk.

She remembered she had left the light on.

'Come,' said Propp. If he was shocked to find his room lit up, it did not show in his voice. 'Please excuse mess. I write book. I stay very, very late. Ho – so cold! You like calvados?' She heard the clank of the empty bottle. 'Good for writing, good for dreams. Hmm.' He made a noise in the back of his throat. 'When we live, it is best to be awake. But when we must sleep, it is best to dream.'

Delphine looked up. The flue was a black pillarbox, rising, rising towards a distant smudgy slit of light. It smelt like paint and liquorice. She could not see her hands, but when she smeared her thumb across her palm she felt a greasy layer of creosote.

Hugging her knees to her chest, she listened to Propp's heavy footsteps as he moved from rug to floorboards. What were all those wires connected to under the dust sheet? Why did he have a wardrobe half-full of clothes that would only fit a young boy?

'I show you something.' A click. The squeal of hinges. The light in the hearth narrowed and flared as his shadow crossed it. 'Eighteen years ago, in Kars, old woman sell me this book. You are artist. Look at pictures. Tell me what you think.'

Delphine held her breath and listened. She could hear the crackle of pages turning.

'She was, uh, houselady? How to . . . She, uh, she rent rooms?'

'Landlady?' said Daddy.

Delphine let out a small involuntary yelp then slapped a hand over her mouth. That was his voice! It was him! Daddy was here!

'*Yes,*' Propp purred, rolling the syllable, giving no indication he had heard her, 'landlady. Thank you. She find book in room.'

'I, um . . . I'm afraid I can't value it.'

It was peculiar hearing Daddy's voice again. The chimney's acoustics gave it a dull, mechanical ring.

'I'm not an antiques expert,' he said. 'I'm a painter.'

'Ah!' Propp's cry was so loud she shrank back from the opening. 'But *this* is why I ask you! Book is pffft. Paper. Leather. Worthless. What do you *see?*'

Delphine could hear the slight squeak in Daddy's nostrils as he breathed. Mother said the war had ruined his sinuses. He was for ever getting nosebleeds. Daddy said the bleeding helped his headaches.

'Well . . . they're perfectly nice woodcuts. Rather . . . conventional. I can't read the text but I presume this is a book of fairytales?'

'Hmm.' Propp's shadow wavered in the fireplace. Delphine leant forward, waiting for him to speak. She ached to drop down into the hearth and surprise Daddy.

But no. If she just waited until they left again, she could get a look under that sheet . . .

'Thank you, my dear friend,' said Propp. 'Interesting. Very interesting.' His footsteps tramped back across the room. 'It is just pastime of mine, collecting books. Now, I expect you curse my name – I keep you from food!' Hinges shrieked. Something clicked. 'Come, brother, let us go.'

She heard Daddy's lighter footsteps move towards the door and her chest near-burst with the need to follow him. She balled her hands into fists.

'Wait,' said Daddy. 'Mr Propp . . . I understand you are a, uh . . . *physician*, of sorts.'

'I am dance teacher.'

'But you . . . your *methods* . . . they can . . . ' Daddy stopped. 'Sir, if I may be candid, lately I find I am . . . less than master of myself.'

'Yet until he admits this, no man may be free.'

Daddy was quiet for a time. 'Do you think you can help me?'

He had never sounded so frail.

She chewed on a knuckle.

Propp cleared his throat. 'What do you fear, brother?'

'I, uh . . . I suppose I fear illness and old age, and uh . . . some misfortune befalling my family, I fear failing in my duty as a – '

'NO!' A great crash made Delphine bite down on her knuckle so hard she drew blood. 'You lie!' Propp was yelling. 'You stand in my room and you lie!' She listened to his heavy, angry breaths, the silence spreading behind them. When he spoke again, his voice was low, bristling with menace. 'Do not ask me to shut your wounds if you cannot stand to be burned.'

Propp took a few steps. She heard the rustle and rip of paper.

'Take. Write.'

'Write what?'

'That which you cannot bear to say.'

'I don't . . . I don't understand what you . . . '

'When I clap hands, write. Not in usual, mechanical way. Do not think. Simply let pencil move. When I clap hands again, stop.'

'But I . . . '

A clap.

What was Propp doing? Why was Daddy letting himself be spoken to like this?

Delphine curled her toes and waited. She felt lightheaded from breathing so shallowly – she was sure the noise would give her away.

A clap.

'Now,' said Propp, 'fold in half, and half again.' He exhaled – a long, wheezing note. 'Please pass to me.' Footsteps. 'Good.'

Propp's shadow filled the hearth. 'This is what I teach. To choose. To wake. To dance.'

She tensed. Propp made a familiar grunt as he knelt. Delphine closed her eyes. She tipped her head back and prayed he would not hear her.

She heard the crumpling of more paper. In a suffocating rush, she realised what he was doing.

A scuff. The chimney came alive with light.

Propp blew. The light flared.

'To warm room for my return,' he said, rising. She heard him unfold a fireguard and slide it into place. 'Let us eat.' He walked away.

The door slammed.

Delphine shuffled to the edge of the smoke shelf that hung over the fire. Ash and dirt fell hissing into the hearth. The kindling had already caught – ginger-blue tongues flickered between the split logs. She dangled her legs over the lip of the smoke shelf and tried to kick a log out of the grate before it caught. The heat against the soles of her sandals rose from hot to stinging.

Her legs weren't long enough. She planted her palms on the cool brick and edged her backside forward, straining to reach the logs with her toe. The space left by the lintel was too narrow to jump down without landing in the fire.

Smoke was making her eyes water. She drew her foot away, wincing, tried with the other one. She clipped one of the logs; it slipped deeper into the grate. Flames lapped from the gaps it left – she felt a sharp pain and tugged her foot clear.

She slid back from the edge of the shelf and tried to catch her breath. She had to act. If she jumped now, before the logs caught, her feet and ankles would be badly blistered but she would survive.

The inside of the flue was lit up, flowing in the firelight. Thick deposits of creosote glistened, disappearing behind rising smoke.

She turned her head and coughed. She was sweating. A sick weight grew in her belly.

What would happen if she crawled into the chimney corner and lay down, her cardigan pulled over her head? Delphine tried turning her back on the flames and getting as low as she could. She blinked away tears. The air was thick with fumes. She experimented with sucking air in and out through the corner of her mouth. She felt lightheaded.

Propp said he wrote in long bouts. He might return and toss more logs into the grate. He might keep it going for hours.

Perhaps he had known she was hiding. Perhaps this was his way of getting rid of her.

Delphine felt a surge of panic. She cried out – she could not stop herself.

'Help!' She beat on the greasy brick walls. 'Help!'

She bent over to cough and breathe. She could barely see.

When she raised her head, she saw, high above, the faint crack of light where chimney opened onto sky.

It was too far. The chimney pot would be too small, probably covered with mesh to stop birds nesting.

But what about the first floor? There was a second fireplace not ten yards above her.

She would never make it. There were no handholds and . . .

She wiped sweat from her face with the sleeve of her cardigan, then took it off and bunched it over her mouth. She glanced up the chimney again.

She had done harder climbs. The cliffs on holiday last year. Onto the roof of the changing huts at St Eustace's. The oak tree in the meadow behind her house.

She should never have touched the key. She should have returned to her bedroom, washed her hands, then come down for lunch. She did not want to make this choice. She did not want this to be real.

She thumped the wall. The pain brought her round.

Mother's favourite phrase was 'needs must when the devil drives'. It meant sometimes you just had to do things whether you wanted to or not. They were never pleasant things.

Delphine stood and pressed her back against the wall. The brick-work was sticky. She flattened her palms, then jumped and kicked out, digging her feet as high as she could into the opposite wall. Her heels skidded. She tensed her legs. Her heels stopped.

Smoke thickened. Flakes of black paper rose around her like snow in negative. Biting her lip, she relaxed her left foot and slid it a little higher up the wall. She did the same with her right elbow. Then she slid her right foot up a little. Finally, she slid her left elbow upwards. With all four limbs planted, she scraped her shoulders a few inches higher.

She stopped to catch her breath. Perspiration glued her vest to her skin. Her eyes stung; she had to keep them shut.

She had climbed barely four inches, and she felt exhausted.

Needs must, she told herself, and slid her left foot a little higher.

Scrape, tense, breathe. She could hardly catch her breath. The flue tapered as she climbed, letting her bend her knees a little.

Whenever she had read about Victorian orphans working as sweeps, the chimneys were always cramped, hellish crawlways, wretched urchins scrabbling with fingertips and knees to reach the top. She had the opposite problem – the bottom of the flue was so wide she had to keep her legs extended to hold herself in place.

Her left heel slipped. She felt the drop in her stomach. She kicked out, slammed her elbows into the brickwork.

For a moment, the house was spinning round her.

She was not falling. Her feet were splayed but secure. She could feel her heart thudding against her chin. Her skinned elbows throbbed.

Don't look down. Needs must.

Scrape, tense, breathe.

She was sure the bricks felt different beneath her soles. Slightly hollow. Blinking away tears, Delphine opened her eyes.

She could just make out an opening above her toes, cut into the side of the flue. It was a few feet wide, just large enough to squeeze through – if only she could reach it. She ground her elbows into the brickwork behind her and squinted at the gap. Her arms were shaking; tremors spread through her back, into her legs. If she slid her feet in first, she'd fall backwards down the chimney. Just imagining it made her woozy.

Gingerly, she lifted her left elbow and reached for the lip of the opening. Her outstretched fingers clutched at air, a clear six inches shy. She replanted her elbow, trying to ignore the pain in her calves. The only way she could think to do it was to push off from the wall behind her and grab the opening with both hands. Then she could scramble through head-first.

It would mean a dizzying instant of holding on to nothing. If she missed her handhold, she would die.

The longer she waited, the weaker she would be. Delphine shifted her weight from her heels to her toes. She coughed, spat. She sucked in a last breath.

Three . . .

The trick with a countdown was to fool yourself. To go before you were ready. Before your body tried to stop you.

Two . . .

Delphine slapped her palms against the tacky wall behind her and shoved. She tucked her legs and swung her arms forward. She felt her toes drop. She was falling.

Her fingers grasped the lip of the opening. Pain slammed through her wrists. Her toes scrunched to a halt. Her sweaty right hand slipped, then found purchase.

She breathed out.

A chunk of wall came away in her fist. Her body swung out in a cascade of mortar; her feet skidded, lost their grip. She saw the black brick vanish, heard it pulverise against the bottom of the flue.

She was hanging by the fingertips of one hand.

Her legs dangled helplessly beneath her. She clawed with her free hand; soot and mortar showered her eyes. She could not see. She was coughing, gasping.

Her fingers found the jagged edge where part of the wall had come away. The back of the fireplace was just a single layer of bricks – it was never built to hold a person's weight. She felt it shudder as she strained to drag herself upwards, her feet scrabbling for toeholds. She had to pull herself into the hole. Her arms were about to give out completely.

She could not breathe. She dry-gagged. Her ears rung. She was blacking out.

Her fingers slipped.

Cold fingers gripped her wrist.

A jolt of shock and revulsion energised her. She pedalled her legs. She scrambled and scraped and kicked and screamed and dragged herself hand over hand up into the gap. She wriggled through the slot between the back of the fireplace and the lintel, emerging in an unlit room.

Delphine crawled out of the hearth and rolled onto her back. She lay there, hacking, breathing. The floorboards felt so good against her head and spine.

But who had grabbed her?

She glanced around. Dust sheets formed a grey mountainscape. A dim, buttery glow leaked from the edges of a door.

She looked at her hands. They were thick with soot and creosote. Blood shone on her fingertips.

Perhaps the lack of air had made her hallucinate.

When she was finally able to stand, Delphine dragged a dust sheet off what turned out to be a stack of wicker lawn chairs. She wrapped it round her filthy clothes and pulled it over her head to hide her hair and face. It dragged behind her as she crossed the room.

The door opened onto a quiet hallway. Everyone was still at lunch. Delphine stepped out, clutching the dust sheet to her chest. She staggered through empty corridors like a ghost.

In the bathroom, steam clouded as she brushed ash from her hair. Her clothes lay in a sticky black grot, ruined.

She was about to take the scrubbing brush from its brass hook when she noticed a scrap of writing-paper stuck to one of her discarded socks. She stooped and unpeeled it.

It was badly charred, but she recognised the elegant handwriting immediately. A few words were still legible, pristine in a dark halo of burnt paper:

r sleeps in Avalon

CHAPTER 5

I CANNOT BEAR A GUN

April 1935

It was a cloudless morning. Delphine and Mr Garforth stood in rippling shade on the east side of the meadow. The wind broke against a bank of elms sleeved in ivy and fell away to the gentle chook and baw of broody hens inside their sitting boxes.

The plywood boxes were arranged in rows of seven, raised from the ground, with sloping roofs, like little beach huts. In front of each one, Mr Garforth had driven a Y-shaped hazel stick into the grass. From each stick trailed a length of butcher's string. He tapped his cane against the side of the nearest box.

'It's ten o'clock.'

Delphine knelt at the first box. Three neat air holes had been drilled in the door. She twisted the latch at the top and the door fell open to form a ramp. A Light Sussex hen, with plump white body and black speckled wings, sat on a nest of hay. It turned one eye towards the light and let out a low, rather surly, cluck. Just as Mr Garforth had shown her, Delphine slid one hand under the hen's warm breast and lifted it clear of a nest containing twenty small olive eggs. The hen pumped its wings and kicked. Delphine placed a palm on its back. She waited. The bird calmed.

'Good,' said Mr Garforth.

Holding the hen in one hand, she tethered it to the first hazel stick, looping the string round its leg in a slipknot. She set the bird down beside a dish of water and closed the box. She looked at Mr Garforth. He nodded. She moved to the second box, turned the latch and repeated the process. Mr Garforth watched as she worked down the line. He leant on his stick, occasionally tilting his head and narrowing his eyes to indicate qualified approval.

She tethered the seventh hen, scattered a few handfuls of mixed grain.

'Why won't you teach me?'

Mr Garforth raised his downy eyebrows. 'I am teaching you.'

'To shoot.'

Laughing, he took one hand from his cane and swiped at the air.

'Come on. There's two more rows to be done.'

'I'm serious.'

'So am I.' He walked to the next row of sitting boxes and tapped his cane against the roof. 'If we don't get them out on time they'll empty their backsides over their own eggs.'

Delphine hid her reddening cheeks by pretending to massage her temples. She worked down the next row of broodies in silence.

When the last hen was pecking at grain, she looked at him again.

'I already know all about guns.'

'How could you possibly know about guns?'

Delphine gazed down at the feeding hens and thought of a sheriff crouched amongst boulders on a windswept mesa, picking off Red Indians with his 1873 Winchester lever-action rifle, their hallooing war cries in his ears and the taste of salt on his lips as he loaded another magazine, took aim, squeezed the trigger. She thought of a detective inspector brandishing his heavy police pistol as he thundered down a wooden jetty after scar-puckered platinum smugglers. She thought of Rogers of the Machine Gun Corps, ripping through Boche with his Vickers gun while the boys dragged Jenkins into cover and used a pocket knife sterilised in a candle flame to dig shrapnel out of his thigh. She thought of pages crackling beneath her fingertips, the taste of butterscotch candies, her toes warm under the quilt, the smell of ink and paper; the refuge; the horror.

'Research,' she said.

'Research.'

Delphine waited for him to say more. When she glanced up, he was watching her with thin, canny eyes the colour of tea.

'Well then, expert,' he said, 'answer me this: when a soldier looks into his enemy's eyes, what does he most fear to see?'

Delphine tutted. 'That's not a gun question.'

'Certainly it's a gun question.'

She hesitated. 'Hatred.'

Mr Garforth shook his head. 'You don't know anything.'

'What's the answer, then?'

'It's no good telling. You have to *learn* it.'

'So teach me,' she said. '*Please*.'

Mr Garforth walked to the third and final row of sitting boxes. 'Give me one good reason.'

Delphine knelt by the first door in line. The latch was stiff.

'We might get invaded.'

'By who?'

The latch gave. 'Bolsheviks.'

'You don't even know what that means.'

'I do.'

Mr Garforth leant forward on his cane. 'Go on, then.'

Delphine lowered the door. She lifted out the soft, white hen.

'Well, I didn't say it would definitely be Bolsheviks. They were just an example.'

'What on earth makes you think there'll be an invasion?'

She fumbled the string and had to grope around for it, hen clutched to her chest.

'Nothing.' She worked the loop over sharp, splayed toes, pulled it tight. 'Anyway, if you teach me to shoot I can help control vermin.'

'Like Bolsheviks?'

'Like foxes.'

'They're not "vermin". I don't like that word. They do what they must to feed their families. They're predators.'

'You still shoot them.'

'Sometimes,' he said, 'but mostly I use traps. A trap doesn't need to be fed, doesn't mind waiting, and while men sleep, a trap is at work. Well-laid traps do the work of twenty men.'

'Poachers, then.'

'The answer is no.'

Delphine moved to the next box. 'You're worried about breaking the law.'

'Nonsense. It's my land and I do as I please.'

'It belongs to the 4th Earl of Alderberen.'

'Do you see him anywhere?' Mr Garforth scanned the horizon.

'So teach me.'

'No.'

'Hey, these eggs are cracked.'

Mr Garforth came and squinted into the gloomy box, grunting as he stooped.

Delphine stood holding the broody. 'Are they ruined?'

He gripped his cane and heaved himself back upright.

'They're not cracked. They're chipped.'

Delphine wrinkled her nose. The hen pedalled its legs; she stroked behind its blood-red comb till it settled.

'I don't understand.'

Mr Garforth rolled his eyes. 'They're ready to hatch, you halfwit.'

'Oh.'

'Yes, "oh".' He retrieved a stub of chalk from the pocket of his waxed jacket and drew a cross on the roof of the box. 'When we come round tomorrow they might be the first of the new covey. Shut the door before they chill.'

Delphine closed the box and tethered the broody to its hazel stick. She watched it pecking at the dirt.

'Do they know?' she said. 'That the eggs they're sitting on aren't their own.'

He pressed an index finger to his dry lips. 'Shh!'

'Oh, shut up.'

His grin exposed yellow dentures. 'They're chickens. They don't know anything. Long as they've got their routine, they're happy. Now, come on.'

Delphine took the last of the broodies from its nest and scattered some more grain. She stood back with her hands clasped behind her tailbone, listening to murmuring clucks and the rustle of beaks in grass. Mr Garforth walked up and down the lines of hens like a colonel inspecting his troops. Every so often he would bend and riffle through a hen's plumage with his thumb. Near the end of the second row, he sat down and took hold of a broody with his big hands. Gently, he rocked it back and forth until it defecated in a short grey spurt.

'Right.' He took out his pocket watch. 'That's time.'

She walked back to the first broody, picked it up and slipped the tether from its leg. Checking that its feet were clean, she placed it in front of its box. The bird took a last few glances right and left, then strolled back up the ramp onto its nest. She lifted the ramp, twisted the latch shut, then moved to the next box. She worked through the boxes in the order she had opened them, each time allowing the hen to walk back in of its own free will, but keeping her hands poised either side in case it tried to escape. She noticed the hen with the chipped eggs returned to its nest with an especially haughty swagger.

When the last box was shut, she fetched a bucket and trowel and began to move amongst the hazel sticks, scooping up chicken poo.

'It wouldn't have to be loaded,' she said. 'You could just show me how to hold it. Like you did before. Uh . . . I mean, I wouldn't be aiming at you this time.'

Mr Garforth picked a bit of hay off of his trousers. He turned and looked across the meadow. Beyond the sitting boxes were the wire enclosures, ready for when the poults hatched. He scratched his backside, his nails digging into a fresh white stain.

He said something, but the wind caught his voice and all she heard was 'father'.

'I'm sorry?'

He glanced back over his shoulder. 'I said what does your father make of all this? Is he happy with the idea of his daughter running round the estate with a shotgun?'

Delphine tilted the trowel; a thick dollop of excrement slid into the bucket. It stunk of ammonia and spoiled milk. Beads of sweat tickled her forehead.

'Daddy is extremely busy.'

'Too busy to ask for permission, yes, I understand.'

She stabbed the trowel into the earth below another chicken poo.

'Actually he's a very famous artist.'

'So you keep saying.'

'He's working on a new project. The Earl has let him use part of the old stables as a studio.' She downed tools and rose. 'Please. Just show me the basics.'

Mr Garforth sighed and clutched at the air. 'I said no. Why do you keep asking?'

She looked him straight in the eyes. 'Because I'm a delinquent and if you won't teach me I'll steal a gun and go shooting anyway. With your help there's less chance I'll kill myself.'

He breathed in very slowly. His eyes went to his boots, which were brindled with hen faeces and mud. When he looked back up it took him a moment to speak. He lifted an index finger.

'Tomorrow, when I do my evening rounds, you can come along. If,' he brandished the finger like a cudgel, '*if* I have to crack off a shot, I'll explain to you afterwards how I did it. Purely theoretical, mind. I've got work to do. But if you want to observe . . . that's my final offer.'

'Done!' said Delphine. She grabbed the bucket and began marching back across the field. 'I'll put these on the compost then I've got to get back. Mother says I have to start taking lessons with a tutor. I expect it'll be some stern governess with fishy breath.' She pulled a face. 'First class is at eleven.'

Mr Garforth flapped his grimy hands. 'Off you go, then. Get cleaned up!'

She turned, and her march became a run. Soon, she had left the wire fences and huts behind and she was racing north over open fields, back towards the house. Sunlight silvered the swerve of a brook amongst ancient grey alders. The smell of fresh-cut grass sang in her nostrils, the wind in her ears one long scream.

In the chimera room, all the animals watched Delphine. Delphine watched the Professor.

He was big – not flabby big, just large – and his cardigan strained to contain his broad shoulders. His hair was messy, his beard patchy brown. The only sound was the hiss of his pencil stub as he sat at a table jotting notes from the selection of books spread out in front of him, tracing sentences with a thick finger before returning to the foolscap in a whisper of lead.

He did not seem old enough to be a professor. The look of him was all wrong. He ought to be a wrestler, or a lumberjack. Perhaps he was another foreign spy, in league with Mr Propp – a mountain-man from the Urals, sent to bump off Lord Alderberen. There was definitely something funny about him – something that itched at her brain.

Delphine felt a slap of recognition. She had met him before.

He was the man from the train – the one with the crossword and the cigar, the one who had offered to pay for her ticket. The memory brought a stampede of associations: the stuffiness of the carriage, the frozen world outside, the hope. She fought back vertigo.

Delphine steadied herself on the Portuguese card table that served as her desk. She gazed around the room. Glass display cases lined the walls, full of novelty taxidermy: a tortoise with three viper heads, a cat with a lion's mane, a scorpion dove, a chimp with bat wings, a unicorn, and a creature that the little bronze plaque beneath called a 'wolpertinger': a rabbit with antlers, fangs and downy aquamarine wings. Each animal was posing in a diorama that implied its natural environment – the chimp-bat hunched on a tropical limb, the tortoise-hydra trudging through red volcanic sand.

Chips of coloured glass glinted in their eye sockets. The animals seemed to be watching her, and she didn't much care for it.

'Excuse me,' she said.

The Professor looked up from his studies. 'Hello.'

'I think we've met before.'

He scratched the bridge of his nose; his eyes and mouth converged on it, as if in conference. 'Anything is possible.'

'It was just before Christmas. I didn't have a ticket. You helped me get away without paying.'

'Did I indeed?' The Professor planted his boulder-like elbows at

73

the extreme edges of the desk and laced his fingers. 'Then it is providential we find ourselves in each other's company once more. Don't interrupt me during my studies and you may consider your debt repaid in full.' He returned his attention to the books spread before him.

'Aren't you going to teach me something?'

He set down his pencil heavily. 'If I must. What would you like to learn?'

Delphine produced a piece of paper. 'I made a list.'

The Professor leaned forward. 'Go on.'

She gripped the edge of the table, inhaled.

'Major sieges: 500 BC to Present, ballistics, what plants cure a fever, what plants can you crush up to make a poison, how to make a pit trap, how to skin an elephant, pressure points that stop the human heart, explosives, ju-jitsu, camouflage, espionage, code-breaking, how to survive if you crash-land in the Peruvian rainforest, how to survive if you crash-land in Arctic tundra, how to survive if you crash-land in the Soviet Union, Russian, French, sword technique, piracy, tunnelling, the Lincoln assassination, squids, the secrets of Freemasonry . . . ' She turned the page over. 'Animal calls, bomb-making, navigation, uh . . . poisoning . . . no, I've said that. Did I say that? How to make different poisons. How to catch a fish when you haven't a net. Sailing. Oh, and how to drive a tank.'

The Professor watched her for a moment.

'Nothing else?'

'No thank you. Sir.'

He lifted a hand, beckoned. Delphine pushed back her chair and walked to his desk. Between her desk and his, a tasselled rug the colour of beef paste lay across bare floorboards.

He slid a book from the bottom of the pile and thrust it towards her.

Delphine took it. The book was crimson and heavy.

'What's this?'

The Professor did not look up from his work. 'Read it then write a one-thousand-word essay on your understanding of its contents.'

She tilted it and read the spine: *Early Assyrian Art*. 'This isn't about poisons.'

'Very shrewd, Miss Venner. Only nine hundred and ninety-six words to go.' He crossed something out in a sharp slash of graphite. 'And don't "sir" me. I'm not a knight and I don't care to be reminded of the fact. You may call me Professor Carmichael.' He glanced up. 'Stop gawping. I have important work to complete and you are disturbing me.'

Delphine walked back to her desk in a daze. The stuffed hybrids watched as she sat down and opened the book in front of her. Its pages smelt of damp hay.

Mother slept. When her eyelids had fluttered during lunch Delphine had bit back her excitement. Now Mother lay in her bedroom, slumped across the made bed, her breathing so shallow it was almost invisible. Delphine closed the partition door and crept out into the corridor. In the alcove opposite, an alabaster minotaur stood with its arms folded, chin raised and askance, a thick ring hanging from its snout.

When she reached the landing, the Great Hall was empty. Everyone was with Mr Propp in the music room, awakening their kidneys. She went down the main staircase, across the chequerboard floor and out the front doors. The day was bright and gusty, twists of cloud scudding across a willow-pattern sky. She crossed the gravel and entered the stables through a side door.

Inside was dark. Drying canvases lay against walls or propped in easels, forming a cramped labyrinth. The air was warm and still and ripe with turps. She pulled the collar of her blouse up over her nose and picked her way over jam jars and slabs of wood rainbowed in daubs.

A narrow alley turned back on itself and opened out into a chamber. Four grey walls faced inwards. In the centre, beneath a single low-watt bulb, Daddy squatted on a three-legged stool with a cigarette in his lips, glaring at a big canvas. The palette in his right hand was a maelstrom of chocolate, russet and dirty gamboge. The colours bled down his forearm, onto the rolled-up sleeve of his shirt. Paint tubes lay around him like spent shells. Three brushes stood in a jar of murky turpentine. His other hand, still wrapped in gauze, yawned hungrily.

'Don't tread on that,' he said, without looking round. He gestured vaguely with his painting hand, fingers opening, snapping shut.

She looked down. The floor was a brittle topography of old paint-stiffened newspaper – crags and gullies and lakes of spilt colour. At the tip of her sandal, an empty tube of Prussian blue lay stamped out like a slug.

Daddy's painting hand plucked the cigarette from his mouth, then felt about on the crate beside his stool till it found the chipped rim of a mug. He lifted the mug to his lips; he swigged, then looked off to one side and said: 'Ah.'

'Daddy, I need to – '

'Shh.' His torso canted left as he put down the mug. He straightened, swept a twist of damp, steely hair back behind his ear. The light of the naked bulb brought out the leanness in his arms and jowls. Delphine's eyes were beginning to water on account of the turpentine. She was sure Daddy ought not to allow flames in such a poorly ventilated space.

He put a fist to his mouth, cocked his head. The canvas, as far as she could see, was a mass of undifferentiated brown behind a few slashes of white. Daddy stared at it as if the act of concentrating alone would drag an image to the surface. Plaits of smoke rose from between his knuckles and folded against the bare beams of the ceiling.

He tipped his head back and groaned. Then: 'Come here, darling. Mind my mess.'

Delphine held her breath. She began picking her way towards him, sticking to patches of bare floor, taking care not to tread on anything that might crack or crunch or squelch. She drew up beside him. He smiled.

'There's my little Delphy.' His painting hand reared up and pinched her cheek. The gauze was rough against her ear.

'Ow.' She rubbed the tender skin.

'Come on. Let's not have whingeing.' He took a last drag on his cigarette then stubbed it out in a terracotta dish.

'Daddy.'

He put his palette down and took a tobacco tin from the crate. He began rolling a cigarette.

'Yes?'

'I need to tell you something.'

Daddy worked the cigarette paper back and forth between the thumb and fingers of his left hand. Dry paint flaked from his fingernails.

'Tell.'

'The first day Mother and I got here. Before you arrived.' Perhaps it was the fumes, but she felt the start of a headache. 'I was walking around the house. I overheard a conversation.'

Daddy stuck the cigarette between his incisors like a toothpick. He retrieved a matchbook from his pocket.

'You've been listening at keyholes again, haven't you?'

'No, I . . . ' She was about to fib, but something in his eyes made her reconsider. 'There was a hole in the wall. The west wing is full of holes. I never meant to spy – they were talking so loudly.'

Daddy flipped open the matchbook and tore out a match. 'Who?'

'I think . . . one of them was Mr Propp.'

He dragged the match down the rough strip. It did not light.

'You shouldn't eavesdrop. We're guests here.'

'Daddy, he said there's going to be a war.'

'Then there probably is.'

He struck the match and it lit with a noise like someone ripping open a present. His face rippled purple and orange. He made a cave with his hand and brought the flame to the tip of his cigarette.

'He said they've been taking trips over the channel for secret talks.'

'Who was he saying this to?'

'I . . . I don't know. An old man.'

'An old man.' Daddy blew smoke over his shoulder. 'Go to the library. You're to spend the afternoon reading silently.'

'But – '

'I won't have you slandering our hosts.'

'But he said – '

'You've told me what he said.'

'You're not listening! They – '

'Out. Now.' He picked up his palette.

Delphine took a deep breath, bunched her fists.

'Daddy, I think the Bolsheviks are plotting to kill me.'

Daddy leant back on the stool. His shoulders began to shake. The tremors moved to his arms and head and it was only when he opened his mouth that she realised he was laughing. He took a pull on his cigarette and swung round to face her.

'Oh, Delphy.' His painting hand settled on her shoulder. Gauze crackled as it gripped. 'One whiff of a foreign accent and you think you're Richard Hannay.'

She tried to slip loose from his grasp. His hand clung.

'It's not a joke! Mr Propp is a spy.'

'He's not a spy. He's a teacher and a thinker and a healer. He's going to make us all well again.'

Delphine stared into her father's eyes and saw only clean burning zeal.

'But I *heard* him,' she said.

'Perhaps you misheard.'

'But he was so angry.'

'Perhaps he had good reason.'

Delphine could feel her resolve melting. What had seemed a minute ago like a fat and damning dossier now felt wispy as a fading dream. She looked down at her sandals.

'I want to go home.'

'Come now, Delphy, what did I say about whingeing?' Fingers grabbed her chin and tilted her head up. He breathed yellow smoke in her face. 'For now, this is our home.' He had shaved unevenly. Black bristles dotted the curve of his upper lip. 'I know it feels new and strange, but you mustn't worry. Everyone here wants to make the world a better place. Be a good girl and play your part.'

Smoke stung her eyes. 'But I'm scared.'

'I won't let anything happen to you. Please. Give the Society a chance. It would make me very happy. You want me to be happy, don't you?'

Her head was pounding. Over Daddy's shoulder, the canvas churned crimson, raven's wing, Passchendaele brown. She let her arms go limp.

'Yes, Daddy.'

CHAPTER 6

UNHAPPY AND FORSAKEN TOAD

April 1935

Mr Garforth hunched over a rumbling cauldron, boiling blood off gin traps. Delphine watched him from the doorway of the cottage. He wore a pair of grubby cloth gloves. Steam condensed on his cheeks and brow, droplets tugging at his whiskers. Using the head of a pick, he hooked out a pair of dripping steel jaws, rinsed them with a ladle of cold water, then tossed them into the dirt with the others.

Mr Garforth bought the traps from Mr Wightman, the blacksmith, for twenty-nine shillings a dozen. They were big enough for rabbits but he used them for rats. He said the smaller traps were apt to amputate a limb, letting the rat escape. He said they were too light, and if you forgot to peg them down a rat might drag a gin off into the undergrowth.

Once he was done boiling the traps he would bury them in the ground for a week to get rid of the scent of humans. Then he would replace any sprung traps along runs or around the sitting boxes. Delphine said it seemed like a lot of fuss. Mr Garforth said there was fuss and then there was fuss, and if rats gnawed their way into a box they could devour all the eggs and strip the broody to a skeleton in a single night. He said he'd heard stories from men back in France who'd had to burn the bodies of horses that had frozen to death on the battlefield, and once the fire was lit hundreds of rats began pouring out of the horses' mouths. He said he knew of a private who lost a hand when a rat bite went bad, another who woke to find a black rat gnawing at his eyelid.

'Gas is nasty, granted,' he said, throwing a gin trap onto the pile, 'but there's not a soldier living who didn't learn to fear and hate rats. If you see one, kill it. They're vermin.'

'I thought you didn't like the word vermin,' said Delphine.

'I don't,' said Mr Garforth, 'and I don't like rats.'

Delphine chewed her twist of liquorice and said nothing. She thought of how she had checked the traps for him that morning, walking through crunchy, fragrant fields, collecting the traps that had caught something, springing and resetting the ones that hadn't. She thought of how she had found the dead weasel, blunt gin teeth champing its spine, and, in front of it, in a plum-dark pool of blood, a shivering infant rat, barely bigger than her thumb. She thought of its downy hair, of how it had not tried to run away.

She had tightened her grip on the coal shovel Mr Garforth had given her for dispatching anything still alive. She had held it above the rat; the shovel had cast a Zeppelin-shaped shadow. She had braced herself for the coup de grace.

Then she had scooped the creature up and carried it back to the Hall. She had put it inside an old liquorice allsorts tin with a saucer of water and a handful of porridge oats. She had stabbed holes in the lid and hidden it under her bed.

She watched Mr Garforth work the fire with a set of bellows. He added more water to the cauldron, then handed her the bucket to refill at the pump.

The rat would probably be dead by the time she got back. Part of her hoped that it was, if only to assuage the guilt she felt every time she looked at Mr Garforth. How could she witter on about defending King and Country when she didn't have the guts to kill a single baby rat?

When she reached the pump she found a white feather had stuck to her sandal. She peeled it off and tried to fling it away, but it wafted back and landed at her feet.

The pump squeaked as she filled the bucket. Delphine dipped

her hands into the icy water, washing them again and again and again.

Later that afternoon, she hid inside the wall and watched the old lady sleeping: the swell and sink of the duvet, the skin that hung from the ancient jaw like gills. Delphine found herself thinking of a shrunken head she had seen at the carnival when she was very little – the smell of damp sawdust and canvas, the hushed dark of the tent, and a scrunched brown thing, rather like a toffee apple, framed by matted hair, its lips fastened with twine. She remembered gazing, transfixed by the sad, lidded eyes, waiting for it to draw breath, to speak. How Mother had scolded Daddy for showing his daughter something so frightening! And so Delphine, not wishing to get him in more trouble, had kept quiet when, for the next three weeks, the head stood watch at the end of her bed, heavy and silent as a bag of suet, vanishing whenever she opened her eyes.

Delphine watched the old lady and felt a prickling wonder. She could not imagine being so old, existing inside such ruin. The old lady turned, made a noise in the back of her throat. Veins tattooed her bare scalp. Beneath mottled amber lamplight, she was a wreck, breaking up on the tide that came with each stuttering breath.

Delphine drew back from the spyhole, rested against the wall. The air in the passageway was muggy and perfectly still.

She heard a whine from the other side of the wall. Delphine put her eye to the spyhole and saw Mr Propp.

He had his back to Delphine. He lowered his dumpy body into a chair at the bedside. The old lady was awake. She was crying. Mr Propp gripped her hand and smoothed her long pale fingers. As he leant in, shadows picked out tiny dents all over his bald head. Tears streamed across the old lady's cheeks. She howled, a faint, ululating sound that made Delphine's skin prickle.

Propp's lips squeaked as he kissed the old lady's brow.

'Shh shh shh shh.' His voice was steady and sonorous. '*Shutov k'ancni.*' He held her.

Delphine felt drowsy. She was falling prey to his mesmeric arts. She told herself to resist, yet a second impulse willed her to succumb.

Part of her wanted to give in to him, wanted to be important enough for him to notice and control.

Slowly, the old lady slackened and fell asleep. Mr Propp rested the back of his palm against her cheek, muttering the same incantation: 'K'ancni. K'ancni. K'ancni.'

He slid his hand away, reached for something on the bedside table. Delphine heard a metallic scrape, like coin on coin. Propp lifted his plump frame from the chair. He took his heavy silk robe from a hook on the door. From the seat of his pinstripe trousers hung a leather holster. In his right hand was a revolver.

'Mr Propp has a gun.'

Mother did not break stride. 'Delphine. *Not now.*'

'He has a gun. I saw.' Delphine struggled to keep pace as they marched through the long gallery that ran west to east along the ground floor, connecting the smoking room to the old banqueting hall. Mother had insisted she 'dress appropriately' for the symposium – a stupid pond-weedy heap of a frock that made it hard to run.

'Saw? *Saw?* What do you mean you "saw"?'

'I saw him put a Webley Mark 6 revolver down the back of his trousers.'

'Oh, don't be so ridiculous!'

'It might have been the new Mark 4 .38. I only saw it for a second.'

'Really.'

Delphine accelerated so she could turn and look Mother in the face. 'Please. I think he might be – '

'Enough!' Mother jerked to a halt and snatched Delphine's wrist. 'You will *not* start again with your, your . . . *fantasies.*'

'But Mr Propp – '

'Very well may have a gun. Many, in fact *most* of Lord Alderberen's male guests will have brought at least one with them for their stay here.'

'Not a shotgun. A revolver.' Exasperated, Delphine mimed a pistol with her free hand and aimed it at her mother's head. 'And he was carrying it with him.'

Mother stopped beside a bust of Cicero. She swatted Delphine's hand away.

'*Even if* I did consider you remotely trustworthy, I don't see what business it is of mine and, more to the point, yours, if Mr Propp chooses to carry his own property about his person. If he did have some underhand purpose in mind, I scarcely think he would have let a nosy little girl stand there and watch while he armed himself.'

'He didn't know I was . . . that is . . . ' Delphine caught herself. 'I'm not sure that he saw me. I was coming down the corridor, towards his room. He was standing there. He must have just locked the door. He had his back to me.'

'Delphine, *please*.' Mother took a step back, silver evening dress hanging from her shoulders like a popped balloon in a thorn bush. 'Not tonight, of all nights.' She hooked a finger through the chain round her neck. 'This is your father's first symposium. It's so important to him.'

'He's not even here.'

'He will be. And until he is we have a duty to be seen as a decent, respectable family.' The magnitude of the task seemed to settle on her like a great, black bird. 'Don't you want him to be happy? Don't you want him to get well?'

'Of course, I – '

'Then please. Just play your part until he arrives.'

And with that, she began dragging Delphine towards the doors, the smoke, the symposium.

The banqueting hall was a long, rectangular room, its oak-panelled walls decorated with zodiac tapestries, paintings of late medieval battle scenes, circular gilded shields of watered steel (Delphine thought they might be Indian) and – bracketed to the wall above the fireplace – a huge, gemmed war hammer. Thirty or more guests jawed and puffed, poets and business owners and composers and politicians and philosophers and old soldiers, tweed and flannel and silver Asprey cigarette cases, eyeglasses on silk ribbons and glass eyes in sallow sockets and white shrapnel scars, walking sticks and gleaming cufflinks and facial tics, pipes and cigarettes and alcohol, sloshing, gleaming, flowing.

Somewhere amongst it all was Propp.

Under her ghastly frock, Delphine was sweating. The rank, warm flavour of cigarettes caught in her throat. She stood with Mother beside the wide fireplace, part of a loose group gathered around Dr Lansley. If only she could slip away, just for a minute, to find Propp.

Dr Lansley stood with his eyes half-lidded, one glove pressed to his chest, the other swishing a cigarillo side to side. His dinner jacket squeezed his figure into a lithe S, deaf-aid cable trailing from one ear.

In the past fortnight, Mother's manner towards Dr Lansley had chilled. They now acknowledged one another with the barest of pleasantries, and were rarely seen in the same room save for meal-times. Perhaps Mother – fool though she was – was finally growing leery of Mr Propp's associates.

An older lady in a flowing green gown turned to address Mother. 'And how are you finding life at Spim?'[*]

'We're very honoured Lord Alderberen invited us.'

Dr Lansley's lips formed a half-smile, his little black moustache glinting.

'Oh, come now, don't be modest,' he said, gazing into the fire. 'Of course Lazarus invited you. Your husband's practically family.' His voice dropped a note. 'I hear he and Arthur were very close.'

Mother sipped her Tom Collins and grimaced as if it were vinegar. 'They served together, yes.'

A silence fell over the group. Alice the maid passed with a tray of drinks. Everyone took one. Delphine gritted her teeth. Without a distraction, she would never get away. She cleared her throat.

'Um, excuse me, Doctor?'

Dr Lansley looked at her without turning his head. Mother pretended to scratch her temple, glaring at Delphine pointedly behind her hand.

'Mother is fascinated by these figures.' Delphine pointed to two oak-carved statuettes either side of the fireplace. They were three feet tall and gangly, clad in mismatched bits of armour. She could

[*] The Society for the Perpetual Improvement of Man.

85

not tell if they were supposed to be human, or if the ragged shapes on their backs were wings. 'She wondered if you knew anything about them.'

Dr Lansley's eyes narrowed. He looked from Delphine to Mother.

'Is that true, Anne? I thought you'd grown tired of my little lectures.'

'Well, I . . . ' Mother coughed into her drink. 'My daughter exaggerates. I mean, I don't really know . . . '

Delphine began slipping away.

'Ah, Delphine, don't wander off.'

'They're Tudor origin,' Dr Lansley said, directing the group's attention back towards the fireplace, 'Henry the Seventh without a doubt. Look how their hands are clasped. Standard-bearers. Ten-to-one they held banners at tournaments. I'd stake my late mother's life on it.'

'Just getting some more Vimto.' Delphine held up her empty glass, but Dr Lansley was passionately placing the statuettes in their proper historical context, and nobody heard.

'Funny little devils,' said the woman in green. 'Like bats.'

Delphine escaped.

She headed for the edge of the room, where the crowd was lighter. She clipped an elbow and someone tutted. She could not see Mr Propp anywhere.

She leant against the wall and found herself next to Professor Carmichael.

The Professor clutched a sheaf of paper close to his face, mouthing words. His champagne-coloured suit was several sizes too small, stretched taut over his wide shoulders. He had slicked back his unruly brown hair with brilliantine; as he squinted in the light of the chandelier, it shimmered like kelp.

'Professor?'

The Professor started, glancing around before locating Delphine at his left.

'God almighty, girl.' He exhaled heavily. 'Don't sneak up on people like that.'

'What are you doing?' She had to shout to be heard over the chatter.

'What am I doing? *What am I doing?* Bugger off is what I'm doing. You ought to be in bed.'

'I'm on important business.'

His frown faltered. 'What's that supposed to mean?'

Delphine hesitated, wondering how much to tell him.

'I'm looking for Mr Propp,' she said.

'Not very hard, obviously. He's just there.'

The Professor nodded towards the centre of the room. Delphine turned to look, but bodies blocked the way. She wedged a heel against the skirting board and lifted herself up.

Two people were ringed in the golden glow of the chandelier: Mr Propp, smiling beneath his white moustache, and beside him, another resident of the Hall, sipping a martini as she tossed her smile from one lucky guest to another – Miss DeGroot.

Delphine glanced back at the Professor. His lips were parted and his eyes did not blink. He looked younger, somehow.

His hands snapped tight round his sheaf of paper.

'Right,' he said. 'Follow me.'

He began shouldering his way into the throng.

Guests sighed and rolled their eyes. Delphine darted into his considerable wake, the crowd closing behind her.

'Well, Ivan, if the rumours are true, you're a *very* dangerous man.'

Delphine followed the Professor to the edge of the circle surrounding Propp and Miss DeGroot. Mr Propp had one hand on his silk waistcoat, patting his belly. He chuckled, his tanned cheeks dimpling.

'No. I do not think this.' His demeanour was halfway between Heidi's grandfather and a small porcelain owl. He was diabolically cunning.

'Such innocence!' said Miss DeGroot. She had the dramatic figure of a treble clef. She wore a crisp silk blouse, sleek black trousers and a cream capelet decorated with blue swallows. Her hair hung in a slick wave of honey. Using the green divan behind her as a point of reference, Delphine guessed she was a little over four feet tall.

'Come now, Ivan. You're amongst friends.' Her soft Canadian accent was punctuated by lapses into something more exotic, as if she had painted over an old voice only for certain words to show through. She jabbed his shoulder. 'Why, in Belgravia I've had *several* gentlemen . . . ' the crowd let out cat-calls and whistles, 'if you'll let me finish . . . I've had several *respectable* gentlemen tell me in *all* sincerity that this little,' she flapped a fur-cuffed satin evening glove at the room, 'ginger group of yours is the guiding hand behind every government in the civilised world. "Watch that Mr Propp," they say,' and here she affected a stiff, military voice, '"He's a downy bird, you mark my words. Makes Rasputin look like Santa Claus." Should I be *terribly* afraid?'

Delphine gripped her glass.

'I hope,' he said, 'you told them how boring I in fact am.'

'But that's just it – when I defend you they think my head's been turned. They think I'm a lieutenant in your black gang.'

'So what do you say?'

Miss DeGroot drew on her cigarette holder and gave her audience a sly smile.

'What can I say? I tell them they're absolutely right and the revolution starts in three weeks.'

Laughter, applause. Professor Carmichael, waiting on the cusp of the group, rocking back and forth on his heels, took a fortifying puff on his cigar. He cleared his throat.

Miss DeGroot, oblivious, was pointing at the ceiling.

'Now when was *this* created?' she asked Mr Propp.

Above their heads, a complex symmetrical pattern spread from the central chandelier. Overlapping layers of circles wove huge, colourful petals, resolving at their farthest extremities into eight damascene discs of black oxidised iron and silver, each the size of a dinner plate, depicting the phases of the moon. It would, Delphine imagined, have looked perfectly boring had several fires not left the ceiling an angry mass of apocalyptic black tendrils, swarming from the centre of the universe, engulfing everything.

Mr Propp gave an exaggerated, distinctly Gallic shrug. 'I am merely dance teacher. For history, you must ask Doctor Lansley.'

'Really? I say, Doctor?' The crowd parted as Miss DeGroot shuffled round the divan towards Dr Lansley, her blond hair holding perfect shape. Delphine had to go on tiptoes to keep her in sight. 'I do beg your pardon.' She grasped one of Lansley's long thin arms, winking at Mother. For an instant, she looked like a miniature Gainsborough Lady. 'Doctor, we require your legendary expertise. We have a sudden yen for a full and frank history of the banqueting-hall ceiling.' The crowd closed behind her as she dragged him back into the centre of the room. 'Do you know anything of its provenance?' Dr Lansley and Mr Propp exchanged a glance. Lansley sucked in his prim chin.

'Ah,' he said. 'You've spotted the "lunar mandala".'

'Is it very old?' Miss DeGroot's eyes widened. 'Was it here before the house? Did the druids build it? Will it bewitch us?'

Dr Lansley swirled his brandy glass and glowered into its amber waters. 'Third Earl. That is, Lord Alderberen's father.'

Delphine had barely seen Lazarus Stokeham, 4th Earl of Alderberen, since her arrival. She had snatched glimpses of a rumpled old man who looked as if he had been poured into his bath chair, but so far the Earl remained a rumour, an idea, like the King, or Death.

The Doctor coughed into a clenched glove. 'The third Earl was a bit of a . . . well, I suppose you might call him an innovator. One of the first places in the country to install electricity – '81 or '82, it must have been. One of the first to have a telephone put in, too, although where the sense is in having one before everyone else I don't know. In any case,' he regarded the scorch marks ruefully, 'as you can see, the electric light system they rigged up was rather unsafe. Laz . . . ah, Lord Alderberen says when he first returned from India the ceiling would occasionally burst into flame, and they'd have to fling cushions up at it to put it out. Still, such is the price of ambition, I suppose. Pioneers rarely hit it in the middle of the bat.'

Professor Carmichael cleared his throat a second time. Mr Propp, Dr Lansley and Miss DeGroot turned to look at him.

'Hello!' Professor Carmichael stuck his cigar between his teeth and thrust out a hand, crossing an invisible threshold into the inner circle. 'Algernon Carmichael. Uh, Professor Algernon Carmichael.'

The crowd fell silent. Delphine felt their disapproval as a cold rush in her tummy. The Professor had breached some strange, unspoken rule. She wanted to run to him, but everyone was watching. What if Propp drew his pistol?

Mr Propp's smile neither widened nor shrank. He reached out and enclosed the Professor's hand in his.

'What is your, ah . . . "field", Professor?'

'Eclectics,' said the Professor brightly.

'Ah. I am very pleased to meet.'

'Oh, likewise, likewise. It's such an honour to meet you at last.' The Professor turned towards the wall of disapproving onlookers, winced. He pumped his arms and let out a high, staccato laugh.

'Sorry,' he said, 'perhaps this isn't the time. It's just that, well, I've been at the Hall almost a fortnight and somehow we haven't bumped into each other . . . quite bizarre! It's like you keep disappearing! The thing is, Ivan – may I call you Ivan? When you *do* have a moment, I've a project that I've been working on for five years now, and I think – well, that is to say, I *hope* – that you'll be rather interes – '

'Actually,' said Dr Lansley, stepping forward, 'we were in the middle of a conversation.'

'Really?' The Professor looked from Lansley, to Miss DeGroot, to Propp. 'Oh, I do beg your pardon. What are you talking about?'

'I'm not inviting you to join – '

'This thing,' said Miss DeGroot, nodding upwards. 'I was rather worried it might be placing us under some species of voodoo curse – that's a tremendously fetching bow tie, by the way.'

'Thank you.' The words came out a little throttled and the Professor had to fan his face with his papers. Delphine followed his gaze back up to the ceiling. 'Curse, you say? I should think the whole estate's cursed, shouldn't you? Entire medieval household, retinue and all – poof! Vanished like a Welshman on a workday. Or so the story goes.'

'Oh! So is this your area of study, Professor?'

Dr Lansley's expression was flat and hard.

'The Professor,' he spat the word, 'is here acting as schoolmaster for the Venner child.'

Delphine felt a jolt of anger. Dr Lansley had wielded her as an insult.

'Mrs Venner invited me here as a tutor, yes, but my primary area of study is . . . Put it this way – what's the first word that pops into your head if I say to you: Lemuria.'

'Um . . . lemur?' said Miss DeGroot.

'Folktale,' said Propp.

'Goodbye,' said Dr Lansley.

'Ah, no, absolutely right, absolutely right.' She saw the Professor nodding, grinning tightly. 'Any wise man would say the same. The stuff of story papers. But uh . . . ' He took a deep breath. 'I, like yourselves, am disinclined to trust the official narratives thrust upon us by the powers that be. Therefore, I have made it my life's work to uh, to . . . My point is this: during my studies of accounts of Ancient Britain, I have uncovered a glaring lacuna.'

Dr Lansley rolled his eyes. 'The only glaring lacuna is the one between your ears.'

The Professor's smile faltered. Miss DeGroot stifled a guffaw.

'But surely,' and here, the Professor made the mistake of appealing to the crowd, 'in this gathering of our nation's greatest freethinkers, no man would deny there exist worlds beyond our own?'

Delphine felt the question hang. Her mouth had gone dry.

The Professor wavered beneath a reproving silence. Dr Lansley sucked in his cheeks.

'Mr Carmichael . . . ' He paused to sigh heavily. 'The Society is a meeting place for great men of science and politics. Not a charitable foundation for, for . . . crackpots.'

'Ah, but I have proof!' The Professor took a step back, flourishing his heap of papers.

Dr Lansley glanced at them. For the second time that night, he and Propp exchanged a look.

'Well. That changes things.' Dr Lansley turned to the room. 'Ladies and gentlemen, the Society for the Perpetual Improvement of Man has a new member. I propose a toast.' He raised his brandy glass. 'To Professor Carmichael . . . the discoverer of Oz!'

Palpably relieved laughter and applause. Dr Lansley drained his glass. Other guests whooped and drank. Delphine felt heat building in her cheeks and brow. Dr Lansley turned his back on the Professor and began talking to Propp.

The Professor attempted a smile.

'All right,' he said, but no one was listening except Delphine. Humiliation made him bigger, somehow; the papers were a wilted bouquet in his giant fist.

She thought of how he had stuck up for her on the train. Indignation blazed in her heart.

'Hey.' Delphine stepped forward. 'Hey!'

Dr Lansley did not respond. She stepped nearer. 'Hey!'

He did not respond. She prodded a finger into his dinner-jacketed back.

Lansley wheeled round with a fencer's grace. When he saw her, his smile turned to a bored scowl. She stared up at his puffed-out chest, his hairy black nostrils. He exhaled from one corner of his narrow mouth.

'What do you want?'

A pulse hammered in Delphine's ear. Her face felt sticky.

'You oughtn't to speak to the Professor like that,' she said. All around, the party had gone quiet. People were turning to watch. She heard the tremble in her voice. 'He's not . . . he's a very clever man.'

Dr Lansley's scowl melted into a smirk.

'Ah, Professor – here's your secretary.' Sniggers, isolated claps. 'What's the emergency? Does the British Museum need an expert to label its new collection from Neverland?'

Delphine clenched her fists. Her vision was narrowing around Dr Lansley's wonky butterscotch grin. 'Tell the Professor you're sorry.'

Dr Lansley cocked his head. The wan skin at the corners of his mouth crinkled.

'Or what? You'll set me on fire?'

Delphine felt a cold hand on her shoulder.

'I do apologise.'

It was Mother.

Dr Lansley nodded. 'Anne.'

'Mother, not now. I'm helping the Professor.'

A woman in a diamond choker whispered something to the man at her shoulder, who snorted into his drink. Delphine glanced at the Professor for support. He did not look grateful.

Very quietly, he said: 'Miss Venner. You're making a spectacle of yourself.' He slapped a coil of slimy hair back from his eyes, grimacing. 'Please, just . . . buzz off.'

Delphine blinked, trying to hide the crushing sensation in her chest.

'Come on, Delphine,' said Mother, 'that's quite enough.'

'No, it's not.' Delphine shrugged loose. 'It's not enough at all.' She glared at Dr Lansley. He raised his hand and she flinched. He saw and chuckled, smoothing his bloodless lower lip with a finger.

Delphine felt an icy rage. She would rip his throat out. She would throttle him with the cable of his deaf aid.

Then she saw it. Past the curve of Dr Lansley's hip, a lump at the base of Mr Propp's spine, smothered in silk robe. The revolver. Everyone was watching. She could unmask him, and Lansley – surely one of his accomplices – in a single stroke. Then they'd bloody listen.

Dr Lansley noticed her staring. He followed her gaze.

Delphine lunged.

The double doors opened with a bang. A glass shattered. Everyone turned to look.

Propp sidestepped out of Delphine's range. Something was going on, past everybody's heads. She heard gasps. She scrambled onto the divan.

A figure stood in the doorway. He was soaked through; his trousers shone like sealskin. His shirt was nearly transparent, save for thick arterial creases lining his arms. Water puddled about his bare feet. His hair hung lank and drooling. Cradled in his shaking hands was something like a live heart dunked in potter's slip, caught in the steel teeth of a gin trap.

'Daddy!'

'Gideon!' Mother ran to his side. 'What on earth are you doing?'

He stared at the mess in his hands. Delphine could no longer see it – people had moved in the way. Water dripped from his brow, nose and chin. Mr Propp cleaved through the crowd with an agility that belied his age and size.

'Near the pond,' Daddy said, then grimaced at some gut-deep pain. 'I . . . I didn't know what to do.' He held out his hands, an offering. Onlookers gasped and groaned. Mother put three thin fingers to her mouth but made no sound.

Dr Lansley was on the other side of the room, jabbing the bell button.

'For God's sake, someone fetch him a towel. Stop gawping!'

Delphine followed Mr Propp through stinking, smoking guests, towards Daddy.

'Come on, Giddy,' Mother was saying, tugging at his shoulder, 'let's get you dry. Come on, Giddy . . . '

'I didn't know what to do,' Daddy muttered, over and over. He glanced down, screwed his eyes shut, chewed at the air. A moment later, he looked again. His agony was almost ecstatic.

At Daddy's shoulder, a silhouette resolved itself into two great eyes, a face. Mr Propp stepped into the light. His voice throbbed like a cello. 'Please, everyone.' He clapped twice. 'Away.'

The exodus was instantaneous. Guests retreated to the edges of the room and Delphine found herself standing alone.

'Brother, please.' Mr Propp placed a hand on Daddy's elbow. The outline of the revolver was clear against his purple silk robe. He leant forward and whispered something in Daddy's ear. Daddy became very still.

Gently, almost tenderly, Propp scooped the gooey mass from Daddy's hands. Daddy stared down into the hollow of his palms. Propp walked away.

As he moved beneath the chandelier, Delphine saw. Mud dripped from something round and smooth – curved interlocking plates like a shoulder pauldron on a suit of armour. Reddish. Bits of straw twitched in the mush. She only caught a flash of it, but in that instant she swore she saw it *move* – flexing, jawing apart as if alive.

Propp walked to the sideboard and calmly dumped the thing into a silver ice bucket. He turned, his eyes closed, and gestured towards the bucket.

'Is dodosh. Um . . . ' He stirred fingers in front of his brow. 'Jean-Leonard! *Comment est-ce qu'on dit "crapaud" en anglais?*'

'Toad, Monsieur Propp,' came a voice from the crowd.

'Ah! *Bien sûr.*' He opened his eyes. 'It is dead toad.'

Whatever the thing was, Delphine knew it was no toad. It was too big.

On the other side of the room, Daddy stumbled. Mother tried to take his arm but he yanked it away. He was beginning to shiver. A dullness had come into his eyes. Delphine had seen it before. Soon, he would sleep.

Alice the maid arrived, wrinkled her nose at the mess and said she would fetch towels. Propp held out the ice bucket for Dr Lansley.

'Please. Remove.'

Lansley glanced inside. His upper lip curled. He snatched the bucket from Propp's grasp and marched off.

Delphine felt washed out and nauseous. She watched Mother try again to take Daddy's arm. This time, he relented. Mother led him out of the drawing room.

A low restlessness agitated the remaining guests – the sort of half-concerned, half-pettish muttering prompted by a late curtain at the opera. Professor Carmichael poured himself a very large whisky. Delphine felt a tap on her elbow.

She turned to see Miss DeGroot, holding a brandy glass.

'You okay?' said Miss DeGroot. She was smiling. 'Delphine, isn't it?'

Delphine nodded, studying Miss DeGroot's eyes for slyness or mockery. Miss DeGroot watched her steadily. Delphine flushed and dropped her gaze, focusing on the blue swallow print of Miss DeGroot's capelet against the white of her throat.

'Here. Don't tell your Mother I gave you this.' Miss DeGroot held out the glass. In the bottom was a dribble of brandy.

'Uh, no thank you.'

'Don't be polite. You've had a rough evening. It'll help you sleep.' She jiggled the glass and the brandy swirled round and round.

Delphine hesitated. She took it, her fingertips brushing the cold silk of Miss DeGroot's glove. She sniffed the brandy, tried to suppress a gag. She shut her eyes and emptied the glass into her mouth. It tasted like Daddy's studio.

When she opened her eyes Miss DeGroot was nodding.

'You don't let anyone push you around, do you?'

Delphine looked down at the carpet, her throat and cheeks burning.

A hubbub arose at the west end of the banqueting hall. Alice had returned. She was pushing a wooden wheelchair. Sitting in the chair, his knees covered by a custard-coloured blanket, was Lazarus Robert Stokeham, 4th Earl of Alderberen.

'What on earth happened here?' said Lord Alderberen, kicking a slippered foot.

Delphine had once read[*] that cobra venom worked by making the blood coagulate, clogging arteries until the heart puffed out and exploded in an eruption of clotting gore. She had long imagined the sensation – the squeezing, aching pain shooting down from the wrist, following a webwork of veins and capillaries to smash, like a crossbow bolt, into the clenched sac of the heart. She felt something close to that now.

She knew the voice, the slippers, and the blue stockings within them. Lord Alderberen had been the one talking to Mr Propp back in the room all those weeks ago. They were in league. Of course they were.

Delphine stared at the puddled space where Daddy had stood. Electric fish glowed in mirror pools. Reflected in the water, the chandelier hung like a trap, about to snap shut.

[*] *Boys' Adventure Weekly*, Issue #312.

CHAPTER 7

THE CURSE OF THE STOKEHAMS

May 1935

A few days after the symposium, Delphine sat by the fire in Mr Garforth's cottage, steaming open letters. The copper kettle gubbled over the flames. She used a pair of coal tongs to pass an envelope through the steam, watching the paper corrugate like the lips of a clam.

She had waited for the postman's van and greeted him at the back door with a curtsey. He had not even asked her name. It had been a masterstroke of espionage.

She practised on Professor Carmichael's correspondence, building up her nerve. One was a typewritten slip, thanking him for his essay: 'It does not meet our needs at this time. We wish you all success placing it elsewhere.' Beneath, scrawled in blue ink, were the words: 'no SAE = no MS return!'. A second contained the Quarterly Newsletter from ENVELOPE.* A final handwritten letter from someone called Walter ('your chum, always') comprised several pages complaining about the author's 'Hellish time' at All Souls†.

When Delphine tried to reseal the letters, she discovered she had

* The Esteemed Neo-Vrilian Epistolary League Of Potential Enlightenment.

† Everything was 'Hellish': the food, the weather, and especially Walter's lack of money. The letter closed with an appeal for a loan 'just to tide me over till the end of term. Of course I miss you blackly. If I can only survive this Hellish year I promise I shall come and visit. Scout's honour.'

held them in the steam too long and the gum had melted. She managed to stick the flaps down with a little paste, but they looked all bendy.

No matter. The Professor had nothing to hide; he would not be looking for signs his mail had been tampered with. Perhaps he would think the postman had dropped his letters in a puddle. Delphine put them back in her rucksack, along with the others, and moved on to the central object of her investigation.

Seven letters were addressed to Mr I. Propp or Mr Ivanovich Propp, including one to 'Dr Propp'. She applied steam cautiously. Delphine licked her lips and ran a butter knife along the back of the first envelope. The flap yielded wetly. The cottage was empty. She had an hour before luncheon, at which point the post would be missed.

> *Dear Mr Propp,*
>
> *I write to thank you for your little visit on the 7th. Since then we have followed your principles as best we can. Although my wife's neurasthenia makes performing the Hidden Steps a challenge on occasion, daily I find evidence of improvement in her mood and vital energy. As for myself, the constipation which was the despair of my three doctors is cured and the pills are no longer necessary. We are both indebted to you for imparting your method and our friends anxiously await your next seminar in London.*
>
> *Yours sincerely,*
> *Mr N. Rouche*
>
> *P.S. I enclose a small donation to allow your Society to continue its invaluable work.*

The letters that followed featured more of the same. Beneath her fingers, they felt faintly warm and damp. They were written on high-quality, thick-gauge paper – the sort she imagined was used by diplomats and viscounts and rich financiers of global intrigues. She found nothing explicitly incriminating, but if Mr Propp was receiving messages from continental spies, it stood to reason they would use code. Perhaps the names of conditions? She jotted down 'rheumatic shoulder' and 'nervous collapse'.

All the envelopes contained cheques, except the last:

Dear Ivan,

    hao chiu pu chien! I am arriving sooner than expected. I hope this not cause you inconvenience. Two travellers back together at last. And share our discoveries.

    Your friend,

    Edmund

She read and reread the letter. The cottage seemed to tilt like an ocean liner. Surely this was a message from one agent to another. And what were those first four words? She thought that 'chien' might be French for dog.

The door swung open and Mr Garforth entered, rain-wet and snorting. He threw his coat off and made a beeline for the fire.

'Oh, good. You've put the kettle on.'

Delphine tried to hide the letter but the sudden movement drew his attention.

'What's that?' he said.

'Nothing. Post.'

Mr Garforth sat in the chair beside the fireplace and slapped moisture from his scalp. His boots came off with a thump. He looked at the heap of opened envelopes.

'Someone's popular.'

'It's nothing.' She gathered them up, trying to remain calm. 'Correspondence chess.'

'You? A chess-player?' He glanced at the kettle. 'That's dry-boiled.'

'Well, you took too long.'

'Nonsense. I'm back early on account of the drizzle. How does that work, then, chess by post?'

'Oh, I don't know,' she said. Mr Garforth raised his eyebrows. 'I mean, I don't care. I'm giving up. It's boring.'

Mr Garforth made an 'umph' sound behind his teeth. 'No patience. Let's have a look.' He reached for the letters.

She clasped them to her chest. 'No, it's stupid.'

'I'll be the judge of that.' He leaned forward, grasping. 'Maybe I can talk some sense into – hey!'

With a flick of her wrist, Delphine cast Mr Propp's letters into the fire. They rolled with the updraft, flared and crumpled. What had she done?

Mr Garforth glared at her. 'That was damn foolish.'

She bit down against the cold panic rising in her chest. He was right.

'Sorry,' she said. 'I didn't want you to see how rotten I am at chess. I'm a bad loser. It doesn't matter.'

He looked at her for a long time. At last, he said: 'Right, then. Fill the kettle.'

Delphine rose, glad of something to do. In the fireplace the remains of Propp's letters flickered like votive candles, secrets vanishing up the chimney in twists of black smoke.

The next morning, a car arrived containing Mr Kung. He wore round eyeglasses and carried a small brown suitcase with a paper tag attached to the handle. The tag flapped in the wind as he stood before the Hall, staring. Delphine watched him from her bedroom window. His mouth was open and he kept putting a hand on his bowler hat to stop it blowing away. He looked like a man about to step into the belly of a whale.

Delphine let the curtain fall back across the pane.

On her bed was a gun catalogue, open at a colour double-page spread of sidelock ejectors. She clothes-pegged it to a wire coat hanger, slipped a powder-blue frock over the top, then hung it in her wardrobe. Another twelve or so catalogues were stashed in a hat box wedged behind a joist in the attic. Beside the hat box was her old suitcase. She had poked airholes in the lid. There was shredded newspaper for bedding, a twig for gnawing, an old Bournville cocoa tin for a nest, a saucer of water and whatever food she managed to sneak up from the kitchen (the previous evening it had been a bit of sausage saved from dinner). Delphine had christened the rat Vicky.

Though Mother had never explicitly forbidden gun literature, she was a capricious god. Texts bearing the whiff of heresy might be seized and confiscated, or torn to scraps. Indeed, any item Delphine betrayed a fondness for became territory ripe for annexation in Mother's neverending war on delinquency.

Like anyone living under an occupying power, Delphine had devised ingenious methods for hiding contraband. She spent many hours in the attic, reading by the light of a bare electric bulb and listening to Vicky rustle and chirp. Her bedposts, it turned out, were hollow, and by unscrewing the bedknob and stuffing a woollen stocking a foot or so down, she had created a secret cache for sweets, matches and beautiful pebbles found on the tideline.

Communications were the war's primary front. Mother was liable to intercept any correspondence addressed to Delphine, so she requested catalogues as 'Miss P. DeGroot'. This was mainly because Miss DeGroot was a part-time resident and seldom checked her letters (she liked to let them build to a suitably impressive stack before opening them, conspicuously, one after another in the drawing room, gutting each envelope with an ivory-handled fruit knife) though, since their exchange at the symposium, Delphine rather fancied that if Miss DeGroot did one day find out, she would approve.

As it was, the rigmarole of the deception – the writing of a short covering letter, the copying of the manufacturer's address onto an envelope, the long walk to buy stamps at the sub post office in Pigg – these small, everyday tasks made her feel like an outlaw, a smuggler. They set a warm rush going in her chest that made her climb the stairs three at a time. Sometimes she became convinced that Mother was onto her, that something in her face had betrayed her; at other times, she felt serenely invincible. When Mother chided her for some imagined crime such as running in the hallway or frowning, Delphine felt her growing collection of secrets snug around her waist like a dynamite belt.

She stepped out onto the landing. The maid Alice was leading Mr Kung through the Great Hall. Mr Kung had his bowler clasped to his chest. He bent over to stroke Zeno, the Hall's resident tortoise, who was in the process of crossing the threshold between two tiles.

Mr Propp emerged from a door beneath the stairs. His flat feet slapped against the black and white tiles. He saw Mr Kung and beamed.

'But what is this? I thought you do not come for one, two weeks! I trust you had pleasant journey?'

'Yes, thank you,' said Mr Kung, bowing slightly. His black hair thinned around the crown like the grass on a batting crease.

Mr Propp said something hearty in a language that might have been Russian or Mandarin. Mr Kung replied with vigour. The two had several rapid exchanges then Propp turned to Alice and said: 'Two coffees, drawing room, if you please.'

'Yes, Mr Propp.' Alice nodded and smiled in that half-impertinent way of hers, and disappeared through a side door.

'Ah, Edmund, my dear friend.' Mr Propp's words echoed up into the domed roof, and down the back of Delphine's neck. Here was the sender of Propp's letter. Propp squeezed the newcomer's shoulder. 'I am glad you arrive. We have so much to do.'

She watched Propp lead him away. Kung's head craned and swivelled as he took everything in. His movements had an urgency Delphine did not like. She could not help but think he was hunting for something.

Professor Carmichael called Delphine to his desk. Without raising his head, he flourished her latest essay, 1,000 words on *Hamlet.**

Delphine took it. The Professor did not let go.

'Not exactly according to Cocker, Miss Venner.' His hand unclenched. 'But a certain originality of thought, nonetheless. Take one.' His fingers tapped a paper bag. 'Go on.'

Delphine stared.

The Professor peered over a pair of imaginary spectacles. He glanced at the bag uncertainly. 'What's the matter? Don't you like 'em?'

---

* Delphine had taken the position that the Prince of Denmark was 'stupid' for not killing his blackguard uncle Claudius while he prayed. 'Hamlet knows the Bible is not true, because he has already met a ghost' she wrote, before conceding that the *true* dilemma facing Hamlet was: 'what's the point of murdering someone if they just end up as a ghost?' She closed her essay by positing an alternative 'more believable' ending, where Hamlet kills Claudius, then himself, the two ghosts 'duelling vigorously on the spiritual plane' before Hamlet finally consumes his uncle's soul.

Delphine teased open the mouth of the bag with a finger. It was full of wine gums.

'Oh no, I like them.'

'Take one, then.'

In the shadow cast by the lip of the bag it was hard to tell which colour was which. Delphine plucked out a red one, put it back, pulled out another red, put it back, and finally found a green.

'Thank you, Professor.' She popped it into her mouth. When her molars met, the jolt of juicy sourness made her toes curl.

'It's not a gift. It's a reward. Rest assured there will be punishments also.' His gaze drifted to the abominations under glass. 'Punishment and reward. The two great engines of pedagogy.' He grinned and made a noise in his throat.

On the desk was a pile of foolscap, the top sheet of which was covered in the Professor's familiar runic scrawl. The title was in block capitals. Delphine read it upside-down: *RAISING MU: HOW TO TACKLE COMMON OBJECTIONS TO LOST CONTINENTS.*

'What's that about?' she said.

The grin disappeared. 'Nothing you'd understand.'

'Is it for the Society?'

The Professor put down his fountain pen. 'I may present it to them at some time, yes. Have you finished your arithmetic?'

'What do you think of Mr Propp?'

'What I think and what I write is none of your business. Your business lies solely with the heady world of long division, which I,' he cupped a hand to his ear, 'ah, yes, I do believe I hear it calling to you. Do you hear that? Now, off with you.'

Delphine walked back to her desk, the dregs of the wine gum snug in the hollow of her back tooth. When she glanced up at the Professor, his patchy beard could not quite disguise the faintest rumour of a smile.

Mr Propp called a special afternoon orientation. Delphine was supposed to be patrolling the box traps for Mr Garforth, but Mother had said the meeting was for all guests and residents.

'Your father needs your support. Your *silent* support.'

Mr Propp sat in a leather club chair, white moustache sagging over the stem of a large black pipe. The residents faced him in a loose horseshoe. Delphine wafted tobacco smoke out of her face, eyes watering. He placed his pipe on the arm of the chair and clapped his hands – big, heavy claps, like someone beating a carpet.

Lord Alderberen permitted smoking anywhere within the Hall, but in the smoking room it rose to a contact sport. Contenders stuffed pipes, lit cigarettes with cigarettes and cut expensive foreign cigars with miniature guillotines. When Propp clapped his hands, all activity stopped. He basked in the fresh silence.

'You are asleep,' he said. He said that life was a war against sleep and everyone, everyone in the room, flinging opprobrium left and right, was losing. 'You are no more master of your destiny than feather in stream. You are, you are, uh . . . *quel est le mot juste?*' He circled his palm, snapped his thick fingers. 'Ah! You are *insensible* to life.'

Delphine sipped her Vimto, stewing.

'You must take dissatisfaction you feel, deep in here,' he beat a fist against his chest, 'and deep here,' he thumped his belly, 'and push up, up,' he mimed a volcano surging through his body, 'until, at last, gets here.' His hands came to rest on his bald head.

He looked right at Delphine. She felt ice water spread through her gut. He was watching her, *searching* her. Did he know she had stolen his post? Was he deciding whether to kill her?

She broke eye contact. The room felt too hot. She could feel a thin apron of sweat glazing her hairline. When she glanced back up, he was still watching her.

The corner of his mouth curled upwards. He looked away.

'When enough suffering, enough *heat* reaches brain, maybe, maybe you generate some energy, mist clears, and for one half of one half of one half of one second . . . you are *awake*.'

Several guests nodded. Miss DeGroot went 'Mmm', as if smelling a pudding. She was having a mauve day, except for a daring tweed sash. Daddy watched with a sad, dogged intensity. His face was pouched and yellow.

'And then . . . ' Propp's hands fell to his sides, making Delphine flinch. ' . . . is gone. But you are no longer fooled. And so you set to work. And you work now with *intention*.

'This is work you must undertake. You must fight every day, every hour, every second. Normal efforts will not do. You do not heat kettle by deciding: "Oh, I will heat for fifteen seconds today, ten seconds tomorrow, maybe another ten at weekend." No. You place kettle in fire and hold there *until kettle boils*.'

Delphine fought the urge to leave there and then. He knew. He was toying with her.

Alice entered carrying a tray with a crystal decanter and a steaming cup of coffee. Miss DeGroot applauded softly at the synchronicity. Propp accepted the coffee then held it up while Alice added calvados. Eventually, Propp said: 'Thank you.' Alice replaced the stopper and Propp stirred his coffee with a silver teaspoon.

'We have new companion.' He placed the hot spoon on the coffee table; little bumps of condensation rose on the glass, forming the spoon's mirror-image. Delphine breathed in the bitter, earthy aroma. She couldn't keep her hands from shaking. 'Please welcome Mr Kung.' He gestured towards the man sitting on a piano stool at the extreme right of the settee. The Society members clapped. Mr Kung acknowledged them with a momentary smile, hands bunched over the bowler hat in his lap. 'Mr Kung comes to us from Inner Mongolia, so for today he is excused from activities. Tomorrow, real work begins, ha!' Propp lifted his coffee to his lips and slurped; a shudder passed through his round shoulders and bald head.

'How exciting!' said Miss DeGroot. 'Later I shall interrogate you mercilessly.'

Mr Kung gave her a bashful chuckle. Residents began to shuffle and grunt, retrieving cigarette cases from clasp handbags, patting pockets for matches.

'I have a question.' The voice made Delphine jump. It was Daddy. He was usually so quiet as to be invisible; the other guests reacted as if a chest of drawers had come to life.

'Please,' said Propp.

'If suffering leads to freedom, should we then be cruel to our fellow man, and thus emancipate him?' Daddy's expression was softly thoughtful – that of a perplexed schoolboy.

'What a splendid idea,' said Dr Lansley, crossing his legs and taking a drag on his cigarette. He turned to the Professor. 'I say, Algernon, you could read people one of your essays.'

'Pipe down, Titus,' said Miss DeGroot. She shot a half-smile at Daddy. 'Interesting question. What's the answer, Ivan?'

Propp rubbed an index finger across the bridge of his nose.

'Misfortune alone does not create change within. Good fortune may distract you from need for change. But suffering alone – this is not sufficient. You must *choose* to suffer. And may I remind,' he lifted an index finger, cutting off Miss DeGroot whose glossed lips had parted, 'when I say "suffering" I use word in very specific sense. I do not say "suffering" to mean "Oh, dear me, I have banged toe on table leg," not this sort of discomfort. No. When I say suffering I mean *deliberate* applying of will, focused upon single activity. For example, dances.' He looked to Mother and Miss DeGroot. 'I do not think dancing can be called "suffering" in normal sense.'

Miss DeGroot opened her mouth as if to comment then apparently thought better of it.

'When person performs Hidden Steps,' Propp went on, 'not repeating mechanically but *fully being within* each movement so no other action takes place except dance, *this* . . . this is true work, true effort, true suffering. This English word, to "suffer", it means, I think, to carry, but also, to *allow*. You must *willingly* carry burden given to you.'

Delphine watched Daddy's face throughout the explanation. He looked like someone gazing into a treasure chest.

'There's more, isn't there?' he said. 'Things you're not telling us. Secrets.'

Propp sipped his coffee. 'Yes.'

'Why?'

He began loading his pipe. 'Every great religion has outside teaching, and inside teaching. Mr Kung – this is true of East as well as West, no?'

Mr Kung seemed a little startled. He nodded quickly.

'Yes, I think so, my friend.'

Propp grunted, satisfied. 'So. This protects religion and protects followers. Wisdom half-understood may be deadlier than gun.' He peered down the pipe stem like rifle sights. 'Wisdom is physical thing. Imagine canister of petrol. If we use for one car, we may travel many miles, see many things. If we divide between now fifty, now one hundred cars, all cars go nowhere. Petrol is wasted. So it is with wisdom.'

'So what about us, Ivan?' said Miss DeGroot. 'When are you going to fill us up with your spiritual gasoline?'

He shook his head. 'You are not ready. You would not understand.' He reached for his matches. 'Or worse: you would go mad.'

Miss DeGroot giggled. Propp did not smile.

He touched a flame to the bowl of his pipe and took several practised puffs. 'Friends, thank you. You may now go. Please, remember as you perform afternoon activities: you must hold yourself in fire. Willing suffering makes freedom, and only way to suffer is to work.'

His audience shuffled and began to rise. Delphine hung back, watching Professor Carmichael approach Mr Kung. He slapped Mr Kung's shoulder with such force that the smaller man's eyeglasses slipped down his nose.

'Good to have you here,' said the Professor. 'Welcome to the Hall.'

'Thank you,' said Mr Kung, listing slightly beneath the weight of the Professor's meaty palm.

'You've picked a good day to arrive. Archery tomorrow.' Delphine saw the grey cotton of Mr Kung's suit bunching as the Professor gave his shoulder a fraternal squeeze. 'You any good with the old bow and arrow?'

'I, uh . . . ' Mr Kung gave a deferential laugh. 'No, not really.'

'Never had a go?'

'No. I do not think I will be so good.'

'Don't try it till you've nocked it.' The Professor waited for a reaction. 'Eh? No? Ah well, you're tired.'

Delphine followed the guests filing out of the south exit. As she walked down the corridor, she heard Dr Lansley behind her, muttering: 'Work? He wouldn't know work if it leapt out from behind the rosebushes and paddled him on his vast, self-righteous backside.'

'You shouldn't speak about our teacher like that.'

She turned to look. Dr Lansley had stopped. Daddy was blocking his path.

Delphine felt shiny and awake. It was finally happening. Daddy was going to pound the stuffing out of him.

Dr Lansley folded his arms. She had to sidestep to see him.

'I'm sorry – what?'

'I said you shouldn't speak about Mr Propp like that.'

Residents bunched in the corridor behind Lansley. He regarded Daddy, lips parted, wet teeth gleaming.

'You're in my way.'

Even with his poor posture, Daddy stood a good two inches taller than Lansley. Beneath his shirt, tendons shivered tight as ballista ropes.

'He's trying to help you,' said Daddy. 'But he can't unless you let him into your heart.'

Lansley went to push past but Daddy sidestepped. Lansley backed away. The two men stood watching each other, breathing.

The corner of Lansley's mouth twitched, curling upwards into a familiar smirk.

'And what's in *your* heart, sweet, tortured Gideon?'

Daddy's painting hand balled and flexed. Delphine waited for it to spring up and bury itself in Lansley's sunken jaw. Her own hand twitched above an imaginary holster. If only she had a gun, God how she would humble him.

As if hearing her thoughts, Lansley glanced at her. The smirk hardened into a grin. He looked Daddy up and down. He ran his tongue over his teeth.

'Daddy.' He dropped the epithet like a gas grenade. 'What *did* you do in the Great War?'

Daddy's fist swayed.

He stepped aside.

Dr Lansley drew himself up to his full height, adjusted his earpiece, then strode smartly down the corridor, swishing past Delphine in a perfume of stale perspiration and hair tonic.

Why hadn't Daddy boxed his ears? Why wasn't he thundering after him, wrestling the Doctor to the floor, pounding his yellow teeth down his yowling throat?

She shot a glare back down the corridor, furious. Daddy was leaning against the wall, gazing down at his paint-spattered brogues.

'Daddy?' Delphine took a step towards him.

Daddy looked up, startled. The rest of the guests were filing by.

'Delphy, go away.'

'But Daddy, I – '

'*Go.*'

She dipped her head and ran. Her legs felt like they were full of custard. As she dashed past white classical statues, Daddy's expression burnt bright in her brain. His eyes had been pinpricks.

He had been terrified.

Back in her room, Delphine took out a fresh piece of writing-paper and wrote at the top: <u>*SUSPECTS*</u>.

Fighting to keep her hand steady, underneath she wrote: *Ivanovitch Propp, Lazarus Stokeham, 4th Earl of Alderberen, Dr Titus Lansley, Edmund Kung.* Professor Carmichael was certainly exonerated – a clear outsider. She hesitated, then added *Alice, maid* and a thick black question mark.

Next she wrote: *MOTIVES*

To unseat His Majesty and usurp our elected government (in favour of <u>what</u>??? Bolsheviks? Anarchists? <u>Germans??</u>).

ORGANISATION

Propp is ringleader. Alderberen may be money man – phaps all are under P's thrall (hypnosis? Drugs? <u>Ask Prof. for books on mind control</u>). Lansley = henchman (supplying poisons to P?). Kung – role unknown (agent for Chinese Communists? ~~*Chinese Boxer assassin*~~ *TOO OLD). Alice – involvement yet to be established (lackey? Unwitting dupe? Commence surveillance <u>immediately</u>)*

EVIDENCE

Conversation between P and A overheard by DV

Suspicious pattern of movements by P

Contraband materials (comm. device?) in P's quarters

Letters to P (destroyed) – poss. codewords 'rheumatic shoulder' & 'nervous collapse'

Arrival of foreign elements at Hall

She tapped the tip of her pencil against the writing-paper. Written down like that, her proof seemed awfully thin. At least, the big swells at Scotland Yard would see it that way. Coming from a schoolgirl, it was liable to get scoffed at unless she built an impregnable case.

She folded the paper into eighths and slipped it inside her bedpost. She had seen the look in Propp's eyes. He was trying to intimidate her. That could mean only one thing.

She was getting close to the truth.

Delphine strolled behind the ha-ha,* walking two of Mr Garforth's ferrets on lengths of string.

In her mind, she was patrolling a trench in the Somme at dawn. Out on the lawn, Professor Carmichael and Daddy were gormless tommies about to get perforated by Mauser fire.

The ferrets, Maxim and Lewis, dove and tussled on fresh-cut grass, tangling their strings, darting round and between her legs, using her ankles as maypoles, flapping their rubbery spines like landed salmon before springing off in pursuit of some new imagined ecstasy. Gusts combed the bright lawns. Alderberen Hall winked and glinted. The music room window was ajar, the glassy notes of one of Mr Propp's harpsichord compositions wafting out across the grounds. Grey, half-obscured figures moved in unison.

Daddy and the Professor were breaking rocks. Mr Propp assigned Spim members explicitly pointless tasks like digging and refilling holes, claiming such work frustrated the conscious mind and ultimately released a person from servitude.

The Professor brought down his sledgehammer on a rock the size of his skull. The rock coughed pale dust but remained otherwise

---

* The ha-ha was a concealed ditch that ran widthways across the south lawn, a gentle slope on the south side, on the north a nose-high stone wall bearded in moss. Delphine considered it an exceptionally poor piece of landscaping, on account of the cover it would afford attackers in the event of a siege.

indifferent. More rocks lay in a wheelbarrow beside him. He rested the head of his hammer on the grass and leant on the shaft. His shirt sleeves were rolled up and sweat shone on his red cheeks.

'Must be murder on the lawn,' he said.

Daddy swung his hammer; a clank echoed off the walls of the house. He lifted his head.

'Sorry, did you say something?'

'Must be murder,' said the Professor. 'On the lawn.'

Daddy looked blank.

'All this hammering.' The Professor gestured at the white dust and rubble around their feet.

'Oh. Yes.'

Looking at Professor Carmichael for too long made Delphine feel piercingly sad. He was thick-shouldered but oddly cowed, as if walking on two legs was an unfamiliar act that had been beaten into him.

He reached into his trouser pocket and pulled out a hip flask.

'Nip?' he said, holding it out.

Daddy shook his head. He raised his hammer and swung again.

The Professor unscrewed the cap. His large hands made the action seem as intricate as removing a cog from a pocket watch. He took a slow swig, gazing round the grounds as he did so. Delphine ducked a little, on reflex. He refastened the cap and tucked the flask back into his pocket. He smacked his lips.

They stood for a while, Daddy marking time with his slow, regular hammer blows. Dust seethed from the boulder's compacted crown. She kept expecting it to shatter, but instead it conceded sulkily, shedding crumbs, slivers. The Professor had his hands on his hips. He was gazing towards the lake.

'Bugger, isn't it?' he said.

Daddy said nothing, but grunted with the downswing.

'That business at the symposium the other night,' the Professor said. 'Nobody thought anything of it, you know.' He examined the back of his hand. 'In case you were . . . Nobody thought anything of it.'

Daddy paused, the sledgehammer trembling above his head. He looked at the ground and took a breath.

'Thank you.'

The Professor rubbed a palm against his shirt.

Daddy brought the hammer down. The rock broke like a sugar lump.

North of the house, Prothero Wood waited like an army.

As she walked the ferrets towards a line of shushing elms and blossom-dappled horse chestnuts, Delphine thought back to February, and St Eustace's, and the night of the fire.

The binding of Eleanor Wethercroft went like this: Delphine spent two days laying the foundations, pretending Eleanor's treachery was forgotten, a silly misunderstanding! Then, under the pretext of a 'surprise', Delphine had led her blindfolded down to the boiler room after lights out, told her to spread her arms – Eleanor giggling at first, shrieking with delight when Delphine slipped the first cool noose over her wrist – and secured her to pipes on opposing walls with two lengths of sailing rope tied with rolling hitches.

The idea was to scare her. The idea was that Eleanor would struggle and sniffle and submit, and Delphine would insist she apologise – for the beastly things she'd said about Daddy, for the awful beastly lies. But Eleanor did not cry. When she realised she had been tricked, she became very still; she hung her head and her long brown hair spilled down over her knees. She waited. She breathed.

Delphine did not move. And she realised what should have been obvious: that she was the one who was scared. She was scared of the girl who stood a full hand higher than her, scared of what would happen once the bonds were cut.

Delphine ran. She scrambled up the steps and when she got to the top she slammed the door. She had abandoned Eleanor in the boiler room, until the fire came.

Delphine stepped over fat, twisting roots, pushing into the shadows. Propp had fooled Daddy, he had fooled Mother, and now he was coming for Delphine.

He was winning everyone's trust, all the while covering their eyes, binding their hands. One day very soon, he would turn and lock the door.

And then there would be no escape.

She saw him.

Mr Propp stood ahead in the clearing, fingers laced over his tailbone. Delphine watched from behind a hawthorn bush, Lewis and Maxim nuzzling around its base, yanking at their strings.

He brushed something from the shoulder of his greatcoat. All around him, lilacs bloomed with lush, stinking abundance. The burial vault was grey and squat, more a bunker. A larch, evidently uprooted in a storm, lay broken-backed across the roof; ivy smothered tree and vault in a carpet of shining, green-black scales. Propp took it all in with an air of professional interest, like a mason surveying a new plot. He used the head of his cane to prod at the wet moss around the base of the tomb. He walked a slow, flatfooted circuit; Delphine shrank back behind the bush.

Apparently satisfied, he took his pipe from his coat and located his mouth through the bristles of his white moustache. He patted his pockets for a box of matches. He cupped the pipe, struck a match and puffed. Smoke oozed between his fingers. He extinguished the match with a flourish, then began walking back into the woods, straight towards her.

She glanced about for cover; if he came any closer, he would spot her. A couple of yards away, the lower branches of two beeches threaded over a shallow basin, creating a pocket of shadow.

Propp paused. His pipe had gone out. As he reached for his matches she picked up the ferrets, darted across open ground and flung herself flat under the interwoven boughs.

Lewis and Maxim squirmed in her grip. She pressed her face into the earth, ears ringing. Over the roar of her breathing, she heard the sigh and crackle of footsteps. She glanced up. Propp was off to the right, shuffling back towards the Hall with his hands in his pockets. Smoke trailed behind him in a raggedy white pennant.

She counted to twenty before crawling out.

The dark granite showing through in flashes was clean and new and uncarved. When she stepped through intermittent light to tease aside a dry curtain of ivy, she found a name:

PETER STOKEHAM, 3rd EARL ALDERBEREN
1810–1884
JOHN 11:44

Delphine backed away and regarded the tomb with what she hoped was a sombre expression. She could not imagine what Propp had found so fascinating.

Maxim and Lewis were at her feet, grappling zealously. The ground was damp and mossy; this was the border of the marshlands, the beginning of labyrinthine trenchworks that covered the final mile between wood and sea. A distant, lazy droning came from the bushes.

All she knew about Peter Stokeham, and all anyone ever said about him, was that he had been Lord Alderberen's father, and he had been mad.

Delphine lay down on the moist ground. She pressed a cheek to the fragrant moss and closed her eyes.

Madness. She wondered what it was like, living with brain fever. Some scientists said that madness was in the blood. They said it was passed down like blue eyes, an incorrigible, marrow-deep part of you.

Perhaps she was mad. Perhaps Propp was a wise, kind man just as Daddy said. After all, his most vocal critic was Dr Lansley, a man who exuded loathsomeness. The thought was at once horrifying, and a bitter relief.

Perhaps Propp would help Daddy, and they would go back home.

She felt a tug on the strings. She opened her eyes and saw the world sideways – a wall of patchy grass on the left; on the right, some distance away, a welter of lilacs. The strings described a pair of taut white lines that ran, like tram wires, from knots on her middle and ring fingers, to the bushes. Again, a tug. She got up.

Ivy wrapped the fallen larch in glossy scales. Maxim and Lewis were nowhere to be seen.

She followed the strings to where they disappeared into the lilacs.

'Max! Lewis!' She could drag them out if it came to it, but they had to learn to follow her commands so that one day she could use them to carry messages or foil burglars or simply terrorise Dr Lansley, gnawing through his deaf-aid cable, lunging at his stupid, rash-stippled throat. Mr Garforth said males were no good as ratters, because they were too big, and got stuck in holes.

The lines tightened. The ferrets were using the extra slack to explore deeper.

She listened. The sweet stench of lilacs was overpowering. Beneath the hum of bees, she heard scrapes, clatters and a soft popping.

'Max? Lewis?' She swept aside lilacs with her forearm. The lines went slack.

Lewis burst from the bushes, his hindquarters flipping up almost over his head, then Maxim followed, a flicker of cream. She crouched and the ferrets galloped into her outstretched arms.

Behind them, the undergrowth crackled with the fast, angry movement of a wild animal.

Delphine ran. Something burst from the bushes with a screech. The ferrets bucked in her clumsy grasp. She heard the thump of wings.

She hared into the woods. She glanced back. A dark shape flickered between the silver birches. She leapt over a snarl of roots and kept running. Her vision was narrowing. She hunched and clutched the ferrets to her tummy, her forearms tangled in string. The pounding of wings grew louder.

She zigzagged through the pine coppice, dry needles crickling under her heels. She leapt the streambed and as she landed, she felt something slip from her grasp. She pivoted on the ball of her foot and Lewis lay U-shaped with the winged creature bearing down on him. She yanked his string and he skidded along the dirt towards her. The air was vibrating as she snatched him up with her good hand. She ran, disoriented, over flat, soft ground. Her hand throbbed, her lungs burned and she could taste copper. She clenched her teeth and ran harder.

Delphine had read tales of rabid dogs chasing hunters through forests. It had to be an infected bat, bloated and enraged by disease.

She ducked, barging shoulder-first through a brake of thorn bushes, branches tearing and crackling and the *huff huff* of the bat's wings drawing closer and closer. Its bite would be fatal. Where could she go? What was she supposed to do?

The woodland floor sloped beneath her, the gradient putting power into her strides, and something slapped her eye and she cried out and stumbled and her left foot skidded in something nasty. She lurched, throwing an arm out, smashing her knuckles into a tree, steering into the stagger, and regained her balance. Sweat streamed down her neck. She swiped the back of her hand across it and her hand came back red.

The hill steepened; her sandals whipped through fragrant air. She glanced back and the creature swooped at her face. She swerved and it surged past her ear and something leathery brushed her throat.

She yelled but the bat was gone. She saw a flash of black off to her right. The creature wove through the trees, wings tucked in for speed, coming for her.

It was huge. Like an angel.

She was going to die. She was going to die and not at the hands of spies or criminals or an assassin sent to protect the interests of shadowy cosmopolitan financiers, but bitten to death by a rabid bat, alone, so close to her parents, an agony of fever, burning, burning.

A haphazard fence marked the edge of the treeline. She was much farther east than she had thought. Wire twisted round slanting posts and through a belt of dry nettles. Beyond was a thick green ocean of wheat. Maybe she could lose the creature in that. The nearest stile was more than fifty yards to the right. Her vision was blurring. She'd have to jump the fence.

She threw her good hand out for balance; Lewis writhed in her sweaty grip. A screech told her the bat was at her shoulder. She lashed her arm back and forth and shrieked through gritted teeth and lost her footing and the fence was lurching towards her and she jumped – a clean launch off her right leg, the creature's panting falling away as the soft wheat spread its welcoming arms, then something yanked her ankle and the ground swung up to meet her and she dropped Lewis and Maxim and threw her arms out and a tremendous crack –

She lay on a wooden board. Her arms were on fire. She tried to lift herself up. The wheat had turned purple. The bat's silhouette spread as the creature descended on her, blotting out the sun. She could not see the ferrets. *I'm about to die*, she thought. She felt no fear. The ground gave beneath her, something clipped the back of her head –

– a brittle purring, like a thumb drawn across the bristles of a broom. Pops. Ticks.

Flat blackness.

Something dry and hooked scraping her cheek –

When Delphine woke up she thought she was dead. Then she thought she was blind.

She was on her back. She was somewhere black and silent.

She lifted her head. A rush of wooziness; the world tipped. She lowered her head. The world settled.

Every bit of her hurt; her arms, neck and face throbbed and ached. She balled her hands into fists. She could not quite close the last two fingers on her left hand. She brushed fingertips across her throat and face. They were still intact. She touched her forehead and noted, with satisfaction, the rough, crumbly texture of dried blood. She probably looked awful.

She listened. She became aware of a rustling, snuffling, and at the same moment a faint tension on the two strings tied to her fingers.

'Max?' she called, and the name rang, suggesting stone, space. 'Lewis?' A patter, like the beginnings of a landslide, then two long, stinky bodies were rubbing up against her face. 'Ha! Hello. Hello, boy.' She reached out to pet them, felt a shooting pain in her shoulder.

She lifted herself up onto her elbows, more slowly this time. A wave of nausea crested, passed. She sat up. She smelt wet earth. She could not turn her head all the way to the right. Her bottom lip had swollen up. Mother was going to be furious.

She twiddled her fingertips in front of her eyes, saw the faint impression of movement. She looked up. Blackness. Whatever hole she had fallen through had sealed itself.

She cursed herself for not owning a lighter, or at least carrying a box of matches. She might be surrounded by all sorts of mysterious hieroglyphics (or more likely, she corrected herself, the remains of a Roman villa) just waiting to be revealed by a lit match raised tremulously above the intrepid explorer's head. Perhaps this was a lost treasure vault of the Stokehams, perhaps the discovery would make her family rich. But then, they were already rich – at least, Mother was.

Delphine scolded herself. This was no time for daydreaming. She had nearly died back there.

She clapped a hand to her neck. Had she been bitten? She had cuts and grazes all over. What if she had been infected?

The thought made her breathing quicken. She had to get home. Gingerly, she stood. She held one hand above her head in case it met resistance but there was plenty of room. She could not put weight on her right foot.

This was real. This was genuine peril and now that it was happening she longed for boredom. She had heard the warnings about naughty children wandering off into the countryside only to fall into dene holes or abandoned tin mines, their putrefied remains winched out weeks, perhaps months later. You died instantly, if you were lucky. Unlucky ones broke an ankle and lay keening in the dark like trolls, till they starved.

'Hello?'

She yelled, suddenly frantic, and realised that she was not, as she had first thought, in a chamber, but at the end of a tunnel. Behind her, it terminated in a heap of what smelt like earth and rubble. In the other direction it stretched into the distance, and since she could make out its bare outline, light had to be coming from somewhere.

'Hello!'

The salutation vanished, a pebble tossed into a well. If she had had a match, she could have struck it then headed whichever way the flame tilted, because that meant fresh air. She resolved to always carry a box of matches from now on. She felt for a breeze. The air was cold and still.

Delphine knelt.

'Come on, boys,' she said softly. The ferrets scampered to her feet. She scooped them up and buttoned them into her cardigan. The day's rigours seemed to have tired them out – they moved like furred treacle.

She tested her injured foot. What had, at first, felt like a railroad spike driven into her achilles tendon now felt like a thwack from a rolling pin.

Delphine began to walk. The stone floor was more or less even underfoot. She sniffed, listened, hoping for clues as to where she was, where she might be going. She smelt damp rock. She heard her own breaths.

The tunnel was two yards wide and at least three high – big enough to ride a horse down. She ran a hand along the wall, traced the edge of stone blocks; mortar crumbled beneath her fingertips. Not a natural tunnel, then. And if someone had made it, they must have made it to lead somewhere.

The thought lifted her spirits. She sped up, even allowed herself to entertain fantasies of a search party scouring the grounds mere feet above her head, thrashing through the bracken with golf clubs and walking sticks. After a few minutes, she was starting to enjoy herself. She came to a T-junction.

One passage led left, the other right. She called down both.

'Hello? Hello?'

Nothing.

Delphine dithered, her optimism draining. She unpopped her cardigan and placed Maxim and Lewis on the floor. Ferrets were bred to burrow underground then find their way back again. Whichever way they chose was surely the road to freedom.

Squinting through the darkness, she watched the two ferrets knot their bodies together and settle down to nap.

'Useless!' She rubbed their backs vigorously, trying to chivvy them into action. 'Come on! Which way?'

It was no good. The ferrets had woven themselves into a chubby pretzel of indolence.

She was starting to feel hysterical. She cried for help, and the low echo made her feel as if the walls were closing in. Her air was running out. She definitely felt lightheaded. Maybe the rabies virus was seizing hold of her wits. It was an horrendous way to die, frothing, baffled, enraged.

She considered praying, then worried it might make God angry. She hadn't prayed for months, not since school – to do so now might draw His attention and remind Him that her spiritual account was in arrears.

With every moment she hesitated, the air seemed to get thinner, her mind weaker. She had to decide.

'Eeny meeny miny moe . . . ' The pendulum of her forefinger settled on the path to the left.

She grabbed Lewis and Max and marched down it before she could change her mind. The tunnel narrowed, curving right. Her sandals splashed through puddles. The thrill of committing herself had set her heart galloping, so she was oddly disappointed when the tunnel ended and her fingers closed around the rung of a metal ladder.

She shook it. The ladder held firm.

Delphine buttoned the ferrets inside her cardigan to leave her hands free. She climbed in short stages, resting in between, allowing her injured foot to hang. Very soon, she reached a ceiling. She pressed a palm against it. It was wood.

Delphine pushed. The ceiling held firm. The light had improved to such an extent that she could see her hand. She felt around. Heavy oak boards. She slapped the wood then, hooking her wrist round a rung, balled her other hand into a fist and pounded the barrier above her. Each blow boomed – there was space above. She was below a floor somewhere. If the boards had been rotten, perhaps she could have punched through, but they felt dry and sturdy. She thumped them again and again, beating her knuckles raw, punishing herself for her lack of preparation, for picking the wrong path, for not knowing the things to say to get grown-ups to *listen* to her, for –

Wait. She froze. Her fist crumpled, shaking. She listened.

There it was again. Noises from above. Movement.

Delphine beat against the oak for all she was worth, and was sucking in air to bellow for help when the roof lifted cleanly away, a hinged trapdoor, and a blast of light turned everything orange-white. She blinked, shielded her eyes.

The first thing she saw was the gun.

'I expect the Hall is in uproar,' she told Mr Garforth, bathing her cuts by the warmth of the fire. 'I expect they've sent out a search party.'

The old man did not look up. 'Well, then you'd bestn't stay for cocoa.'

'Oh, well I'm sure five minutes won't make a difference.' She winced at the sting of the washcloth. 'Since I'm here.'

Mr Garforth rolled his eyes. The table was covered with gun parts from a pre-war Belgian hammerless that he was struggling to re-assemble. He took a jug from the countertop and poured milk into a saucepan.

'You're an idiot,' he said, 'by the way.'

'You're lucky I wasn't killed.'

'*I'm* lucky?'

'You must've known it'd break sooner or later, a flimsy bit of board.'

He set the saucepan on the stove. 'I didn't think anyone'd be so stupid as to go jumping up and down on it.'

'I didn't jump, I fell.'

'There you go,' he said. 'An idiot.'

Delphine dropped the washcloth back into the bucket and pulled on her long cotton socks.

'I think I have rabies.'

'There's been no rabies in England for years.'

'A bat chased me.'

Mr Garforth looked back over his sloping shoulder. 'What are you talking about?'

'A bat. In the woods. It was huge.'

He stared at her for a long time. 'A bat.'

'It chased me all the way down the hill. I thought I was going to die.'

Mr Garforth lowered his head. He narrowed his eyes and his whiskers moved to the rise and fall of his chest. The cottage filled with hissing and spluttering. He swore and returned to the foaming pan of milk.

Delphine watched his back. Through his shirt, his shoulder blades formed a dark chevron.

'What is it, anyway?' she said.

'What's what?'

'The place I fell into.'

'What do you mean, "What is it"? It's a bloody great hole, what d'you think it is?'

'All right.' She took a breath. 'I suppose what I really mean is *why* is it? Why is there a tunnel going all the way to your cottage?'

Mr Garforth stirred the milk faster. 'No idea.'

'Don't tease.'

'I'm not teasing. The master's father built them before I arrived.'

She sat up sharply. 'There are more?'

'They go all over the estate. Well, those where the roof hasn't caved in.'

'Gosh.'

'That's not an invitation to go exploring. They haven't been used for years. They're very dangerous.'

'Of course.'

Delphine gazed at the uneven black and terracotta floor tiles, tracing the repeating diamond design with her eyes as if it were a maze. Several tiles were missing, creating dead ends from which she had to backtrack.

'I wouldn't want to, anyway,' she said. 'They were full of horrible insects.'

'Eh?'

'You know – creepy-crawlies. I felt them on my face while I was coming round.'

'You dreamt 'em.' Mr Garforth appeared at her shoulder with a steaming mug. 'Don't spill it.'

She lifted it to her lips.

'And don't burn yourself,' he added.

Delphine blew. She looked from her cocoa, to the maze, then to Mr Garforth.

She said: 'Was Lord Alderberen's father mad?'

Mr Garforth set his mug on the table and sat with a grunt. He picked up a screw.

'Who told you that?'

Delphine shrugged.

Mr Garforth tried the screw in the top of the buttplate. After a couple of twists, it popped from his fingers. He swore, then groped around until his hand settled on a screwdriver.

'I never knew him,' said Mr Garforth, a bit too loud, 'but as I understand it, his only crime was wanting a bit of peace and quiet. If that's what passes for madness these days then argh, damn it all!' The head of the screwdriver slipped and scored an ugly line across the walnut gun stock, while the screw pinged loose and rolled off the table.

Delphine put her cocoa down by the fire, walked over and retrieved the screw. She held it up to her eyes, as if she were a giant clutching a tiny, naughty man.

'Do you want me to have a go?'

Mr Garforth glowered. 'Give me that.' He moved to snatch the screw; she pulled her hand back. 'Stop fooling around.' Delphine hesitated. She placed the screw on the table.

She watched as he tried for a third time to fit it into the buttplate. A tremor worked its way from his hand, through the screwdriver and into the screw, which rattled testily. He tightened his grip; the shaking increased. He slammed the screwdriver down.

'Useless! It's rusted to bits.'

Delphine nodded gravely. Mr Garforth ploughed his fingers through the final greasy strands of his hair.

'Um . . . since it's broken, can I have a look? You know . . . just to see?'

Mr Garforth pinched his nostrils, tapping the bridge of his nose with his forefinger. He stared at the dark window. He pushed his chair back.

'Do whatever you want.' He picked up his cocoa and walked to the fire.

Delphine waited, then took Mr Garforth's place at the table. Sitting hurt. The chair was still warm. She picked up the screw and examined it. The thread was a little worn at the tip, but otherwise it looked fine. She glanced over her shoulder at Mr Garforth. He was sitting with his back to her, watching little purple flames claw at a new log.

Lining up the holes on the buttplate and stock, she slotted the screw into position then took the screwdriver and began to twist. The screw rotated in place, refusing to bite. She pushed; the black bruise on her tricep sang. The screw yielded; three more turns and it sat snugly in the plate. Delphine sorted through the bits till she found the second screw. Once she had twisted it into the base of the stock, she turned to Mr Garforth.

'I've done it.'

He did not look up from his bible.

She held up the gun butt, polished iron scrollwork flashing in the firelight. 'Hey, look. I did it.'

Mr Garforth put a finger to his lips. As the finger lowered, she saw his lips were moving, silently reciting. She watched for a moment, then felt a little embarrassed and turned back to the table.

Over the next fifteen minutes, Delphine rebuilt the shotgun piece by piece. Pain left her, utterly. Her mind was empty as a jug. When she was finished, she took it from the table, heavy and whole. She looked down the breech then shut the gun with a sure, true click.

A hand gripped her shoulder.

'Good.'

She looked up. Mr Garforth nodded.

'They don't make 'em like that any more,' he said. He stepped round the table and pulled out the second chair. 'Simple. Reliable. No fancy business to clog or wear out.'

'I like it.' She held it out for him.

'It's yours.'

She nearly dropped it. She blinked and wobbled.

'No.'

'Well, if you don't want it – '

'No, no – I do, it's just . . . ' She put the 12-bore down on the table. Her hands felt too light without it. She looked at Mr Garforth. 'I don't understand.'

'Not yet you don't.' He set the bible down, next to the gun. His quiet time had changed him; he seemed calmer, softer. His lips formed a half-smile. 'There's one condition.'

'Go on.'

The half-smile vanished. 'Stay away from the woods for the next few days. Till I've sorted your bat problem.'

She scratched the back of her neck. 'Okay.'

'And no playing in the tunnels.'

She narrowed her eyes. 'Hey. That's two conditions.'

'I mean it. Promise me. I'll know if you've gone back on your word.'

'Fine.' Delphine looked the old gamekeeper in the eyes. 'I won't play in the tunnels. I promise.'

CHAPTER 8

UNDERWORLD

June 1935

Т he tunnel entrance was half her height, cut into a bank of soft brown clay set back from the beach. The stonework bore an orange corona of rust from the old iron grate, which lay half-buried in silt, like the rib cage of some furnace-born horror. The tunnel looked like a sewage outlet and stank of putrefying fish. She dropped down on all-fours, switched on her electric torch, and peered inside.

She was not *playing* in the tunnels, she reminded herself – this was research.

Professor Carmichael had assigned her a book on horse breeding (in retaliation, she suspected, for her disparaging remarks on Malory* in a previous essay). *The Modern British Breeder* was so punitively dull she had passed into a kind of trance while reading, and it was with groggy eyes that she began a section on the old stables at Alderberen Hall.

What she read next snapped her awake:

Latterly, the Earl's contribution to modern equestrianism has been almost entirely overshadowed by the manner in which it ended. After the fire of 1854, the Earl – never a gregarious man, even in his prime – retreated from public life completely. During this period, he commissioned a great deal of building work: the widening

---

* 'He manages to make war and swordfights boring. I hated all the swooning.'

and extending of old smugglers' tunnels beneath the estate, the construction of corridors within the house hidden by internal walls, and the long overdue relocation and expansion of the Stokeham family mausoleum. Although the tunnels seem to have been built to accommodate horse and rider (perhaps for ease of transport between the stables and the railway station), in 1855 the Earl dismissed Mr Mercer, the stablemaster upon whose expertise and dedication the success of the Alderberen breeding programme had been predicated. The stables entered a rapid decline, losing all of their prized studs to theft, anaemia and mystery ailments, before the remaining stock was sold off and the stables closed.

Construction work continued until the Earl's death in 1884, providing employment for a large number of labourers, each of whom he furnished with a pony and a parasol to ease their burden in hot weather. This, alongside his sacking of Mr Mercer, is often held up as proof of his diminishing mental faculties, but the affection in which his workers held him is evidenced by the fact that many moved to the village and remain there to this day. Throughout the last years of his life, the Earl was rarely seen or heard. He moved about the estate by means of his passages and tunnels, often going for long midnight strolls, his valet walking twenty paces ahead, holding a lamp, the master's face always obscured by a high collar and wide-brimmed hat. By day, he lived in five rooms of the Hall's west wing, receiving correspondence and delivering orders by means of a letterbox. Such behaviour earned him the nickname 'the Silent Earl'.

Rumours abounded as to the cause of his reclusiveness, ranging from absurd fancy to the basest libel: the Earl had been disfigured by syphilis, the Earl was a vampire, the Earl was gradually turning into a woman, the Earl was leading a double life as a London upholsterer – one Leopold Speed – and had fathered a second son. Though it is beyond the purview of this modest volume to speculate as to the true nature of his Lordship's burden, a note in Mr Mercer's diary, dated one week before the fire, records that her Ladyship had twisted her ankle dismounting a visiting Holstein mare, and was confined to her bedroom. Perhaps the Earl blamed himself for letting his young wife ride so soon after childbirth. Certainly he may have concluded that her lack of mobility counted decisively against her in the tragedy that followed. It is this author's humble opinion that gossipmongers looking for scandal in the Earl's retreat from society ignore the simplest explanation: he stayed indoors because he was grieving.

Not just madness, but accusations of vampirism? And his young wife dead in a fire not long after giving birth to their only son. No wonder he had filled the Hall with paintings of her.

Most pertinent of all was the book's suggestion that Lord Alderberen's father had built the tunnels to transport horses. As a diligent student, Delphine had a responsibility to find out more.

She had a duty to her country, too. What if Mr Propp were using these tunnels to meet his contacts from across the channel? She must at least check the entrances for signs of use.

The long library had big leather books marbled with damp, containing maps of the Hall and grounds. Design sketches in faded brown ink showed structures like the mausoleum and the ice house. None appeared to show the tunnels, but then most were more than fifty years old. At last, in a thick new album stuffed with photographs (mainly studies of trees, but including several pages of hunting parties in the field, reposing on wicker chairs in bowler hats and tweed waistcoats, the grandeur of their moustaches matched only by the circumference of their paunches) she had found a foldout hand-drawn map behind a sheet of glassine paper, depicting the entirety of the Alderberen estate: to the north, Prothero Wood and the ocean, to the west, the village of Pigg, to the south, the railway station, and, sinuating from the Hall like the arms of an octopus, four trails of red dashes signifying, according to the legend: *tunnels*.

They all appeared to begin at the house, but getting below stairs was a trial worthy of Orpheus. The housekeeper Mrs Hagstrom ruled everything her side of the green baize door. She was impressed by no one, serene in her judgements, strong and terrible as a valkyrie. If she had a weakness, Delphine could not yet guess at its nature.

Delphine had decided to search for the tunnel entrances across the estate. Surely Mr Garforth would see no harm in her observing from a safe distance. How could she avoid them unless she knew where they were?

One tunnel apparently emerged inside the boat house, but after jemmying the lock (the wood was splintered anyway and it would have fallen off sooner or later) and slipping inside, hunting amongst the humid funk of mildewed canvas, listening to punts bump and knock, she found no sign of an entrance. Perhaps it was under-water.

The mouth of the western tunnel, near Pigg, was a sandstone arch blocked with dirt and smashed bricks. It had obviously been that way for some time – beech roots had threaded into the soil, binding it together. She dug at the pile for a few minutes before giving up.

When she found the northern tunnel, near the beach, she stood back, observing. Surely it would make no odds if she shuffled an inch closer. Soon, she was ducking inside. After all, she had obeyed Mr Garforth's edict about staying away from the woods. She would just have a quick glance, for the purposes of her essay, then leave.

The stone floor was slimy with mud; ragworms squelched beneath her splayed fingers. Pools flashed in the torchlight. She found a sprat, twitching forlornly. This section obviously flooded at high tide. The stench got thicker as she went deeper. The ceiling dripped. She had to duck right down and squirm forward on her belly. Sharp nodules of rock scraped her breastbone, her bare knees, her raw and freezing hands. If Lord Alderberen's father intended these tunnels for horses, he must have bred them very small indeed.

The crawlway ended in a ladder of iron stemples leading up. She stood. Now she had come all this way, it seemed silly to turn back – ungrateful, almost. She needed both hands. She switched off the torch.

The dark was liquid. She slipped the torch into her rucksack then felt for the first rung. Her hand slid over lichen-greased rock. The rung was gone. She spider-walked her fingers up the wall. They closed round cold, wet metal.

The stemples were slippery. The only grip came from blisters of rust and, on the lower rungs, the occasional barnacle. Delphine climbed, the sure weight of her drawstring bag swaying between her shoulder blades. Her hand found a ledge. She swung her bag onto it, hauled herself up.

She switched on her torch. Ahead, a long, vaulted tunnel led into darkness. She pulled the bag tight on her shoulders, spat, and marched into the unknown.

* * *

According to the map, the tunnel ended beneath Alderberen Hall's wine cellar. Delphine stood at a crossroads, breathing damp, chilly air. Other tunnels branched off into the darkness. A ladder led up towards a trapdoor.

Delphine picked a tunnel and followed it. It was wide and airy and apparently not very deep underground – through corroded ventilation grilles in the ceiling, she could hear the wheezy *ee-wits* of lapwings. The tunnel curved and the damp atmosphere increased. Delphine's feet were aching and she thought she might be getting blisters.

The beam from her electric torch was beginning to dim. She would have to go to the village to buy new batteries. It had just occurred to her that they might not last till she found an exit when the light winked out.

For a dizzying moment, she did not know which way was up. She steadied herself against a cold stone wall. She shook the torch.

Her eyes began adjusting. Faint threads of light from a ceiling grate caught the curve of the walls. There was something up ahead.

Dragging her fingertips along the stonework, she edged forwards. Hard black lines sharpened into the bars of two sturdy iron gates. Metal flaked under her thumb as she felt for the lock. They were rusted shut. She gave them a few experimental kicks; they did not even wobble. She pressed her face to the bars.

In the darkness she could make out broken, half-shapes – things that might have been smooth clods of earth, things that seemed to shift and cower as she peered at them. She heard rustles, clicks.

'Pow!' she yelled. Her voice shattered and faded.

As she stepped back from the gates, the torch clipped the wall and the tunnel blazed with light. She was blind. She threw an arm up to shield her eyes. She heard scuttling, a clatter, breaths. Rats? Or her own panicked stumbles echoing back at her?

As her eyes adjusted, she squinted in the direction of the torch-beam. The tunnel was empty.

CHAPTER 9

THE INSCRUTABLE MR KUNG

June 1935

Delphine walked the track into Pigg, buzzing with secrets. Rain had fallen that morning and the big walnut tree over Mr Wightman's shop was fragrant and dripping. Outside the forge yard, an upended pram rusted beneath a sign for Spratt's Patent Dog Cakes. The pram's wheels had been removed; horse parsley sprouted through a rip in its black belly.

She entered through a fog of brushwood smoke. Mr Wightman was shoeing cartwheels. He had finished the dreary bit with the machine and the rollers, and was heating each iron tyre on a bonfire to make it expand. She watched him hammer a tyre onto a wooden wheel then douse it in water; it hissed like a goose and coughed great bushes of steam as it shrank and tightened. He repeated the process, shoeing four more wheels of different sizes. Without waiting to be asked, Delphine tossed sticks onto the fire when she felt the heat dwindling.

When he was done, Mr Wightman stepped back and rubbed his buckled forehead with a rag. He rolled himself a cigarette, then snatched a twig out the fire and blew on the end for a light. He paused between drags to take the cigarette from his mouth and frown at it sceptically, as if he thought it were somehow trying to cheat him. Once he was halfway through, he looked at her.

'All right?'

She wiped a twist of hair from where it had caught in the nook of her eye, and nodded.

'Good.' Mr Wightman's head had a deep dent just above his right eye. He said it was from where he'd been kicked trying to shoe a horse with the misleading name of Punch. He wore a leather apron and a shirt with the sleeves rolled up, exposing forearms decorated with glossy pink-white scars.

Delphine loosened the drawstring on her bag and rummaged through a drift of envelopes until she had retrieved one, two, three, four large keys. Mr Wightman held out his hand. She gave him them one at a time. His skin had the same tough, grainy texture as a pig's. He held each key to the light, like a jeweller.

'I'll get them done this afternoon.'

'Thank you.'

He tipped his head back and took a long pull on his cigarette. 'So they've got you running errands for them?' He looked at her.

'Yes.'

'Not got domestics for that?'

'No. I mean, yes, but I said I'd do it.'

'Do you want me to send my bill to the Hall?'

'No. I have some money. They gave me the money.'

'They've been losing a lot of keys lately.'

'Yes.'

He dropped his cigarette and scrunched it out with his heel. 'How's the crab hook?'

'Good, thank you.' A fortnight earlier, Mr Garforth had given her a birthday gift – a broom handle with a bit of thin iron rod attached to one end, twisted into a hook. He'd had Mr Wightman make it for her, and though it was clearly the work of a few minutes, she treasured it because it had been her only present. Mother had given her a smart blue skirt, a hairbrush decorated with a butterfly and an atlas for her studies, but those didn't count because they were things Mother thought Delphine ought to have, not what she had wanted.

'See you later, then,' he said.

She walked out of the forge. Wiping her nose, she sniffed the webbing between her thumb and forefinger. A metallic tang mixed with woodsmoke mixed with vinegar.

She only ever borrowed the keys. It was not stealing, and besides, she was acting in the defence of the realm. If she was to gather the proof she needed, she had to get access to every room in the house – especially the locked ones. Time was running out. She had not managed to get back into Propp's study, nor his bedroom, but when she did, his ticket to the gallows was all but assured.

She closed her eyes and, for a while, walked blind. Her bag felt light. As she reached the edge of the village, she heard voices.

Two children – a girl, perhaps ten, in a frayed, sloe-blue frock, and a boy around six, naked except for a pair of red underpants, his hair wild like a savage's – stood by an open gate, engaged in passionate, noisy debate over the terms of their game.

'You be the Queen Snake,' said the boy, 'I'll be the clockodile. And I have to catch you.' He made snapping gestures with his rigid, tanned arms.

'No, *you* can be the crocodile, and I'll be the hunter.'

'No, you can be the clockodile and I'll be the hunter. No, the tiger!' The boy began to spin.

'No, I'm the tiger.' The girl started giggling. 'And you're the *monkey*.'

'No! You're the monkey and I'm the bunky.' The boy chuckled like a drunk, whirling.

'There's no such thing as a bunky!' The girl tried to grab the spinning boy but he twisted out of her grasp and spun faster. She laughed, piercingly, explosively. 'Tommy, stop!'

'I'm a monkey, I'm a bunky, I'm a lunky, I'm a tunky,' round and round and round, and the girl, perhaps his sister, fell crippled with hysterics, suffocating, collapsing in the dust as he danced and danced.

Delphine watched these strange, thoughtless creatures as she might have watched tribesmen from the Peruvian jungle or Martians, their rituals and their happy, untamed weightlessness utterly opaque to her.

The girl rolled over and spotted her. For one impossible second, Delphine believed the girl would say, 'Come, play with us', and the two children would teach her how to be a snake, a queen, a tiger, a clockodile – the knack of it, the magic.

The girl's expression became solemn. She stood and, as if noticing dirt for the first time, brushed down her frock. She looked to the boy.

'Come on, Tommy.'

She grabbed his little brown hand and led him swaying through the gate.

Delphine watched the gate click shut. She imagined the rich, vast land beyond. A gust rushed across the village. The trees of Pigg exhaled.

She had her afternoon planned out:

i. memorise all genera of the order *Chiroptera* native to the British Isles, ready for Professor Carmichael's test
ii. eat the Mars bar she had wrapped up in her hankie (disguising the action, if necessary, by pretending to blow her nose)
iii. use her new keys to search the rooms on the east wing first floor for evidence
iv. help Mr Garforth with his feeding rounds

As she opened the door to the long library, she heard a *whap*, like someone hitting a tennis ball. Mr Kung turned to look at her. He was at one of the bookcases, dressed in a crisp suit. He had just slapped a book shut. It sat between his palms. He looked a little like a vicar about to lead the congregation in prayer.

Delphine felt herself wince under his gaze. Most adults in the house did not see her – she was like a spectre, or a servant – but he was looking straight at her. He smiled and let the book dip. She nodded.

'Hello,' he said, giving equal weight to the two syllables.

Delphine nodded again. Mr Kung nodded. She waited for him to turn away, but he continued to stare. She nodded a third time, then, clasping her hands behind her back, walked over to the Nature section. Mr Kung watched. Delphine turned her back and pretended to scan the shelves for *A Guide To British Animal Life*. She could feel his eyes on her. She felt sure he sensed her anxiety – that, in some horrible way, he was feeding off it.

She heard footsteps. She froze, then realised they were heading not for her, but the far door. Out of the corner of her eye she saw him exit with quick, purposeful strides, hands behind his back, just like hers. The door clicked shut.

Her heart was galloping. Had he been holding his hands like that to mock her? She counted to ten, then dashed to where he had been standing. She scanned the shelves for the book he had been reading.

It took her several sweeps. The spine was dismal grey-brown, and blank. Its dullness worked like camouflage. She took it to the window, where the light was better.

The book was plain, with no title. The first page had a brown water stain and a signature she could not read. The next couple of pages were blank. On the next, she found the title: *Transportation And Its Practice – A Guide By A. Prentice.*

Her shoulders sagged. What had she been expecting? *The Opium Smuggler's Compendium*?

Delphine stood on tiptoes and slid the book back on the shelf. The letter, the channel, the tunnels. The old Earl's supposed madness. Delphine felt as if she were teetering on the precipice of something.

As if something dark and hungry were about to burst out of hiding.

CHAPTER 10

BETTER DROWNED THAN
DUFFERS

June 1935

Delphine walked from the powdery dunes down to the hard
sand of the beach. Razor clams and whelks crunched
beneath her feet. The full moon sat low in a cloudbank,
burning.

She snagged a dry tangle of seaweed with her crab hook and
hoisted it high above her head. It hung against the moon like a fright
wig, gnats and bluebottles scribbling at its edges. She spun it once,
twice, and hurled it back towards the dunes, where it crashed and
slewed apart.

The distant sea was sleek, stippled with milk-bright flakes. Delphine
imagined it surging inland, filling the crooked channels of the salt
marshes, inundating the woods, flooding the secret chambers beneath
the estate and finally seething through the corridors of Alderberen
Hall itself, tearing down fine brocade and fittings and portraits,
washing conspirators from their beds then receding, dragging the
whole rotten edifice with it, leaving only mud – miles of stark, honest
mud.

On the dark sand left by the ebbing tide was a pair of black
leather shoes. The beach was empty. She claimed salvage rights.

She sunk her crab hook into the sand, dragging it behind her as
she began a loose circuit of the shoes. They were smart men's shoes.

Indeed, they appeared to have been recently polished. They sat side by side on a folded newspaper.

Her crab hook scored a spiral winding inward. She stopped.

The laces were clean and black. She picked up the shoes. Apart from a few grains of sand in the stitching around the toe, they were immaculate. The soles looked brand new. It was as if a shoemaker had left his workshop door ajar and, spotting their chance, his latest creations had made a break for the seaside. The surrounding sand was packed into muscular ridges; there were scuffs that might have been footprints, but they petered out after a couple of yards. She was about to pick up the newspaper, imagining it might contain some vital clue, when she noticed a man in a grey suit, standing in the sea.

The tide was a long way out. She only spotted him because he reached up to steady his bowler hat. After that he stood still, one hand on his hat, the other by his side. He had his back to her. The water was up to his calves. His trousers were not rolled up.

Delphine watched. The man did not move. He was camouflaged, grey suit against grey sea.

She put down the shoe, then reached into her bag and retrieved the field glasses she had found lying around at the back of a locked chest of drawers in Dr Lansley's room. She put the cold metal to her eyes, twisting the eyepieces until the image focused.

His black hair glistened in the moonlight.

She watched. He stood, as if waiting. She considered shouting.

He took a step, wobbled; the slack hand went out for balance. He took another step. He began to walk.

The water was up to his knees. Delphine knew he would give in and turn back – this early in the summer, the sea was perishing.

She stood on the flat, wide beach, the full moon blazing. Any moment, he would turn and spot her. He might think she was trying to steal his shoes. The water was up to his backside.

She had a crazy thought: *He's not going to stop.*

She tweaked the focus. His outline sharpened. Water was creaming round his waist. The fingers of his left hand trailed in the water.

Mr Garforth had warned her about the lethal riptides in this area.

Breaks in the sandbars created currents that could drag even strong swimmers away from the shore in less than a minute. It was the kind of grisly warning that Mother came out with all the time.

The water was up to Mr Kung's belly. His left hand was submerged. The field glasses made it feel as if she were watching a scene in a film.

She lowered them. Mr Kung was still there.

'Hey!' she called, startling herself. The word came out small and hoarse. He did not react. 'Hey!'

A gust frilled the smooth water into dragon scales. Mr Kung waded deeper.

Delphine turned and ran.

She hammered on Mr Garforth's door and peered through the thick window. The cottage was dark.

Moonlit nights brought out poachers. Mr Garforth said the problem had got worse over the past few years, on account of jobs being scarce. He said they worked in gangs. He said he understood that a man must feed his family and that he felt no ill will. Then he told her about the time he had surprised a man setting snares for rabbits and winged the fellow as he ran away. When Mr Garforth finished the story, his eyes got a faraway look and he chuckled.

She hared across the marshes towards Prothero Wood, hoping to catch Mr Garforth patrolling the feed run. It had rained earlier and the ground was doughy. She vaulted trenches, silver ribbons of water flashing beneath her feet. The wind was picking up. Ahead, a belt of ash trees lapped at the damp air.

She took a shortcut between dense-packed trees and dropped onto the track bisecting the wood. She squinted against the darkness. Pussy willows curled and rose on either side, forming a tunnel that looked as if it had been left in the wake of a monstrous, slithering crocodile.

Since the incident with the bat, she had been wary of Prothero Wood. She steered clear of the tomb, but she could not avoid the wood entirely – she had to walk through it each day to reach Mr

Garforth's cottage. Her senses sharpened when she entered. It felt very much like enemy territory.

'Hello?' she shouted. 'Hello?'

Nothing. Cracks of sky glowed through the branches overhead. The moon was a headlamp in fog.

She hesitated. Snug in the belly of the wood, listening to the slow shhhhhh of the wind, she started to doubt herself. Maybe she had misunderstood. Maybe she had imagined it. The thought calmed her.

But she had seen Mr Kung, standing there. She had watched him through binoculars. What if she did nothing, and he died?

Delphine fumbled for a plan. Mr Garforth could be anywhere on the estate. She could run round till sunrise and still not find him. By the time she got to the Hall, it would be too late. It might already be too late.

She sprinted along the track, not sure where she was going. The track eased left then lurched right, dipping through slush and then flattening out. A shrew scurried across her path and she had to leap to avoid it; she skidded and when she looked up she saw Daddy.

He stood side-on to her, in the middle of the track, breathing smoke. He had no coat. His back was bent and his unbuttoned shirt cuffs hung like tattered bandages. He lifted an open palm to his mouth as if yawning; a red point of light sharpened between the first two knuckles. He lowered his hand, sighed smoke. His eyes were closed.

'Daddy.'

He snapped upright. He cast around in the darkness, then found her. His face was pale. He tossed his cigarette to the ground and stomped it out.

'Hello.'

'Mr Kung is in the sea.'

Daddy squinted. 'Sorry?' He shook his head. 'What do you want me to come and see?'

'Mr Kung is in the sea. *With his clothes on.*'

'Oh, right. Oh, well then.'

'You have to come quickly.'

'Right.' Daddy raised his arms slightly and glanced around.

'Now!' Delphine swiped at the air, then turned and began running again. When she glanced back, he was following with clumsy, flat-footed strides. She slowed to let him close the distance then scrambled up the bank into the shortcut. She heard the gasp and crash as he beat his way through a holly bush.

'Where are we going?' he said.

'The beach!'

Once they were out on the salt marshes Daddy found momentum, pumping his arms. Delphine accelerated to two-thirds her normal speed and led him through the easy route – firm ground and plank bridges, no jumps. He kept pace. A crosswind kept trying to spin her clockwise, ruffling the reeds. The moon was out from behind the clouds, turning the dunes to caster sugar.

She pictured reaching the crest to see Mr Kung in a stripy bathing suit, perkily towelling himself off. Perhaps nocturnal bathing was normal in China. Perhaps he had just got overexcited – from what she remembered from her atlas, Inner Mongolia was a long way from the seaside. Or what if there was no trace of him at all? Daddy seemed to be in one of his placid moods tonight, but if word got back to Mother that she had faked an emergency – and worse, that she had exerted Daddy unnecessarily – the showdown would be apocalyptic.

Delphine fell onto her hands and knees as she hit the summit. The shoes were still there. She peered at the sea. The water was choppy – it was hard to pick out a figure amongst the slump and crunch. She moved to take out the field glasses then, remembering Daddy, angled her body to hide the bag as she removed them.

She saw Mr Kung. He was up to his shoulders. He still wore his bowler.

'He's there! He's there!' called Delphine, pointing frantically.

Daddy staggered up towards her. He had a scratch on his forehead and his ankles were painted with mud.

'Where?'

'There!' said Delphine. She looked. Mr Kung had gone. 'Oh my God.'

'Where?'

'He's gone under! He's gone under!' She was dashing down the dune, windmilling her arms. As the sand levelled out she broke into a sprint, focusing on the point where she had last seen him, but the sea was swelling, shifting, and she began to worry she was running towards the wrong spot. She slowed, searching for landmarks she could triangulate by, then something crashed into her shoulder from behind and she hit the sand.

She landed face down. When she lifted her head she saw Daddy running faster than she had ever seen him, stampeding towards the waterline.

'Where is he?' yelled Daddy.

Delphine scrambled to her feet. 'I don't know! He went under!'

Daddy did not hesitate; he ploughed into the sea with a chain of splashes like a Vickers gun strafing a pond. He lurched forward as the water dragged at his ankles, then drove himself onwards with sweeps of his lean forearms.

'Where is he?'

Delphine halted at the water's edge. 'Somewhere here, I think!' She waved her arm back and forth, indicating a wide cone.

Daddy was waist-deep, paddling with his arms. He looked around.

'I can't see him!'

'He was deeper! He went under!'

A blast of wind lifted the water into spikes. Daddy dived.

Delphine could not believe it. She stood at the water's edge, stunned and alone.

Daddy surfaced, mouth wide, filling his lungs. He dived. He came up again, swum a yard deeper, plunged. When he rose a third time he was gasping, tendrils of hair whipping droplets as he cast about.

'I can't see him! It's too dark!'

A stammer pinned her tongue to the roof of her mouth: 'I duh . . . ' She clenched, took a breath. 'I duh-duh . . . '

Under again. Water rolled fizzing to her feet. She willed herself to step forward, to run in and help him, but her legs did not move. Another four seconds passed. Daddy did not surface. He burst up, spluttering, wiping hair from his eyes. He was treading water. He dived.

This time he came up quickly.

'I can't . . . see him!' Daddy was weakening – she heard it in his voice. At night, the sea was freezing; dipping your head underwater felt like clamping it in a vice.

He dived. He came up breathing raggedly. He slopped hair out of his eyes, screamed. A wave lifted him up. He looked around. He was alone. He took a breath and ducked back under.

Delphine had her cardigan balled up in her fists. The tight, trapped feeling had spread from her tongue, down her jaw to her shoulders and chest. She wanted to yell at him to give up. He surfaced, coughing, slapping about for purchase. He let out a wounded cry. When he went under again, Delphine could not tell if he had meant to. His head tipped back and he sank.

A wave hid the place where he had gone under. When it had passed, he was still missing. She stared. Her vision narrowed. It was crazy to believe this sucking, plunging sea held two living men. They were gone. Her bladder tingled. She was going to collapse.

Daddy broke gasping, went under, surfaced, found his footing. Water streamed from his hair and nostrils. He was walking. He was yelling. She thought he was calling to her, but she could not make out words. His mouth was wide; his teeth glowed. He held something in his arms: driftwood wrapped in black canvas. As the water got shallower, his burden pulled him down to a stoop.

'Gah . . . ah . . . gah . . . ah . . . ' Every breath was a hoarse roar. The tide was dragging at his legs. He shook water out of his eyes, looked around. He spotted her. 'Help me!'

She ran into the sea. It was scalding. She gasped at the pain. Daddy staggered; the driftwood fell from his arms. She ran for him, steadied him. She looked down at the thing floating at his feet.

It was Mr Kung.

He was face down in the shallow water. She grabbed him under one of his arms. Daddy was huffing, shivering. He caught hold of Mr Kung by his other arm and, together, he and Delphine pulled Mr Kung out of the waves and onto the sand.

They laid him on his back. His spectacles were gone. His eyes were open and crusted with sand, cataracts of froth purling in the corners.

Blood and foam ran from his nostrils. Bloody water flowed from his mouth. His skin was the colour of tallow. He was not breathing.

'Help me pick him up,' said Daddy. Delphine caught hold of the sodden lapels and heaved. Once they had lifted Mr Kung upright, Daddy swung him round and began squeezing him in a bear hug, letting his head loll.

Lots of water came out of Mr Kung's mouth. It splattered brightly against the firm sand. Daddy squeezed again. More water came out. Mr Kung's lips were slack and mauve. Phlegm hung in a silver beard. His eyes stared blindly. Daddy hugged him again and again. Water came out and each time Mr Kung shrugged as if to say it is no good, I am doing the best that I can.

Delphine wrung her hands in wretched, trembling prayer. Daddy lowered Mr Kung onto the sand, rolled him onto his back and shook him.

'Hello!' Daddy said. 'Hello!' He slapped Mr Kung across a shining cheek – gently, at first, but then harder, and harder, as if interrogating a spy, left, right, left, right, and Mr Kung shook his head, no, no, no, no. Daddy thumped Mr Kung in the chest and water arced from his mouth.

Mr Kung spluttered.

Delphine shot a look at Daddy. Daddy's eyes were wide. He thumped Mr Kung again. A little more water came out. Delphine looked down at Mr Kung's pursed, purpled lips. Something black hung from the corner of his mouth.

'In his mouth!' she said.

Daddy grabbed Mr Kung's chin and tilted his face upwards. He squeezed the cheeks so Mr Kung's lips popped open in a prim 'oh'. His teeth were bad, ranging from cream to mahogany. Daddy plunged two fingers into Mr Kung's throat; he hooked out a thick, dark clot of seaweed with a long tail that kept coming. The strand snapped; Daddy cast it aside and dug in again. This time, he pulled carefully, pinching thumb and forefinger to tease out the delicate flukes.

Mr Kung coughed. His face tightened. Bloody water welled up in his mouth. He inhaled it, gargled.

Daddy scraped the last of the weed from Mr Kung's mouth. Mr

Kung tried to breathe, and again he choked, froth streaming down his face.

Delphine looked around for some way to help. She ran to the sea, scooped up some water, then knelt over Mr Kung's head. She tilted her hands and poured a little water onto either eye, washing away the foam and sand. It made him look worse. His naked eyes were pink and sightless, pupils rolled back.

Mr Kung made a strangling noise. Daddy gripped his shoulders with pale, tendon-mapped hands. He looked at Delphine.

'I can't save him,' he said. He gazed around at the empty beach. Something brought him smartly to attention. 'You have to go to the house and get help.'

'But it's over a mile away.'

'I can't save him.'

'But what do I say?'

Daddy pounded a fist against the sand. 'Get Dr Lansley! Bring him here now!'

Delphine sprang to her feet. She began sprinting back towards the dunes. The wind sliced across her sopping arms and legs. She remembered her bag and the electric torch inside. Perhaps she could signal the Hall for help.

But who would be paying attention at this hour? They'd all be drunk, except Alice, who probably hadn't even heard of Morse.

There was nothing for it but to run – over the dunes, across the marshes, through the woods, past the north shore of the lake and over the lawns. She had timed herself before. She would treat it as a challenge. If there was ever a day to beat her personal best, this was it.

'Do you know I think it's my first memory? Reaching for the beautiful amber paperweight on my Papa's writing desk, straining with my stumpy little arm and realising it wasn't quite lo – '

'Doctor Lansley, you have to come now!'

Miss DeGroot cut off mid-flow. She stood by the globe in the corner, one arm slung round its latitudes like a chummy Atlas.

Everyone stared.

Delphine dripped onto the rug. She could feel stiff spikes of hair hanging down across her brow. Dun gloves of dry mud ran halfway up her forearms. She had fallen twice crossing the marshes. Her wet feet tingled in the heat of the hearth.

Mother, rising: 'Delphine, what on earth is the meaning of – '

'Doctor Lansley has to come to the beach!'

Miss DeGroot's mouth shifted into a smile. She looked at the other guests, delighted.

Dr Lansley, from the settee: 'How *dare* you burst in here and start making demands of me!'

'You have to come!'

'I will do no such thing!'

'Mr Kung is dying!'

'Get out of this room this instant!' Lansley stubbed out his cigarette. He gathered his hearing aid and wires in one hand and rose. 'Look at the state of you!'

'He's *dying*!'

'Do not test me, child.'

'What's wrong with you?' She cast around at the other adults. 'He's going to die!'

'Delphine.' Mother's voice was thin and firm. 'You have ten seconds to explain yourself.'

'He's in the sea!' She looked to Professor Carmichael. 'Please, Professor. Tell them! Tell the Doctor he has to come!'

The Professor frowned. 'Steady there, Titus.'

'Shut up.' Dr Lansley advanced round the coffee table, moustache writhing.

'Wait,' said Miss DeGroot. 'Give the girl a chance.'

'Miss Venner.' The Professor eyed her carefully. 'Is this a prank?'

'No!' She threw her arms out. 'Daddy dragged him out of the sea. They're down on the beach now and they need a doctor or he's going to die!'

Invoking Daddy brought them all up short. Dr Lansley hesitated. Everyone looked at him.

He glared. 'Is this true?'

She met his gaze, glaring right back. 'If he dies, it'll be your fault.'

Lansley's chin retreated into his neck. He looked at the Professor.

'Ring for Mrs Hagstrom. Have her start the car and meet me outside the front door in three minutes. We'll take the horse track. Patience – ' he looked to Miss DeGroot '– fetch towels and my coat off the rack. I'll get my medical bag. You,' he shot a gloved finger at Delphine, 'be waiting in the car when I arrive. You will give clear, concise directions when asked, otherwise you will remain absolutely silent, is that clear?'

Delphine looked into the fire.

Professor Carmichael prodded the bell button. 'Had I better come?'

'No,' said Lansley and Miss DeGroot together.

The Professor's shoulders slumped. He trudged back to his chair.

'Right.' Dr Lansley grabbed a bottle of brandy on his way out the door. He stopped, looked back at Delphine. 'I pray, for your sake, this is not a lie.'

Mother stood very straight. 'Did Daddy ask for anything else?'

Delphine shook her head.

'Well . . . ' Mother looked away. 'Be careful, please. Off you go.'

Delphine hesitated, just long enough to indicate she was leaving of her own accord.

The car rattled and jounced along the track, branches clatter-scraping off the bonnet. The rain-softened earth made the going a little easier, but even in the dark Mrs Hagstrom was a bracingly fearless driver, accelerating with a blind faith that bordered on zealotry. Delphine had stared the first time she had seen the house-keeper behind the wheel, knuckles shining as she swung the car out of the garage, but no one else at the Hall found it the least bit remarkable. Mr Garforth said that during the Great War, Mrs Hagstrom had driven a bus.

Dr Lansley sat in the front, black bag on his knees. He took a cigarette from a fresh packet, tapped the end against the dashboard, then slid a matchbook from his breast pocket. In the back, Delphine sat hunched and malevolent.

Mrs Hagstrom pulled up at the top of a stone slipway.

'Turn the car round then follow me,' said Dr Lansley, climbing out the passenger door.

Delphine saw Daddy a way off, still knelt over the body.

'Hey!' she called. He turned and waved both arms. She ran to him, Lansley following, Mrs Hagstrom bringing up the rear.

As they got close, Daddy yelled: 'He won't wake up! There's water in his lungs and he won't wake up!'

'Move,' said Lansley, making shooing gestures. He and Daddy locked eyes. Daddy stepped back. 'You,' Lansley pointed to Mrs Hagstrom, 'roll up a towel and give it to me.' He knelt down beside Mr Kung and popped open his medical bag. Delphine hung back, watching.

Lansley took a small red torch from his bag. He grabbed Mr Kung's face and shone the light in his mouth and eyes. He pushed an index finger deep into Mr Kung's throat and moved it round. Mr Kung jerked and something thick like egg white came out. Lansley pulled at Mr Kung's tongue. Mrs Hagstrom handed Lansley the rolled-up coat; he stuffed it underneath Mr Kung's shoulder blades, then pulled Mr Kung's head backwards.

'Give me some bloody room.' Lansley stood. He grasped Mr Kung's arms by the elbows, lifting them over the head. He counted: 'One, two.' He lowered them to either side of the chest, pressing them against the rib cage. After two seconds, he lifted them again and repeated the procedure. He turned to Mrs Hagstrom. 'Get the smelling salts from my bag.' To Daddy: 'Pour him a capful of brandy.' Delphine braced for her instruction but Lansley went back to pumping the arms and counting.

Mrs Hagstrom held a little bottle between thumb and forefinger. She scrutinised the label.

'Is this it?'

'Yes,' said Lansley. 'Go on then.'

Mrs Hagstrom knelt with a grunt. She pulled out the stopper and wafted the bottle beneath Mr Kung's bloody nose. Mr Kung's chest was moving. Delphine heard his throat rasp wetly.

For a minute or two, Mrs Hagstrom swayed the smelling salts while Dr Lansley lifted and lowered Mr Kung's arms. Daddy stood on the periphery, his teeth chattering, capful of brandy quivering in his upturned hand.

Daddy said: 'Is it working?'

Dr Lansley hissed through his teeth. To Mrs Hagstrom, he said: 'Get a towel. Dry him as best you can and then get another one and cover him.'

Mrs Hagstrom unfurled a towel and began rubbing at Mr Kung's legs. As she worked upwards, Mr Kung's trousers rode up, exposing pale, hairless ankles. Delphine winced. She wanted to call out, to shout to him to wake up.

Lansley lifted the arms, and Mrs Hagstrom leant over and wiped Mr Kung's face. Most of the blood came off, leaving an oily sheen. Mrs Hagstrom threw the towel aside. She laid the second one over Mr Kung's belly and legs. Mr Kung's feet poked out the bottom, big toe bulging mushroom-like through a hole in his black socks.

Lansley went on pumping Mr Kung's arms. After a while, Mrs Hagstrom stood back; with Daddy and Delphine, she watched and waited. Lansley shook his head.

'It's no good. This man needs a hospital.'

Mrs Hagstrom rubbed her hands together. She glanced at Daddy. 'Shall we, sir?'

Daddy set the cap of brandy on the ground, twisting it into the sand. Lansley stepped back. Daddy grabbed Mr Kung under the armpits. Mrs Hagstrom and Lansley took a leg each.

Mrs Hagstrom turned to Delphine. Sand crusted her upper lip.

'Run ahead to the car. Open the doors.'

Delphine took off across the beach. She spread her numb arms and sand rolled beneath her. She was running through no-man's land at midnight; to the east and west, Vickers guns and MG08s cackled and spat. If she flagged for even an instant, thousands of rounds would shred her legs. The thought relaxed her. She had the queerest feeling that if she closed her eyes and went limp, she would fly.

She leapt onto the slipway and scrambled to the car. The handles were freezing. She opened all four doors and slumped against the bonnet. Looking back across the beach, she saw the three adults with

Mr Kung slung between them like a drunk. Dr Lansley had his heavy medical bag under one arm and Mr Kung's bare foot under the other. Mrs Hagstrom marched hard and straight, leaving deep black footprints. Daddy had his eyes closed. Together they threw a crazy, gangling blue shadow, a giant landcrab rampaging beneath the glare of the full moon.

They reached the car and bundled Mr Kung into the back. Daddy bent over, wheezing. Mrs Hagstrom dropped into the driver's seat. Dr Lansley got into the back, Mr Kung's head in his lap.

'Hospital. Now.'

The engine growled throatily, then the car lurched and began accelerating up the slipway. Delphine watched it buck as it hit the first rut, headlamps making the trees dance and flash. The sound of the motor faded. She and Daddy were alone.

The wind had died. The ocean was calm as a plate.

Daddy staggered down the slipway. His shirt was open to his stomach. Delphine wanted to speak, but her mouth was dry. She walked in his deep footsteps.

Daddy walked back to where Mr Kung had lain. He took the capful of brandy. He held it up. In the moonlight, his hair gleamed like chains. He drank the brandy, picked up the bottle and began walking towards the dunes.

Delphine walked over and picked up her crab hook. Mr Kung had left three dents – his buttocks, back, and head. She hacked at the sand. Her skull ached. She thought she might cry, then the feeling passed, like a sneeze.

She watched the sea for a while, glassy, replete. When she turned inland, Daddy was a way off, standing over Mr Kung's shoes.

He stooped, pushed the shoes aside and picked up the oblong of crumpled newspaper beneath them. He turned the paper over in his hands. He found a seam. He peeled away a layer and let it fall. The wind caught it, skimming it towards the sea. Daddy peeled a second layer, a third.

When he rose, Daddy held a book: small, grey-brown. He looked at it from several angles, as if unsure how to make it work. He looked like he might drop it, then he lifted the brandy bottle to his mouth. Brandy spilled over his lips, running down his cheeks, his neck, following the line of his collarbone, soaking into the stiff dark hair around his heart. He poured until the bottle shone clear. He ran the back of his sleeve across his face, then tucked the book beneath his armpit.

Delphine watched him trudge away. The beach was quiet. She felt hollow, papery. She remembered the sting of the brandy Miss DeGroot had given her and wished she could feel that burn now. She wished Mother was there, to fuss and brush sand off her clothes and lead her safely home.

A piece of newspaper tickled her ankle. She looked down.

As her eyes focused, she saw it was not newspaper after all, but a crumpled page of densely-scrawled notes and crude diagrams. She grabbed the corner. Numbers and English words stood out against a mass of squirly symbols – were they Chinese? She was so exhausted, she could barely read. The wind snatched at the paper. One word caught her eye, repeated again and again across the page:

DELLAPESTE

DELLAPESTE

DELLAPESTE

INTERLUDE 1

June 1935

The man known as Ivan Propp attached brass electrodes to a tiny, shivering, hairless creature, and prepared to transmit. A candle burnt in a tin holder on his desk. He poured himself a second glass of 1865 calvados and dragged the dust sheet off the rest of the apparatus. The little chubmouse, blind and pink, scratched at the walls of its glass prison with its antler nubs, mewling to its brothers and sisters in the cage on top of the cupboard. Ivan sipped his calvados and grimaced. Sending a cross-channel wire was *une activité très désagréable*.

He found himself thinking in French more and more these days. Russian came to him only when he wrote, and the language of his homeland even less – only when he made a conscious effort, and sometimes on waking, and as he passed into sleep, as if that part of his life had already crossed the threshold and was waiting for him to join it.

He lifted the black earpiece to the side of his head. His index finger hesitated over the Morse key. Inside the larger glass partition of the telegraph apparatus, the mother chubmouse scrunched her eyes shut. She was the size of a Christmas pudding. Two patches had been shaved into the sandy fur on her fat back. Electrodes winked in the candlelight. She chirruped – he thought it had started, waited for the beeps in his ear, but it was just pre-message anxiety. These fleshy, docile creatures were not so insensible. They knew what was coming.

Just as he was reaching for his pocket watch, the mother chub-mouse's jaw began to tick. In his ear, the ready signal cycled: MESSAGE BEGINS . . . MESSAGE BEGINS . . .

He took a pencil and transcribed. As the message continued, the mother chubmouse whined and bucked and stropped her antlers against the glass, overcome by a weird, disembodied torment. The electrodes read her discomfort as discrete units of current – a dot or a dash – and the equipment beside her compartment converted this into sound.

He spent a moment translating.

GIRL STILL MISSING STOP REQUEST MEETING TO DISCUSS STOP GUNS NEEDED URGENT STOP KIND REGARDS AS STOP

He reread the message, then screwed it up. Glancing towards the empty fireplace, he briefly contemplated the journey. The calvados had dampened the knifing pain in the small of his back, but as he placed his palm on the desk and tried to rise several ancillary pains replaced it. He dropped the balled message in his ashtray and touched a match to the top.

In its glass compartment, the baby chubmouse flinched at the sudden, flaring light. He waited till the message had burnt away to black flakes. He drained his glass, then placed a finger over the Morse key.

Pardonnez-moi, mon enfant.

He began to tap. With each stroke, the hairless chubmouse pup convulsed, as his finger completed the circuit and sent electricity through its plump and wrinkled body. In the box alongside, the mother chubmouse lay inert – it was not her child.

But he could picture a creature, in a land so distant yet so dizzy-ingly close, writhing at each stab of the key.

MESSAGE BEGINS . . . MESSAGE BEGINS . . .

Ah, what agony to be a mother. To be so awake, to love so honestly. For what was love, if not feeling another's suffering as your own?

ACT TWO

July–September

Threescore years and ten the Lesser Threshold takes
and holds in trust until the traveller's return.
The angel and the lower creature are exempt:
the former because he inhabits an unchanging, supermun-
dane vessel, the latter because it has no soul.

– Transportation And Its Practice, A. Prentice

CHAPTER 11

IN BALANCE WITH THIS LIFE

July 1935

Rain fell into the gravemouth, dripping from the wings of black umbrellas. Hunched and shivering beside Mother, Delphine watched it drum the lid of Mr Kung's coffin as men with ropes lowered him into the ground.

Mr Propp began to sing. He stood at the foot of the grave, dressed in black, a fist to his heart. Alice stood beside him, holding a brolly over his shining head. Propp sung in a minor key, in a language Delphine did not recognise. The scale sounded Middle Eastern, full of strange intervals, ululating, mournful.

The stench of grass and wildflowers and wet July earth was stifling. Delphine pushed her shoe against the sodden ground; brown water pooled around the toe. She glanced at Dr Lansley, on the opposite side of the hole. He had a leather glove pressed to his mouth. He regarded the pit with a look of disapproval. He seemed to despise Kung for giving up so easily.

Propp finished his song. He stepped forward and tossed a handful of dirt onto the coffin. It landed in a clod and washed away. Dr Lansley stepped forward, soil balled in glove. A big wedge of earth broke loose beneath his foot. He wobbled. Dirt sloughed into the grave. Miss DeGroot, wrapped in black satin, grabbed his collar and pulled him back.

Everyone took a step away. Dr Lansley stood in the rain, fruitlessly slapping his sopping sleeves, blowing a spritz of moisture out of his thin moustache. One leg of his trousers was painted in mud.

'I'm going for a bloody drink.'

Delphine spent the afternoon on the beach, watching the sea. Warm rain fell, fragrant with heather. It pelted her scalp and her ears and the nape of her neck, and she barely felt it. Spume washed over broken shells. She watched the waves, kept expecting Mr Kung to break the surface, kelp slopping from beneath his bowler hat, a boyish smile on his face as he strode shoreward, ready to reclaim his shoes.

As the tide went out, she walked to the pits she had dug at the mouth of the marshes. She plunged her crab hook into syrupy silt, dragging it around till she felt the scrape of iron on chitin. Most of the time the crabs gripped it with their pincers, clung on even as she lifted them dripping into her bag. It was their tenacity that did for them.

Why had Mr Kung killed himself? And why, if he really was a foreign spy, did she feel so sick and shaken by it?

Her shadow began to lengthen. Chunks of petrified tree jutted from the mud like rotten teeth. She took her bag filled with the day's catches and headed for the tunnel.

Delphine followed the tunnel from the beach to the wine cellar. At the top of the cellar stairs, she pushed a long brass key into the lock and opened the door. Finding out which keys fitted which locks had been a long, risky process.

She stuck her head out and looked both ways. The corridor was empty.

She locked the door behind her and headed left, past the game larder, where woodcock, teal, partridge, goose and pheasant hung glumly. Next door was the gun room. She unlocked the door with a second, smaller key, stepped in and shut it behind her.

A leathery smell hung in the cool, still air. On three walls, shotguns and hunting rifles of various sizes stood vertically in racks. Two locked glass cabinets housed vintage guns: a double-barrelled French flintlock from 1760, a British Navy seven-barrelled Nock volley gun, a mahogany case containing a pair of silver-gilt blunderbuss carbines from the Caucasus. A punt gun with a two-inch barrel ran the length of the left-hand wall. She had read they could take down a flock of geese in a single shot.

She took a shotgun from the rack: a Westley Richards hammerless ejector, barely two years old. She squinted down the sights, stepped and swung, tracking the trajectory of an imaginary bird. The flesh beneath her collarbone ached. Shooting still hurt like blazes, but she was getting stronger. She wiped a smudged thumbprint from the walnut stock, then slotted the gun back in place.

She went over to a set of office drawers. They were supposed to be kept locked. The front of each drawer was labelled with an index card. She slid out the drawer marked '3', opened a couple of cartons and slotted her leftover cartridges into the gaps.

A cough from the hallway.

She cast around for refuge. The gun room was all display cases and empty space. She flicked off the light and as the filament died she threw her back to the wall beside the door. The door opened inwards, hiding her.

'Hello?' A man's voice, hushed, querulous. It was Professor Carmichael.

She bit her lip.

He took a step into the room, pushing the door wide as he entered. She dodged before it could bump her shoulder.

'Hello?' The floorboards creaked as he shifted his weight.

She noticed her spoils bag lying in the middle of the floor. Amongst all the wood and steel and leather, the green canvas was obvious. The thump of a shoe. Another. The far wall filled with his shadow.

'Can I help you?' A woman's voice from the corridor: loud, common. The Professor's soles scraped as he turned. Pressed against the wall, Delphine exhaled thinly.

'I, uh . . . '

'Mr Carmichael.' It was Mrs Hagstrom. 'How did you get in there?'

'Uh, uh, it was open.'

'"Open", he says. So if it's not barred and padlocked that's an invitation for you to come and go as you please?'

'I'm sorry, I – '

'"Sorry", is it. That's the song now.' Delphine could hear a *whap whap* as of a blunt object striking an open palm.

'It's Mr Propp,' said the Professor. 'Pay, uh – Miss DeGroot is concerned as to his whereabouts. I was looking for him.'

'In the gun room?'

'Yes.'

Mrs Hagstrom stomped forward and grabbed the door handle. Delphine flinched. She could hear Mrs Hagstrom's panting through the inch of pine.

'And is he in here?'

The Professor audibly sagged. 'No.'

'You're sure?'

'Mrs Hagstrom, may I – '

'Mr Carmichael – '

'Actually, uh, it's Profess – '

'*Mr* Carmichael.' Mrs Hagstrom inhaled. 'If Mr Propp needs a place to contemplate life's great mysteries, you can rest assured it won't be down here. If he wants to fritter away his days ogling his belly button that's his lookout and his folly, but the moment he comes my side of the green baize I shall be after him with a carpet beater, inner peace or no. Some of us . . . ' she swept him from the room and slammed the door, 'have work to do.'

Delphine heard her sorting through the big ring of keys like a gaoler. There was a reassuring *clunk-clack* as she relocked the door.

'Now,' said Mrs Hagstrom, her voice clear and strident, 'off with you. Go on! Off! Off!' Delphine listened to Mrs Hagstrom herding the Professor down the corridor. She allowed herself to exhale. So, Propp was off on his travels again.

A blast of damp heat hit Delphine the instant she entered the kitchen. She had sneaked round to the north side, to make it look as if she had come into the house via the servants' entrance, but the ruse was unnecessary; the room was such a commotion of clanking and yelling that she could have entered through the chimney and no one would have noticed. The shelves were heaped with apparatus like a wizard's laboratory: copper pans, tureens, jelly moulds, weights and balances, whisks, ladles and heavy-bottomed pots. At the far end, several geese turned on a spit above the range, dribbling fat that hissed as it hit the flames, while behind them black kettles thrummed with water.

Mrs Hagstrom stood a short distance from the fire. She had her sleeves rolled up. Sweat glued hair to her brow. She bellowed commands without looking up from her work, the thwack of her blade keeping time.

Delphine wove round the back of Alice, who was cracking egg after egg into a pudding bowl, and presented herself to Mrs Hagstrom. The heat from the range was incredible; it came in waves, a physical thing that pushed against exposed skin. With the flames, the clouds of moisture and the clangs of industry, standing in the heart of the kitchen was like standing on the footplate of a steam engine.

'Ah, Miss Venner!' called Mrs Hagstrom, the bang-swish-bang of the cleaver hacking her speech into a platter of discrete, confusing clauses. 'A perfect disgrace, as usual, sauntering in, a whisker before, dinnertime, your skirt splattered, with muck the likes, I've never seen. And here I was, thinking your Mother, had forbidden you, from leaving the, house without her, permission. You look as if, you've been crawling, through a sewer pipe,' the cleaver arcing down through another shallot, 'and surely that can't, have been *your* bag, I saw a minute, ago just lying there, on the floor of the gu – '

Delphine slammed a lobster on the table like a telephone receiver. Its pincers were tied with parcel string. The lobster and Mrs Hagstrom exchanged bemused glances. The cleaver hung in mid-air. Mrs Hagstrom looked at the cleaver, set it down.

'Come with me,' she said.

This, then, was Mrs Hagstrom's weakness.

In the laundry room, Delphine handed over the lobster and two crabs – haggled down from four – in exchange for use of the servants' bath, a change of clothes, and Mrs Hagstrom's silence. The air in the laundry room was warm and damp and cloying. The crabs were cold from the sea. Mrs Hagstrom put them in a bucket. She stood over the bucket, looking down.

Ten minutes later Delphine emerged from the bathroom in the scratchy blue housedress Mother had insisted she wear tonight. Her skin felt tender.

Mrs Hagstrom snatched up Delphine's hands, inspecting the fingernails.

She released them. 'Hmph. That'll have to do.'

Delphine held out her muddy clothes. Mrs Hagstrom tumbled them into a ball which she wedged beneath her armpit.

'Don't think you can go making a habit of this,' she said. 'Next time I may be occupied by my duties – which are many and arduous – and you'll be left to make your own excuses. Now, get yourself to the dining room. What with all these distractions dinner'll be ash and cinders. Go on, before I come to my senses,' and she shooed Delphine upstairs.

Delphine's belly growled but no one was starting.

Lord Alderberen tapped his spoon against the rim of his wine glass and kept tapping until everyone fell silent. He set the spoon down. Vapour rose from his tomato and shallot soup, bathing his rumpled bluish face.

'Noble colleagues – if I may say a few words before we begin the evening meal.' His head bobbed in a steady trickle of affirmation. He looked to Propp, who nodded for him to continue. Lord Alderberen usually took meals in his bedchamber. His presence at the dinner table was both awkward and momentous.

'We have,' he said, in a voice with the wavering quality of a gramophone recording, 'all of us, been affected profoundly by the events of last week. But in times of great adversity, we also find cause for great hope. Mr Propp and I have always said that the Society, if it is to be an engine for *real* change and not yet another cabal of pompous drawing-room philosophers, must demonstrate its efficacy through action. Rarely has this efficacy been demonstrated so resoundingly as on Wednesday, where quick thinking, skill, and grace under fire ensured that Mr Kung reached hospital with a minimum of delay.'

He lifted his glass. 'A toast.'

Everyone raised their drinks. Delphine shrank back in her chair, cheeks glowing.

'To Dr Lansley.'

To Lansley, repeated the diners.

Delphine was dumbfounded. No one objected. Even Daddy said nothing. Lansley accepted their praise, circling his glove like a traffic policeman.

Delphine was about to protest when she caught Mother's glare.

Propp gripped the arms of his chair and rose. 'My dear brothers and sisters, I add only this: you see now why we must work. You see now how very little time we have.' He regarded the guests with his big, dark eyes. His gaze came to rest on Delphine.

Under the table, Delphine curled her toes. She refused to look away.

Propp sat. He picked up his spoon. When he lifted the first spoonful of soup to his lips and blew, everyone else started to eat.

After dinner, Delphine went below stairs and ate supper.

Mrs Hagstrom cut up some sandwiches and piled them on two plates: half were goose and half were crab. She laid out some butter and a jar of plum jam and more bread, and strong, hot tea in a big green pot that took both hands to carry. Alice and Mr Garforth and Mr Wightman the blacksmith and Mr Garforth's assistant Reggie Gillow shuffled onto the long benches either side of the table and began to help themselves. Next to the doorway sat a little black woodburning stove, its seams creaking as it heated up. On a corner shelf, the wireless crooned softly.

'Nice of you to join us this evening, Martin,' said Mrs Hagstrom.

Mr Wightman nodded. He was wearing a checked cotton shirt with the cuffs buttoned back and his hair had been combed flat across his dented head. He had been at the Hall a lot recently, undertaking minor repair work on a room in the east wing where the rain got in.

'Ta, Mrs H, this is lovely,' said Reggie. Reggie had not lost his job over the pheasant business, so either he had been innocent, or – and this was the explanation Delphine thought more likely – Mr Garforth had not had the heart to sack him. The sun had brought his freckles out; they jostled as he chewed.

Mr Garforth tutted. 'Don't talk with your mouth full, boy.'

Alice was beaming. 'Reggie doesn't get anything like this at home, do you, Reggie?'

'Just greasy tea and a clip round the earhole.'

'Well, if you don't watch your manners I'll make you feel right at home,' said Mr Garforth. 'And *elbows*.'

Reggie slid his elbows off the table. 'Sorry, Mr G.'

Delphine munched on a jammy doorstop and gazed over Alice and Reggie's heads at framed photographs, pristine against the lime-washed brick. The largest picture showed a pair of dray horses chained one behind the other to a game waggon, on which dead pheasants hung in dozens from long metal bars. She could not see the grass for corpses – they carpeted the ground. A man was looking into the camera with a sullen expression. He had three pheasants in each hand.

A small, typewritten card tucked into the corner of the frame read: *November 1888. Assistant Keeper Mr H. Garforth recovers the last of the weekend's bag. Over two days' shooting, six guns (Lord Alderberen, Sir N. Goole, Cpt. B. Hunstanton, Mr M. Rao, Mr B. Khan, Rev. J. S. Coe) accounted for 2,686 pheasants, 80 partridges, 74 hares, 134 rabbits and 1 woodcock.*

Delphine examined the young Mr Garforth. He wore a black coat with a high collar and six brass buttons down the front. Beneath the pushed-back brim of his bowler hat, his face was tanned and lineless.

The photograph to the left showed a youth in a pith helmet, squatting with his rifle across his knees in front of a felled water buffalo. In the background, amongst tall dry grass, an Indian servant smiled uncertainly. The caption read: *Mysore, 1869. The young sahib shows off his first trophy.*

Tucked away in the top-left of the display was a photograph that looked to have been taken in the orangery. The washed-out, blurry image showed a dozen men and women dressed in kimonos, holding fans and parasols; at the front of the group stood a slight man in black evening dress, clutching a katana in an elaborate gilt-iron scabbard. He stood with one shoulder dipped, looking past the camera as if someone had just called to him. Delphine had to squint to read the little card in the corner of the frame: *March 1853. The 3rd Earl of Alderberen and servants prepare for the annual Birthday Play.*

Her chest clenched. She stared at the figure at the front of the photograph. His face was a blot of white.

She had always assumed no photographs existed of Lord Alderberen's father. Wasn't he supposed to have been a recluse? Hadn't he hidden himself away, because he was deformed, or a vampire, or a lunatic?

'Don't eat with your mouth open,' said Mr Garforth, flicking a clot of crabmeat from his whiskers. He was always grumpy at Sunday supper, partly out of tiredness (the walk to church was a round trip of eight miles), and partly because Mrs Hagstrom insisted on tuning the wireless to Radio Luxembourg, which he disapproved of because it carried advertisements for the pools on the Sabbath.

Delphine swallowed her last mouthful of bread and jam.

'I thought the old Earl didn't like to go out.'

'What are you talking about?'

She pointed at the faded photograph. Everybody turned to look. Mr Garforth peered over his shoulder, craning his neck until his eyes found the picture.

'Well?' she said.

Mr Garforth took a piece of bread and began to butter it with the easy grace of a barber stropping a razor. 'That was taken before the fire.'

Alice helped Mrs Hagstrom clear the plates away. Mrs Hagstrom laid out a coffee cake cut up into fingers, a dish of bourbons and a bowl of oranges.

'So, Henry.' Mrs Hagstrom took an orange from the pile. 'I suppose it's too much to hope that you might have passed a broom round that grubby cottage of yours since I last came by? Place was like a coalmine.'

'I'm *fine*, thank you.'

She jabbed her fingernail into the peel and tore off a strip. 'You're a man, is what you are, Henry, and a proud one at that, one who'd rather live in squalor than admit he needs help. When was the last time you had visitors?'

Delphine thought Mr Garforth's cottage was very tidy, thank you very much. Mr Garforth dunked a bourbon into his tea and looked murderous.

'I'm supposed to have the afternoon off Wednesday,' said Mrs Hagstrom. 'I'll be round with the mop and duster, if only to save you from yourse – '

'No. Muriel.' Mr Garforth held up a palm. 'Can't let you do that.'

She ripped off more skin. 'I insist.'

'That's very kind, but no.'

'Henry, you can't go on living as you do.'

'I get by.'

'I'm coming round and that's that.'

'No!' Mr Garforth slammed a palm against the table. Delphine's cake fork bounced off her lap and hit the floor. She ducked under the table to retrieve it.

The first thing she saw was Alice's little white hand smoothing Reggie's thigh. She flushed and began groping about on the cold tiles for her fork, unable to focus. Muffled through a layer of oak, she heard Mr Garforth say: 'Please. Just leave me be. I'll tidy the clutter in my own time.'

After everyone had finished, Mr Garforth took out his pipe while Reggie and Alice and Mr Wightman lit cigarettes. Mrs Hagstrom took a bottle of scotch whisky from the cupboard and poured everyone a glass. She let Delphine have a drop watered down in a mug. Delphine sipped it and felt needling fire across her gums and tongue. Delphine asked for a cigarette and Mr Garforth gave her a look, so she leant back and listened to the wireless and smelt his tobacco, mild and wafting like a hayloft in summer.

Somewhere behind her head, a maple-cased wall clock tocked dully. Mr Garforth said that, back in the old days, the Hall employed a clockman whose sole job it was to patrol the house winding the various timepieces. Now, Lord Alderberen barely kept enough staff to make dinner.

'He was a good man.'

It took Delphine a moment to realise that the speaker was Mr Wightman. He gazed at the barred slit of a window on the far wall.

'Shy, maybe. Not mad.' At this, Delphine worked out who he was talking about. 'His Lordship's father never needed *tunnels*. The village was ailing. He knew we wouldn't take charity. He invented jobs. The tunnels were just an excuse. His wife had passed. Young Master Lazarus was packed off to India. He became father to all of us. He was lonely.'

Mr Wightman refilled his glass with whisky. He opened his tobacco tin to reveal a few loose brown threads. Alice nudged Reggie, who took a pack of Player's from his shirt pocket and tapped one out onto the table. Mr Wightman accepted the cigarette. He struck a match against the white brick.

'Did you know him?' said Alice.

'Nope. Before my time.' He touched the flame to the tip of his cigarette. 'But I lived amongst them as did – my father included. I never heard anyone speak ill of his Lordship. No one had a bad thing to say.'

'I don't wonder no one had a bad thing to say,' said Reggie, making a face as he sipped his whisky. 'They never saw him.'

'Is it true he never left his bedroom for thirty years?' said Alice. 'And that he took all his meals through a special letterbox?'

Mrs Hagstrom hissed. 'Don't be so stupid, girl.'

'Father said the letterbox was for letters,' said Mr Wightman. 'Correspondence in, instructions for the workers out. He took his meals through a hatch. And it wasn't just his bedroom. It was most of the west-wing first floor. His Lordship liked his privacy. After the fire, the only person allowed into his chambers was Mr Cox, his valet.'

'I reckon he was sneaking out,' said Reggie. 'All those tunnels. I reckon he had a bird.'

'I reckon you'd best keep your opinions to yourself, lad,' said Mr Garforth.

'All the stories of her Ladyship say she was a remarkable woman,' said Mr Wightman. 'A little quiet perhaps but, oh, what a beauty. She was dearer to his Lordship than . . . well, you've seen all the portraits. They were all done after the fire. He filled the house with her. All the pictures of him he had taken down and destroyed. That photograph was down the back of a wardrobe for twenty years. It was like he thought if he didn't exist, she could live.'

A bell jangled in the adjoining room.

'That's me.' Alice finished her whisky and stood. She ducked through the archway. Delphine watched from the table as she fastened her white bib apron in a smudged looking-glass.

Mrs Hagstrom shook her head. 'We're run ragged in this house. So much for giving everyone jobs.'

'Muriel, that's enough,' said Mr Garforth.

She held up her sinewy hands. 'Well, hang me for being honest. If it weren't for the dailies, I'd of dropped down dead years ago. Half the Hall's under dust sheets. For the number of staff we struggle by on, you'd think we were working for the village doctor.'

Alice returned carrying a silver tray with scalloped edges. On the tray sat a pot of tea, a tumbler of scotch, and a brown glass bottle. Delphine squinted at the label. In Dr Lansley's familiar, regimented hand she made out the words: *tincture of silver*.

Mr Wightman knuckled at his eyes. For a strange second, Delphine thought he was crying.

'That's the problem with this country,' he said. 'Everything's gone to ruin. All the good men, all the gentlemen and hardworking lads, got nobbled in France. All that's left are bank managers and soft-bellied Sunday golfers.' He sucked on his cigarette and it glowed like his forge. 'The old master lost his wife. He could've took the coward's way out, but he didn't. He soldiered on. Even in his misery, he was always looking for ways to help others.

'Same with his Lordship. After what happened with Arthur . . . ' He took a sharp breath and drained his glass. 'The whole Stokeham bloodline's cursed. But they fight it. They won't give in to fate.'

His hand was shaking as he ground his cigarette out.

'Oh, but you can't escape your fate,' said Alice. 'A fortune teller told my Uncle Jack that he wouldn't go on holiday this year. He went to Southend just to spite her and got hit by a trolleybus.'

Delphine imagined the shriek of brakes, the dry thud as Uncle Jack went down. She saw blood, broken teeth. She remembered Mr Kung gasping on the sand, froth pooling in his eyes.

All at once, her whisky tasted of cinders.

'I've got to go.' She was rising, clutching at her collar. 'Thank you. Sorry.'

The bell rang again.

'Delphine!' said Mr Garforth.

'I've got to go!' She spilled out into the corridor, unable to breathe. She stumbled towards the stairs. Her lungs tightened.

In unison, the Hall's clocks began striking the hour.

CHAPTER 12

THE BRAT OF HEAVEN

July 1935

Delphine was lying on her tummy in the treehouse, poring over Mr Kung's crumpled notes. The crabbed Chinese characters were giving her a headache. Some of the larger ones looked like crude little maps. And there was that word: 'DELLAPESTE'. Did she recognise it, or had she just stared at it for so long that it felt familiar? She slapped the page aside and heard weeping.

Delphine pressed her face flat to the floor. From somewhere in the surrounding alders and sycamores came the curt, squeaky calls and liquid trills of a goldfinch. She relaxed. She had mistaken birdsong for . . . No. There it was again. Someone was beneath her.

She slithered from the clubhouse to the crow's nest. She held her breath.

She pulled herself up and peered over the rim of the barrel. Diamonds of midday sunlight studded the woodland floor, shifting in the wind. Amongst glossy fronds of hart's tongue fern, a woman sat with her hands over her face, softly crying. Delphine saw the golden hair against the shoulder of a navy blue prefect's jacket and recognised Miss DeGroot.

Over the past couple of weeks, Miss DeGroot had begun affecting a swagger stick. The lion's head pommel lay beside her in the undergrowth. She had kicked off her chocolate-brown walking boots. She wept without ostentation.

She dragged a forearm across her eyes.

'If you're going to stare, at least toss me a peanut.'

Delphine dropped back inside the barrel. She clamped a palm over her mouth. Perhaps Miss DeGroot had been talking to herself. Perhaps someone was coming. Delphine's heart squeezed in her chest.

'I know you're up there. I can hear the boards creaking.'

Delphine held herself rigid, eyes screwed shut. If she kept still, Miss DeGroot would give up and walk away.

'Hey. I'm not mad at you. Just trying to be neighbourly.' A sigh. 'Okay. Have it your way. I plan on crying for a solid forty minutes, so I hope you weren't hoping to leave any time soon. Ah. There you are.'

Delphine stuck her head over the parapet. Miss DeGroot was standing, looking up at the treehouse.

'Hello,' said Delphine.

'Hi.' Miss DeGroot folded her arms. 'Nice cabana you've got here.'

Delphine had a tingly sensation in her belly. 'Thank you.'

Miss DeGroot's eyes were pink. The soft lines over her cheekbones glistened. She sniffed, then snorted unapologetically.

Delphine havered, then, with a weightless feeling, she said: 'You can look inside, if you like.'

A corner of Miss DeGroot's smile steepened. She looked down at her fingernails.

'You don't have to humour me. I was just kidding about the crying jag.' She swatted the air. 'Go on. Enjoy your freedom while you still have some.' She began walking away.

Delphine kicked loose the rope ladder. It unfurled with a clatter. Miss DeGroot spun round. She laughed and put a hand to her mouth.

'That's quite the red carpet.'

'It's safe. I repaired it.'

Miss DeGroot prodded the ladder with her stick. 'Okay, then.' She glanced at a paper bag lying next to her boots. 'I've got a bag of maple candies I can trade for sanctuary. How's that?'

'Acceptable.' Delphine folded Mr Kung's notes and tucked them inside her sock. She shuffled to the edge of the treehouse. Miss DeGroot placed a foot on the first rung.

'I'm not supposed to be exerting myself. I'm supposed to be an – ungh – invalid.' She thrust her swagger stick upwards. Delphine grabbed the cold brass pommel and helped pull Miss DeGroot the last few feet. She reached the top sweaty, panting. 'Wow. What a swell place.' Delphine caught a whiff of perfume: lemon, cedarwood. Miss DeGroot rolled onto her back and lay catching her breath, taking in the clubhouse (four driftwood walls beneath a rusting corrugated-iron roof) and the crow's nest (an old rain barrel with the bottom knocked out of it). Grey-green oak moss coated a seam where one of the walls met the tree. In the opposite corner, cobwebs crisscrossed the papery husk of an abandoned wasps' nest. 'How long it take you to build?'

'It was like this when I found it.'

Miss DeGroot half-closed her eyes. 'I like it.'

The treehouse filled with goldfinch song and the quiet gasp of wind through leaves. Delphine was not sure what to say. She looked at the old wasps' nest. A lattice of silver filaments hung across its underside. She could hear Miss DeGroot breathing. The hairs on the back of her neck prickled. She inhaled the scent of wet leaves and old wood, tinged with perfume. In the lower half of the web, a spider had caught something fat and struggling.

When she glanced back, Miss DeGroot had stretched her legs. She was sucking on a candy.

'So,' she said, 'what do you think about up here?'

International spy rings. Secret codes. The invasion of Britain. Giant rabid bats. My father.

Delphine turned out her bottom lip. 'Nothing.'

'You seem to have taken a shine to the harbourmaster's son. I saw the two of you gabbing down by the quay.'

Delphine's cheeks glowed. 'I was buying a *knife*.'

'That's okay, sweetie. No need to be embarrassed.'

Delphine prised up a loose board and retrieved a blade folded into a crude scrimshaw handle.

'There.' She slammed it down on the floor beside Miss DeGroot's head.

Miss DeGroot glanced over and laughed. 'Okay, okay, I believe you.' She held her palms up. 'No offence intended. Good for you. Boys are the dullest.'

Delphine snatched up the knife, wondering if she had been a bit rash. What if Miss DeGroot told Mother? She was placing it back in its box when she felt Miss DeGroot's eyes over her shoulder.

'Is that an air rifle?'

'No, it's . . . ' Delphine stopped herself. 'Yes.'

Miss DeGroot gazed at the double-barrelled shotgun tucked inside the floor compartment. She rubbed her palms together.

'I had one back on the farm. Used to sit up in the hayloft and use the old pump for target practice. Once my brother Stanley was fetching his bathwater and I got him right in the seat of his pants.' She mimed looking down sights, the kick of the trigger pull.

'Was he all right?'

'Naturally.' Miss DeGroot lay down again and sighed theatrically. 'Life was simple back then. You hid in barns. You shot your family.' She patted the paper bag. 'Have a candy.'

Delphine picked out a hard brown candy and sucked on it, glad of the distraction. The sweetness was so intense she felt a headache coming on.

Miss DeGroot closed her eyes. She extended her arms and slid them up and down like someone making a snow angel.

'We must seem ancient to you. Do I seem ancient?'

Delphine glanced at Miss DeGroot. Up close, she did look older. Fine cracks radiated from her eyes and her skin had the sickly cast of semolina. Her blond hair was thinning at the scalp.

'No.'

'You're a sweetheart. And a liar.'

Delphine bit her lower lip.

'Do you love Mr Propp?'

One of Miss DeGroot's eyes snapped open. 'That's a very strong word.'

Delphine wrinkled her nose.

'I'm sorry.'

'Don't be. I'm your guest. It was a fair question.' Miss DeGroot squinted at the corrugated-iron ceiling. 'I should say all Spim is founded on the doctrine of *amour-Propp*. Of course, Ivan says that none of us *can* love – not while we're asleep. Oh, we all *think* we do. But when you look at it, what we call "love" is just a cat's cradle of demands and rewards. Real love doesn't make you feel good. You have to pay. Real love is sacrifice. It costs you.' She let out a short, mirthless laugh. 'Huh. Perhaps I do love him.'

Delphine drew in the dust with her fingertip. 'You don't think he's wicked?'

'Now, what on earth would make you say that?'

Delphine felt her face getting hot. 'I heard somebody say so.'

'Who?'

'I don't remember.'

Miss DeGroot's gaze hung on Delphine a moment longer.

'Well, maybe they're right. Maybe everyone we place our trust in is destined to betray us. I honestly don't know any more.' She draped a forearm over her face. 'Oh gosh, he's really done a number on our heads, hasn't he?'

'What about Dr Lansley?'

'What about him?' Miss DeGroot slid her arm from her eyes. 'Young lady, I do believe you're trying to shake me down for gossip.'

'No, I'm just . . . I . . . ' Delphine clenched her fists, breathed in. 'Can you keep a secret?'

'No.'

'Oh, uh . . . '

'But at least I'm honest.' Miss DeGroot lifted herself up onto her elbows. 'Look, I know the Doctor isn't exactly a teddy bear, but he's not good with . . . well, anyone, really. Try not to take it personally. You know he saved dozens of lives during the war? Lost his hearing, too. Small wonder he's a little cranky.'

'I have evidence suggesting Mr Propp is a spy.'

'Is that your secret?'

Delphine nodded. 'And I think Lord Alderberen and Dr Lansley are in on it.'

Miss DeGroot tilted her head forward. 'Why are you trusting me with this?'

'I don't know. I thought . . . you might believe me.'

Miss DeGroot closed her eyes. She smiled and brought a finger to her cheek. A tear rolled over her knuckle.

'You're a nice girl, you know that?' She sat up. 'Okay. Tell me about it.'

Delphine told her everything. She talked about the secret passages and tunnels, about overhearing Propp and Lord Alderberen on the first day, she even – after picking at a splinter in the floor – admitted to opening Propp's post and finding the letter from Mr Kung. All the while, she monitored Miss DeGroot's face for signs of scepticism, anger, or boredom. Miss DeGroot nodded and watched. She did not smirk.

'He left this on the beach.' Delphine slid the folded paper from her sock. 'It was wrapped round a book my father took.' As she passed it to Miss DeGroot, she realised that her hand was shaking. 'I can't read it.'

Miss DeGroot studied the page. She folded it in half, running her thumb along the crease, and lay it on the floor beside her.

'You must be exhausted.'

'I don't know what to do.'

'Listen.' Miss DeGroot reached out and closed her fingers over the back of Delphine's palm. They were soft and clammy. 'I believe you.'

Delphine breathed out long and hard.

'I believe everything you've told me.' Miss DeGroot gave Delphine's hand a squeeze, then let go. 'I know it's hard to understand, but all the adults here . . . we're broken. Me, the Doctor, Lazarus, your father. Look at that professor of yours, shut away in the chimera room, surrounded by beasts while he waits on a letter from the latest handsome young undergraduate he's mooning over. Dreaming of a hidden country they can run away to together.' She shook her head. 'The island of Dr Morose!

'I'm sure those men like to dream they could take over the world. Making trunk calls at the dead of night, playing kingmakers. But that's all they're doing – playing. Maybe Ivan really is a spy, who knows? If he is, this is the best place for him. Away from London, away from anyone of any influence whatsoever.'

'But . . . '

'The symposium? Oh, darling, no one of any account goes there. Important people are too busy running the country.'

Delphine sagged. 'You think I've imagined it all.'

'No. Absolutely not.' She picked up Mr Kung's notes. 'I'll look at this. I'll think on what you've said. And if you find anything more, or . . . you just need somebody to talk to, you come find me, you hear?'

Delphine placed her hand flat on the floor. She could feel her palm pulsing against the warped wood.

'All right,' she said.

Miss DeGroot stretched and yawned.

'Why were you cry – '

Delphine was cut off by approaching voices. Miss DeGroot scrambled into the crow's nest. She grabbed a leafy branch and pulled it down across her face. She beckoned for Delphine, who joined her on the battlements.

Down in the woods, Dr Lansley was pushing Lord Alderberen in his wheelchair. The wheels eek-eek-eeked as they traversed bumpy ground. Lord Alderberen clutched a tartan blanket spread across his knees. Walking alongside, hands tucked into the pockets of his silk waistcoat, was Propp.

'Speak of the devil,' said Miss DeGroot. 'Here come the girls of Radcliff Hall.'

'What?'

'Shh!'

The wheelchair progressed in a succession of jerks and hiccups; Dr Lansley was grimacing with the effort. The sound of snapping twigs grew louder. She could make out Lansley's part of the conversation, since, as usual, he was noisiest.

'Well, that's as maybe, but . . . No, it's not that I disagree, I just . . . Well, I'll have to take your word on that, won't I, because as you keep telling me, I can't make the trip. Damn it, Lazarus, can't you wheel yourself for a bit? It's like ploughing treacle. Steady, there's a dip here . . . '

Delphine glanced to her right. Miss DeGroot had vanished. She heard footfalls on the hollow floor and suddenly Miss DeGroot was beside her, brandishing the shotgun.

'What's the betting I can still hit Titus in the backside at thirty yards?'

'No!'

'What, don't you think I can manage it?' Miss DeGroot barged her way into the crow's nest. 'Come on. I bet you a pack of Du Mauriers. Right in the hiney.'

'Please, you can't.'

'Pshaw! Just watch me.' She swung the gun towards the approaching trio and squinted down the sights.

Mr Garforth had made Delphine swear to keep her gun unloaded unless preparing for a shot. She would never dream of breaking her word, but experience had broadened her definition of 'preparing'. After all, shouldn't she always be prepared? When the perfect bird presented itself, she didn't want to be fumbling for cartridges. In a sense, her whole life was a preparation for the next shot, and thus the only true negligence was leaving her shotgun *unloaded*.

Miss DeGroot inhaled.

'Pull.'

Delphine slammed her forearm into the muzzle just as it kicked. The right barrel sent up a tremendous report. The shot rang through the woods, goldfinches scattering. She saw, through smoke and falling leaves, Dr Lansley sprawled face down in the dirt.

Delphine stared. The treehouse seemed to lurch.

A second later he was staggering to his feet. The shot had gone comfortably wide.

'Jesus Christ!' Slapping earth from his tweed lapels. 'Jesus Christ, what the Hell was that?'

Delphine dropped into the sanctuary of the crow's nest. Miss DeGroot lay on her back, hands clamped over her mouth, laughing silently till the tears streamed into her hair. The woods echoed with Lansley's swearing.

'Oh my,' she said. 'Oh my, girl. That was *fun*.'

CHAPTER 13

BIG GAME

July 1935

Delphine followed Propp round the north shore of the lake. He was climbing a small hill on the water's edge, towards a dome of grubby, mossy brick. The maps all referred to it the same way: 'the ice house'.

She sliced through a black clump of candlesnuff fungus with her crab stick. In the late evening sun, the woods rippled with amber light.

Mr Propp's disappearances were beginning to bleed into one another. He was away more than he was present. He sometimes talked vaguely about seminars in London, but he never took a motor car – Delphine had checked – and the station was too far to reach on foot, especially for one so old and portly.

After dinner, when Propp pulled on a dark grey greatcoat, slid his stick from the bronze umbrella stand and left the Hall through a side door, Delphine followed him. She kept her distance, pantomiming intense absorption in flowers or clusters of reeds. She watched him through the field glasses. They were still speckled with sand from the beach. When she twisted the focus knob, it crunched.

At the crest of the hill, he stopped. Delphine crouched in a patch of yellow rock-rose, congratulating herself on her consummate veldtcraft. Propp shielded his eyes as he looked back towards the Hall. Above him, great anvil-shaped clouds hung with scarlet and magenta peaks and dark underbellies. In the dwindling sun, his tanned, bare head winked like a doubloon. When he turned and continued round the far side of the ice house, out of sight, she balled her fists.

He was unaware. She had him.

She waited for him to reappear.

Five minutes passed.

Delphine began to get fidgety. She had cramp in her thigh from squatting. She threw glances into the woods. What if he had circled round?

She sat. Something flickered in the trees. A red squirrel was corkscrewing up the trunk of a horse chestnut. She pressed a palm to her chest, exhaled.

Ten minutes passed. No sign. He had vanished.

Delphine stood as casually as she could. She made a point of not looking towards the ice house. Her right leg throbbed with pins and needles.

She ambled to the lakeside, pretending to admire the way the orange sun flowed molten into the water. Gnats seethed above the rushes. She scythed through them with her crab hook, then turned and began wandering up the hill.

Up close, the ice house was in even worse repair than the tomb. Spurts of yellow stonecrop dangled from cracks in the age-blackened brickwork. Moss clung in dark, sweaty clumps. Set deep in an embrasure was a door.

It was made of thick oak planks banded with black iron. Above a three-inch keyhole was a door knob bigger than her fist.

Surely Propp hadn't gone inside?

She scanned the lawns, the distant driveway. They were deserted.

Delphine knelt and peered through the keyhole. Blackness. She listened. Silence. She sniffed. Musty sourness.

She stood and stared at the door. There had to be a way in.

She kicked it. Her heel bounced off the oak. It was like kicking a church. She brandished her crab hook and spent a few fruitless minutes trying to find some angle whereby she could fit it inside the keyhole and pick the lock.

There was probably nothing inside. The door looked rusted shut and the lock was so sturdy she doubted even a shotgun blast at point-blank range would shift it.

The light was fading. She shivered. Across the lake, Alderberen Hall was turning a dirty beige.

She gave in.

'The whole thing's a rum business,' Delphine said later that evening, lifting the kettle off the fire with her crab hook.

Mr Garforth was at the table, refilling the lamp with paraffin.

'Don't talk like that,' he said. 'You sound like an old colonel.'

'Beats looking like one.'

'Rubbish. I ent got the jowls.'

Delphine set the kettle down on the worktop. 'The what?'

'The jowls. The jowls.' He slapped his palms against his cheeks and smooshed them up and down. 'I'm too young in the face.'

'Too soft in the head, more like.'

'Watch it.'

She took the lid off the little blue teapot and poured in hot water.

'How much tea you got in there?' he said.

'Two spoonfuls.'

'Stick in another.'

She replaced the lid. 'No.'

'Go on. It's one spoon per person, then one for the pot.' He put down the paraffin canister and moved as if to get up. 'Go on. Else it tastes like dishwater.'

'Then you're not brewing it long enough. Two is plenty. If you make it too strong, you spoil the flavour.'

In front of the fireplace hung wet clothes, socks and longjohns and impossibly huge underpants, filling the cottage with sweet damp mist. Mr Garforth sat with his back to her. He was barefoot, wearing a pair of loose brown cotton trousers held up by braces, the top three buttons of his shirt undone. The hearth made noises like a game of marbles.

Delphine stood by the teapot, using a teaspoon to tap out a march against its spout while whistling a loose pastiche of Battle Hymn of the Republic.

'That'll be ready now,' said Mr Garforth, without turning round.

She waited until she had completed a full verse and chorus before pouring the tea. She added three spoonfuls of brown sugar for Mr Garforth then a splash of milk in each mug.

'There you go.' She set his down in front of him.

He picked it up and blew. Wisps of steam peeled from the surface. She watched him take a sip.

'Aah.' His chair creaked as he settled back into it. Delphine glanced at her reflection in the window and realised she was smiling.

'Fearlessness,' she said. 'That's what a soldier most fears seeing in his enemy's eyes.'

'Not even close.'

'Drat.'

'So,' he said, 'what mischief have you got yourself into today?'

She levered the lid off the biscuit tin and pushed a digestive into her mouth. 'Mwuffin.'

He swatted the air and shook his head, disgusted. 'You've got the manners of a Zulu.'

Delphine chewed through the mouthful as fast as possible and swallowed. 'Actually, the Zulu people are a race of *proud warriors*, and two, I've been busy doing schoolwork.'

'A likely story.'

'I know it is.' She grabbed a second biscuit then patted the lid back down. She walked round so she could see his face. 'So . . . you know by the lake, the ice house?'

Mr Garforth stared at the table.

'Hello?' she said. Sometimes he dozed off in the middle of the conversation. He could go to sleep with his eyes open.

He sniffed, looked at her. 'Yes?'

'So you know it?'

'Of course I know it.'

'What's it for?'

He opened his mouth, let his upper dentures fall onto his tongue, sucked them back into place. In the firelight, his ears looked like they were melting.

'It's not for anything. It's a ruin.'

'Someone must have built it.'

He took a sip of tea. 'I suppose they must.'

'Well, what did they build it for?'

'What do you think someone builds an ice house for?'

Delphine hesitated. 'Ice?'

'Yes, well bloody done.' Mr Garforth thumped his mug back down on the table, sloshing tea. 'Now, will you please stop going on about it.'

'All right. There's no need to yell at me.'

'This is my house and if I want to raise my voice, I will,' he said.

Delphine's face felt hot. She looked down into her tea.

'Sorry.'

'Don't go anywhere near it. It's not a bloody playground.'

'I wasn't going to,' she said. 'I just wanted to know what it was for.'

'Nonsense. You wanted to break in. You wanted to poke your nose around and pry and interfere. You won't listen.'

'I do listen.'

'Liar!' He rounded on her, jabbing his finger. 'I told you to kill rats. You took one as a pet. I told you not to go in the tunnels. You went in the tunnels.'

'I never!'

'After everything I've done for you, you'd stand here in my own home and lie to me.'

Delphine focused on the white hairs in his nostrils. No one used the attic except her. She checked she was alone every time she used the tunnels. She had been *so* careful. He was bluffing. He had to be.

'You're wrong,' she said. 'I never went in those tunnels.'

His nostrils swelled and shrank. The little hairs shivered.

'Swear on your mother's life.'

'I swear I never went in the tunnels.'

'On your mother's life.'

'All right, then.'

'Well?'

She looked him in the eyes. 'I swear on my mother's life I never played in the tunnels.'

'Not played. Went.'

Delphine threw a hand up. 'Played, went. Whatever you like.'

He glared at her.

'Right,' she said. 'Fine. I swear on my mother's life I never went in the tunnels, there, are you satisfied?'

'Get out.'

'What? I said I never did it.'

'Go on.' He turned his back. 'I can't stand to look at you.'

'Why are you being so horrible?'

He did not answer.

Delphine stood clutching her mug of tea. Mr Garforth plucked at his side whiskers with long, dirty fingers. Half his body was glutted with shadow. She set her tea down beside the sink.

She opened the door, waited. Mr Garforth closed his eyes. Delphine stepped into the night, slamming the door behind her.

CHAPTER 14

THE BATMAN

July 1935

One morning before sunrise Delphine stood at the edge of a field, listening to the motion of the wheat. She knelt, unclasped her hands.

'You're free,' she said.

Vicky looked up at her uncertainly.

Delphine placed Vicky on the ground. She ran a knuckle across the back of the rat's hairy ears.

'Run.'

Vicky did not move.

'Go!' Delphine gave her a nudge. 'I'm setting you free, stupid. Go on. Boo!' She lunged. Vicky darted into the stalks and was gone.

Delphine rose and looked out across a rippling golden ocean. The wind pressed at her back, insistent, like a dare.

When Delphine entered the stables, Daddy was in a corner with Miss DeGroot. He was showing her a selection of canvases propped against the wall. She was cooing and touching his arm.

The room was hot. All his things were stacked neatly: canvases, brushes – sorted by size – paints, rags, jars of turpentine, the dull, greengrey book Mr Kung had left on the beach. The floor had been swept – she saw now it was stone, with shallow drainage channels leading to circular iron grates.

'Such bold strokes!' said Miss DeGroot meaningfully, stepping back like a carpenter. She tugged on her gold silk neckerchief. 'Like *chasms*.'

'It's not finished yet,' said Daddy.

'Oh, but you mustn't touch it!' She clutched his elbow. 'This is raw, undiluted.' She drew a sharp, scintillating breath. 'The utter dominance of the line.' She held the sentiment for a moment, then exhaled, replete. 'Did you say you fought?'

Daddy seemed thrown by the abrupt switch of topic. 'Oh. Yes.'

'Really. You look far too young.' She cast a glance back over her shoulder and spotted Delphine. 'Ah! Your other masterpiece.' She turned him like a show pony.

Daddy's sleeves were rolled up. He had black paint on his fingers. 'What do you want?' he said.

'I need to speak to you,' said Delphine. She had made up her mind. Whatever the truth behind Propp, Alderberen and Lansley's intentions, she felt ruin looming like a stormfront. She would demand the family leave. She would make it impossible to stay.

'Not now.'

Miss DeGroot rolled her eyes. 'Ignore him. He's in a mood because his latest painting doesn't need him any more.' She crossed the room, grasped Delphine's hand. 'And how are *you* today?' After the incident in the treehouse, Delphine had expected a flicker of embarrassment, perhaps a wink acknowledging their conspiratorial sisterhood.

Instead, Miss DeGroot squeezed. 'Good to see you,' she said. She marched back to Daddy. 'You have a surprise for your daughter.'

Daddy buried his painting hand in his trouser pocket. He dropped his gaze.

'Another time, perhaps.'

'Oh, come on! Don't be such a sourpuss! No time like the present and no present like time. We might all be dead tomorrow.'

Daddy sighed with his whole body. 'I made you something.'

Delphine felt a momentary weightlessness. She fought it back. 'Did you?'

Daddy nodded. He blew out the corner of his mouth, a strand of steely hair rising, dropping.

Miss DeGroot smiled one of her laidback, worldly smiles.

'Why don't I fetch it for you?' She pointed at Delphine. 'Close your eyes now.'

Delphine looked at Daddy. To her surprise, he smiled.

'Go on, Delphy.'

She closed one eye. 'Okay.' She closed the other.

'And keep them shut!' Miss DeGroot's voice, with its warm vowels and faint, borderless twang, moved to the back of the room. 'Peep and you'll ruin the magic.'

'I won't.'

'Cover your eyes so I know you're not cheating.'

Delphine pressed her fingers to her eyelids. Purple blotches swelled in the darkness.

'Marvellous!' Miss DeGroot sounded genuinely delighted. She began rummaging through a heap of heavy-sounding objects. Delphine smelt tobacco smoke. Either Miss DeGroot or Daddy had lit a cigarette.

There was a *shhhhhh* noise, then a clatter and lots of bangs.

'Whoop, there we go!' called Miss DeGroot. 'You've got so much trash. Aha!' She fell quiet. Delphine waited. Quick footsteps returned to Daddy. 'Now . . . *very* slowly take your hands from your eyes and hold them out in front of you – don't peek, now! That's it. Bring them down and make a bowl. A little lower. There!' Delphine's cupped hands trembled. 'In your own time, Gideon.'

Something hard pressed into the moist flesh of her palm. She kept her hands as still as she could manage. She heard Daddy smack his lips. He stepped away.

Delphine waited for instruction.

'Well?' said Miss DeGroot.

'Can I look?'

'Feel it first.'

Carefully, Delphine tipped the object into her left palm and brought her right hand over the top. The thing was a little bigger than a bar of soap. One side felt rough, like a scab, the other smooth, like a tooth. It was light. Delphine frowned.

'Can I look now?'

'Don't you want to guess what it is?'

'I can't.'

'Have a go.'

She ran her fingertips along a network of interlocking grooves. 'Pine-cone?'

Miss DeGroot hooted with laughter. 'As a present? Give your daddy some credit.'

Delphine felt a jab of resentment. Before things got bad, Daddy used to bring her all sorts of treasures: conkers, little rusted keys, beautiful peculiar stones. Mother had fussed, insisting on washing them, but Delphine received each like a rare and fragile artefact plundered from the tomb of an ancient king. She laid them out, curated them, speculated on their origins, invented histories. A pine-cone, especially one this big, would make a fine gift. The best gift.

'Go on,' said Miss DeGroot, 'try again.'

'I don't know.'

'Stop thinking at it. Let your intuition do the heavy lifting. Perhaps you're an undiscovered latent.'

She exhaled heavily. 'Is it a hairbrush?'

'No!' This time, she heard Daddy chuckle too. 'You can do better than that!'

She closed her hands tight around the object. Tough notches dug into her skin. An image of Mr Kung patting Zeno flashed into her mind.

'Is it a tortoise?'

Silence.

Miss DeGroot said flatly: 'You peeked.'

Delphine opened her eyes. Sitting in her palms was a small tortoise, carved from bark.

'Oh!' She almost dropped it.

Miss DeGroot stood clutching Kung's book, a cigarette perched in her lips. Mazy tentacles of smoke wafted through her blond hair. Her expression softened.

'You really did guess, didn't you?'

Delphine lifted the tortoise up to her eyes. It was carved from a hunk of black poplar, the thick grey bark forming the shell, the light smooth wood beneath compromising the tortoise's head, legs and belly. It was covered in a thin coat of matt varnish. It was quite, quite lovely.

She looked at Daddy. 'Is he really for me?'

Daddy smiled. He looked almost bashful.

'Who else would it be for?'

Delphine stared numbly.

'Can I give him a name?'

Daddy nodded. She looked at the tortoise. Her mind was blank.

Daddy crushed her to his chest. She smelt linseed oil and the woody fug of sweat. The air went out of her and she focused on the hard, light tortoise balanced in her hand.

His grip relaxed. Delphine stepped away. Sometime during the hug, Miss DeGroot had made her silent exit.

Delphine tested her balance. She felt like an empty tube of paint.

'Daddy. Who's Arthur?'

He took his hand away. 'You know who Arthur was, darling. He was Lord Alderberen's son.'

Delphine watched his eyes. She felt the taboo between them like a physical thing, thickening. She pushed at it.

'Did you fight with him?' She licked her lips. 'Beside him, I mean?'

'Yes,' said Daddy. 'I was his batman.'

'What's a batman?'

'It means I helped him with things.'

'Like a servant?'

Daddy paused. 'Like a friend.'

Delphine looked across at the canvas Miss DeGroot had been admiring. It was a mass of jagged black lines and dirty swirls. She could make out something like a scarab's mandibles.

'Did he die?'

'Yes.'

She waited for more, but apparently it wasn't that kind of story. Daddy looked at his shoes. The studio was mausoleum quiet. Daddy walked to the pile beside the wall and dug out his tobacco tin. He rolled a cigarette, lit it.

He said: 'You were good, on the beach.' She met his eye. He nodded. 'You were good.'

'You didn't see him. Not at the beginning. He was just . . . standing there. Like someone queuing at the pictures.'

Daddy squinted against coils of smoke.

'The balance of his mind was upset. The Kwan-Dong army burned his house down. They burned his whole town down to the foundations. Killed his family too. He had a daughter – about your age. We were his last hope.'

'Daddy, I think . . . ' She looked away, remembering Mr Garforth's glare, the lacerating cold of the wind as she had left the cottage.

'Go on.'

She eyed Daddy's expression like someone preparing to jump a ravine. She thought of Kung's notes, of the conversation she had heard all those months ago, of Propp, prodding at Peter Stokeham's tomb. Miss DeGroot might be right – perhaps the *whole* country wasn't in danger – but those things had still happened. She hadn't imagined them.

'I know you don't think so, but . . . I think the Society is bad somehow. Maybe not all the time. Maybe they don't *all* mean to be, but . . . I've been gathering proof. Something dark is coming.'

Daddy took a long pull on the stub of his cigarette. She waited for him to shout, or laugh.

'I know exactly what you mean,' he said. 'Sometimes I feel the same way.' He thumped a fist against his stomach. 'Down here. The dread. Like you've been kicked by a horse.'

'Yes!'

'It's a trick.'

'What?'

'Delphy.' Daddy tossed his cigarette butt to the floor. 'Fear stops you from burning brightly. When I went in the sea . . . it all got washed away. I can think better. I can *see* better.' He beamed. 'I'm almost *clean*. Soon, you and me and Mummy, we can leave. Just a little longer and . . . we can go home.' His eyes sparked at the word. 'Won't that be nice?'

Delphine thought for a moment. 'I'd like that.'

'And we will live happily ever after.'

'But Daddy, I – '

187

'And if you ran away . . . ' He clutched her shoulder. 'If you abandoned me . . . you would spoil all that. Do you understand?'

Delphine thought of the dank tunnels that ran under the estate, Mr Kung's vomiting water on the beach and Propp's singing before a sucking, flooded grave. She looked into Daddy's furious blue eyes. She thought of her bedroom.

She nodded.

'So you won't make a fuss?' said Daddy. 'You'll work hard and listen to Mr Propp?'

'Yes, Daddy.'

CHAPTER 15

LOVE LIES BLEEDING

July 1935

S he had been tracking the mother and children for almost half an hour.

Delphine lay in the amaranth bed with her shotgun. Heavy fuchsia tassels hung either side of her head.

The bitch stoat shuffled in the long, dry grass, a sleeve of caramel. Behind it, half a dozen kits hopped, gnashed and boxed clumsily.

Delphine looked at the mother through freshly blacked gun sights. She adjusted for gravity, imagining she was a sniper, pretending it was other than a dreadfully unsporting shot.

But the point – as Mr Garforth had always insisted – was not to show off one's gunplay. The point was simple extermination. Whether by shotgun or snare or shovelhead or gin trap or the introduction of a larger predator, all that counted was death.

The bitch stoat rose up onto its hindquarters, bucked and sprang into the air. Grass splashed as it landed. It rose again, undulating crazily. Delphine glanced over at the kits; they were mimicking their mother, tilting up onto their back legs, fainting like duchesses. She thought of Lewis and Maxim. She thought of Vicky. Her trigger finger tingled. She granted a five-second stay of execution. Another.

She did not notice the rabbit until it was yards away. It lingered, apparently intrigued. The bitch stoat writhed, ecstatic. The rabbit blinked.

The stoat attacked.

The rabbit bolted. The bitch covered the tussocky ground in bright, springing strides. The rabbit bounded towards the treeline, widening the gap, then stupidly, suicidally, swerved left, letting the stoat cut the corner and make up lost ground. The kits looked up from their rough and tumble, vaguely aware that their mother had gone. One trotted a few feet, lost its nerve and returned to its brothers and sisters.

Delphine considered firing. It was certainly a harder shot now, the stoat zipping diagonally across her field of vision, its black tail disappearing behind white sprigs of crow garlic. To shoot would be to grant the rabbit a sudden, celestial reprieve. It would live on, perhaps siring its own children, some of whom would survive to have children in their turn, some of whom would feed the children of predators, whole dynasties rising and collapsing at the twitch of her index finger.

She brought the muzzle round and aimed at the kits. Two were watching their mother; the rest were romping in a listless, perfunctory way. The tendons in her wrist tightened. She pictured the impact, the splatter pattern.

Mr Garforth said a bitch and her kits worked the area round their den systematically, devastating birds and ground game. He said if you disturbed them, they would move, and you rarely got a second chance. Once, on a patrol, he squeaked twice, and when a stoat popped out of an old mole run he blew its head off.

The bitch stoat accelerated up a hump and launched itself, catching the grey rolls of the rabbit's throat in its teeth. The rabbit made a noise like a baby crying. The stoat gnawed and kicked. Slowing to a lollop, the rabbit shrieked then lay down and closed its eyes. The stoat straddled the fat, hot body, massaging the rabbit's head with its forepaws, shh, shh. There was no blood. The stoat wriggled for a while, then fell still.

Delphine felt her lungs pushing against the soil. As she squinted through the dark nick of the sight, she wondered if her own life fell within the crosshairs of some looming, silent creator, and, if so, whether He would shoot.

The bitch stoat snapped its head up, then squeaked and ran to its kits, leaving the dead rabbit behind. In one lithe brown mass the stoats threaded through the grass and into their den, in the shade of an ash.

Delphine blinked, surprised. Stoats were tenacious little beasts, reluctant to abandon good grub without stashing it – bravery was their downfall, really, made them easy to lure into traps, easy to shoot.

Something was coming.

She heard a swish. Dr Lansley came striding through the tall grass, swiping a stick back and forth with gusto. His back had a pronounced concavity that became especially noticeable when he walked; he looked as if he were marching against a strong wind.

She shrank into the amaranth. Through purple columns, she watched Lansley cross the scrub. He stopped, prodded the rabbit carcass with his stick. His tongue came out, triangular, purple. He blenched, moustache curling like a leech put to a candle. Delphine held the gun to her chest. Her heart pumped softly against the barrels.

Dr Lansley glanced around. For an instant, he was looking straight at her – *through* her, she realised – then he continued, adjusting his course towards the old orchard. She waited till he had his back to her then dropped onto all-fours and began to crawl after him, following the amaranth bed to where it met the hedge.

Lansley tugged at his lapels and hoisted himself over the stile. She counted to ten. She peeped over the hedge.

The orchard was a sea of low, sprawling apple trees in knee-high grass. A narrow, flattened path meandered towards a dry-stone wall at the far end, in which was set an arch and a wooden gate. Lansley's stroll became increasingly vigorous – he thrust his stick at trees or the cottony heads of thistles, as if naming them. He stopped, turned round.

Delphine ducked. She did not think he had seen her. She listened. The day was slow and windless. Even the birdsong had a washed-out quality.

She put down the shotgun and pushed her way into the hedge.

A branch snagged her stupid, dowdy box-pleated skirt; she went to grab it and the branch snapped with a firecracker report. She froze.

When she dared move again, she found a gap in the foliage. Peeling leaves aside, she peered through.

Lansley was smoking a cigarillo, oblivious. They were his latest affectation. One elbow rested on the head of his stick and his gloved hands worked back and forth over each other in an odd, compulsive washing motion. He glanced about the orchard, then down at his gloves. Delphine relaxed her fingers, letting a few leaves swing back into place, and watched through the gaps. Lansley took out a cigarillo tin, opened it; the lid flashed in the sun. He tucked the tin back into his breast pocket and patted it; his hand remained on his chest for some time. He scanned the orchard once more, then continued towards the gate in the distance.

He was heading for the chapel. He had to be.

She reversed out of the hedge, almost toppling onto her backside, and picked up the gun. In the scrub, the mother stoat and its kits were back around the dead rabbit, nibbling, stripping. Beneath their pelts, muscles flowed like water.

Delphine took the wide route around the orchard, following a dry streambed down past dense-packed silver birches, her shoes kicking up clumps of mud. The rows of birches scrolled by at different speeds, gaps opening and closing as she moved. She paused, scooped a clod of sandy soil out of the bank and smeared it laterally across her cheekbones. The book* said camouflage worked by breaking up the lines of the face. The dirt felt cool.

The chapel was a small, boxy building of grey stone. It was surrounded by a low wall. Delphine approached from the rear. Long-term servants of Alderberen Hall were buried here. There were a few simple graves, the grass round them recently cut, and a white marble sarcophagus guarded by four winged cherubs, inscribed with the name *Rutherford Cox*. Mr Garforth had his plot reserved; he had shown her the exact rectangle of earth, tracing its limits with the tip of his cane.

* *The Boys' Bumper Treasury Of War* (1934).

'Once I pass,' he had said, 'this slice of land will be mine for all time.'

Today, a single stem of larkspur grew just beyond the border, trembling with flowers that went from mauve to a deep sunset blue. She looked at it and felt a tugging that was close to grief.

On the corners of the chapel, alternate cornerstones jutted out like vertebrae. It was a short, easy climb, but it required both hands. She broke the shotgun, took out the cartridges, and slotted it into the slipcase she had borrowed from the gun room. Slinging the case over her shoulder, she vaulted the wall, ran to the foot of the chapel and began to climb.

The stonework was warm from the sun. From nearby came the *kek kek kek* of a sparrowhawk. When she reached the roof, she put her hands out, steadied herself. Set into a carapace of moss-tinged slates was a little dormer window, its shutters slumped and shattered. Edging along a thin strip of mortar between the roof and the gutter, she stopped in front of the window and lowered herself through.

The sounds of the orchard faded. She was in a cramped loft, two-thirds of which was taken up by a wooden dome, its rafters and supports. This was the void, the gap behind the chapel's elegant domed ceiling. The air was cooler than outside; she smelt old wood and a musty, salty scent that might have been damp stone or bird muck. She pulled the shotgun from its case and used the muzzle to tear through cobwebs.

Parts of the dome had rotted away. Delphine crouched and put her eye to one of the thumb-sized holes.

Below, she saw Lansley standing at the altar. Behind him, beneath a gothic arch, was the war memorial, covered in names of estate workers and men from Pigg who had died nobbling Germans. One name loomed above the others, edged with intricate gold leaf scrollwork: *Arthur Stokeham*. Lansley took out a cigarillo, seemed to think better of it, tucked it away. On the altar, the stub of a candle sat in a tarnished tin holder. A tapestry hung down the front, showing a bull and a sword and a pool. Lansley exhaled, and the hiss of his breath filled the space, seemed to roar.

He reached beneath his jacket and took out his watch. He flipped it open with practised efficiency, lifted it right up to his face.

Delphine breathed through the corners of her mouth. A rafter was digging into her shins.

Lansley produced a handkerchief and wiped sweat from around his jowls. He smoothed gloved thumb and forefinger over his little moustache again and again, checking his reflection in the lid of his pocket watch. He gripped his lapels, stood with his thumbs out, gazing down the aisle like a shipyard owner posing for a photograph. He sat down in one of the pews. He stood, turned away from the door, worried at a piece of dirt on his cuff and glanced back over his shoulder.

He kept wincing, as if chewing on an ice cube, then he would relax his face before putting on a smile, a frown, a half-smile. He looked as if he did not quite know how to be human, as if he were practising the various emotions. He took out his pocket watch for the umpteenth time and blinked at it. The chapel echoed with the clack of the latch lifting.

Lansley put away the watch, straightened his back, lifted his chin, winced again, turned so he was facing the entrance side-on, became absorbed in one of the stained-glass windows.

Delphine heard the door open. Dr Lansley's features shifted beneath the new light source; a shadow fell across the altar.

'You came,' he said.

The sound of slow footsteps on stone floor. The door shrieked shut and slammed with a boom.

Lansley's lips were parted. From this angle, she could see a star-shaped bald patch left by his aggressive combing. In the light of the stained glass, it burned.

The footsteps stopped. Lansley glanced about him, as if he had lost something. Delphine still could not see who had entered. Lansley took a deep breath.

'Hello,' he said.

He and Delphine waited for a reply. Delphine gripped her shotgun, pressing the barrels to her cheek. This was it. This was the moment.

Footsteps, faster. Lansley looked shocked – he stepped back. A figure marched down the aisle, marched right up to him, and stopped. She was half a head shorter than him. She was wrapped in a tan shawl. She let the shawl fall away. She and Lansley were almost touching.

He raised his hands slowly, as if it were a bank robbery. Neither he nor the woman said anything. He was breathing, and looking at her. His hands sank.

The woman touched her brown hair, sunlight silvering individual filaments. She grabbed the back of Lansley's head, pulled him forward and kissed him.

And by 'she', that is to say – as Delphine saw clearly now – Mother.

Delphine squeezed the trigger.

A loud unbroken tone, like a death ray. Delphine opened her eyes and saw clouds of roiling dust. She was on her back. The air hung thick with the maple-bacon tang of gunpowder. She pulled the neck of her cotton vest up over her mouth, took a breath. Her lips tasted salty wet. She lifted her vest away and saw a bloody crocus. All she could hear was ringing.

She sat up, felt a sharp pain beneath her ribs. The world felt distant and unreal. She groped through a yellow fog until she found the shotgun. There was a new hole in the chapel dome. Her hands were bloody. She crawled to the window and back out onto the roof, not caring if she was seen, not caring if she fell.

The sun hurt her eyes. All birdsong was submerged beneath the single, constant note filling her ears. She was vaguely aware of two figures running pell-mell towards the orchard.

The shotgun slipped from her slick fingers and she let it fall; it landed in the graveyard with a clatter. She walked back along the guttering, climbed down the wall and jumped the last ten feet. The impact thudded through her heels and made her teeth slam together. Colours seemed too bright – the grass was a garish, roaring green, her grubby fingers bright pink against it.

She grabbed the shotgun and ran.

Delphine squatted in the lee of a haystack, rocking. Her heart was a bundle of sticks.

Lansley kissing Mother. Why hadn't Mother resisted him? She had seemed so unnatural, so *compelled*.

Delphine tried for tears, but none came. There was just an icy, hollow feeling.

She took out the box of Swan Vestas she always carried with her now, and struck one. She watched it burn down till it reached her fingers. She let the pain grow to a fine white point. When she dropped the match, her mind felt clear. She lit another and let it burn down. She took a piece of hay from the ground and lit one end. It shrivelled and blackened in moments. She made a little heap, pulling hay from the stack, and set it on fire. She held her hand over the flames, close enough so the heat tightened her thoughts like a winch.

As the ringing in her ears died down, it broke into bits. All the little fragments rang at different pitches, fading in and out.

Was this the madness, finally? Was her birthright coming to claim her?

Then she realised – the sounds came from inside the haystack.

They were rats.

An hour later, Delphine marched beneath a purpling sky with her electric torch, the ferret box and a cricket bat. The box had airholes drilled in it and hung from her shoulder by a leather strap.

The fields were northeast of Alderberen Hall, shielded from the sea by a narrow belt of trees. By the time she reached them, it was almost night. Capped with the last shafts of light, haystacks stood dark and massy and silent, like a herd of sleeping diplodocuses. She walked to the nearest and set the box down. She flipped the lid. Behind the ringing in her skull she could hear rustles, squeaks. She took out Lewis and Maxim, gripping them like stick grenades.

'Careful, Max,' she said, and kissed him on the head. She hurled him into the air. A black smudge arced through the sky and landed on top of the haystack. 'Careful, Lewis.' She kissed Lewis, then flung him, too.

Delphine took the torch and the cricket bat. She swept the beam around the base of the stack, looking for runs. She found a hole and put the torch down facing it. The squeaking grew louder. She lifted the bat.

Bodies poured from the hole. Screaming.

She hit them with the bat. She hit them again and again. Their stomachs burst. Some got away. The bat left pits in the earth. A rat writhed, slapping its tail in the dirt; she pounded it flat. When her arm got tired she switched to a two-handed grip.

They kept coming. She beat them and beat them. She felt as if she were watching herself. They died in ones and pairs, and she despised them for it.

When they stopped coming, she stood panting over a trench lined with bodies.

Max scampered out of the run, chirping. She dropped the bat and caught him round the haunches just as Lewis appeared. She made a grab for Lewis but he ducked back into the run. She called for him, waiting with her hand poised above the hole, and when he stuck his head out a second time she snatched him up.

Lewis had been bitten on his nose. His pale fur was dappled with dark flecks.

Delphine looked down at the bloody bat, the bright pool thrown by the torch, the corpses. The pain and fear and confusion had receded, leaving only a steady, pounding hate. There were plenty of haystacks left. The ferrets wriggled in her grip. Her muscles trembled.

She walked to the next haystick, kissed Lewis and Maxim on their warm, wet heads, and began again, a mantra forming to the rhythm of her swings:

Lansley, Lansley, Lansley

CHAPTER 16

GOOD AUTHORS TOO WHO
ONCE KNEW BETTER WORDS

August 1935

Delphine squatted at the edge of the lake, prodding the corpse with a twig. The afternoon was hot, fragments of sun glowing beneath the water like clinkers in a bucket.

The reeds hid a cracked terracotta bowl with steep edges. Inside, the frog's crisp, shrivelled body was like a seedpod. She blew gently and it shivered.

Off in the distance, in front of the house, guests were doing complicated calisthenics while Mr Propp sat in a lawnchair watching. Every so often he rang a bell and everyone had to freeze till he rang it again. It was like a game, except nobody was smiling. Professor Carmichael looked like he might cry.

Delphine drew her pocket knife from her sock and used it to saw a stick into pieces, then tied the pieces together with fishing line to make a miniature raft. She set the raft on the bank and added a layer of balled-up tissue paper, loosely secured with a couple more loops of fishing line. She swept the desiccated frog into her palm, then sat it in the middle of the tissue paper, like a deva on a lotus. She unscrewed the canister she had stolen from Mr Garforth's store-room and drizzled paraffin onto the pyre. Droplets ran over the frog's dry flesh, beading on its back and lips.

She noticed a toad* watching from the sticky mud. She went over and picked it up; it was fat and wet and cool.

'No civilians.' She carried it a short distance along the bank, one hand cupped over its head like a sunhat, feeling its soft, squat legs kick at the heel of her palm. She set it down on a little headland and it lolloped into the clear water with a plop. She sniffed her fingers. They smelt of gunpowder.

She returned to the frog and stood over it for a few moments. She weighed up various pronouncements but none felt appropriate. Eventually, she placed her palms together and said, in her head:

This court finds you guilty of adultery. The sentence is death by immolation.

She picked up the raft by its corners and lowered it onto the water. It settled, then began to turn, very slowly. Across the frog's black body drops of paraffin winked like garnets.

Delphine wrapped some cotton wool round the end of a twig. She splashed on a little paraffin then struck a match and lit it. The cotton wool blackened and vanished, flames licking invisibly in the bright sun. She touched it to the funeral raft.

Nothing happened. Then the air above the frog's head warped and fluttered. The crumpled tissues transformed from lilies to black dahlias. She knelt to get a closer look. The frog tilted, its throne furling, compressing like bellows. When she shielded her eyes she could see a soft yellow outline. Something in the frog's head popped and hissed.

'Viking, was he?'

Delphine turned. Lord Alderberen sat in his wooden wheelchair, squinting from beneath a wide-brimmed straw hat. He was wrapped in a camouflage-green double-breasted jacket and had a cream blanket spread over his knees.

'I used to burn things, y'know,' he said.

She stared at him, a coldness rising in her chest. His skin had a

---

* Professor Carmichael had recently explained to her that a common cause of death for elderly toads was being eaten alive. He said that flesh-eating flies laid their eggs in the hollow of the toad's back and, being old, the toad was unable to dislodge them. When the eggs hatched, the young maggots ate through the toad's eyes and consumed the living brain. 'Which can't be much fun for the old boy,' he had concluded, popping a pear drop into his mouth. 'Poor sod.'

bluish tint. His eyes were gluey and yellow. He was not looking quite at her face.

He frowned, blinked at his lap. Now she finally confronted him, Delphine was surprised at how brave she felt.

As he watched her, he nodded constantly. Some days, he brought it under control until it was the barest quiver. Sometimes, like now, it became a sequence of violent pecks, as if he were attempting to hammer in a nail with his chin. He gripped the hand rims of his wheelchair.

'Remind me of your name,' he said.

'Delphine, uh . . . '

'Delphina?'

'Delphine.'

'Hmm.' He bobbed his head, yes, yes, as if he thought this exceptionally apt. He coughed. His eyes widened as he struggled to bring his palsy under control. 'And, uh, how are you enjoying your stay at my house?'

'I hate it.' She threaded her fingers behind her back. 'Sir.'

Lord Alderberen put a fist to his mauve lips; his throat made a squelching noise.

She wiped her forehead. He was so frail and papery. She breathed in the sweet stink of burning paraffin. She wondered if she could push him into the lake; everyone would think it was an accident.

His eyes pinched. He tensed, then gasped and flopped back into his chair like a trance medium at the end of a séance. The process repeated. Sweating, he pulled a crimson hankie from his left breast pocket.

'Are you all right?'

'Dying,' he said, dabbing at the folds of his throat. He caught sight of her expression and smiled. 'Not now. Slowly.' He folded the handkerchief into triangles and tucked it back inside his pocket.

Delphine shot a couple of sly glances over her shoulder; a fine undertaker's thread of smoke rose from the raft. She began using the point of her toe to scuff an arc in the dirt. The sun was warm against the nape of her neck.

'I watch you, you know,' he said.

She looked up sharply. He had his head to one side and was rocking.

'Capering about the grounds. Up there in your barrel like the Rector of Stiffkey. Used to be Arthur's, that treehouse. Oh, don't look so surprised. I watch everybody. It's one of the perks of being ignored.' He paused for a moment and let the latest wave of convulsions subside. 'Makes me smile. Seeing you so carefree. I missed out on all that.'

Delphine narrowed her eyes. Was he making fun of her? How could anyone think she was carefree? She scratched her scalp and looked away.

'You'll be old one day. Then you'll understand. I'm expected to spend my twilight sipping quack medicines and sprinkling bonemeal round the aspidistras – busywork till I feel the tap from the bony finger.' Briefly, the nodding turned to a shaking of the head. 'They'll do it again, you know. Send another generation into the mincer.' He thumped the arm of his chair. 'Perpetual improvement, my eye! Look at them!' He flapped an arm at the rich people doing jumping jacks on the lawn. 'That's not improvement! It's nigger-driving!'

He gazed at the old ice house across the lake, breathing through his nostrils, his purple lips pressed into a thin horizon. The bottoms of his eyes began to glisten. When he spoke again, his voice had dropped to a quavering murmur.

'I'm sick of all these Young Turks with schemes for changing the world. What I want is someone who'll stop it from changing.'

Gradually, he brought his breath under control. Delphine watched the veins around his throat flex and contract.

'Why do you let us all live at your house?' she said.

'My house, is it? Yes, I suppose I have a piece of paper that says as much.' He glanced at his hand. 'When you're near the end, ideas like money and property start to seem rather silly.'

Delphine took a breath. She lowered her voice.

'You're a Bolshevik, aren't you?'

Lord Alderberen let out a dry laugh that fell in three stages. 'Living here? In the Winter Palace?' He laughed again, did the exact same laugh.

She felt her face get hot. She had said something stupid and she did not understand what.

Lord Alderberen's drooping mauve face began to shudder. He clutched his wheelchair.

A strange pressure built in Delphine's gut and chest and behind her eyes. She had imagined confronting him so many times. She had pictured herself delivering the accusation before a roomful of witnesses, his blustering denial, his sobbing confession. Now she was finally alone with him, watching him shake and twist, she had to fight the urge to comfort him.

'Are you all r – '

'It's almost time,' he said, giving himself over to the nodding, shutting his eyes. 'I'm ready to leave this wretched body behind. I'll be going to a better place. I'll be with Mother.' He slumped forward in his chair.

'Delphine!'

She turned. It was Mother, dressed in tan hip-jacket and trousers. The dregs of a gin and bitters sparkled in her hand.

'You should be studying,' she said, 'not pestering our host. I'm so sorry, Lord Alderberen.' Her voice dropped half an octave as she pivoted to address him. 'Apparently my daughter is such a prodigy she can read books half a mile away. Come along, Delphine.' Mother lifted her glass and rattled the ice, like Propp ringing his bell.

Delphine balled her right hand into a tight, sweaty fist. Mother began to walk away. She glanced back over her shoulder. '*Delphine.*'

She did not look Delphine in the eye. Delphine saw the hand come up and grip the back of Lansley's slimy head, the sun against mousy hair, the hungry way Mother kissed him, a pig gobbling slops. Her nostrils stung with the salty-acrid scent of cremated frog.

'Delphine.' Mother shot a smirk at her daughter. 'Come, let's walk. I hardly get to see you these days. You can tell me what the Professor has been teaching you.'

Delphine held her ground.

'Now,' said Mother. 'This is not a negotiation.'

'____ off.'

Mother's smile hung in the air like gunsmoke. Her eyelids fluttered. Lord Alderberen made a quiet, throaty noise, a trapdoor closing.

Delphine glowered into Mother's twitching hazel eyes. Very quietly, she said: 'You're drunk, Mummy. Go and play with Mr Lansley.'

Mother stood there a moment longer, looking as if she were about to say something. At last she closed her mouth, gave a little nod, turned and walked away. It was the queerest thing. Delphine watched her getting tinier and tinier, till she was only a speck.

CHAPTER 17

FALL

September 11th 1935

I t was the day before the killing started.

Dr Lansley opened his black bag and screamed.

Everyone in the smoking room turned to stare at him. Delphine sat cross-legged on the carpet, her rucksack beside her, reading about the Frankish conquest of Italy in Volume V of Gibbon's *The History Of The Decline And Fall Of The Roman Empire*.* She did not look up.

Miss DeGroot paused in the act of sucking a date, gauzy green scarf wound round her throat. She coughed, quietly, into a hand-kerchief, hacked up something, wiped her lips. Her swagger stick lay on the floor beside her. She leant over the back of the leather sofa.

'Florence,† what on earth's the matter?'

---

* 'A torrent of Barbarians may pass over the earth, but an extensive empire must be supported by a refined system of policy and oppression; in the centre, an absolute power, prompt in action and rich in resources; a swift and easy communication with the extreme parts; fortifications to check the first effort of rebellion; a regular admin-istration to protect and punish; and a well-disciplined army to inspire fear, without provoking discontent and despair.'

† Miss DeGroot had been trialling this new pet name for over a week (apparently a reference to Florence Nightingale), eliciting steadily more vehement reactions from Lansley. That, in this instance, he did not even seem to notice, can be read as a direct index of his distress.

'It's another one.' He lowered himself into a chair at the bridge table. His hands were trembling so violently he could barely slide a cigarillo from the tin.

'Another what?'

'A rat, a bloody dead rat in my medical bag!'

From behind his copy of *The Times*, Professor Carmichael spluttered.

'Something funny, Carmichael?'

'No, nothing, nothing.' The Professor turned the page with a flourish. 'Just a very droll caricature of Roosevelt.'

Lansley patted down his jacket for a light. Miss DeGroot stretched out on the sofa and popped another date into her mouth.

'Perhaps the cat likes you,' she said. 'They leave them as presents, you know.'

'We haven't got a cat,' said Lansley. He put the cigarillo in his mouth. It was bent at a right angle. He tried to straighten it and it snapped clean in half. 'Damn.'

'Florence, language. There are children present.'

'If you call me that one more time, I'll break this table over your head.'

'I thought doctors took an oath forbidding that sort of thing.'

Lansley tossed his broken cigarillo into the wastepaper basket. 'It's a doctor's duty to kill nasty little parasites.' He flipped open his cigarillo tin but it was empty. 'Damn it.'

Miss DeGroot yawned loudly. 'Oh, for goodness' sake, help yourself to one of Ivan's. The box is over there on the shelf. I'm sure he won't mind.'

Dr Lansley glanced across the room. He snapped his fingers.

'I say, you, child. Look at me when I'm talking to you.'

Delphine sucked all her anger deep inside. She slipped the red ribbon bookmark between the pages and raised her head.

'Fetch me the cigar box,' he said.

She put the book down, slid her hand into the mouth of her rucksack, and stood. She padded across to the shelf. The cigar box had a polished rosewood veneer; a bat was carved into the lid. She stood over it for a moment, her back to the room.

'Come on, come on!' Lansley clapped his hands.

Delphine turned and carried the closed box over to Lansley, placing it on the bridge table. He glared at her as she walked back to her spot on the rug.

Miss DeGroot plucked another date from the glass dish on the table next to her. She held it up and turned it, like the world.

'Are you looking forward to the symposium this weekend?' she said.

Lansley paused, licked his moustache. 'Are you talking to me?'

'Yes, dear.'

'Well, then you know the answer.'

'Oh, Flo, you're such a pill.' The leather sofa croaked as Miss DeGroot leant back. 'It's going to be the party to end all parties.' She chuckled, then smothered it with a date.

Dr Lansley inhaled sharply. Delphine watched his opera-gloved fingers reach for the catch on the cigar box. They got within an inch, then paused.

'You know,' said Lansley, 'if Lazarus actually attended his own damn symposiums he'd see what a waste of time they are.'

Miss DeGroot pursed her lips, pushing the date out before sucking it back in. 'You always seem very happy, making eyes at Lord Wolfbrooke. Hoping he'll name a paper after you?'

'He's the worst of all. Chuntering on about natural selection and "improving the stock". You can tell he's spoiling for another war.'

'Aren't you? I thought you said Britain needed more warriors and fewer stockbrokers.'

'As a *deterrent*. Wolfie thinks war's like a social laxative – you take it and it purges all the bad elements from your system. I told him: you want to see who does best on the battlefield. It's the rats every time.'

He flipped the little silver latch and lifted the cigar-box lid.

And screamed.

Behind the pages of *The Times*, Professor Carmichael let out a series of stifled, snorting coughs.

'It's a warning, I tell you.'

Delphine lay on her side in the gap between walls, eavesdropping. The hole was an inch from her eye.

She could barely believe it. After fruitless months of listening in on conversations about cricket scores and stomach pain, or requests for more fruit cake, finally she had *caught* them.

'Calm down, man,' said Lord Alderberen. He, Mr Propp and Dr Lansley sat facing each other, their chairs arranged in a triangle.

'I will not – ' began Lansley, then one of the others must have indicated he was shouting, because he continued, more quietly, 'I will *not* calm down. I have watched men claw their own organs back into their rib cages. I am not given to hysterics.'

'Please, please.' Propp's voice was deep and steady, like an idling motor. The dry *pop-pop* of lips puffing on a cigar.

'Look,' said Lord Alderberen, his consonants crisp, 'all I'm saying is, if you look at it *rationally* – '

'*Three* in my medical bag,' hissed Lansley, stamping his calf-leather Oxford against the floor, 'two in my coat pocket, one in my riding boots, one when I opened my *umbrella* . . . '

'I did not know you wear riding boots,' said Propp.

'I mean, for God's sake, I found one rolled up in my washcloth. In. My. Washcloth.'

There was a long silence, into which Propp exhaled, *hah*.

'I keep my room locked at all times,' Lansley said. 'Don't you understand?' His two companions left a pause which indicated they did not. 'They're sending us a message. They want us to know that they can *get at us*.'

All three stopped to digest this. Delphine pinched her nostrils to stifle the beginnings of a sneeze.

'Well, why are they targeting you?' said Lord Alderberen. 'Why not me and Ivan?'

'I don't know.'

'The only other people with keys to the rooms are Alice and Mrs Hagstrom. Surely you're not insinuating one of them is . . . Titus, they've worked for me for years.'

'I insinuate nothing. The facts speak for themselves. There is a traitor among us.'

Delphine's breathing quickened. *And she's closer than you think.*

'Hmph.' Lord Alderberen sat back in his chair. 'Sounds jolly fishy to me.'

'Mmm.' Propp sounded as if he had a pipe between his teeth. Delphine inhaled through her nostrils, thought she caught a whiff; it smelt like burning hair. 'Maybe not so fish. Today I visited library. Prentice is missing.'

'Don't be silly,' said Alderberen, 'it's just been miscatalogued.'

'No,' said Propp. 'I walked room twice. Book is gone.'

'Well, what if it is? Three-quarters of it is the purest fudge anyway. No wonder he published under a pseudonym. You'd have more chance jumping into pools at random than following . . . Oh. Oh my.'

'What?' Dr Lansley rose from his seat. 'What's wrong? Are you all right, old man? Is it your heart again?'

'I'm fine. Sit down. I just had a thought . . . You don't think Kung was trying to . . . '

'Yes,' said Propp. 'I think exactly this.'

'But how did he know?'

Mr Propp made a small, noncommittal noise. 'Your father's library is world famous.'

'Also,' said Lansley, 'evidently he did not know. If he did, he'd still be alive.'

'Still,' said Alderberen, 'he knew enough. He knew to try, didn't he?' He let the innuendo hang.

'Well,' said Lansley, 'now he's gone. And the book's somewhere at the bottom of the ocean.'

The hairs on Delphine's neck prickled.

'This I doubt,' said Propp. 'This I very much doubt. He would not risk damaging it.'

'If he had it in the first place,' said Lansley.

She listened to the three men breathing. In her mind, she saw Daddy on the moonlit beach, retrieving a grey book from the sand.

Propp said: 'You are correct. We speculate.'

'It's worse than that. It's scaremongering.' Lord Alderberen coughed up something wet. 'A few dead mice and we're up on a chair clutching our petticoats.'

Lansley snorted. 'Mice don't fire shotguns.'

'What in blazes are you talking about?' said Alderberen.

'Someone shot at me – twice.'

'Oh, poppycock – that was just the wind.'

'The wind doesn't blow a hole in the chapel ceiling!'

'What were you doing in chapel?' said Propp.

'That's none of your damn business.'

'Oh,' said Alderberen. 'So now you don't trust us, either? Come on, man. Pull yourself together.'

'That's your solution, is it?' said Lansley. 'Stick our fingers in our ears and go la la la? If they're onto us, we're buggered.'

'All right,' said Alderberen. 'Supposing they are. Why on earth would they want us to know they've got an inside man? Why tip their hand like this?'

'Two possibles,' said Propp. 'One, they feel very assured. Two, they feel very afraid. Either way, very careless. We may use.'

'That's it.' Lord Alderberen's slippers settled on the floor. With a shuddering effort, he stood. 'I'm going to talk to them. Face to face. Get this whole ugly knot untangled.'

Propp sighed. 'Not wise.'

'Hate to say it,' said Lansley, 'but I'm with the Fat Owl of the Remove on this one. Knots don't send death threats. They'll take you as a hostage, Stokeham or no.'

'Why don't we pre-empt them?' said Lord Alderberen. 'Say they can have her?'

Delphine shivered. Her nails dug into her palms.

'No,' said Propp. 'Not possible.'

Nobody said anything for a while. Lord Alderberen sat back down.

Propp said: 'I will speak to them.' He rose.

'What?' said Lord Alderberen. 'Now?'

'Yes.'

'But you just said it was a bad idea! What on earth will you say?'

Propp's voice dropped to a murmur, his accent thickening. 'My dearest friend, you must not worry. Wait here. I will speak to them.'

He walked slowly out of Delphine's view. She heard the door click shut.

Lansley spoke almost immediately. 'He's insane.'

'No.' Lord Alderberen sounded like he was talking through his fingers. 'Very sane. Also: very arrogant.'

'You're even starting to sound like him.'

'What's that supposed to mean?'

'Why has he got so much power over you?'

Lord Alderberen exhaled heavily. 'Don't be absurd.'

'Prove it, then. Overrule him. Tell them what happened. Say that Propp acted alone, without your authority. Give up the child.'

A freezing river poured down Delphine's back. She clamped a hand over her lips.

'Are you mad?'

'I think insanity's a very relative concept these days, don't you?'

'But he'll never consent. And what if they don't accept our apology? What if handing her over isn't enough? Surely we should just keep mum.'

'Neither of those things need concern us unduly.'

'What on earth do you mean?'

Lansley drew a long breath. 'We'll give them Propp too.'

This time the silence held for what seemed like minutes. She listened to the sound of her own breaths, felt them hot and damp against her fingers.

When Lord Alderberen spoke, it was in a whisper.

'You forget your place.'

She heard the catch in Lansley's throat as he inhaled.

'No, my Lord. You forget yours.' He stood. As he continued, his voice rose. 'Quite amazing, the things a man will tell his physician when he believes himself to be on the verge of death. The unburdening of the soul.' He began to walk around the room. 'Like draining a boil.'

'If you're threatening me . . . '

'I am *reminding* you. Did Arthur sacrifice himself for this, this . . . picayune stalemate?' The toes of Lansley's calf-leather shoes spun to face his master. 'You are the *last* of the Stokeham line in England. You have a responsibility to assume control of this house and not let some dusky, jumped-up goat farmer come wandering off the steppe and use you as a foothold in his desperate scramble for significance. We were supposed to be gathering an elect for the new world. Now it's all star jumps and watering your many-petaled iris.'

'It's a lotus, Lansley.'

'I don't care what bloody flower it is! That's precisely my bloody point! Once, we dreamed we could be nation-makers. Propp's turned us into bloody botanists.'

There was a pause.

'So instead of kowtowing to Propp, I should kowtow to you?'

'Lazarus. You know I have only your best interests at heart.'

'Spoken like a true Machiavellian.'

'Do you *want* to die?' Lansley was shouting now. 'Because you know that's going to happen, don't you? This isn't about negotiating any more. Propp is prepared to sacrifice all our lives out of pig-headed sentimentality.'

'No! Right from the beginning, the whole *purpose* of the Society was to –'

Lansley brought a foot smartly down. 'He doesn't care. He's *turned*. And we've just sent him to speak on our behalf. I mean, do you know what he's going to say? I don't.'

Lord Alderberen was silent for a time.

'Perhaps you're right. We must . . . make plans.'

'The time for plans is long gone. We must stop him.'

Alderberen's chair moaned as he let out a sigh. Very quietly, he said: 'Agreed.'

Delphine rolled away from the hole. Putting a palm on the dusty floor, she stood. Blood rushed to her head; the ringing in her ears swallowed all other sound. For a moment, she thought she would pass out. She slapped a palm against the wall with a dull bang. She thought she heard a voice react, the upward inflection of a question, but she did not care.

She would gather up her evidence and go straight to the police. She would have Scotland Yard breaking down the door. Mother and Daddy had been bewitched. Why else would Mother have done that *thing*, touching Dr Lansley? Propp couldn't charm the whole of England. The authorities would see him with eyes unclouded by his exotic glamour. He and Alderberen and Lansley would hang for treason.

She negotiated the darkness with the grace of practice, stopping at last at the door. She pressed her ear to the crack in the door frame and listened.

Silence. She turned the club-shaped key in the lock and stepped out, into the smoking room.

A hand gripped her shoulder.

'And that,' said Dr Lansley, 'is quite enough of that.'

CHAPTER 18

TRIAL OF THE PROFLIGATE

It was not like in *The Champion*. She tried to pull free and he grabbed her by the scruff of her cardigan.

'If you misbehave, I shall hurt you.'

He marched her to the bell button, rang for Alice.

It was nothing like *The Champion*. She did not flatten her captor with a hook to the jaw. She waited, meekly. She thought private, angry thoughts but did not act on them.

Alice arrived. She gave Delphine a curious glance.

'Yes, Doctor?'

'Fetch Lord Alderberen. Mr Propp too, if you can find him. Tell them to meet me in the study. Tell them . . . ' He wet his lips. She felt his fingers relax slightly. 'Say I've solved the rat problem.'

She twisted free of his grip and ran.

'Hey!'

She kicked aside the heavy double doors and ran south, down the west gallery. Several windows were open and a cold breeze swept about her throat. Afternoon sun fell across the hallway in hot golden slabs. She ran past white busts with blind stares, footsteps resounding.

She glanced back as she opened the door to the music room. Lansley was marching, not running.

'Where are you going?' he shouted.

She ran through the music room, past the black harpsichord and the grand windows. She ran into the hallway heading east. She pumped her arms, accelerating down an empty corridor. She ran onto the chequerboard floor of the Great Hall. At the foot of the stairs was Daddy. He was caught in a sunbeam, half golden, half dark.

He turned, smiled.

'Delphy!' His face fell. 'Whatever's the – '

She barrelled into him. He caught her.

'Oh daddy they're after me I heard them talking they're going to ah ah to take me away to give me to the to the ah across the channel oh daddy don't let them take me don't let them t – '

'Shh shh shh.' He rocked her side to side. 'There, there. It's all right. You're safe. It's all right.' She closed her eyes and tried to lose herself in the swaying. She heard the door open. Footsteps.

Daddy's chin lifted from her crown.

'Ah,' he said.

She breathed in. She breathed out. She pushed gently away from Daddy's chest and turned to face her pursuer.

Lansley had broken a sweat. A slash of dark hair hung over his brow; his fingers rose and flicked it back into place. His hearing-aid cable was a sinuous black tendril trailing from his ear to the battery on his hip. He tugged his lapels and glared at Delphine.

'Come with me,' he said.

She clutched Daddy's arm. 'No.'

'What's going on?' said Daddy.

'I am not going to ask you again,' said Lansley.

Delphine looked up at her father. 'He hit me.'

Daddy looked from Lansley, to Delphine, then back to Lansley. 'What do you want with her?'

Lansley let out a little furious gasp.

'Your daughter, sir, has been breaking into rooms – '

'I never!'

'*Shut up!*' Lansley screamed the words, rocking forwards onto his toes, spittle flying from his mouth. 'Your daughter has stolen keys, spied upon guests in their private quarters – '

'He's a Bolshevik! I heard them plotting to bring down the British Crown and – '

'Delphy.' Daddy stopped her with a stern forefinger. He turned to Lansley. 'Now, Mr Lansley – ' Delphine noted with pleasure how Lansley flinched at the title *Mr* ' – would you care to explain what is going on? What is Delphine talking about?'

'How *dare* you – '

'Perhaps I.' A voice rang from the top of the stairs. They all turned to look. Propp was descending with that mild, waddling gait, hands behind his back, a slight smile beneath his white moustache. His brass buttons glistened in the sunlight, black patent-leather shoes silent against the soft red carpet. Down he came.

'And how are you today, my dear companion?' he asked Daddy.

Daddy's eye pinched. He nodded.

'Very well, thank you.'

'Wonderful.' Propp's tone was warm, deep, lulling. He stopped two steps from the bottom, slightly above Daddy's eye level. 'I wish to speak to your daughter for short time.'

Delphine felt a palm at the base of her spine.

'Of course,' said Daddy. He gave her the faintest of shoves.

She wobbled, shot him a look.

'Go on,' he said. 'You and I can talk later.'

'Daddy?'

He pushed her again, more forcefully. 'Don't be rude, darling. Mr Propp would like to speak with you.'

Propp smiled and bowed. He beckoned Lansley with a tilt of his bald head.

She backed away from Lansley. 'Daddy, don't let them take me.'

'Delphine, what on earth is the matter with you today? Mr Propp is asking for five minutes of your time and you're pitching a tantrum.'

A strong hand gripped her wrist and twisted it behind her back. Another dug into her armpit. Lansley leant in to her ear.

'Come along, young lady,' he sang quietly. She could smell the juniper tang of his hair tonic.

'Daddy! Help me!'

Lansley began pushing her towards the stairs.

Daddy frowned. 'Look here, don't yank her about like that – '

Mr Propp approached Daddy and placed a hand on his shoulder.

'My brother, be at peace. Youth is full of fire. I will find what distresses her so. She will settle.'

'Daddy!' Her legs folded beneath her. Lansley grunted, hoisted her upright, dragged her up the steps. 'Daddy!' She was screaming. 'He's hurting me! Daddy, he's hurting – ' Lansley wrenched her wrist round on itself; she howled.

Daddy was talking: 'I'm so sorry. I don't know what's got into her.'

'Brother, I understand.'

Her sandals slipped on plush carpet. She called and called, even as she realised it was hopeless.

'Thank you,' she heard Daddy say. When she looked back, he was walking away.

It was not like *The Champion* at all.

They did not tie her to the chair. They did not produce gleaming instruments of torture, one by one, from Lansley's medical bag.

Alice brought coffee and a dish of ginger snaps.

They were in Lord Alderberen's study, the room on the other side of the peep hole. There were two doors, one leading to his bedchamber, the other to the hall. The hall door had a letterbox. These were the rooms in which the Silent Earl had spent his final years – stewing, losing his mind. Delphine sat in the sagging leather club chair. On the wall was a painting of a matador – a very bad painting, the bullfighter clutching some sort of dishcloth, the crowd pink smudges.

Delphine inhaled, felt the shiver in her breath.

Propp leaned back in his chair. Alderberen sat to his right, a loose-woven shawl across his shoulders. Propp dipped his ginger snap into his coffee and sucked it. Brown droplets collected at the tips of his white moustache.

'Well?' Lansley was standing in a corner.

Propp placed the half-eaten biscuit on the lip of his saucer. He turned to Delphine.

'Now, my dear child.' His face softened into a smile. 'What were you doing in the wall?'

Lansley clutched his brow. 'What do you think she was doing? She's a spy, she's a bloody spy.'

Alderberen squinted over his little gold-rimmed pince-nez. 'Doesn't look much like a spy.'

'They generally don't. That's generally the *whole bloody point*.'

'She's a child, Lansley.'

'Children can be spies.' He rounded on Delphine. 'Now, the game's up, you little devil. Do you understand? It's over. Who put you up to this?'

Delphine forced herself to meet his gaze. He was shuddering with rage. She could trace the dark lines of sleep deprivation around his eyes, see the ridge of his yellowed teeth beneath the dry lips that Mother had kissed, chewed upon, pushed herself into.

'I'm going to ask you one last time,' said Lansley. 'Who put you up to this?'

She looked him dead in the pupils.

'The League of Ovaltineys.'

He hit her. Something hard clipped her eye. Her head bounced off the back of the chair.

'Who was it?'

Delphine clutched her watering eye. Propp and Lord Alderberen looked on gravely.

'No one,' she said. 'I was just playing, I – no!' Lansley raised his hand and she cried out, hated herself for crying out.

'Please,' said Mr Propp.

She bit her lip, swallowed back a stammer. 'Ah-ah-all right. Just make him stop.'

Propp gestured for Lansley to sit down. Dr Lansley adjusted his cuffs, glaring at Delphine. He stepped back.

'Now.' Propp opened his palms towards her. 'In your own words, please.'

Delphine looked from Propp, to Lansley, to Alderberen. She breathed out.

'I was playing in the passageway. I hardly heard anything.'

'I see. You do this many times?'

She shook her head.

'How many times?'

'This was the first time.'

'Oh.' Propp put down his cup and saucer. 'First time just today, yes?'

'Umm hmm.'

'Mmm. So today for first time you find door, you find key to door, you explore, yes?'

'It was open.'

'Hmm?' He cupped a palm to his ear. 'Again?'

'It was open.' The club-headed key, threaded on a string, lay cold and spiky down the back of her knickers, poking her in the bottom.

'Open. Ah. And what did you hear?'

'Nothing, really. I wasn't really listening.'

'Do not test me, girl,' said Lansley.

'"Nothing, really",' said Propp. 'Are you sure?'

Delphine lifted her head to look him in the eyes, but he was gazing into his coffee.

'Yes.'

'So why, then,' said Lansley, 'did I find her wailing to her father that we were all of us guilty of treason, that we were a pack of Guy Fawkeses plotting to bring down the country?'

Mr Propp chuckled gently, the skin around his big eyes creasing. He looked at Delphine.

'Is this true?'

'I was joking. It was just a game.'

His smile vanished. 'Are you sure?'

'Yes.'

'Doctor.'

Propp looked away. Lansley stepped forward and cuffed her across the temple. He stepped back.

'Now,' said Propp. 'Think again.'

Her hands were shaking. She focused on the pain. Her thoughts sharpened.

'Fine. Here's what I heard.' She was staring past him, staring at the armchair's worn headrest with its crosshatching threads. 'After you left the room, Dr Lansley and Lord Alderberen said you're out of control. They said they're going to stop you. They said – '

Lansley hit her again. The glow of the backhand lingered hot against her temple. He stood over her panting.

'Stupid little girl!'

He was blocking out the light. She sat scrunched on one side of the armchair, shielding her head. She lowered her arms in an attempt at defiance. Lord Alderberen squeezed Propp's bicep.

'Pure fantasy, of course, Ivan.'

Lansley turned to face them. 'We'll have to get rid of her.'

Delphine tried to appear dazed. She slid a hand towards her sock.

'What do you propose?' said Lord Alderberen.

'I have an old friend, the headmistress of a school, just outside Carlisle. It is a fine, hard place. I'll tell Mrs Hagstrom to place a call. The term has barely started. I'm sure they will take her.'

'Ah,' said Propp. He shook his head at Delphine. 'You must forgive us. We should never have let child live alone in house. This must be very lonely.'

He smiled under sad eyes. She felt sick. He was trying to charm her.

'So you leave,' he went on. 'You make friends. You study. I,' he placed a hand on his heart, 'will take care of your mother and father. Your father is great man. His healing is almost done. By Christmas, you return home. This, I promise you.'

It took all of Delphine's self-control not to spit at him.

'Well, that's that, then.' Lord Alderberen's doughy blue face was utterly expressionless. Lansley was lying, and Alderberen knew it. They weren't going to send her to a school. They were going to hand her over to their friends across the channel, along with Mr Propp, and by the time her parents realised it would be too late.

Delphine pretended to scratch her ankle, drawing the pocket knife out of her sock. She sat back, knife snug in her palm.

'I'll explain to Anne,' said Lansley. 'I'm sure she'll be relieved finally to be rid of one of her burdens.'

Delphine met his gaze. She thumbed open the blade.

'When my Daddy finds out what you've done, he's going to kill you.'

Lansley snorted. 'Oh yes, all England cowers before the wrath of

219

a frustrated painter. Pah! He's no father. He knows what he's done.'

'*Lansley.*' Lord Alderberen's voice had a note of warning.

'He knows what he is. I think you do, too. He has to live with that, and it's burning his insides out. He should've drowned himself with Kung.'

She jumped forward and swung the knife. Lansley jerked back. The blade swished across the front of his shirt, snagging something as it went. Lansley stared at her. She lunged with the backswing. He slammed his shoulder blades into the wall. She missed.

'She has knife,' said Propp, the words curiously uninflected. He did not rise from his chair.

Above the black smear of his moustache, Lansley's eyes were dirty little gobstoppers. They kept flashing from her face, to the knife, and back again. His arms were spread like a wrestler's. Delphine felt unreal, gaseous, smoke wafting round a white-hot ball of hate. She wanted to skin him. She wanted to pin him to the wall and drag out his gut ropes.

'What are you going to do?' said Lansley, and it was unclear if he meant this as a taunt or a genuine enquiry.

She had no idea. The scrimshaw handle felt greasy beneath her fingers. Her phlegm was thick. Lansley breathed through his nostrils in short, rasping starts, bracing to counterattack.

She kept the blade between them, tip swinging like a compass needle.

'Don't trust them, Mr Propp!' she said. 'They're planning to betray you. They're going to hand you over to your friends across the channel, as a prisoner.'

'She's raving!' said Lansley, spit flying. 'She doesn't know what she's talking about!'

She caught a flash of movement out the corner of her eye. She looked, but it was just Mr Propp, sipping his coffee. Lansley swung with a wide right hook. She slashed at his arm but it was a feint; his left rose through her open guard and connected with her chin. Her head snapped back. He tripped her, bringing her clattering to the floor.

A knee to her back emptied her lungs. She tried to breathe in.

She could not make room. She felt the knife slip from her grasp.

Lansley was speaking: 'Ring for Alice. I want my bag. The girl is hysterical. She needs a sedative.' He shifted his weight and the pressure on her chest increased. Lights popped at the fringes of her vision. 'What are you waiting for? Put your bloody coffee down and *get the maid*!'

She heard Propp rise with a grunt. The room was growing darker.

'I'll need some way to restrain her, too,' said Lansley. His voice sounded far away. 'Oh, don't look at me like that, you supercilious old goat. Fat lot of good you are in a scrape.'

Beside the skirting board, a dead woodlouse lay curled up like a tractor tyre. Propp murmured something. She tried to inhale, felt her body convulse at the lack of air. Someone smeared a rag over her mouth and nostrils. The pressure on her back eased. She inhaled compulsively. A sweet scent entered her nostrils. She was sinking into the floor. The room was high above her.

Chloroform.

It was exactly like in *The Champion*.

CHAPTER 19

THE SLEEP OF REASON

Delphine's head felt fuggy and thick. She tried to scratch her ear; coarse rope snatched tight round her wrist.

Mattress springs creaked as she lifted her head. Her wrists and ankles were tied. She was in her bedroom. The bed had been dragged into the middle of the floor.

As she shuffled up onto her elbows, she felt a bruise on her tricep. Dr Lansley had injected her with something. Chloroform wouldn't have kept her out this long. He must have administered a tranquiliser. From that moment, her memory became a mesh of bright shapes like sunlight through leaves, a sense of heat, fragments of conversation that might or might not have been real. She remembered being carried, slung over a shoulder, a corridor jouncing upside-down. Mother, crying. She remembered Mrs Hagstrom, an argument – something about salmon-paste sandwiches? Had Mrs Hagstrom tried to bring her some food?

A surge of nausea forced her head back down onto the pillow.

The curtains were drawn. The house was soundless. She curled and uncurled her fingers. She felt like the last person on Earth.

She restaged the fight over and over, cursing herself for stupid errors. Maybe, deep down, she had never wanted to land the coup de grace. She hated Lansley, right to her marrow she hated him, but now, in the dim and the quiet, part of her was glad the blade hadn't connected. What would it have achieved if she had slashed his throat? She thought of his glove whipping through air, the heat of the blow. Her stomach churned. She just wanted him to go away for ever, to never come back, to never have existed.

Maybe she did want to kill him. She just didn't have the guts.

Delphine came round with a start. She had fallen asleep again.

Where was everyone? How long had she been unconscious? Hours? Days? The thick drapes admitted no light. Her mouth tasted of soap.

Miss DeGroot. When she heard that Delphine had been tied up, might she not realise that Propp and Alderberen and Lansley really were spies? Might she not come to the rescue? What about Daddy? Or Mother? Would they really sit about and let her lie here?

She imagined Mr Propp's account of events, backed up by Lansley and Alderberen. He would tell Mother how Delphine had tried to murder Dr Lansley. Lord Alderberen would insist that the police needn't be involved, before looking grave and conceding that Delphine could no longer stay at the Hall. Dr Lansley would offer his 'professional opinion' and the matter would be closed.

Perhaps she was mad. Perhaps the blood madness that Eleanor Wethercroft and Jacqueline Finks-Hanley and Prue Dunbar had taunted her about was real. Perhaps Daddy was mad, and his madness had mixed with the Stokeham madness that hung in the corridors like choke damp, and now both strains were blooming and fruiting in her ravaged brain.

What was going to happen to her? She tried to organise everything she knew. Propp, Alderberen and Lansley were not the united front she had supposed. Alderberen and Lansley were plotting to betray Propp – because he refused to hand over a child, a girl. They couldn't be talking about her, could they? Yet she was the only child in the house – and now, she was a prisoner.

But why on earth would Lansley believe she was a spy? He seemed paranoid, raving. Had their dealings with Bolshevik cells gone awry? And had Propp believed her when she revealed his conspirators' treachery?

She screwed her eyes shut. It was all so baffling. When she examined it, really scrutinised the pieces one by one, the structure collapsed. None of it made sense. And if she was wrong about the spying, might she not have been wrong about Mother and Lansley? What on earth would Mother see in such an ugly, slippery man, with his shaving rash and his deaf aid and his preposterous, snivelling ways? What if Delphine had made a mistake?

She thought on it and thought on it until the walls of her skull pressed in like a fist. If she was mad, her entire thinking process was tainted. Even her thoughts at this moment were the thoughts of a lunatic. No madman could ever correctly diagnose his own lunacy. If she was mad, she was doomed anyway. Therefore, the only rational course of action was to proceed as if she were sane.

Delphine lay back and allowed herself a half-smile at the logic of this. If she was mad, let her be wholeheartedly mad, floridly so. They would catch her and drug her and shave off her awful hair and keep her in a nice soft bed away from the school tests and the world with its maze of invisible boundaries, and she would eat and drool and doze in a grey, grey haze.

If she was not mad, she had to escape.

She and Mr Garforth checked his traps every couple of days. If a stoat got caught in a gin, eventually it would chew its own leg off and limp off to die in the wilderness rather than let you catch it. Even wild animals knew it was better to die free than spend your last few days trapped and helpless.

Most of her important possessions – the shotgun, her rucksack, the tortoise Daddy had carved her – were in the treehouse. The rest were at the cottage, easily pinchable. She could live in the woods. Mr Garforth had taught her how to trap things, how to shoot, how to fish. By day, she could sleep in the tunnels. Let Lansley and Propp and Alderberen try to follow her. She would kill them all before letting them take her.

How much better would things be if she just killed Lansley? She could bury his body in Prothero Wood. Who would ever know? They would think he had just gone missing.

A second, hived-off part of her brain watched these thoughts with delirious fascination. Was she wicked, to fantasise like this? Did everyone think this way sometimes? Was God listening in to her thoughts, and would He punish her for contemplating such evil, brutish things?

Her scalp itched. She moved to scratch it and a noose ground into her wrist and she remembered that it was all very well to plan a murder when she was drugged and bound to a bed.

The ropes round her wrists were fastened with clove hitches tied off with double thumb knots. She glanced at the bedstead. A double thumb knot secured either rope to opposing bedposts. She gave a few experimental yanks but only succeeded in pulling her restraints tighter.

She looked down at her ankles. She could not make out the knots used but her feet had been tied to opposite ends of a single piece of rope, fastened to the centre of the bedframe with a simple cow hitch. She rubbed her ankle against the mattress. The restraints had a little give. Perhaps her arms and legs had been tied by different people. She kicked her left heel against the noose holding the opposite foot. With her socks on, it was hard to get a grip.

She rubbed her ankles against one another. Little by little, she rolled her socks down til she was able to pin down the loose material with her heel and drag, first her left, then her right foot out of the socks.

Her ankles were tied to the middle of the rail, and when she brought them together both bonds went a little slack. It hurt to keep craning her neck forward, so she lay back and worked from touch alone. By snagging her big toe round the noose on the opposite foot, she was able, with agonising slowness, to tug it down, over her ankle bone, towards her heel. Rope fibres sawed into her skin. Her soles were cramping. She kept stopping to catch her breath – the effort of concentration was exhausting.

For there to be enough room to slip the noose over her heel, she had to pull her big toe from inside the loop and try to nudge the rope round her heel with the tips of her toes. Her toenails offered no grip at all, because she bit them. The noose kept reaching the widest part of her heel, then slipping back. The third time it happened, she swore and shook her fists till the whole bedframe rattled. She calmed down and tried again. The coil of rope slid over her quivering tendon; she focused on keeping her foot as straight as possible, pointing like a ballerina's. She nudged the rope forward, forward.

Her toes lost their purchase and it slipped back. She gasped.

Please God. Please help me. Please.

She was begging God for help minutes after wishing for Lansley's grisly death. If God existed, hypocrisy would only arouse His contempt. She stopped her petition. She would escape without His help.

She started again. She pretended it was just a game. Her toes dragged the rope closer and closer to her heel. The noose tightened as it reached the widest part. Delphine relaxed, let her upper body go limp.

I can do it. It's just a game. I can do it.

Her foot slipped. She pinned the rope in place with her toe.

It's just a game. I can do it.

She stared up at the ceiling and imagined she was a moth.

I can do it.

The rope slipped over her heel. She pulled her foot free.

Relief washed through her. She moved her freed leg in wide circles. All of a sudden her remaining restraints felt all the tighter, all the more unbearable. With one foot free, the cow hitch – a basic over-and-under knot anchoring the rope to the bedframe – sagged loose, and it was relatively straightforward to kick the slack noose over the end of the bed, then draw her left leg upward and rub the knot against her knee until she had worked it down over her heel.

She bicycled her untied legs. The wrist restraints were another matter. Whoever had secured them knew exactly what they were doing – she suspected Lansley. Delphine tried to stretch her legs back over her shoulders, as if she could pick apart the impregnable knots with her toes. Blood rushed to her head. She saw green and white pinpricks of light. She gave up, puffing, dots of sweat standing out on her brow.

It was no good. Even if she had an extra pair of hands, the knots were probably too tight to untie. She would need a stout pair of shears, or a knife.

She lifted herself up onto her elbows again. Lansley and Propp weren't likely to have left a knife in here for her. Next to the wardrobe, on the writing desk where she did her schoolwork when the grown-ups wanted her out of the way – or rather, more out of the way than usual – were several pencils and a sharpener. Could a sharpener blade do the trick? Doubtful – it was too small. Besides, it was screwed in place. How would she unfasten it with her hands tied?

She rattled the bedframe again, heard it clang. The noise made her jerk upright. The bedposts were hollow. She had stored things inside them.

Delphine strained to reach the bedknob, but the rope round her opposite wrist was too short. She tried to flip onto her shoulders and unscrew it with her feet, but she couldn't balance properly. She had an idea. She swung her legs up over her head, then pushed with her elbows and flipped over the back of the bedstead, her bare feet touching down on the floorboards, her wrists now tied in front of her.

Well, it was progress of a sort. She still couldn't reach either bedpost with her hands, so she lifted her right leg and, balancing against the bedstead, began trying to shunt the bedknob round with her foot. It would not move. She had screwed it down tightly for the express purpose of deterring casual snoopers. She took a couple of deep breaths. If she panicked, she would sweat, and if her foot became moist she might lose her grip.

She placed the ball of her foot against the smooth metal, working it back and forth with gentle, coaxing movements, as if petting a mouse. Warming to its role, the bedknob began squeaking very quietly. At last, she kicked at the right-hand side of the bedknob and it twisted cleanly upwards, wobbling at the top of its thread before dropping to the floor with a stunning report.

She leant over and peered into the hollow bedpost. There was a length of parcel string, three marbles – including a beauty with an oxblood twist through its middle – the end of a Nestlé's chocolate bar wrapped in foil and, right at the bottom, a packet of England's Glory matches.

She hoisted her foot up over the bedpost and tried fishing for the matchbox with her toes, but the matches were at least a foot deep, balanced on top of a wadded-up blue stocking. She tried pushing her tongue inside, but only succeeded in nicking her cheek on the bare metal.

She licked blood from the corner of her mouth and forced herself to think logically. What could she use in the room to hook out the matchbox? Her gaze fell on the wardrobe.

The bed was deceptively heavy. Its iron feet growled as she dragged it, inch by inch, towards the wardrobe. Someone was bound to hear. She felt veins standing out in her throat as she tensed and heaved it another fraction of an inch, stopped for breath, tried again.

At last, when she was close enough, she peeled the wardrobe open with her toes and kicked at the frocks inside until one fell from the rail, its hanger clanging against the pine floor. She dragged the frock out (a horrendous thing the colour of sunburn) and, with a bit of faffing, managed to tease the wire coat hanger out from inside. She used her feet to lift the coat hanger up into her bound hands, where she flattened it into a long, straight ellipse with the hook at one end. Then she gripped it in her teeth and leant over the hollow bedpost.

The hook was too wide to fit in the hole. She squashed it flatter, tried again. This time, it slipped in smoothly. Holding the coat hanger in her teeth meant she couldn't see what she was doing, so she had to work by feel and sound: the subtle vibrations working up the wire, the scrape of metal, the rattle as she tapped the box. When she thought she had it, she eased her head back up.

Twice, the hook emerged empty. On the third time, she saw the tip of the matchbox before it toppled, *shuck*, back into the hole. Delphine wanted to scream. She wanted to rip the bed to pieces then smash the pieces with a sledgehammer. Instead, she bit the inside of her cheek, hard. The pain was calming.

On her fourth attempt, the matchbox rose from the hollow bedpost, teetering on the cusp. She tilted her chin and the matchbox flipped onto the bed.

She dragged the bed the couple of feet to the writing desk and grasped sheets of paper with her toes. She passed the paper up to her hands and tore it into strips, then wrapped them in spirals around the hook of the coat hanger. Soon it was swathed in a ball of paper the size of two fists.

She picked up a match, struck it, and lit the paper. Golden flames lapped up fuel. She pulled the rope holding her right wrist taut and held the improvised torch beneath it. Fibres blackened, recoiling. She yanked. The final strands split. She transferred the coat hanger to her right hand and held the guttering flame under the rope securing her left wrist. She pulled. It held fast. The flame went out. She braced her foot against the bedstead and wrenched.

The rope broke. She was free.

Delphine stepped back from the bed, panting. Her arms felt like they were on springs. Rope hung from her wrists in charred bracelets.

She tried the door to her bedroom. It was locked.

She fished the club-headed key – the one that opened the hidden passage – out of her knickers, then unscrewed the second bedknob and drew out her bunch of copied house keys. The two doors to her bedroom – one connecting it with her parents' room, the other leading out into the corridor – were locked. She had a key for the connecting door, but she knew from trying it before that the opposite side was blocked by a heavy Indian travelling chest, probably dragged there by Daddy (on Mother's orders) for that express purpose. She did not have the key to her bedroom because she had never needed it. It had never been locked before. Besides, if she stepped out into the corridor she would be apprehended immediately.

That left the window.

Two ledges across, the ivy was glossy and lush, turning from apple green to deep lipstick red as it cascaded down the wall. It was much thicker than when she had arrived at the Hall. Back then, she had thought it would never bear her weight.

Today, it would have to.

Even if she fell, wouldn't that be an escape? Delphine climbed onto the end of her bed, folded her arms across her heart, closed her eyes, and let herself drop backwards. The mattress caught her with a whump. She lay still, heart thudding, and imagined the wind against the nape of her neck, the fall, the black pit, the silence. That'd teach them.

Delphine got up from the bed a little fast, felt the room fade and return. She glanced around, gripped by a sudden urgency, afraid that she would lose her nerve. The effects of the sedative Dr Lansley had administered numbed the edges of her perception. Nothing felt quite real, and this, she discovered, made her strong.

She did not feel brave exactly, just dizzy and heedless. The fear, the peril – these things seemed to belong to another, frailer girl.

She fished her jottings out of the bedpost, pulled a chair up to her writing desk, took a fresh piece of lined paper and sharpened a pencil. She touched a finger to the tip and wondered why Lansley had not thought to confiscate it, given that it was perfectly designed for puncturing an eye. The keen scent of pencil shavings woke her up.

She wrote with slow, neat strokes, licking her lips between words. She imagined the reaction as one of the grown-ups read it aloud to the others, the falling faces, the gasps – a swoon? No, too much. Too Malory. But certainly a cry of anguish, certainly a fist pounding the desk in repentant fury.

If you are reading this note then the situation should be obvious. I am no longer a resident at Alderberen Hall. I have decided to repair to London to seek my fortune as my present circumstances have become unbearable. Do not attempt to find me. I assure you I have taken great care to cover my tracks.

She paused, savouring her slyness. When she wrote, she felt older, stronger. She powered towards the letter's climax.

It has come to my attention that Dr Titus Lansley is an ADULTERER and SPY. He has tried to seduce my mother Mrs Anne Venner and she in her weakness has succumbed. He has also plotted to collude with enemies of the British Crown and in this endeavour he has been assisted by Mr

Ivanovitch Propp and Mr Lazarus Stokeham alias the 4th Earl of Alderberen, BOLSHEVIKS to a man. You will find enclosed sufficient proof to see that they ALL HANG.

When she came to the end of the sentence, she was pressing so hard she nearly tore the paper. She felt like she ought to add more. She spent a full five minutes trying to formulate a sentence to the effect that, should Lansley, Propp and Alderberen try to shift the blame to others, Mr Henry Garforth, Professor Algernon Carmichael and Miss Patience DeGroot were residents of impeccable moral character and in no way involved, but she could not summon the same right-eous fire, and, if she was honest, she was not one hundred per cent sure that Mr Garforth *was* innocent. Why, after all, had he turned on her so sharply that night? What was he trying to conceal? In the end, she simply transcribed the key points from her notes, before signing the letter:

Sincerely,
Miss Delphine Venner

She folded the paper in half, ran her thumb along the crease till it was cleaver-sharp. She set it down on the desk. She began to write 'DADDY' across the back in large capital letters; she got as far as 'DA' before changing her mind. She took a rubber and erased the big silver arc of the 'D', adding instead two stiff, dark horizontal lines, like bayonets, to form the 'F' of 'FATHER'. She brushed twists of india-rubber from the warm page, placed the note on her pillow then walked to the window.

The curtains were puce and thick as quilts. She dragged them aside.

The sun was blond, the sky the colour of unripe sloes. It looked like late afternoon. A whole day *had* passed, then. No wonder she felt so hungry.

She unfastened the window latch, hooked her fingers beneath the frame and lifted the sash. It stuck two inches up. She slipped her palms underneath, bent her knees and pushed. The wooden frame resisted, shuddered. Paint fell in hard black flakes. She took a breath, gritted her teeth and tried again. Again, the heavy sash rattled. It sighed upwards and she felt cold wind on her cheeks and eyes.

She took a last look around the room. Sunlight picked out dust seething above the carpet. An empty glass sat on the dresser beside her bed. Two moisture rings had stained a neat Venn diagram in the pine. If she waited any longer she would lose her nerve.

She planted a foot on the sill, gripped the sides of the frame and lifted herself up, ducking beneath the sash. The wind slapped her face, wet and freezing, stinking of loam.

She felt out behind her for the pane, rested her fingertips against it, straightened up. The gravel below tipped and surged. She wobbled, widened her stance.

She was standing on a wide stone sill. There was no reason to feel giddy, no reason why she shouldn't keep her balance. She made herself focus on the horizon. In the distance lay Prothero Wood, the brown ribbon of the saltmarshes, the sea.

Out of the trees rose the dark rip of a large bird.

She squinted, trying to get a sense of scale. It looked almost buzzard-sized. It climbed with laborious, lurching strokes.

She looked back at the gap between her sill and the next. A small jump. A trivial thing, really. She braced herself, taking big, fortifying breaths. The hard part was over. She could do this.

Out over the woods, another bird appeared. Then another. Then another.

The trees were haemorrhaging ink. At first she thought the woods were on fire, then she saw silhouettes against the pale blue sky, a scattergram of living Vs.

She heard a noise like the *pop-pop* of radio static, like someone blowing bubbles in milk with a straw, like ripping.

Black shapes. Dozens. More than a hundred.

And then she realised.

They were not birds.

They were bats.

CHAPTER 20

THE FOLORN HOPE

Without thinking, Delphine took a step back. Her heel slipped from the sill. Pitching forward, she looked down. She felt her gut plummet. She flailed her right arm and grabbed the underside of the sash, yanking herself back from the precipice. She stood on the sill, trembling. After a moment spent steadying herself, she clambered back into the room.

The pine floor felt good beneath her feet. The bedroom was unchanged. On the wall above her bed was the largest of three butterfly paintings, a rabble of red admirals across a meadow of cornflowers, tiger-oranges and blacks against muted blues and greens. The breeze through the open sash caught the note on her pillow and made it flap. She turned back to the window.

The creatures flew with ponderous drags of their wings. They were just like the thing that had chased her through Prothero Wood. They were far too big for bats. Together, they blackened the sky.

She did not remember moving but she found herself pounding on the door to the hallway.

'Let me out! Something's coming! Let me out!'

Like most of the doors in Alderberen Hall, it was big and old and her fists hardly made any noise against it. Her shouts sunk into the soft furnishings. The thick walls that had let her drag an iron bedframe the length of the room without attracting attention now muffled her calls for help. She pressed her lips to the keyhole.

'Help!' She yelled till her throat burned. 'Something's coming! Look out the window!' She stopped to catch her breath. She listened for a reply, footsteps, anything. 'This isn't a trick! For God's sake, look outside!' Beating against the hard wood, she decided to change tactics. 'I've started a fire! The room's on fire! I'm going to burn myself to death and all of you too!' The heels of her fists cramped with a cold pain. She clawed at the door; varnish squeaked beneath her fingernails. 'Daddy? Where are you? Daddy!'

She slumped against the door frame, hoarse, exhausted. Even if they had heard her, they probably thought she was throwing a tantrum. She listened to her breath hissing in and out. A sour sort of freedom descended upon her. She was utterly alone. She had no one to rely upon but herself.

She lifted her cheek from the coolness of the door, and stood. She looked round her bedroom. There was nothing she could use to break down the door – that would take a sledgehammer, and even if Lansley had been thoughtful enough to leave her one, she doubted she could put enough force behind the blow to smash out the lock. The heaviest thing in the room she could lift was the green glass paperweight on her desk – it was the size of a goose egg, with a weighted base.

She retrieved her frock from the floor. She took the paperweight from the desk and wrapped the dress around her hand several times.

When she reached the window the creatures were still there, closer. They were big as dogs, flying low above the lawn, the sun throwing deformed shadows. A crackling, popping wall of sound grew louder, louder. She swallowed the sick feeling round her tonsils and climbed out onto the sill, the frock-wrapped paperweight clenched in her fist.

The jump to the adjacent sill was less than a yard. She looked at it and her head swum and her fingertips went numb and she wanted to wee. When crossing the marshes, she had done jumps twice the size without thinking. Even though she was only one storey up, Alderberen Hall had such high ceilings that the drop was thirty feet.

She stared at the gap, and an eerie sort of calm sluiced through her chest and stomach. Her panic felt like an argument going on in another room – she was aware of it, but it was hard to get caught up in. She spent a moment watching her feelings, curious at her own detachment. Was this the tranquilisers, or bravery, or madness? Was she even awake?

Beneath the sound of wingbeats she could hear a rapid clicking in high-low scattergun bursts. All those times she had entered the woods, they had been roosting there in their hundreds. Perhaps they were migrating and had rested in on the estate after a long flight across the North Sea, and now, something had got them agitated.

Several creatures at the front exchanged some kind of signal then peeled off, pumping their great leathery wings as they climbed. They were not graceful; flying looked like a struggle, a torment, even. One of the creatures seemed to stare right at her. It spat a peal of pops and screeches to the others; they yawed away from the main group.

They were coming for her.

She watched. She knew she should be afraid, but she could not summon the emotion. The best she could manage was a memory of how she had felt that time at the tomb, a fast black shape at her heels, flickering through the trees. She had the strangest sensation that what happened to her was none of her business.

She turned away from the advancing horde, told herself to concentrate. She was in danger, even if she could not feel it. She focused on the other sill, counted to three, lost her nerve. She counted down again. She jumped.

Her heels hit the sill; her momentum carried her forward. She stopped, gripped the window frame.

The creatures were over the lawns.

She stood beside a big window like the one she had escaped through. The drapes were drawn. Delphine tightened the florid peach frock round her fist, hefted the paperweight and punched a hole in the glass. The pane fell away in fat, jagged triangles. Using the dress to shield her hand and wrist, she knocked away the biggest, sharpest slivers, then reached through and undid the catch.

Winged shadows blackened the gravel path.

She lifted the sash and, holding the dress above her head, ducked and jumped through the closed curtains into the room.

Glass crunched beneath her sandals. The room was gloomy, uninhabited. Dust-sheeted furniture formed strange, snow-smothered mountain ranges. She picked her way between them, letting paperweight and frock drop from her grasp.

The popping, ripping sound was like thunder. Behind it, she heard the *whumph whumph* of wings. She tried the door. It did not open.

She heard the scrape of claws or hooves on the ledge. The light in the room changed. She rattled the door knob. A body was pressing into the drapes.

The door gave.

She burst into the corridor and slammed the door. Snatching up her keys, she moved to lock it. There was no keyhole. She glanced around for something to block the door with. There were a few paintings on the wall – a portrait of a vinegary, wax-faced old dowager dressed in Flemish lace beside a spinning wheel, a landscape of a busy port cluttered with sailing ships, a still life of a milk churn – but nothing with any mass.

'Help!' Her cry echoed stupidly off the walls. All the doors were closed. She ran for the landing. 'Help! Help!'

Out in the Great Hall, light from the portico windows fell slantwise across the east side of the grand staircase. She ran to the balustrade and leant over. At the foot of the flowing red stair carpet, Mrs Hagstrom stood holding a yellow duster and a tin of polish. She looked up. She had a red mark on the bridge of her nose. Her sweaty forehead shone in the sunlight.

She and Delphine stared at each other for three long seconds. Delphine was dumbstruck – seeing Mrs Hagstrom made the experience of a few moments ago feel bluntly unreal. She had imagined it. Of course she had.

The doorbell rang.

Mrs Hagstrom glanced towards the entrance.

'Don't answer it!' Delphine rocked forward on her toes.

Mrs Hagstrom raised a dark eyebrow.

'Shouldn't you be in your room?'

ding dong

'Don't answer it!' She could hear her own voice and it was shrill, cracked from screaming – the voice of a frightened child. 'Please! There are . . . things. Outside. Bats.'

Mrs Hagstrom set down her duster, jaw tight with disapproval. She snorted like a bull.

Something began to hammer on the door.

'Miss Venner – '

ding dong

ba ba bang

' – I can't simply stand here and *ignore* it.' She began to walk across black and white squares, towards the door.

Delphine grabbed a vase off a plinth and held it over the edge of the balustrade. The vase was tall and blunderbuss-shaped and covered with a repeating pattern of mauve diamonds wreathed in vines.

Mrs Hagstrom stopped.

'If you open the door, I'll drop it!' Delphine said.

'Will you, now? And then what?'

ba ba bang

'Miss Venner, that vase – '

ding dong

' – is over two hundred years old.'

'If you open that door, it'll be a two-hundred-piece jigsaw, I swear to God.'

Mrs Hagstrom glanced down at the floor. She closed her fingers round empty air, clenched them for a moment, let them go limp. She looked at Delphine.

'I was one of the few who spoke up for you.'

'Then *listen*!' The vase was growing heavy in her sweaty palms. 'Why would I lie? There are things coming towards the house!'

'Things.'

ding dong

She took a breath. 'Monsters. I know it sounds stupid, but – '

Mrs Hagstrom shook her head.

'Miss Venner,' her voice carried as she marched towards the door, 'I don't know a lot, but it's my understanding that "monsters" aren't in the habit of ringing the doorbell.'

'No! I'll drop it.' Mrs Hagstrom was not even watching. Delphine heard the clunk of the bolt being drawn. She heard the door open. She heard a cry.

'Gah! Argh! Shut the door! Shut the door! Jesus Christ, what took you so . . . ' Pant pant. The speaker was Professor Carmichael. The *clump-schlack* of Mrs Hagstrom shutting and bolting the door. 'Have you seen it out there? Bats! Hundreds of 'em!' Pant pant. 'Ruddy great things, like . . . like . . . '

From the corridor behind her came the sound of smashing glass.

'Get everyone downstairs!' Delphine said. 'Get to the gun room!'

Thuds came from many directions at once. Then ticking, continuous, like hail.

Black rags flurried from the Great Hall doorways. Mrs Hagstrom fell to her knees. Creatures thumped their wings and took off, filling the space. They rose towards the domed ceiling in tight spirals like flakes of burnt paper, hissing, crackling. The Professor stared, his bristled jaw slack, his face strangely calm. Mrs Hagstrom clutched at the Professor's jumper, trying to yank him down.

Delphine gaped. The things had *faces* – sharp, hairy faces, like pine martens', set between flared velveteen ears.

Something black and sinuous unspooled from one of the creatures as it flew. It snagged Mrs Hagstrom's thigh and began winding round her and the Professor – some sort of sticky cord.

She struggled. The cord pulled tight, binding her and the Professor together, pinning their arms to their sides. The creature at the end of the line landed directly beneath Delphine.

She felt the vase slip – a sudden weightlessness in her gut, as if she had fallen with it. It dropped through churning air, blasting apart on the floor.

The creature looked up.

Mrs Hagstrom hollered a single word:

'Run!'

Delphine turned. Down the corridor, a door swung open. More of the bat-dog creatures capered out, stooped and clumsy. They walked erect, skitter-hopping on taloned feet. The tips of their wings ended in long black hooks. One of them spotted her.

If she had not been drugged, perhaps she would have screamed. She ran across the landing. The air boiled with torn sou'westers caught in a tornado. She sprinted for the east wing.

A black shape swooped for her. She dived, skidding on her chest. When she glanced back, the thing was spreading its huge wings, curving steeply upwards before its feet touched down on the floor. More landed behind it. Their eyes shone like wet berries. Their wings folded and they gave chase.

She scrambled to her feet and ran into the corridor heading east, back the way she had come, the clatter-scrape of claws on floorboards close behind her. She could smell the thick, slightly musty rug beneath her feet.

What about the Professor and Mrs Hagstrom? Were they dead?

Delphine made for the long library. She had to reach the gun room. She didn't care what these beastly things were – giant rabid bats, some exotic species of monkey, perhaps – if she had a shotgun, she could take them down by the dozens.

No use heading there directly – they'd catch her in seconds. If she made it to the library, she could slip into the hidden passage behind the bookcase and work her way downstairs undiscovered.

She could sneak from the smoking room to the green baize door northwest of the banqueting hall, with its steps leading down to the servants' quarters. She had no idea whether the hallways along the way would be swarming with . . . what had she said to Mrs Hagstrom?

Monsters.

The ground whipped from under her. Her chin bounced off the floor. She bit her tongue and cried out.

She had tripped on a ruck in the carpet. When she glanced back the creatures were coming. What she had taken for smooth torsos were quilted leather jackets worn over serge trousers cut off at the knee. They were wearing *clothes*. The fur on their faces flashed bronze in the electric light, their teeth like chips of glass. She pedalled her legs and started to crawl backwards but she was too slow and they were almost upon her and the frontrunner spread its horrible ripped-bodice wings and she raised her arms to shield her face.

A patch of light spread between her and the monsters. A door had opened inwards. Standing in the doorway was Dr Lansley.

'Up – now!'

He stepped out into the hallway. In his right glove he held a heavy brass poker, the end decorated with several vicious flukes, like a grapnel.

The bat-monsters hesitated.

Lansley steamed into them with an underarm tennis swing, embedding the poker's spiked tip in the throat of the leader, lifting it off the floor. He pivoted and dashed its head against the wall.

Its three fellows skittered backwards. Lansley wrenched the poker from the convulsing body. Purple blood flecked the wallpaper like rain shaken from a brolly.

He turned to her. 'What are you waiting for? Move!'

Delphine scrambled to get up, slipped. Lansley grabbed her arm and yanked her to her feet. There were more creatures clattering down the corridor.

He dragged her into the room, slammed the door and slid a bolt across.

A bang sounded from the other side. Another.

She was in the chimera room. She saw her own pink face reflected in a multitude of glass cabinets. Her hair was heaped up on one side of her scalp and her chin was grazed. She winked. The battered girl in the reflection winked back.

In the centre of the windowless room stood Dr Lansley, dark blood soaking the sleeve of his tweed hunting coat. He was panting and shaking. In a corner, standing over a wheelchair with his back to her, was Mr Propp.

Propp turned slowly. His face was sunken and pale.

Delphine glanced at the wheelchair and saw that it contained not Lord Alderberen but the old lady with the bare scalp and fine white cowlick; the old lady she had watched sleep so many times. Under other circumstances, she might have felt surprise.

The old woman had a loose knitted woollen blanket draped over her legs. Her eyes were half-open but she was staring vacantly into the middle distance. Her lips were parted; her chin gleamed wetly.

Lansley's breaths worked up to a crescendo.

'Well, they picked a bloody good time, didn't they?' he screamed, swiping at the air with his poker. Little spots of congealing blood studded the floorboards. 'Fine, you said! Don't worry, you said!' For a moment, Delphine thought he was going to strike Propp.

His arm went slack.

'What's going on?' she said.

Lansley glanced back at her over his shoulder. 'Are you going to tell her what's happening, then? What you've done?'

Propp sighed with his whole body. He slipped a rough hand into the pocket of his waistcoat. He ran a finger across the length of his moustache.

'Dr Lansley is right. I am at fault.'

'Oh, that's bloody big of you,' said Lansley. 'That's bloody magnanimous.'

Two sharp bangs rattled the door.

'In truth, I am not sure how this has happened. For now it is enough for you to know it is not these creatures you should fear but their masters.'

The clicking noise was building, like a carpet of insects frothing over a jungle floor.

'Professor Carmichael and Mrs Hagstrom are out in the Great Hall,' said Delphine.

Propp looked grave. 'Then I fear they are beyond our help.'

'Where is everybody?' she said.

Propp shook his head. 'I do not know.'

'Where's Mother?' She tried to feel panic, or love. 'Where's Daddy?'

'I do not know. I am sorry.'

Lansley rushed at her, reaching into his pocket. She raised her arms to defend herself. Something clattered to the floor at her feet.

'Not much, but better than nothing,' he said.

She looked down. It was her pocket knife. She went to pick it up but Lansley dropped and snatched it and the point was at her throat. He met her gaze. He was so close she could see the thick brown fibres in his irises.

'One stroke,' he said. She felt a breeze as he flicked the blade from left to right. 'Snick. Across the windpipe.' He turned the knife round in his hand, closed his leather-gloved fingers over the blade. He held it out. Delphine grasped the handle. Lansley did not let go. He took a couple of very deep breaths, huffing and puffing like someone lowering himself into a hot bath. He looked at her. 'If you're going to use a knife, don't wave it around like a feather duster. Go for their throats. Remember. One stroke.'

He released the blade and walked away. She saw the seam of his hunting jacket on his unguarded back, felt the knife in her hand.

Lansley went back to passing the poker from palm to palm. He spoke to his reflection in the glass cabinet.

'In a moment, Mr Propp and I will distract the vesperi in the hallway. I suggest that you use that opportunity to attempt an escape. If you stay, you will certainly die.'

She glanced at the door. The popping was rising to a crescendo.

'Those things . . . are they from Hell?'

Lansley sniffed. 'Not as you understand it.'

'Where, then?'

Propp reached beneath his coat and slid the revolver from its holster. Delphine started at the drawn weapon, took a step back. Lansley was pacing.

'We must haste,' said Propp. He broke the barrel and began chambering rounds. His hands were shaking. His fingers slipped and a cartridge rolled across the floor. Delphine stooped and picked it up. A .38 hollowpoint. Nasty. So his revolver *was* a Mark 4, after all.

Delphine pursed her lips. 'Dum-dum rounds.' She tossed the cartridge back to him.

The men stared at Delphine.

'We need to get to the gun room,' she said. 'We can arm ourselves.'

Propp pushed the barrel up and the stirrup lock shut with a solid click. 'We cannot stay here, this is true. We leave now or not at all.'

Lansley weighed the poker in his fist. 'We'd never make it. Besides, Mrs Hagstrom has the only key.'

'I've got one.' Both men gawked at her. 'I've got keys to most of the rooms. I made copies.'

Propp smoothed his white moustache.

'So. In this case I must entrust you with great responsibility.' He walked across the little beef-paste-coloured rug to the old lady in the wheelchair. 'Take her. Get her away from house.' Then, apparently seeing Delphine's confusion, he added: 'She is my sister.'

'Are you out of your mind?' said Lansley. 'It'll be hard enough escaping alone. You can't ask her to drag a wheelchair as well.'

'So perhaps you think we should surrender? Hand child over?'

Delphine's chest froze.

Lansley glanced from the old lady to Delphine. He shook his head.

'Damn your eyes. You were right all along, pompous oaf that you are. We can't negotiate. They're animals.'

Propp turned to Delphine with those huge grey eyes. Propp the Bolshevik. Propp the deceiver.

'Will you help?' he said.

Delphine looked at Propp's sister in the wheelchair, pale and limp as a burst chrysalis. Her feet were propped on the wooden footrests inside mustard-coloured socks.

Bangs shook the door. It sounded as if the creatures – had Lansley called them 'vesperi'? – had found something to use as a battering ram. The bolt was barely finger-width; already the screws were working loose. A few more blows and it would give.

'What about my parents?' she said. 'What about everyone else?'

Propp and Lansley exchanged a look.

'We will do our best to find them,' said Propp. 'Perhaps they flee already. But if you do not escape, everyone in house will die, I think.'

'Why?'

'Because vesperi will have what they came for. Once that is so, they gain nothing by letting us live.'

'What *are* they?'

'Beasts,' said Lansley, blinking rapidly. 'Quick, tenacious. Some understand English. No real intelligence to speak of, but a rudimentary, savage cunning. Poor discipline. Given to cowardice. Beasts.'

'I think . . . I think one attacked me in the woods once.'

'What? When?'

'Just after Easter. It chased me.'

'I knew it!' said Lansley. 'They've been watching us for months! Why the Hell didn't you say something?'

'I did! *No one bloody listened!*'

BANG

The wood round the bolt splintered.

'Look,' Lansley said, 'we don't have time for this. You're right,' he was talking to Delphine, 'the gun room is our only hope. With weapons, we can bed in, hold them at bay.'

'No,' said Propp. 'She must run. She cannot stay.'

Delphine fixed Dr Lansley with a hard stare. 'I want to fight.'

Lansley rolled his eyes. 'With the greatest respect, young lady, you failed to best an unarmed man in his late forties. I hardly think you will fare much better against waves of bloodthirsty skinwings.'

'I will if I'm holding a twelve bore.'

The Doctor tipped his head back, regarding her down the broad slope of his nose.

'Good. With that attitude you might just live through the next half-hour.' He turned his attention to the bat-winged chimp sitting on a branch inside its display case. 'Propp's right, though. You can't stay.'

'I'm not leaving.'

'We don't need an extra gun – we can use the corridors as choke points, counteract their numerical advantage. What we need is for someone to fetch help.'

Propp laid a hand on his sister's shoulder. The old lady bleated dreamily.

'She cannot escape alone. Please.'

'I'm not abandoning everybody!'

BANG

The door coughed slivers of wood. The bolt jangled loose on its screws.

'Can we *please* postpone the strategy briefing till we've worked out how to escape from this bloody room?' said Lansley.

'Once we're out there it'll be too late,' said Delphine. 'We need a plan.'

'We have plan,' said Propp. 'Doctor and I head for gun room. You take my sister, run.'

'That's not a plan. I can't just stroll out the front door.'

'Why not? Is quickest way.'

'I'm dead over open ground. They'll run me down in seconds.'

'We have no choice.'

'Then we'll die.'

'Will you *shut up!*' Lansley brought the poker down so hard it lodged in the floor. When he tried to pull it out, he levered up a floorboard.

Delphine looked from the gap in the floor, to the glass cabinets, to the locked door. She grabbed the Portuguese card table and tipped it onto its side.

'Quick,' she said, stepping behind it. 'I know this room inside-out. Do exactly as I say.'

CHAPTER 21

BEASTLY THINGS

The bolt housing broke from the door frame with the clean report of an icicle snapping. The door swung open.

Delphine watched from behind the card table. Vesperi darted from either side of the doorway, forming a pack. Some clutched javelins, some small hooked knives. Others carried coils of black rope. She stared at their horrible grasping hands. Fur on their knuckles gleamed with the lustre of iced tea.

The tallest stopped, its huge ears twitching. Its snout was a snarl of dark cartilage ringed with rigid gills. She watched the quick in-out of its chest beneath its sleeveless quilted leather jacket, a chip of red glass winking on the breast. Slowly, Delphine became aware of a mass of bright eyes focusing on her. The clicking dropped to a murmur.

The tallest raised its chin. It spat a noise at her – a flat *puk* that ricocheted off the upended tabletop like a tossed bottle cap. She glanced at the empty ground between them: a few yards of bare floorboards, and that ugly pale brown rug, spread like a welcome mat. The scene floated ghostly and reversed in the line of glass display cases, bat-monsters superimposed over a scorpion dove, a unicorn. One of the cases stood slightly forward from the rest.

The tallest vesperi whipped a bootlace tongue across the yellow spines of its teeth. Its wings hung bunched and leathery behind it. She could feel her mind reeling against it, rejecting the evidence of her senses, rejecting the earthy, oily musk wafting across the room. They could not exist, they did exist, they could not, they did.

The tallest vesperi took a step forward. Behind the card table, she tightened her grip on the pocket knife. *One stroke. Snick. Across the windpipe.*

The creature glanced about the room. The wheelchair sat empty in a corner. The creature clicked to its fellows. Warily, they advanced on the barricade.

At Delphine's knee, the old lady lay hidden in her blanket, nodding, gazing at her curled fingers. The clicking did not disturb her at all – she seemed soothed by it.

The tallest vesperi glanced across at the display cases, stopped short. At first, Delphine thought it was startled by the taxidermied monsters, then she realised: it could see Propp's sister reflected in the glass.

The creature squealed.

The javelin-bearers raised their weapons and the pack surged forwards. The dagger-bearers ducked and struck out in front. A vesperi flung its javelin; Delphine snatched her hand away and the javelin struck the tabletop, its shaft shattering on impact. A deliberately low throw. A warning.

The pack was dividing, preparing to flank the barricade. Propp's sister cooed with delight.

The dagger-wielders hit the tasselled rug and fell. Their chins thudded into the floor. Behind them, javelin-bearers stumbled into a depression left by the collapsing rug, which disguised a hole where Lansley had wrenched up the floorboards. As vesperi tried to pull themselves out, the rearguard blundered into them, trapping the frontline beneath a mound of struggling, flapping bodies.

The hole was shallow. It had halted the charge but already the vesperi were scrambling out.

Delphine stood.

'Now!'

In the display cabinet, the unicorn shuddered. It slid forward till its horn struck the glass – *tink*. The fallen vesperi started at the noise. The cabinet whinnied. Too late they realised what was happening. A shadow fell across the pit. One vesperi managed to drag itself clear before the great glass display case tipped, moaned, and bore down on the rest with a final cacophonous smash.

Gasping, greased with sweat, Propp and Dr Lansley stood in the gap left by the fallen cabinet. Propp raised his pistol and took aim at the one remaining vesperi. The monster lay on its backside, breathing in rapid fits. It saw the gun. Its short, downy throat tightened. It began crawling backwards, hooked wings scraping along the floor. Its ears had scalloped edges, as if they had been cropped. Delphine watched, horrified, fascinated.

'No.' Lansley placed a hand on the barrel of Propp's pistol. He pushed it down. The vesperi shut its eyes and exhaled. 'Save your ammo.' Lansley marched round the cabinet, glass crunching beneath his boots. The vesperi was unarmed. Lansley stood over it. The creature looked up at him with flinty little eyes, grasping a tin ankh fastened to its breast.

Lansley stamped on its leg.

Delphine felt the crunch. The vesperi rasped. Lansley swung the poker into its head and the sound stopped.

He turned. 'Time to go.'

Delphine tried to stand and discovered that her legs were shaking. She frowned. The room whirled; she felt as if she were on a carousel.

Propp was beside her with the wheelchair.

'Quick,' he said. 'Help me.'

Delphine used the table to steady herself. She and Propp picked up his sister and sat her in the wheelchair. Delphine smelt urine, partly masked by talcum powder. Propp flung a loose-knit blanket over the old lady's head. 'To protect,' he said.

Lansley had the poker raised; the spiked end was the colour of dead roses.

'Remember, no detours,' he said. 'We head straight for the master bedroom. Every second we're out there, we're exposed.'

Propp gripped the pistol in both hands and advanced on the doorway. His sleeves were rolled up and his throat growled as he breathed. Delphine glanced at her pocket knife and tried to believe she was ready to use it. Propp hesitated.

A vesperi peered round the lip of the door frame and he fired.

The report boxed her ears. When she opened her eyes a vesperi lay dead in the doorway, the skirting board pebbledashed with blood and skull fragments.

Delphine gripped the wheelchair handles and made herself think about guns. .38s were such a waste at this range. Far more punch than necessary, no spread – unless you counted the enlarged exit wound from the expanding tip.

It was as if Propp was expecting to face something far bigger than bats.

Lansley was at the door. He turned to Propp.

'Hear anything?'

'No. Go, go.'

Lansley stepped into the corridor and there was the *whumph-whumph* of wings and a tarry rag launched at his head. He jerked aside – the creature snagged his deaf-aid cable, pulling him off-balance. The wire went taut; the brick-sized battery slipped from its holster and clipped the vesperi's temple. Dazed, the creature slashed at Lansley and missed. Lansley clubbed its head into the wall and was still clubbing it when Propp grabbed his arm.

'Enough.'

Delphine tilted the wheelchair's front casters off the floor, feeling the old lady's weight shift to the back of the seat. Her palms were slippery. She pushed the chair towards the doorway. From under the cabinet came rustling, pops.

Lansley gathered up the wire and his deaf-aid battery, fastened it back into the holster. Between breaths he was swearing.

Delphine stepped into the corridor. She looked both ways. Thuds and claps and shrieks came from far rooms. West was the long library. East led back to the Great Hall.

'Ready,' muttered Lansley, and it was unclear if he meant it as a question, if he had meant to say it out loud at all. Delphine spun the wheelchair to face east.

A vesperi stepped from a doorway, threw a wiry forearm up over its muzzle. Propp shot. He missed. In the cramped corridor, the report was deafening. The creature recoiled. Propp fired again, hit it in the gut, blew a hole right through it.

He shouted something, beckoned for her to follow. Her ears rang; she felt as if she were underwater. Propp and Lansley ran towards the Great Hall.

She shoved at the wheelchair; after some resistance it started to move. The hardwood floor was slick with blood – she could smell it, loamy and clotting. Her bare toes skidded as she pushed the wheelchair and its passenger down the corridor, gathering momentum. Her throat was tight. Her legs felt floppy. Propp and Lansley had an exchange she couldn't hear; her ears were ringing from the gunfire. She felt sure a vesperi must be right behind her. She braced for the cold thud of a javelin hitting her back. God, for a shotgun.

Ahead, Lansley was shouting something – from his rhythm and intonation it sounded like a countdown as they approached the doorway to the landing. She saw the fluttering black shapes ahead. They were going to do this, they were going to charge into the storm, and Lansley was lifting his poker like a battle mace, and over the tone in her ears rose his guttural war cry, so pained and naked that it sliced through her anaesthetised dullness and her heart wanted to split down the middle and the only way she could stop terror from ripping her apart was to scream too.

One of the wheels thumped over something, maybe a body. She didn't stop.

Out in front, Dr Lansley charged onto the landing, his tweed jacket stained bruise-black up to the elbows. He cocked his head and a javelin flashed over his shoulder; another struck the stone balustrade beside him and splintered. Propp followed him; as Delphine reached the end of the corridor Propp flattened himself against a wall and aimed his pistol at a vesperi coming in to land a few yards away.

The beast's wings rucked like a paper fan snapping shut and it hit the plush red carpet in a sprint. Propp fired; the revolver bucked and the shot went over the creature's head. The vesperi whipped a dagger from its belt. Farther down the landing, two more vesperi landed. Lansley lashed at the air with his poker, driving back an assailant.

If they tried to make a stand here, they would be dead within a minute.

'Keep moving!' she yelled.

As she ploughed out onto the landing with the wheelchair, she was no longer a little girl pushing an old lady hidden beneath a pale blue rug, but a tank commander advancing beneath an almighty barrage, bulletproof, thunderous. A vesperi raised its hooked dagger to gut Propp. She blindsided it; the wheelchair knocked it sprawling. Propp shot it point-blank. The chair's momentum carried her forwards; she could not bring it about in time and the left footrest whacked into the wall. From under the blanket, the old lady let out a yodelling howl. Delphine wheeled the chair back, twisted it to face the right way.

She heard a noise like a flag in the wind then a vesperi was upon her. Wings wrapped round her head, trapping her with hot huffing breaths that stank of creosote.

The pocket knife slipped from her grasp.

She drove a fist through the gap between the creature's wings and clutched at its back. Her fingers found the neck of its jacket. She tugged but its arms were locked round her head. Its fangs were a fraction of an inch from her eye; she pulled again at its jacket and the fangs snapped shut, peppering her face with spittle. She cried out and lurched forward, driving the vesperi back-first into the wheelchair handle. The vesperi croaked, unlocking its arms. She stepped back and it fell to the floor, winded.

She looked at it, then at the pocket knife beside it. *One stroke.* She grabbed the knife. The skinwing was on its back, clutching its throat, making a retching noise. She had to finish the job, otherwise it would rise and kill her.

Something slapped the base of her spine. She spun round, knife ready.

It was Lansley.

'Follow us or die.'

He grabbed one of the wheelchair handles and helped her get it moving again. Propp appeared beside her, gasping, the armpits of his pinstripe shirt black with sweat. A smear of blood divided his forehead like a giant eyebrow.

Ahead, at the top of the grand stairway, two more vesperi readied javelins. One had a weasel snout, the other a crush of folded cartilage. More vesperi circled beneath the white hollow of the hall's domed ceiling, waiting to alight. In the air, they were cumbersome abominations. She saw they needed plenty of room to land and especially to take off again.

The two vesperi lifted their weapons. Propp fired.

'No!' Lansley called out to him too late. The shot went wide; she saw the puff of dust as it ricocheted off the balustrade. The vesperi flung their javelins at the wheelchair. Delphine dropped flat, tipping the wheelchair onto its back. She skidded on the carpet; the chair rattled as something glanced off a caster.

She scrambled to her feet and heaved the wheelchair upright, trying to ignore the old lady's whimpering moans. Propp thrust his revolver at the now unarmed vesperi and moved as if to shoot. The creatures turned and fled.

'I must reload,' said Propp.

More vesperi were clambering up the stairs, thumping their wings for extra lift. Delphine glanced back and saw even more emerging from the corridor she had just left. The two groups exchanged trills and pops.

Down on the ground floor, there was no sign of Mrs Hagstrom or the Professor.

'If wishes were horses, Ivan,' said Lansley. 'For Christ's sake, come *on*!' He roared and lunged upward, batting a vesperi out of the air; it fell like a smashed kite, clipping the balustrade and tumbling to the chequered floor below.

She was less than halfway across the landing, not yet at the top of the stairs. The wheelchair was getting heavier and heavier. She could hear the old lady crying. Her legs wanted to crumple beneath her. Delphine dipped her head and dug her bare feet into the carpet. The wheelchair began to pick up speed. The faster it got, the harder it was to steer.

Lansley was at the top of the stairs, cursing, thrashing at anything reckless enough to get in his way. A javelin sailed past him, hopelessly wide; he turned to see where it had come from and a second caught him a glancing blow across the throat. He staggered with the force of the strike; blood welled over his collar. He wiped a palm across the wound, grunted, looked at his soaking red glove.

On the stairs, several vesperi stopped and aimed their javelins at the newly stationary target.

'Look out!' shouted Delphine. She spotted the earpiece of his deaf aid, swinging loose, cable caught in the crook of his elbow. 'Look out!'

He did not even look up.

Propp hit him like an express train. Lansley's eyes bulged as the two men collapsed and a volley of missiles swished over their heads. Some javelins hit the carpet and bounced, some lodged in the thick pile, quivering. One went long and hit the portrait of Lord Alderberen's mother,* spearing her through the abdomen.

Delphine clattered past them, wheelchair ploughing into the embedded javelin shafts, snapping them under its tyres. The Great Hall was wretched with monsters. Light flickered as splayed wings flashed past the portico windows, so that when she glanced directly at them it was like looking up at the projectionist's booth at the pictures. When she looked back, Lansley and Propp were disentangling themselves and struggling to their feet. She slowed to wait for them, the wheelchair handles tugging at her arms as it tried to keep rolling.

Lansley saw her stopping and his face exploded with fury.

'Go!' He shook the gore-spattered poker at the east corridor. 'Run, damn your eyes!' He threw an arm round Propp's shoulders, helping the old man up. He looked at her again. 'Are you deaf? *Go!*'

Something on the ground floor caught his attention. He let go of Propp, who began hobbling away, and turned to face the front door. His expression went slack. Lansley held up his palm, *stop*, like a traffic policeman, then sidestepped in front of Propp. Delphine heard a thunderclap; Lansley looked up sharply.

The Doctor stared at the alabaster frieze. Delphine almost let go of the wheelchair to run to him. A thick finger of wine lengthened from a spot on his brow. It coated his open eye, his trim moustache.

---

* Anwen Stokeham (nee Prothero-Lloyd) 1833–1854. The one mention of her Delphine had found simply stated: 'quiet, Welsh; died in house fire'.

With something like relief, Dr Titus Lansley dropped and rolled down the long, carpeted stairway, finally coming to rest at the boots of a scar-nosed beast in black riding coat and breeches, holding the walnut grip of a smoking flintlock duelling pistol.

The thing was bat-like, but big as a man, muscled, too heavy to fly. Lowering the pistol, it glanced back at the open Great Hall doorway. There stood a tall figure in the broad-brimmed hat, heavy ankle-length overcoat and skull-white bird mask of a Venetian plague doctor. Coloured glass lenses flashed in the eye sockets as the white beak moved slowly up and down.

The figure raised a leather-gauntleted hand and pointed directly at Delphine.

Something brushed Delphine's shoulder and she snapped back into reality. Propp was at her side.

'Come.'

She ran.

A vesperi blocked the entrance to the east-wing corridor but she dipped her head behind the back of the chair and accelerated. The old lady cawed softly from beneath her blanket. A hiss, a flicker of movement then a *badump-badump* and the chair jumped as it ran the creature down. One of the vesperi's wings caught in the spokes, dragging it several feet down the corridor before the leathery membrane split, leaving the thing a ragged bloody heap against the wall.

She risked a glance back, saw Propp gasping and staggering, bronze-black vesperi heads gaining on him. Her palms were slick with blood and sweat. Her lungs ached. Several doors were open; ticking, bubbling and the sound of breaking glass came from inside. At every noise she braced herself for the dagger raking her throat, the puncturing blow, the close, pungent breath. The door to Lord Alderberen's parlour was the last on the left. If she had to scrabble to fit the key in, they would be on her before she could turn it.

As she approached the door, she saw it was ajar – which was worse. Vesperi were probably inside. She dug her heels into the carpet, shut her eyes and mouthed a prayer. As the chair slid to a halt she mule-kicked the door. It swung open and crashed against the wall.

The room was empty.

The red leather club chair lay upside-down, with the matador painting impaled on one of its legs. Fragments of something white, porcelain perhaps, shone against the royal blue rug. The door to the master bedroom was closed. She tilted the chair onto its back wheels and rolled it in after her. She was about to slam and lock the door when she remembered Propp.

While she waited for him, she tried the door to the bedroom. It opened.

She let it swing wide.

The room was smaller than she had expected. She collapsed against the end of a four-poster bed that took up most of the floor. Alderberen Hall's pervasive musk of stale smoke and sweat intensified as she tried to catch her breath. She scooped hair out of her stinging eyes. The bed was covered in a red silk quilt edged with tassels of dirty gold. On the bedside table lay a straight razor crusted with white stubble and shaving cream, a little oval mirror, a brown bottle containing Lord Alderberen's tincture of silver, and an ivory rook from a chess set. A pine hatch was set into the wall. Above her head, a showy oriental lampshade hung like a colossal glowing spider. The plush carpet was the colour of tonsils.

Her lungs burned. Beside the Chinese lampshade hung a second, darker lampshade. It shuddered and jawed open.

She fell. Her legs were gone. The hanging vesperi dropped. It touched down, wings spread, with a soft *whumph*.

When it rose, there was a grace to the motion, as if it had just been knighted. She scrambled onto her knees.

Its muzzle was a lattice of pink frills that flexed in time with the creature's breaths. A bloom of white pin mould brindled the corner of its mouth. From its belt swung a loop of black rope. It regarded her through sharp amber eyes, waving its hooked dagger side to side. Delphine watched the blade, remembering how the mother stoat had danced to lure the rabbit. She clasped her pocket knife.

One stroke. Snick. Across the windpipe.

The room was too bright. The vesperi stepped towards her. To pin the thing down and slice open its throat, as Lansley had told her, would be to accept it as real. And Lansley was dead. Oh God, he was dead – she had fantasised about it for so long and now it had happened. She tried to feel terror but none of it had any weight. She was riding pillion in her own body.

The vesperi took another step. She felt a nauseous fascination. The thing was breathing, pulsing with life. She could see the stitching in its cut-off trousers, the silvery hairs twitching in its outsized ears. Worst of all, she could see it watching her, could feel the workings of mutual intelligence – it looking at her looking at it looking at her looking at it.

What does a soldier most fear to see when he looks into his enemy's eyes?

She looked away. Under the great bed, tartan slippers sat next to a stoneware chamber pot decorated with elephants roaming the savannah.

The knife wobbled in her grip. She inhaled through her nostrils and opened her mouth to cry out –

The vesperi's open hand swung for her throat. She swiped with the pocket knife but the hooked dagger caught it, easily flipping it from her slick grasp. Delphine snatched at air, desperate.

The skinwing ducked under her guard, brought the hooked dagger to her throat and swung round behind her. Its thin fingers dug into her shoulder. A slow, wet breath condensed inside her right ear.

From the adjacent parlour, she heard Propp's voice: 'Hello?' He would see his sister in the wheelchair, alone, and the door, ajar. His voice dropped to a whisper. 'Hello?'

She tried to inhale; the blade bit into her windpipe.

One stroke. Snick.

The vesperi hissed, *ssss, ssss.* The edges of her vision were closing in. This was it. The pocket knife lay on the puce carpet, just out of reach. She was going to die like Lansley. She drew a thin breath, gagging.

She heard a floorboard croak in the next room. She tried not to flinch in case she panicked the creature into slitting her windpipe. She could hear Propp's exhausted breaths beneath the closer, thinner breaths of the vesperi, and a metallic scraping, as of someone sorting pennies.

He was reloading.

The vesperi held its breath. A faint shadow appeared at the threshold. The door swung inwards.

Propp stepped into the room. The grip on her shoulder tightened; the blade pressed into the soft flesh of her neck. He looked her up and down, blinked languidly. His hypnotic grey eyes glanced past her shoulder. Beneath his white moustache, his lips puckered.

'Let her go,' he said, with a slow nod.

At her ear, the vesperi pop-chirruped a response. Propp plucked at a thread on his shirt sleeve. Dried blood had crusted in the wrinkles under his jaw. It streaked his face like war paint. He raised the revolver. She felt the vesperi duck behind her, using her as a shield.

'It is me,' Propp said. He touched a finger to his cheek. 'It is Ivan. Let her go.'

He was a dreadful shot. Surely he wasn't planning to . . .

He closed one eye.

'No!' she said. She felt the sting of the dagger breaking skin. Propp straightened his pistol arm. The room was receding.

She threw her head to the left. The Webley punched. The dagger dropped to the carpet at her knees. She sunk forward, gasping, kneading her throat. Her hands came away wet, dark red blood picking out the creases of her fingers. The ringing in her ears was louder than ever, her nostrils full of salty, gammony fumes.

She lifted her head. Propp lowered the pistol. His arm was shaking. She glanced over her shoulder and saw a thing of twitching gristle, a blackberry splatter painting the embossed cloverleaf wallpaper.

He had risked it. He had taken the shot.

Propp wheeled his sister in from the parlour, shut the door and, with difficulty, slotted the bolt home. Delphine stared at him. He smeared a fist across his moustache, snorted.

'We have perhaps one minute.'

Delphine could barely speak. 'You could have killed me.'

'I could have. I did not.'

'Where are these things coming from?'

'Through channel,' Propp said. From next door came clattering, ticking. 'Ah. They arrive. You . . . ' Tenderly, he peeled the blanket

257

from his sister. Her head hung to one side, fine white hair spilling over a shrivelled cheek. She chewed at the air. 'Both of you must go now.'

'And you'll head for the gun room?'

Propp shook his head.

'What?' Delphine got to her feet, steadying herself against the four-poster bed. 'But you said . . . you have to!'

'Come.' He guided her towards the pine hatch beside the bed. He tugged the handle. The hatch slid up into a recess with a rumble of counterweights, revealing an empty shaft and a cable. Propp reached over the bedside table to a button panel. He pressed the top one. An electric motor began turning an axle that wound the cable. Mr Propp placed a hand on Delphine's shoulder. 'I never reach gun room alone.'

'You're not alone. I'm here.'

Fists began pounding the door. Propp smiled.

'You must take her.'

'No.'

Propp put the revolver to Delphine's forehead. 'You have no choice.'

She swatted it away.

'Don't be so stupid! You're not going to shoot me. Stop being such a coward. This is your fault. We need your help.'

'I am trying. Please, take her. She cannot protect herself.'

Into the open shaft rose a wooden dumbwaiter car.

'Ivan!' An unfamiliar male voice sang out from the corridor.

Propp pressed an index finger to his lips. He nodded at the dumbwaiter.

'Quick,' he whispered.

Propp pushed the wheelchair to the hatch. Delphine helped him lift his sister. They took an armpit each. She was heavier than she looked. Delphine grunted. Together, they rolled the old lady into the car.

Propp turned to Delphine and whispered: 'Now you.'

'What about you?'

'There is no room for three.'

'But Mother. Daddy.'

Propp looked at her for a long time. Trying to read his big grey eyes was like trying to read the wind.

'I will do what I must to protect those who remain.' The banging on the door grew louder. 'If you fail to escape, everyone in this place will die in penalty.'

Delphine climbed into the dumbwaiter car, lying beside Propp's sister, who was humming tunelessly to herself.

He handed her the spool of black rope from the dead vesperi. 'Perhaps useful.'

Delphine hugged it to her chest. It was slightly sticky.

Propp held up a bloody palm. 'Farewell.' He closed the hatch.

The dumbwaiter car had been built for holding multiple platters of food, plus side dishes, condiments and wine orders from the cellar, but with two passengers it was cramped. She lay in the darkness with her cheek against the cold wood. From the other side of the hatch, she heard two great blows shake the bedroom door.

'Ivan?' The unfamiliar voice was nearer. 'Open up, old friend. What's the matter? This is no way to treat me in my own home!'

The grinding electric motor started up; the wooden car began its rattling descent.

'Come on, man, don't be a silly ass! Open the door.'

As she sank into the shaft, Delphine listened for Propp's answer.

A single pistol shot rang out. Delphine jumped; behind her, Propp's sister gave a little moan. After that, there was only the rumble of the motor, and the car scraping against the walls of the shaft as they went down, down, down.

The wine cellar was bog-black. She crawled around on her hands and knees, too exhausted for tears.

She couldn't find the trapdoor.

'Please,' she murmured. 'Please.'

It had to be here somewhere. Vesperi might burst in at any second. Her knuckles brushed against the corner of a wooden box, its surface furry with splinters. She felt out its dimensions. It was an old tea chest, a sack draped over the top, which meant . . . she backed up a few feet, swiping at the floor with her palms. Her fingertips found a groove. She ran her hand along it till she came to a familiar notch, like a big keyhole, deep enough for two fingers. She wedged her index and middle finger into it, squatted on her hams and pulled. The trapdoor resisted. She heaved. The trapdoor began to lift. Her fingers slipped from the notch but she caught the lip of the trapdoor with her other hand and shoved it open.

The shaft leading down smelt of rotten eggs. Delphine felt her way over to Propp's sister. She tied the black rope round the old woman's stomach, then used a rolling hitch to fasten the other end to the iron hasp of a heavy trunk. The rope's tacky surface made it hard to pull the knots tight. Feeding the rope over her shoulder, she began to lower the old lady down into the tunnel below.

The rope sliced Delphine's palms. She groaned with effort. If she lost her grip, Propp's sister would drop like a body on the gallows. She paid out the line inch by inch, breathing through gritted teeth.

She felt the rope slacken; the old lady had touched ground. Delphine tried to untie the rope from the trunk but the knot had pulled too tight. She sawed through it with her pocket knife.

Before she climbed onto the ladder herself, she felt her way back to the tea chest and pulled the sack from on top. She draped the sack over the raised trapdoor. If vesperi came down here, it might disguise her means of escape. Or draw their attention.

Deafened, palms stinging, her head pounding, her legs weak and numb, Delphine climbed down the ladder. The darkness pulsed with stars.

CHAPTER 22

THE OLD LIE

The story came out of her in a gabbling rush. She told Mr Garforth about the black cloud that had smutted the horizon, the coarse ungainly monsters smashing their way into the house and swamping Mrs Hagstrom and the Professor, the beast with breeches and duelling pistol, the death of Dr Lansley, the masked stranger, Mr Propp alone in the master bedroom, the pistol shot, and her slow escape through the tunnel, dragging the drooling old woman on her blanket. Mr Garforth sat, not saying anything. He did not laugh, or get angry, or call Delphine a liar. Her throat felt sore from where the dagger had nicked it, and when she was done it felt sorer still.

'There are my parents, Professor Carmichael, Miss DeGroot, the servants, maybe others. They were all in the Hall.'

Mr Garforth nodded. With Delphine's help, he had put Propp's sister to bed in the adjacent room, where she had immediately fallen asleep. The kettle began to whistle. He filled the teapot.

'You knew this would happen, didn't you?' she said.

He exhaled.

'You think I'd have sat here while they came for you? If I'd known?'

'But you believe me. About the monsters.'

He glared into the dying fire. 'I told you. I know everything that goes on in these woods.'

'Why didn't you tell me?'

'Because it's none of your business! You're a child. It was for your own good.' He glanced at her grazed and bloodied body. She saw him grimace at the welts on her palms. 'I never thought they'd make it through.'

'Who? Through what?'

'The vesperi, the harka – any of the beasts throwing their lot in with Stokeham. Someone must have let them in.'

'No one let them in,' she said. 'I told you, they broke through the windows.'

'Not into the Hall, you ninny. Into the *world*. Someone must have opened the channel on our side.'

Delphine threaded her fingers then used them as a cradle for her forehead. 'What.'

'Just leave it. This is estate business.'

She stared at a knot in the table, lines banding round it like ripples spreading from a black island.

'What matters now is you're safe,' he said. 'Once you've rested I'll get you as far as the village, then you can ca – '

'Hush. I'm thinking.'

She concentrated on the gentle weight of her brow against her fingers, the throb of her rope-burned palms. The table had nicks in it where Mr Garforth had slipped with his tools. She listened to his breathing, the purr at the end of each out breath, and began to copy its rhythm. At the edges of her attention, she swore she heard ticking.

She looked up.

'There's another world?'

'This won't solve anything.'

'I nearly died.'

Mr Garforth poured the tea. 'You wouldn't understand.'

'Then it won't matter if you tell me.'

He banged the pot down, slopping hot water. 'Where d'you learn to be so damn stubborn?'

'My Mother, who may be dead.' She let the riposte hang. 'Now – what did you mean, someone "let them in"?'

Mr Garforth set a mug down in front of her. He turned his chair round and straddled it with his arms folded over the back. He gazed out the window.

'They're from Avalonia. It's got older, truer names, but they don't care to learn those.' He unfolded his arms and rested his grubby fingers on the lip of the table, like a pianist. 'It's not part of this world. It's somewhere else entirely. There are pathways – channels – that connect there and here. One is on this estate.'

'And that's how these . . . vesperi got here?'

'To the best of my knowledge. Never been there myself.'

'But Mr Propp and Lord Alderberen and Dr Lansley – they have.'

Mr Garforth chewed his dentures. 'Not Lansley – too young. Mr Propp and his Lordship say they have, and I've no reason to doubt them.'

'Why did they . . . I mean, how did you, uh . . . '

'Why would they tell someone like *me*, you mean? A lowly game-keeper.'

'Head gamekeeper.'

'I'll let you in on a secret.' He lifted his mug to his lips with both hands, sipped. 'You can learn a lot if you're still and quiet and act harmless. They spoke as freely in front of me as you would a dog.'

Delphine frowned. She slid her fingers apart.

'No,' she said. 'You're lying.'

'Excuse me?'

'I don't believe you. Mr Propp isn't so foolish and you're not so good an actor.' She slapped her brow, trying to shake off the fog around her thoughts. 'That first day I reset the rat traps – you knew I'd spared one.'

'I could see it in your eyes.'

'Oh, balderdash. I'm an expert liar. You *knew*.' She took a slurp of tea, watched him over the rim of her mug. 'You knew about the tunnels too.'

Mr Garforth sniffed and turned away.

'I followed you,' he said. 'Watched you go in.'

'That's funny.'

'What's funny?'

'Just how I purposely only ever went in them on a Sunday, yet somehow you managed to watch me from a church *four miles away*.'

Mr Garforth sipped his tea and watched the fire.

'All right,' he said. 'All right.' He put down his mug. 'The truth.' He stood, took his cap from a hook by the door. He picked up his shotgun. 'The bloody truth.'

In the middle of the silver birch spinney behind the cottage was a thicket of brambles. Mr Garforth parted them with his stick and hooked a rusty iron ring lying flat in the grass. Delphine watched the sky for vesperi.

Mr Garforth grunted. His knees cracked. A circle of sod lifted from the surrounding earth. His palms slipped on the shaft of the stick. He swore out the corner of his mouth. Taking a breath through his nostrils, he lifted and pushed. The lid, hinged on one side, jawed open. He stepped forward. The lid reached its apex, then toppled wide.

'You first,' he said.

Delphine climbed into the hole. The ladder was cold. Mr Garforth climbed in behind her. He pulled a piece of twine and the hatch closed above him.

At the bottom of the ladder he switched on his electric torch. They were in a tunnel with a low ceiling. Mr Garforth started walking.

'This isn't on the maps,' said Delphine.

'There's a lot not on maps,' said Mr Garforth. The torchbeam flashed over brown, clayey puddles. Their footsteps sloshed.

The tunnel was cool and quiet. Soon, it split in two. The left fork led away to the west. Mr Garforth took the right.

The ground began sloping upwards. They came to a set of iron rungs hammered into the rock. Mr Garforth switched the torch off.

'Up,' he said to the blackness. She listened to the *clang, clang, clang* as he began to climb.

Delphine clambered out the trapdoor into a building large and dark as a barn. Canvas had been tacked across the high windows.

'Where are we?' she said.

'Old hunting lodge,' said Mr Garforth. He clapped his hands three times. 'Gentlemen.'

A swarm of shining eyes slammed open.

CHAPTER 23

THE LITTLE GENTLEMEN

'They're refugees,' said Mr Garforth, spooning sugar into warm water. 'They don't want a war.'

Delphine sat in the cottage, surrounded by foot-tall red beetles – fourteen of them.

The scarabs stood erect, hunched beneath segmented carapaces, watching her with bright, swirling eyes. Their pupils were smoked blue marbles floating in milk. Beneath the eyes was a tangle of complicated mouth parts: wet hooks around a moist proboscis.

Mr Garforth did not have enough cups so he poured the sugar water into bowls. The beetle-things sat three or four to a bowl, dipped their crimson proboscises into the water, and fed.

Delphine wrinkled her nose and did her best to hide her revulsion.

'Can they . . . understand us?'

'Of course. They're not animals.'

'What are they?'

'Not what. Who,' said Mr Garforth. 'And there's not the word in English for their kind. Out of respect, I call them the Little Gentlemen.'

At this, the creatures ticked and popped in a similar manner to the vesperi, but higher-pitched, like cards riffling. The noise made her scalp crawl.

'They help me on the estate,' said Mr Garforth, 'and I keep them safe.'

'They've been watching me, haven't they? I felt them – in the tunnels.'

'I knew you wouldn't listen. I asked them to keep an eye on you.'

Delphine thought of climbing the chimney – the cold grip round her wrist that had saved her from falling. Had that been them, too? She was shocked that a little thing could be so strong.

'I saw one,' said Delphine.

'Your father.'

'He found something by the lake.'

'Wasn't one of ours,' he said. The Little Gentlemen tick-chittered restlessly.

'There are more?'

'Of course there are more. You can't control a threshold without one.'

'Threshold?'

'One end of a channel. That's how the Gentlemen came here. It's *why* they came here. They don't want to pick sides. They don't want to work as slaves. They want to live out their days in peace.'

'God.' Delphine squeezed her head between her palms. 'So, what are we going to do now? Shall we call for the police?'

'And say what?'

'That monsters are . . . ' She caught his expression. 'All right, Bolsheviks. We'll say the Hall has been overrun by Bolsheviks.'

'This is exactly why I shouldn't have told you.'

Delphine ruffled her hair. 'Fine. Burglars. Fifty burglars with rifles.'

'Fifty?'

'Ten, then.'

'And they'll send what,' said Mr Garforth, 'twenty men? How long d'you think they'll take to get there – two hours, three? What chance have twenty coppers got against an army?'

'Well, what should we do, then?' She slammed her palms into the side of the table, shoving her chair back. One of the legs caught a loose tile and the whole chair tipped; she dismounted and it clattered to the floor. 'What should we bloody do?' She kicked the chair and it skidded a couple of feet. She kicked it again. Several of the Little

Gentlemen curled into spheres. 'While we're just sitting here, they're killing everyone and my parents are *dying*, they're dying and you won't even ring for a policeman!' She brought both fists down on the table. 'Damn you!' She kicked the chair again and this time it bounced, a leg snapping off, rolling to the foot of the fire. 'Damn you, you stupid old man!' She looked down at her hands. They were filthy, covered in tiny cuts. She was breathing fast. Her fingers felt numb.

'That's it,' she said. Florescent streaks ebbed in her peripheral vision. 'I'm getting my gun and I'm going back.'

'No you're bloody not.'

'Watch me.'

'Don't be selfish. You'll get killed.'

'If Daddy's dead I don't want to live any more. I just want revenge.'

'You're a child.'

'I'm thirteen.'

'Exactly.'

She took a couple of quick, shuddery breaths.

'Mr Garforth. I am going to fetch my gun and my hook and my good boots, then I'm going to walk back to the Hall and start killing.'

Mr Garforth slipped his rough hands together, rested his chin on his knuckles. 'How quick can you reload a shotgun?'

Delphine shrugged. 'About five seconds.'

'I reckon that's about how long you'll live.'

'Then . . . well, fine.' She folded her arms, glared into the fire.

'So you're happy to die, just like that? For nothing.'

The dying embers looked like a distant shining city on a hill, covered with snow.

'Yes.'

'I don't believe you.'

'Well.' She inhaled, tried to get the tremor out of her voice. 'I'm going anyway. So if you don't want me to die, you'd better come up with a better plan.'

The cottage was silent, save for the plop and trickle of proboscises.

'I have a better plan,' he said.

She looked at him over her shoulder. 'I'm listening.'

* * *

When Mr Garforth was finished, Delphine squatted on her hams amongst the Little Gentlemen. She dunked a finger in the sugar water and sucked it.

'All right,' she said.

'Not now.'

'What do you mean? I thought you said – '

'The deal is . . . ' He lowered his voice. '*The deal is:* you rest and you eat and then you decide.'

'I've decided. I want to go now.'

'You don't *get* to go now. For starters,' he jabbed a thumb at the window, 'there's a big ball of fire in the sky that makes little girls very easy to see.'

'But – '

'I'll tell you what I think: doing anything but running away from here as fast as you can is madness, and it'd be a terrible sin, bad as murder, if I let a child give her life so cheaply, without at least trying to make her see sense.'

Her chest clenched. 'I've made up my mind.'

'Then you've nothing to fear from a little more considering.' He gripped the back of his chair and began to get up. 'Best-rested is best army – you know that, don't you? Can't fight tired, can't fight hungry. Besides, if you want to do it proper, our friends here need time to do some spying.' He gestured at the lumps of living crimson armour.

'If it's too dangerous for me to go in daylight, why is it okay for them?'

Mr Garforth folded his arms. 'Gentlemen.'

The scarab-creature by Delphine's foot stood. Its dark red proboscis extended and started to vibrate, sending up a high, oscillating drone until it began to blur. The other scarabs rose and joined in. Delphine felt the buzz in her nostril hair, down the nape of her neck. She stepped back. The pale fluid in the creatures' eyes grew agitated; it began fluxing green, turquoise, magenta.

'What's happening?' said Delphine but Mr Garforth shook his head.

Flamelike, the blurring spread from each creature's proboscis, over its hinged mandibles, across its glowing eyes, its banded thorax, its spindly arms, the glossed maroon plates of its carapace. With each creature, the last things to be consumed were the bristled hooves of its feet, hooked foretalons smearing, fading.

The Little Gentlemen had not disappeared. They were enveloped in a kind of heat haze. Trying to focus on them made her eyes go funny. They were burgundy smudges, fragments of boulder glimpsed through steam.

'You see now why everyone and his horse wants them as spies,' said Mr Garforth. 'They know the tunnels, the secret passageways, the nooks, the dark spots – places I doubt even a busybody like you's managed to unearth. They'll tell us how the land lies.' He ambled to an old pine cupboard. 'If you're still certain when the time comes, I'll do everything I can to help you. I'll lay down my life beside yours. That's my word.'

'Thank you.'

'Don't thank me.'

'I'm going to fetch my gun,' she said.

'Can't do that. They might have left lookouts.'

'They don't know these woods. I do.'

'Still.' The cupboard squealed as he opened the doors. 'If you get spotted, that's it, we're jiggered.' When he turned round he was holding a double-barrelled shotgun. 'Here.'

She accepted it. The muzzle was extended and slightly tapered. 'Nice.'

'Good goose gun, that,' he said. 'Full choke in the right barrel, half in the left. Throws a tight pattern at range. If you must go out and clear your head, head down towards the beach. I 'spect they won't have come that far, not out in the open.'

She broke the barrel and two cartridges popped from the breech, clattering across the tiles.

'Jesus. It's loaded.' She pushed them back into the breech and shut the gun: *chuk*.

Mr Garforth looked at her.

'May God forgive me.'

CHAPTER 24

SO MUCH FOR OPERATIONS IN SALT-MARSHES

D elphine gazed out across the acres of mud and flooded trenches. She thought of the Battle of Albert – almost 20,000 British men killed in a single day. What was her life against all of theirs?

She glanced at the shotgun, cold and cumbersome in her grubby hands. Mr Garforth was right – she was an idiot for wanting to go back there, for thinking she could make a difference. Dr Lansley had thought he could fight them – had shown more bravery than she would have ever imagined – and look how he'd finished up. Even wily old Propp had lost in the end.

She spat. Pink, coppery phlegm fizzled in the dirt. Terns swept past the sun, shrieking.

In *The Art Of War*, Sun-Tzu said: 'If forced to fight in a salt-marsh, you should have water and grass near you, and get your back to a clump of trees.'

Staring over the shining, treeless expanse, Delphine thought what stupid advice this was. How could you *not* be near water and grass on a marsh? And how were you supposed to get your back to a clump of trees when there weren't any?

She and Professor Carmichael had argued in roistering, passionate volleys over Sun-Tzu's reputation as a master strategist. The Professor had said that all modern military tactics were footnotes to Sun-Tzu.

Delphine had said she didn't care, that Sun-Tzu was an idiot who said vague, obvious things like 'don't be too hasty, but also don't be too cautious', and why didn't he explain how to dig a pit trap so soldiers fall into it, or how to train hawks to drop vials of acid on enemy generals, or how to fight with blades attached to boomerangs. The Professor had said he didn't think they had boomerangs in Ancient China. Delphine had said that wasn't the point – the point was it was stupid, boring book.

Professor Carmichael was probably dead now. Mrs Hagstrom too. She had watched them drop to their knees in a gale of black wings. What about Daddy, and Mother? Were they slumped against a wall somewhere, run through on javelins, heads hanging slack and grey, their hair matted with blood?

If she returned to Alderberen Hall, she would die.

She had seen the size of the swarm rising above Prothero Wood. There had to be more than a hundred of them. And who was that figure in the bone-white plague mask, the one standing in the door when Dr Lansley had been shot?

What had Daddy said about Mr Kung? *The balance of his mind was upset.* And so he had walked willingly into the sea, thinking he could travel to another realm.

Perhaps it had finally happened, just as Eleanor Wethercroft and Jacqueline Finks-Hanley and Prue Dunbar had said it would. Perhaps she had snapped. There had been no monsters. Daddy and Mother were safe. Dr Lansley was still alive.

But if she had imagined it all, where had she found the double-barrelled shotgun? She closed her eyes and pushed the thought away.

Behind the sound of her breaths and the rush of the sea rose another sound. A familiar sound. A sound that made her breath catch in her throat.

Ticking.

She wheeled round, scanning the sky. To the east, behind a poplar windbreak, a dark shape climbed in a slow, thumping spiral.

Delphine half-ran, half-fell into the trench. Freezing water splattered up her legs.

No, no, no . . .

She pressed herself to the trench's gooey wall and peered over the top. The thing was still there. It was using the heat from the cornfields to gain altitude. Any moment it might break back towards the Hall, or strike out northwards, over the marshes.

It's not real . . . it's not real . . .

A pulse galloped in her ears. It looked real. It sounded real.

But if this monster was real, then all the others were too. Daddy and Mother and the Professor and Mrs Hagstrom and Miss DeGroot were in mortal peril. Dr Lansley was dead.

If it was real, she could kill it. That was the final test.

She slipped her finger over the trigger. Terns screamed. The monster continued to rise.

The girl with the gun crouched waiting.

INTERLUDE 2

G ideon smelled lemons again.
     He pushed twists of tissue paper up his nose and pressed on with his painting, angry at the intrusion. It was all in his fancy.

The attic made a better studio than the stables. More compact. More focused. He added a little more dark sienna to the blue he was layering up on the cell floor. A splodge of Chinese yellow clung to the corner of the palette like pus squeezed from a boil. Perhaps that was where the scent of lemons was coming from. No. Don't be stupid.

The electric bulb dangling from a low rafter picked out the ridges of his brushstrokes, patterning the canvas with little glowing 7s. It reminded him of the evening sun bronzing the sea in Valencia, the rumbling wagons heaped with lemons, the feel of cool dimpled skin beneath his fingers, hitching a ride up into the hills with his easel and a couple of cocas wrapped in wax paper and a flask of iced tea. Lizards basking on hot flat rocks, shadows oozing from the silver lime trees. The blood-drenched sunset. The suffocating stars.

Enough. He sipped his tea. His lips puckered.

A phrase from Debussy's *Préludes* was repeating in his head. Was it in his head? Perhaps Mr Propp was playing piano downstairs.

Gideon tore up more tissue paper and plugged his ears. There, that was better. He massaged a crick in his neck. He rolled a cigarette.

He thought he felt an impact through the floor. Just a door slamming. He closed his eyes. Deep inside his stopped-up head there was only him and the thunder of blood.

He smoked his cigarette and the attic filled with oily meshes. The tobacco made his pulse race and he returned to the canvas with vigour.

Through tissue-blocked ears he was sure he heard gunshots. Was everything all right downstairs? He pushed the question aside. Dr Eliot said that phantom sounds and smells were like uninvited guests: greet them with a smile, but don't offer them a room for the night. When they see that they're not welcome, they'll leave of their own accord.

Gideon wiped a hand across his mouth. He could feel gems of perspiration clinging to his top lip.

Dr Eliot had said he was to do mental arithmetic whenever he felt his mind was out of balance. Dr Eliot said simple exercises helped to restore order. Mathematics took as its focus objective truth, and truth was axiomatically the highest form of mental health. Try reciting your multiplication tables, he said.

Gideon squinted at the canvas and saw 7s. Every brushstroke was a 7, the angle of the painted window frame was a 7, the fallen woman's hair was a writhing carpet of tiny tessellating 7s.

He multiplied 7 by 7 and got 49. If you rotated the number 4 clockwise by 45 degrees, it was two 7s mirroring each other. That made 779. If you subtracted the number of 7s (2) you got 777, the number of God. 49 and 2 was 492. 492 plus 777 equalled 1269. And if you took 1269 from 1935 you were left with the number of the Beast.

'I am calm and happy,' he said. His voice sounded distant and foreign.

He began unbuttoning his shirt. He was not giving in to this nonsense again.

He thought of Delphine, how she walked with the heavy steps and twitching vigilance of a soldier. *He* had done that to her. And

Anne. He had always meant to protect her, but his sickness was crushing her. Worst of all, she blamed herself.

Disembodied sensations scratched at the roof tiles. Gideon clenched his fists. He lay on the warm attic floor, shuddering. Tears ran into the tissue paper in his ears.

The Debussy grew louder and louder in his head. He heard a van backfire; a ewe miscarried, disgorging a steaming purple cadaver. All the smells and tastes and sights and sounds in the world were being sucked towards the house.

His body seethed with digits. He was the Hall. He could feel its bleak geometries deep in the black earth.

Time sped up and he saw that all creation was a great plunging cycle of birth and torment; millions burnt to atone for his sins, and he could hear them screaming, broken on the wheel. He was the axle; it turned around him.

The 7s were turning to 6s. He had to stop the cycle.

He rummaged through brushes and empty milk bottles and rags scabby with paint until he found his art scalpel. He held the blade up to the light, felt himself losing his nerve. He pictured Anne's horror when she heard the news, Delphy weeping. God! But wouldn't they live better lives without him, without his sickness dragging them down?

He stared at his wrist. Bluegreen veins roadmapped a pale and freckled arm. He took a deep breath, placed the blade against his skin, and the light went out.

Gideon blinked. He was in darkness. He swayed, unsure which way was up. Had he gone blind? Was this Hell?

A voice spoke to him in the secret language God teaches the dead. Gideon's breath stopped in his throat.

'Arthur?'

ACT THREE
September 12th 1935

What is a dance? No more than order cloaked in chaos.
Like all of nature – like a tree, like the wind – it appears wild,
but when we explore deeply we discover it arises from Law.
The dancer may seem to be dragged first this way, then that,
by the vagaries of whim, but in actuality, every step is planned.
This, then, is the essence of dancing: to ride the changing winds;
to surrender to fate and, in surrendering, to become its master.

– *Meetings With Mephistopheles*, I. G. Propp

CHAPTER 25

PARABELLUM

On the floor in front of the hearth, Mr Garforth rolled out a map. He placed a mug on either end.

'This is a plan of the Hall.'

'I can see that.'

His bloodshot eyes thinned. 'You promised you'd listen.'

'We've gone through this.'

'And so will we again.' He slapped the paper. 'You'll enter here.'

The map was yellow and wrinkled. It showed a plan of all three floors. The ground and first floor looked like dumbbells: the square east and west wings connected by a long rectangle of rooms and corridors. The servants' quarters, underground, were a smaller block. In the bottom-right corner, separate from the rest, were the stables and the generator room.

'So you'll come through here,' he tapped the dark line that marked the door from the cellar to the corridor below stairs. 'Along here,' his finger drew a line east, past the gun room and the game larder, 'is where they are being held.' He circled the pale box of the scullery.

'Is my father there?'

His hand slid from the map. 'Let's hope so. The only hostages they saw were in there.'

'How many?' The heat of the fire was making sweat stand out on her brow.

'Lots. They're tied up. Three vesperi on guard in the room. More patrolling the corridor.'

'How do I get past them?'

'At nine p.m., the Little Gentlemen will shut down the generator. The rest is up to you. Whatever you do, *don't* waste time trying to get into the gun room.'

'But I could give guns to everyone,' said Delphine. 'We could take back the Hall.'

'You're going alone because you're fast and small. If it comes to a standing fight, we'll lose. We're not raising an army. We're saving lives. That includes yours. You're none of you trained soldiers.'

'Daddy is. Professor Carmichael is.'

'So was Dr Lansley. Look what happened to him.'

'Why didn't the monsters just kill everyone?'

Mr Garforth dug a fingernail into his whiskers. 'Maybe they still plan to. Maybe they need information first. What did you say Mr Propp said? Something about handing over a child?'

'Yes, a girl. I thought he meant me, but . . . why would they be after me?'

'Promise me,' said Mr Garforth. 'Get in, get out. By the time they realise what's happened, you'll be long gone.'

'All right,' she said. 'But what about the three guards? How do I distract them?'

Mr Garforth swept his hand across the map. 'Throw 'em some bait.'

CHAPTER 26

FORGIVE ME, COMRADE

s Delphine reached the end of the tunnel, the light was dying. Her satchel of grenades thumped at her hip, the sawn off shotgun weighty in her hand. The safety of the cottage lay behind her. At the top of the ladder was the Hall. The cool air reeked of wet clay.

Her torch threw a dimming ginger circle over the ladder. She looked at the shotgun. She looked at the ladder. She looked at the shotgun.

In her head, she heard Mr Garforth reprimanding her. He never let her cross so much as a puddle till she had ceremoniously broken and unloaded the gun, showing him the smooth cold cartridges snug in her palm like exotic eggs. If she rolled her eyes, he would launch a diatribe cataloguing the grim fates of those who, like her, thought themselves too busy for caution; folk like Ned Nevins' lad, who dropped a shotgun climbing onto the back of a hay cart after the harvest festival and blew his face off – yes, the safety was on – who survived, after a fashion, living blind and hideous in an attic, spooning pap into his ruined mouth. She had heard the story so many times – three, in point of fact – she could barely look at a stile without the Nevins boy's milky, shot-pocked eyes rising in her imagination like the glowing links of Marley's chain.

She thumbed the locking lever (oiled by Mr Garforth so it moved smoothly) and broke the sawn-off barrels, holding a palm over the breech to stop the shells jumping out. She balanced the gun on her forearm like a bird of prey. She switched off the torch.

Her satchel swung as she climbed the ladder. She was going back. After everything that had happened, she was going back. Her head swam. Her fingertips felt numb.

She stopped beneath the heavy oak trapdoor. She listened.

There was only her breathing.

She felt about for the latch and drew it. Slowly, slowly, she raised the trapdoor with her head.

Blackness. She smelt mould and vinegar. She listened again. Nothing. She lifted the trapdoor a little farther and the sack covering it slid back with a hiss. She placed her shotgun on the floor and switched on the torch.

Dust motes swam bronze and aquatic in the torchbeam. Cobwebs hung from the wine racks like seaweed.

She crawled out and gently lowered the trapdoor. The dust coating the floor was gritty, damp and salted with mouse droppings. She wiped her hands as best she could on her knickerbockers. She picked up the shotgun, checked the shells were in place and shut the breech. It closed with a satisfying *clop*.

The wine cellar was three small rooms linked by stone archways. There were bottles of Lacryma Christi and bottles of calvados, clarets and champagnes, and in the dying torchlight they seemed to breathe. Set into one wall was the dumbwaiter shaft connecting the cellar with the kitchen, dining room and master bedroom above. A mahogany barometer lay on its side, the face smashed in. She crept past ale kegs stamped with the local brewery's mark, a pair of bull's horns. At the foot of the stairs, she stopped.

A flight of steps led up, lined with wooden struts. At the top was a door.

She crept up the creaking stairs. Fishing in a slip pocket of her bandolier, Delphine pulled out a long brass key. On the other side of the door was the corridor that linked the kitchen to the servants' quarters, game larder and gun room. She put her ear to the keyhole and listened.

Something was coming.

She held her breath. Footsteps padded from the larder, past the door. They stopped.

Beneath the sawn-off barrels, her palm grew slick.

The footsteps continued.

Delphine crept back down the stairs and shone her torch on the glass face of a carriage clock. It was almost nine o'clock.

She walked across the black cellar to the dumbwaiter, brushed dust from the panel. The button for the kitchen was smooth and black and humped.

She placed a jam-tin grenade in the dumbwaiter car, struck a match and pressed the button with her thumb. Somewhere in the shaft, a motor started. The car began to rise. Just as it was about to move out of sight, she touched the flame to the fuse.

She ran back through the cellar and up the stairs and at the door she paused. She held her breath

The clocks struck nine.

In the kitchen, two vesperi, one with a triangular notch docked from her soft dark ear, were talking.

They spoke in short, crickling bursts. The first vesperi, the shorter, ran his stubby fingers along the ridge of the smooth oak worktop. He looked at his hand. He said something to the second vesperi. She snapped a retort.

The second vesperi opened a drawer and took out a whisk. She shook the whisk and it rattled. She slotted it into her belt.

The clock on the shelf began to chime. She wheeled round, noseleaf flaring as she chirruped an alarm call. A second clock on the wall beside the range made a straining noise, then a tiny pair of doors snapped open. A figurine dressed all in red puttered out along a set of wooden battlements. It stopped before a silver bell, tilted back as if surprised, then began striking the bell with a hammer.

A third clock went off, a fourth.

An animal groan came from the open hatch at the far end of the room.

The vesperi's hands went to their daggers. The second vesperi pop-whistled instructions to her partner.

Something was rising. The first vesperi held back but his comrade advanced, her blade out in front of her.

The hatch opened onto a shaft. In the darkness, a cable was moving. Rising into view was the lip of a wooden box.

Her wings fanned. She approached on talontips.

The box was lit from within. It stopped with a shudder.

It was open at the front. Inside, something fizzed and smoked – a stub of black rope, stuck in a tin.

She squinted.

The lights went out.

The bomb went off.

Delphine heard the concussion, trains shunting in a distant yard. A couple of seconds later, the door rattled in its frame. She waited.

Chittering. Several sets of footsteps passed the door, moving rapidly from left to right, dashing for the kitchen. She let them fade, and as the clocks finished chiming she opened the door.

Her eyes were used to the dark. The corridor was clear both ways. Clutching her sawn-off, she crept east, past the gamey pong of the larder and the locked gun room, to the open doorway of the scullery. She pressed her shoulders to the wall, clutched the shotgun to her chest, listened.

Soft, steady weeping. A cough.

She hugged the abbreviated barrels, whispered the simplest prayer she knew:

Dear Lord, please.

She swung into the room.

To her left, people tied to chairs: Mother, Professor Carmichael, at least eight. Alive. Gasps. To her right, a lone vesperi raised its hooked dagger. She rounded on it.

It stared at her gun. The brindled fur covering its scalp and cheekbones ranged from chestnut to black with ruby notes.

The creature looked up. Its nostrils were little sideways mouths that flexed and pinched. It tossed its dagger onto the stone flagging, then slowly raised its palms. Its eyes were hazel, like Mother's.

A chair leg scraped.

The shotgun bucked and the thing's head burst like a gourd, painting the wall. She felt warm fluid on her cheeks and chin. The lower half of a torso slumped. One leg skittered and danced against the stone floor.

Delphine.

Through the ringing in her ears she heard groaning. She reached for her bandolier and discovered that her hand was shaking.

'Delphine!'

She turned. Professor Carmichael was struggling against his bonds. He was perched on a chair far too small for him, wrists bound behind his back. She watched the motion of his lips. 'Untie us.' He had a bruise on his forehead the size of an egg.

Everyone was here, just as the Little Gentlemen had said, everyone, except . . .

She set down her satchel, took out her pocket knife and began to go from person to person, slitting their bonds. Besides Mother and the Professor there was Mrs Hagstrom, Alice the maid, the blacksmith Mr Wightman, Reggie Gillow, and two gentlemen she vaguely recognised from previous symposiums – most likely they had arrived early, hoping to catch the ear of Mr Propp – all ashen, shivering, drunk.

Mother barely noticed when Delphine set her free. Her gown was torn round the throat. She stared into space with the hollow calm of one who expects only misery.

Delphine looked about. There was no Lord Alderberen, no Propp. No Miss DeGroot either. She gripped Mother's shoulder, shook it.

'Mother?' she said. She could barely hear her own voice. '*Mother.*'

Mother looked up. She blinked at Delphine, glancing around as if seeing the room for the first time.

'Oh God,' she said. 'What are you doing here? I thought . . . I didn't know . . . '

'I came to save you.'

Mother stared. Her thin arms swept out and she dragged Delphine to her greedily, clutching, hugging.

'Oh, you silly girl,' she said, rubbing her wet cheek against Delphine's hair. 'Oh, you silly, silly girl.'

Delphine wriggled and Mother let her go.

'Where's Daddy?'

Mother wiped her eyes.

'I'm so sorry, Delphine. I don't know.'

CHAPTER 27

THE RUNNING OF THE BULLS

Mr Henry Garforth grimaced at the freezing pain in his knees, the arthritis cramping the swollen knuckles of his right hand. He knelt amongst dead lilacs, holding the ferret in place while he peered into the clearing. In front of the burial vault, two minotaurs loitered with flintlocks. The harka bullmen were seven foot tall, glossy chestnut-skinned and swollen with muscle, their horns decorated with the complex martial insignias of House Dellapeste. The rifles looked dainty in their thick fists. Brass rings gleamed in their muzzles. They scanned the treeline with hard, intelligent eyes.

The door to Peter Stokeham's tomb was open.

In the moonlight, the ivy-wrapped fallen larch looked like the shattered neck of a dragon.

Henry Garforth tightened the final loop of string around the ferret's belly. The string was attached to a smoke candle. He struck a match and lit the fuse. White smoke began churning out. He slapped the ferret across its furry haunch and it ran from the bushes, trailing smoke.

The harka guards raised their rifles. Henry reached into his kitbag and lit a second match.

One of the harka squeezed the trigger. An instant later, its rifle let out a crack and white smoke frothed from the pan. The shot hissed through empty air.

The second guard took aim, tracing the ferret's path, fired. The ferret jinked left and the shot thudded into the grass.

The first harka was already running, pursuing the trail of smoke as the ferret zigzagged towards the bushes. Its partner moved as if to follow. Henry let out a grunt as he flung a grenade towards the vault.

The condensed milk tin clanked off weathered stone and landed in the grass. The harka turned ponderously round. The grenade was at its hooves. It poked the unfamiliar object with its rifle. The harka threw its huge arms across its face.

Henry dropped flat.

The homemade grenade exploded. Chunks of hot horseshoe ricocheted off the granite tomb with crazy zinging noises.

Henry rose, his elbows protesting, and dashed across the clearing after the first harka. He could see its huge silhouette thundering into the trees after the ferret, slashing at smoke and foliage with the bayonet tip of its rifle. Henry heard a mechanism snap shut. The creature toppled, bellowing, clutching at the steel jaws that had gnashed into its ankle. It groped at the mess of blood and shattered bone, trying to prise the trap apart. Henry stepped from the bushes and pushed a gun to the flat ridge of bone between its great horns.

A shot rang out in the dark wood. He reloaded.

Henry returned to the clearing just in time to see two vesperi bounding out of the vault, spreading their wings and taking off. As they wheeled towards the Hall, he swung his shotgun past them and fired. One beast jerked, its wing shredded, and spiralled into the treetops. Henry fired his second barrel. The remaining vesperi's silhouette wobbled, glided out of view.

'Damn.' That meant reinforcements would be on their way soon. At least more trouble for him meant fewer vesperi at the house.

He broke his shotgun and the spent shells popped out like fat red crickets. He took two cartridges from his pocket,* slotted them into

---

* 1¾ oz. magnum loads of No. 1 shot, handloaded by the Little Gentlemen back at the cottage. They had become so skilled at measuring out powder and shot – by *weight*, not volume, he would remind them – and ensuring the seating wads fit snugly, he no longer had to supervise. The extra charge in each cartridge rattled his jaw – it was like firing an elephant gun.

place and closed the gun. Behind him, the bushes were full of glowing lights. As he tramped over grass, the Little Gentlemen followed, emerging from the undergrowth with pliers and wire-cutters and lengths of fuse and traps and a stack of aluminium washing-up bowls. Their huge eyes left ghostly trails.

Henry trained his gun on the mouth of the vault. He gave the woods, and England, one last look, then stepped inside.

CHAPTER 28

PATIENCE

D elphine peered into the dark and silent corridor. She ducked back inside the scullery.

'It's clear,' she whispered.

Her torchbeam picked out glassy eyes, wet teeth. Delphine had given Mother the satchel to carry, explaining that it contained home-made grenades; with the strap across her thin shoulder, Mother looked like a schoolgirl. Professor Carmichael held an empty port bottle, slapping it into his big palm like a cosh.

Delphine gave Mrs Hagstrom a second torch, which the house-keeper accepted solemnly. Delphine fixed her with a stern gaze.

'I'll take you as far as the cellar. Once you're inside, lock the door behind you and go to the room with the ale kegs. There's a trapdoor under the sack. It leads to a tunnel.' A murmur rose from the group. 'Keep going until you reach the beach. Then run to Pigg. Call the army, call the navy. Tell them it's an invasion.'

Mrs Hagstrom frowned at the torch in her palm. She snapped her fist shut.

'And where will you be?'

'Rescuing my father.'

'No you bloody well won't.' The blacksmith, Mr Wightman, elbowed his way to the front of the group. His shirt sleeves were rolled up. The darkness turned the dent in his skull to a black pit. 'This is no place for a twelve-year-old.'

'I'm thirteen.'

'Thank you for untying us. The men will take over from here. Give me that gun.'

'One step closer and I'll give you both barrels.'

Mr Wightman moved to take the sawn-off and she aimed it at his head.

'You're mad.' He turned to the others. 'She's mad.'

Mother stepped out of the crowd. She looked Delphine up and down. Something in her expression had hardened. The old keenness had returned to her eyes.

'I'm going with her.'

Mr Wightman threw incredulous glares at the other men.

'Are you just going to stand there? They'll be slaughtered.' He waited for someone to agree. 'Well, I won't have it.' He turned to Mother and folded his scarred arms. 'You can't go.'

Mother faced him squarely. 'And how do you intend to stop us?'

She crossed to where Delphine stood and placed a hand on her daughter's shoulder.

Mr Wightman hiked his folded arms a little higher. 'You won't shoot me.'

'No,' said Mother. 'Just ignore you.'

'You're not coming with me,' said Delphine.

'That goes for you too,' Mother said, not unkindly. 'I've made my decision.'

Professor Carmichael looked around the room. Beneath his green sweater, his shoulders rose and fell as he sighed.

'I'll go too.'

'You can't,' said Delphine.

'Nonsense. I can do what I like.'

'But . . . but . . . ' She couldn't very well threaten to shoot him too. 'You're too big. They'll spot you immediately.'

'Well, perhaps that'll provide the distraction you need. Ah! Don't bother with your counter arguments, Miss Venner. My mind is made up.'

'All right,' she said. She pulled herself upright. 'Well, then. Follow me.'

She switched off her torch and stepped into the corridor. She thought she saw a flicker of movement at the far end, held her breath, listening. Through the ringing in her ears, she heard the guests clustered behind her, panting, the rasp of Professor Carmichael's blocked sinuses.

'Okay,' she whispered.

She had gone a few paces before she realised nobody was following her. She glanced back. 'What's going on?'

'It's Alice,' said the Professor. 'She won't move.'

Delphine returned to the scullery. Alice was sitting on a chair, fingers knitted across her eyes, shaking her head. She breathed in jagged sips.

'Come on, now,' said Mr Wightman. 'You're going to get us all killed.'

Alice began to rock. Delphine thought she could make out the mumbled edges of the Lord's Prayer.

'Please, Alice,' said Delphine. 'We have to go.'

Alice shrank into herself.

'What are we going to do?' said the Professor.

Delphine felt fabric brush her arm, then Mother was at Alice's side. Mother laid an arm around Alice's shoulder. Alice whimpered and flinched. Mother leant in very close. She spoke briskly in Alice's ear:

'Alice, dear. You've been working too hard and you've exhausted yourself. All this is just your worn-out brain playing tricks. We're going to take you to the village for a good, long rest, and when you wake up, you'll realise it was all just a silly dream.'

Alice did not reply.

'Alice, dear?' said Mother, her voice growing louder. 'It's time to go. Now, do you think you can help me walk, because I've hurt my ankle and I'm not very good on it.'

Alice opened her eyes. She looked at Mother.

'Please,' said Mother. 'I don't think I can manage on my own.'

Alice nodded. 'All right, Mrs Venner.'

'Thank you, Alice. That's very kind of you.'

Alice got up from her chair and let Mother lean on her – though Delphine noticed that Mother did not lean very hard. 'We're ready,' Mother said.

Delphine stepped into the dark hallway. Moving on the balls of her feet, the sawn-off at her waist, she led the group back east, towards the cellar.

Once they were gone, she and Mother and the Professor would head back to the gun room. She was breaking her word to Mr Garforth, but he had wanted her to abandon Daddy just to save idiots like Mr Wightman. She had to try. No matter that Mother couldn't shoot – in tight corridors a trench shotgun would do the aiming for her.

Delphine reached the cellar door, gingerly turned the key in the lock.

'Okay,' she said. 'You're free to go.'

A shout made her spin round. In the gloom, she saw a short figure.

Miss DeGroot stepped out of the shadows, holding a handkerchief to her mouth and a hand up in apology.

'Sorry,' she whispered.

'Patience!' said the Professor. 'God almighty, I thought you were . . . Where have you been?'

She did not answer. Delphine turned back to the cellar door. She lowered the sawn-off, touched the door knob and felt a small cold pressure against her temple.

'Put down your gun.'

Delphine swallowed.

'Now,' said Miss DeGroot.

'This isn't funny,' said the Professor. 'Pay . . . oh God.'

Delphine felt a shadow fall across her.

'What are you doing?' she hissed. 'We have to go.'

'Drop the gun,' said Miss DeGroot.

'But – '

'Last warning.'

Delphine crouched. She set down the sawn-off.

'Good girl.' She heard Miss DeGroot kick it across the floor. 'Now turn around slow.'

Delphine turned, her hands raised, to find a hulking minotaur filling the passageaway. Her gut sank. It breathed in deep, grating tides. Its hide was Guinness-black, its horns a harp. Fluid glistened in the pinks of its eyes. It stooped and picked up the sawn-off at its hooves.

Miss DeGroot stepped away and trained her gun on the entire group. She had pulled a pearl-grip baby hammerless – a pistol that, even in her satin-gloved hand, looked petite. The grip fitted inside her palm, the barrel extending just past her index finger. It was a pop gun, a piece of jewellery basically – the kind of dinky joke gangsters' molls were always pulling in stories.

It scarcely qualified as a gun at all.

Mother spoke: 'Patience, what the Hell are you – '

'Shut up.' Miss DeGroot jabbed the snub nose at Mother. She turned to the looming bullman. 'Now do you believe me? Come, lieutenant – let's take them to your master.'

CHAPTER 29

VOYAGE AU CENTRE DE LA TERRE

H enry followed stone steps that curved downwards. Moisture clung to bas-relief carvings of smocked peasants bowing before minotaurs. As he descended, a beery smell grew stronger.

The Little Gentlemen followed with their tools and fuses and big aluminium bowls, negotiating each deep-cut step with precise hops. Henry reached the bottom, and stopped.

He listened.

'Sounds like those vesperi were the last two on guard,' he said. 'They weren't expecting a counterattack. Right. Two need to stay here and rig up some frustrations. Also – we need a channeller.'

One of the scarabs extended a skinny arm from within its wine-coloured shell. Henry nodded. Two more took the sack containing the traps. The rest of the Little Gentlemen followed him down into the tunnel. The tunnel went south for some time, before opening out into a grotto.

Henry put down his shotgun. He flashed his torchbeam around the chamber. Six lifesize statues – two harka, two vesperi and two human – stood facing inwards, water dripping onto their heads, their faces striped with milky trails of limestone. Set into the floor where their gazes met, surrounded by a low ridge of stone, was a pool.

He walked to the edge, boots splashing through puddles. The pool was in the middle of the chamber, its waters thick and black. Bubbles swelled like toad gullets before coughing gouts of vapour: *pah*. It stunk of yeast and burning peat. The dark waters churned clockwise.

Carved into the ridge surrounding the pool was a basin, in which lay a creature identical to the Little Gentlemen, except coral-white, its segmented shell lustrous with steam.

He grasped the creature lying in the basin. It was almost too hot to hold, but his old hands were callused and tough. Gritting his teeth against the pain, he pulled. He felt resistance, then it clunked loose. Immediately the pool became flat and still. The scarab bucked in his grip. He placed it on the stone floor and pressed a boot to the hard ridges of its thorax. He broke his shotgun, removed the cartridges and slipped them into his pocket. He closed the breech, turned the gun butt downwards, and drove it into the creature's skull.

Mouthparts crunched. He hit it again and again.

When he looked up, the Little Gentlemen were watching, motionless.

'I'm sorry,' he said, 'but we're at war.'

A loud snap echoed from the top of the stairway.

'We have less time than I thought,' said Henry. He took the map from his pocket and studied the wall. 'Set charges here, here and here.' He indicated the places with a piece of chalk, marking large white crosses. The Little Gentlemen split into teams and got to work, unstacking the aluminium basins, cutting fuses. The last of their number, the one who had put its arm up, stood waiting before Henry. He picked it up, gently. 'If you'll excuse me.'

Henry set it down on the lip of the inert pool. The scarab regarded the stone basin through big, luminous eyes.

'Never you fear,' said Henry. 'I won't abandon you. You'll be all right.'

Even as he said it, he felt stones in his belly, a cold hard hunch that he was wrong.

The creature lay down in the socket. Nothing happened. It looked up at Mr Garforth, then its irises shrank and its eyes turned to oil rainbows. The pool groaned, heaving and slopping.

Slowly, its black waters began to churn counterclockwise.

CHAPTER 30

BAL MASQUÉ

Ten people sat round the edges of the banqueting hall, tied to chairs with wrists behind backs. Delphine's crown throbbed from where the minotaur had walloped her for walking too slow. Beneath the eight silver moons of the lunar mandala, forty or more vesperi gave off a musk of cured meat and tar. No two were the same shade of black-brown. They had the keen muzzles of pine martens, with complicated fanning layers of cartilage, like giant leaves. She breathed through her nose, glaring at Miss DeGroot, who stood by the roaring fire, cupping a very large glass of cognac.

In the centre of the rug, bound at the wrists and kneeling, was Mr Propp.

The collar of Propp's shirt dangled raggedly. His right eye had swollen to a slit. Each time he inhaled, he winced.

Oil lamps burned around the room, casting a gentle, fluxing light across the antique shields and oak panels, picking out the jewels in the great polished warhammer. A minotaur – Mr Garforth had called them *harka* – stood guard on either door, one armed with Delphine's sawn-off. Their thick snout rings rested upon their upper lips, rising and falling as they breathed.

Her bandolier lay crumpled by the sideboard. On the far side of the room, silent now for ten minutes, sat the masked figure she had seen in the Great Hall doorway. She recognised the uniform from the oil painting above the smoking-room fireplace – the ankle-length leather coat, the wide-brimmed hat, the smooth, bone-white beak. A plague doctor.

The masked stranger drummed leather-gauntleted fingers on the arm of an antique chair. The beakmask had little grooved fangs carved along it, as if clenched in a furious rictus.

To the right of the chair stood the monster which had shot Dr Lansley. Dressed in old-fashioned coachman's garb, it had the splayed ears and hard, furtive eyes of a vesperi but was much bigger, its nose-leaf a sprawl of broken ridges. Fur grew unevenly across its face and head, exposing red blotches that might have been welts or ringworm scars. A pair of tattered, useless wings sprouted through holes in its jacket. From its belt hung a cudgel and two pistols. Three fingers of its right hand had fused into a claw.

On the masked figure's left stood a tall, slim man in black riding cloak, tawny silk waistcoat and breeches of rich ultramarine. The skin across his high cheekbones and long neck was tanned, and his silky hair was the colour of chocolate. His only blemish was the wart on the end of his chin, accentuated by the way he held himself, head up, eyes half-lidded. It was this man who broke the silence.

'Ugly.'

His lower jaw jutted out to eject the word.

Miss DeGroot ceased studying the play of light in her brandy glass and turned slowly to face him. As she turned, Delphine watched her expression change from one of vacant fatigue to a smile, starting with the corners of her mouth and only after some apparent effort spreading to her eyes. She looked at the slim man.

'Did you say something?' The fireplace was heaped with logs; about her head, stray and shining blond hairs danced in the heat.

'Ugly.' The two syllables seemed to lodge in his throat. He regarded the floor darkly. 'Vulgar. Tawdry.'

'What is?'

'Address *me*!' The masked figure stamped a heavy riding boot against the hardwood floor, but – confusingly – it was the elegant thin man who spoke. '*Not the herald!*'

Miss DeGroot's eyelids fluttered. She made a show of rotating an extra five degrees to face the chair. She tilted her glass towards the masked figure.

'Forgive me, Peter. I'm still getting used to your . . . puppetry.'

Delphine's stomach lurched. Surely the person in the mask couldn't be Peter Stokeham?

Again, the beakmasked figure in the chair began to gesture but it was the slim, cloaked man on the figure's left who spoke.

'For the last time,' the slim man said, the masked figure thrusting a palm towards him in time with his words, 'Mr Cox is my Tongue.' The leather gauntlet swung towards the grotesque bat-monster. 'Mr Loosley is my Fist. Do not stare at my Tongue. Look at *me*.' And here, the masked figure in the chair leaned forward, pressing fingers to puffed-out chest. 'I am the one who speaks. They are merely my agents. And do not address me as "Peter".'

'Understood,' said Miss DeGroot. She tilted the cognac to her lips, hiding her expression. 'You are fond of rules.'

Delphine's heart clenched. Why was Miss DeGroot doing this? Was it an elaborate bluff?

'Ugly.' The slim man – was he Mr Cox? – spoke again, and as he did the masked figure behind him rose, with none of the decrepitude of a man more than a hundred and twenty-five years old. Delphine glanced between the two strangers, straining to make sense of their relationship.

Firelight played across circular lenses of tinted red glass set into the beakmask's eye sockets. The mask tilted. Its little carved teeth emerged from shadow, and, for an instant, the bird became a wolf. 'Look at it.' As Cox spoke, the masked figure pointed at a painting beside the fireplace: panels of colour separated by stripes and swirls, suggesting cobbles, a crowd, the curve of a naked breast. 'Since I have been away, that boy has littered my house with degenerate rubbish. Mr Loosley.' The beakmask turned to the monster. 'If you please.'

Vesperi scattered out of the way as the bat-monster crossed the room. It had nothing of their slender frame – it rippled with sinewy power. Miss DeGroot flinched and stepped aside as the creature known as 'Mr Loosley' tore the painting from the wall. It kicked through the canvas, then dashed the frame against the floor until there was only kindling. It – she could not bear to think of something so grotesque as a 'he' – gathered up the pieces and flung them into the fire.

'Peter,' said Miss DeGroot. 'You promised me something.'

The masked stranger – could it really be Peter Stokeham, the Silent Earl? – turned to face her. Again, Mr Cox spoke. As far as Delphine could tell, he did so not on the masked figure's behalf, but somehow *as* the figure.

'Give me the child.'

Delphine's throat closed. She strained her wrists against her bonds.

'That was not one of our terms,' said Miss DeGroot. 'I helped you get here. I even anticipated your guests' escape bid and cut them off. I've done all you asked of me and more.' She sipped her brandy and eyed the faceless stranger over the rim of her glass. 'It's time you kept your word. Stokeham family honour demands it.'

'I want the child,' said Cox.

'I'm sure Ivan can help you with that, can't you, Ivan?'

Without opening his eyes, Propp shook his head. 'They shot Dr Lansley.'

Miss DeGroot threw a glance over her shoulder. 'What? Where is he?'

'Patience. He's dead.'

The surface of Miss DeGroot's brandy began to flutter. She looked round the seated captives, as if she suspected a lie. She turned to the figure in the mask.

'You said no guns. You promised . . . '

'To take every precaution against unnecessary loss of life,' said Cox. 'And so we did. Including that of our soldiers. The Doctor's death was an unfortunate accident – the type that befalls all who find themselves between Mr Loosley and his target.'

'They killed him,' said Propp, his voice breaking. 'They killed Titus.'

Miss DeGroot gazed at the expressionless, bone-white mask. Gradually, the confusion left her face. Her brandy became millpond-still.

'No, Ivan. You did.'

Propp opened his eyes and looked up at her. 'Patience. My dear friend. I forgive you.'

Miss DeGroot turned. She walked until they were face to face. With Propp on his knees, she was slightly the taller. She cupped her brandy goblet, holding it up like a gravedigger's lantern.

'You forgive me,' she said quietly. She half-closed her eyes. 'How brave. How very spiritual you must be.' She snatched her free hand into a fist and shook it gently between them, a silver bracelet flashing on her wrist. 'I shall treasure your forgiveness, Ivan. Just as I treasured your promise of a cure.' She pressed the fist to her breastbone, and her eyes became thinner still. 'Just as everyone who trusted you treasured your promises. Now . . . ' Miss DeGroot closed her eyes, her forehead almost touching Propp's. Her voice was so low Delphine could barely hear her. 'Titus is gone, and that is a tragedy. I never wished for harm to come to anyone, but the past can't be changed. Let's make sure no one else is harmed.' Her eyes flicked open. 'Tell them where the child is, Ivan.'

She held his gaze, her eyes inches from his – held it so long that even Delphine had to glance away. At last, she stood back.

Mr Cox sniffed approvingly.

'Make amends, Ivan,' he said. 'Don't draw these innocents into your game. Give us the girl.'

Propp hung his head. 'I cannot.'

Miss DeGroot slung her brandy glass into the fire, where it exploded in hissing blue flame.

'Damn you, Ivan!' she said. 'Of course you can! Of *course* you can!' She exhaled sharply through her teeth and put her hands to her temples. 'Please. I . . . I don't want things to get worse. You can put an end to this. You can correct your mistake.'

'They will kill everyone,' said Propp.

'Oh, don't be so theatrical,' said Mr Cox. 'We gain nothing from unprovoked murder.'

'You lie. You gain silence.'

Miss DeGroot stood panting, blond cowlick bobbing with each breath. 'He has a point, Peter. Prove that you keep your promises. Cure me.'

'One does not administer the honours like a spoonful of medicine,' said Cox. 'There are protocols and proprieties and . . .'

'Yes, yes, yes, your letter explained it all quite thoroughly. Now – are you going to turn me into an immortal monster or aren't you?'

Mr Cox folded his long thin arms. The figure they all seemed to think was Stokeham nodded, impassive behind the mask, then spoke through Cox:

'Mr Loosley. The box.'

CHAPTER 31

A LITTLE MORE THAN KIN

The scarred beast known as Mr Loosley set a small lacquered pine cabinet down in the centre of the room. The cabinet was about two feet tall, standing on four brass legs. A key winked in Loosley's dark palm. The monster unlocked the door and took out a jar.

Delphine glanced over at Mother, who sat on a piano stool, wrists bound behind her back. Mother held her right arm at a funny angle, as if she had injured it. When Delphine caught her eye, Mother nodded and raised her eyebrow. A little baffled, Delphine returned the gesture in a show of solidarity.

She tensed her wrists against their knots. Even if she got her hands free, she was hopelessly outnumbered. But what else was there to do? Needs must.

'I suggest you sit down,' said Mr Cox, tamping tobacco into the bowl of a long clay pipe.

'I'll stand,' said Miss DeGroot. She unclasped her silver necklace and dropped it on the floor, fine chain pooling round an oval pendant.

'As you wish. In your own time, Mr Loosley.'

Mr Propp began shuffling on his knees towards her. 'Patience. No.'

Loosley stepped forward and struck Propp across the jaw. On the settee, Alice let out a whimper. Propp moaned.

Loosley backed away from Propp, snarling, and unstoppered the jar. Delphine watched, her mouth gummy. Nothing happened. She squinted. Iridescent in the air above the jar, a butterfly.

No, a hornet.

It bobbed fatly, wings shimmering in the hearth light. It was the biggest she had ever seen. Delphine blinked, her eyes dry and sore from staring. When she looked again, Loosley was smearing a lard-like substance on Miss DeGroot's neck, dipping a claw-hand into a small earthenware pot. Loosley put the lid back on the pot, wiped its hand on a purple handkerchief, and retreated.

The hornet emitted an oscillating drone as it swayed in thermals above the fireplace. It was huge, big as a hummingbird. Delphine felt sick.

Miss DeGroot closed her eyes and tilted her head back. Moving in broad, lazy sweeps, the hornet drew closer. It landed on her throat. She gasped.

The hornet dipped its proboscis into the thick white paste. The entire banqueting hall fell silent, forty vesperi watching with what might have been reverence, or terror, or both. Delphine curled her toes inside her stockings. The roots of her hair tingled, and an unpleasant tickling sensation ran across her forearms. The huge hornet twitched its wings.

It plunged its stinger into Miss DeGroot's neck.

In the fluctuating light of the fire, Delphine swore she saw the hornet's black abdomen pumping obscenely. The hornet withdrew its stinger and flew away, reeling, love-drunk. Loosley swung the jar overarm, caught it and jammed the stopper back in.

Miss DeGroot rubbed the spot where she had been stung. She smiled woozily.

'Well, now . . . that wasn't so bad.'

Mr Cox exhaled a wreath of pipesmoke. Miss DeGroot rested a palm against the fireplace. Her other hand went to her throat. She took a couple of convulsive, clucking gulps. Her lips worked, purpling. She grasped at the air, pivoted and fell, cracking her head on the wall as she went. She writhed. She stopped moving.

'I did tell her to sit down,' said Mr Cox. He turned to Propp.

'People are so very poor at acting in their best interests. A kind of bloodymindedness, wouldn't you say, Ivan?'

'Stop this.'

Loosley belted Propp with a claw-hand.

'*Do not! Look! At the herald!*' Cox was screaming in Propp's ear.

Propp spat clotted blood. He turned to Stokeham.

'Please,' he said, a red droplet running from a cut beneath his eye. 'No more.'

'Where is the child?' said Cox.

'I told you. I do not know. I sent her far away.'

'This.' As Cox spoke, the masked Stokeham held up an index finger. 'This is precisely what I mean. I give you every opportunity to end our mutual suffering – to *save lives*, no less – and instead you play games. Ivan, please.' Cox and Stokeham's gestures began mirroring each other. The beakmask swayed left and right, unreadable. 'I know she was here just yesterday – your "dear friend",' they both gestured to Miss DeGroot prostrate by the skirting board, 'told me so. We've been chatting for some time. Do you know,' Cox and Stokeham turned to the rest of the captives, 'he tried to fake his own suicide? Fired a shot just before Mr Loosley broke the door down. Red candlewax, here,' Cox drew a snaking line down his forehead, Stokeham tracing a finger between the mask's red lenses, 'then sat himself slumped in a wheelchair, as if he'd blown his brains out. Everything he does is theatre.' The pair turned back to Propp. 'You simply cannot help but lie. You are an incorrigible mountebank.'

Propp raised his eyes piously. 'I am dance teacher.'

'Your impertinence will be the death of you, boy. I will not permit a tealeaf-reading gypsy to dictate terms to me under my own roof. Presently my staff are searching the Hall room by room. There can be no hiding place because I *built* every one of them.'

'Well, you didn't think to look in the tunnels!'

Everyone in the room turned to stare at Delphine.

Mr Cox raised an eyebrow. He began marching towards her, vesperi dividing to let him through. Behind him, the birdmask swivelled, turning its tinted sockets upon her. A cold sickness spread from her chest into her throat. Stokeham gestured and Cox spoke:

'What did you say?'

'I said you didn't think to check the tunnels, did you?' But already her bravado was dying in her throat. 'I got out and I got back in.'

Cox stopped in front of her. 'Who is this?'

'Leave her alone!' said Mother. 'For pity's sake, she's just a child.'

Delphine stared into Mr Cox's cobalt-blue eyes. His face was sharp and young. Even his wart gleamed.

'My name is Delphine Venner,' she said, 'and when my father finds you, he – '

'Don't look at the herald!' Cox lunged at her, flecks of spit peppering her cheeks. 'Look at *me*, damn your eyes!' Stokeham punctuated each of Cox's syllables with a boot stamp. 'Look! At! Me!' Mr Loosley was striding across the banqueting hall towards Delphine.

'No!' Mother rocked forward on the piano stool. 'Don't you dare touch her!'

'Enough!' Cox silenced the room with a flourish of his arms. Mr Loosley stopped. Cox turned, walked back towards Propp. 'Enough of this, this . . . circus. Ivan, you will tell me where the child is. I will execute one of your followers every ten minutes until you do.'

Gasps and moans from the guests. Alice the maid began chattering hysterically.

'You can't do this!' cried one of the gentlemen guests. His ceramic dentures sat oddly in his mouth, adding a slurping sibilance to his speech. 'My editors expect me to place a phone call at ten p.m. precisely. If they don't hear from me, they'll know something's afoot and call for the police.'

'Perhaps you doubt my resolve,' said Cox. 'Mr Loosley,' Stokeham clapped hands at the monstrous valet, 'bring in that feckless son of mine.'

Mr Loosley left the room with two vesperi. They returned dragging Lord Alderberen. He had been stripped to the waist. His doughy bluish skin was patterned with damson welts and black bruises. His trousers were torn. He sobbed dryly.

The vesperi dumped Lord Alderberen at the boots of Stokeham.

'Dear friend,' said Propp, looking up into the beakmask. 'Please. Show your face. Speak to me. Not to talk through puppet.'

Mr Cox breathed, glowering. 'Your request for unmediated contact disgusts me. You don't understand at all, do you? This is precisely why you would never have received the honours. Ah, come now, don't look so shocked. Isn't that what this is all about? What other bounty would make kidnapping my daughter worth the risk?' Mr Loosley rolled up its cuffs, exposing lean, mutilated forearms. 'Anything to keep your marrow from the maggots, eh?' *Slap.* 'Admit it, damn you!' *Slap.* 'Admit it!'

Cox and Loosley backed away. Cox was panting. 'Dogs like you have brought this once-glorious country to its knees. England used to treat the world as a master treats his hounds. Our justice was swift, dispassionate. Now we're down in the kennels, fighting over scraps. Our finest men died on the battlefields of Europe, and in their place rise cabals of cosmopolitan adventurers: rats who scurry and pilfer but know neither the harrow nor the sword. Even now, the great rural estates are fading, the powerhouses of northern industry, and little lanterns of Britishness gutter and snuff in India, Ireland and the Orient.

'Well. I bring a new way. Mr Loosley.'

The two vesperi grabbed Lord Alderberen by his bare arms and wrenched him up onto his knees. Delphine was surprised at their strength. Lord Alderberen's face was wet. They turned him towards Stokeham.

'Look at you.' Cox spat the words. 'It sickens me to think I once called you my son.'

The sturdy buttons of Stokeham's overcoat gleamed as the beak-mask regarded a rumpled, greyblue old man. Lord Alderberen moaned.

'Stokeham blood finds its truest expression in you, Lazarus. Cowardice is the family's Habsburg jaw. Your whole line has been a failure, culminating with that supreme defective, Arthur. Smothering him in his crib would have been a mercy. For dogs like you and Ivan, death is a mercy.'

Stokeham clapped. Mr Loosley unhooked a duelling pistol from his belt, uncapped a powder horn and tapped out some gunpowder.

'No!' Delphine jerked forward, kicking and scrambling. Three vesperi turned, their eyes widening. One drew its dagger; the other two grabbed her shoulders, their thin fingers biting into her flesh. She tried to wrench loose but they dragged her back down, chair legs creaking beneath her. 'Don't do it!'

Loosley withdrew the cleaning rod and slid it back into place under the barrel.

'You can stop this, Ivan,' said Cox. He took a puff on his pipe. 'Where is the girl?'

'Oh!' Propp rolled his head. 'No, no, no . . . He did not know. It is not his fault.'

'Where is the girl?'

Loosley took five paces back, raised the gun.

'No,' said Propp. 'Shoot me. He is your *son*. Take me.'

'The girl, Ivan.'

Lord Alderberen tried to twist his head away. His false teeth were missing; he babbled, smacking his gums. His upper lip retreated into his skull.

'You will regret,' said Propp. 'For as long as you live, you will regret.'

'Regrets die,' said Cox. 'I am for ever.'

Stokeham turned to face the door. Mr Cox took a step back. Against the glow of the fire, he became a silhouette.

'Don't!' said Delphine.

Propp closed his eyes.

Lord Alderberen breathed a single word:

'Mercy.'

CHAPTER 32

THE ISLE IS FULL OF NOISES

Gideon Venner was very ill.

Half-deranged, he walked weightlessly through empty corridors. The sling round his shoulders jankled with firebombs: turps-filled milk bottles stuffed with rag wicks. He sloshed turpentine over the rug as he went. Arthur had explained. There were 7s in everything. He was setting them free.

The carpet felt cool beneath his bare feet. Its pattern of orange swirls pointed the way. Doors hung torn from their hinges. He walked into the library. Books had crawled from the shelves and lay scattered across the floor like strange, beached crustaceans. Ripped pages quivered in the breeze from the jagged window. Spines scintillated in the moonlight.

He lit a firebomb. Smoke rose in dirty yellow twists. He held it above his head. He was the sun. Shadows stretched and swung. He looked up and watched smoke fold against the ceiling's sunken panels. He was upside-down and the smoke was falling – darkness pouring out of him.

A mosaic showed Arthur slaughtering a bull. Gideon planted his heels and threw the milk bottle.

Glass broke with a high sweet note. Golden ivy bloomed up the wall, dripped onto the floor, spread to the edge of the bookshelves. A wave of love burst against his skin.

Sweat soothed his forehead. His hands tingled.

There was a noise at the door. Angels had appeared. They ran towards him, their black wings spread, gabbling in one of the seven forgotten tongues of Heaven. He lit another firebomb, the wick curling shyly. He threw the bottle and the angels' dark flesh peeled away. They grew fierce new plumage, waving arms in praise of God. They were perfect. He had freed them.

He watched as they lay down to sleep, and then they were gone.

He was surrounded by light. The flames pointed to the open window, urging him to jump.

'Can't leave yet,' he said, or Arthur said, or God said. His eyes welled. He had to free everyone. He understood now.

Salty smoke bathed his wounds. He followed the path Arthur had left for him between the flames.

The milk bottles chimed against his heart. The heat on his back made him strong. He would find them – Anne and Delphy and Mr Propp, everyone – and he would set them free.

Gideon walked into the burning corridor, full of love.

CHAPTER 33

GOOD SERVANT, BAD MASTER

Cox and Loosley stood over the slumped body of Lazarus Stokeham, 4th Earl of Alderberen. Loosley hooked the smoking pistol into its belt. Cox's face was a picture of disgust.

'Typical Englishman. Incapable of meeting his death with dignity.' He sucked on his pipe, grimaced. 'Consider yourself disinherited.'

Loosley pop-clicked a command and two vesperi hoisted Lord Alderberen by his armpits. Delphine saw a spreading darkness around the old man's crotch.

Loosley had shot deliberately wide.

'Dump this cur and his wheelchair outside,' said Cox. 'I never want to see him again. The Alderberen dynasty is over. This is the age of House Dellapeste.'

The vesperi began dragging him.

'Please!' Alderberen's words were gummy and slurred. 'Let me prove myself! Don't leave me again!' He tried to dig his heels in as they pulled him across the Persian rug. It rucked up beneath him. 'Please! Oh God! Oh Jesus! Mother!' A third vesperi struck him on the temple with the pommel of its dagger. He went limp.

A glossy smear led from Cox and Loosley to the door. Cox glanced at Stokeham, who observed with folded arms, blank as an ivory chess knight.

A wheezing vesperi appeared at the door. The harka with the sawn-off clumped over and listened as the vesperi chitter-pipped something. The harka returned to Stokeham and spoke in heavily accented English.

'Endlessness. The vault has been taken.'

Delphine jolted upright in her seat. Her head ached, and it was hard to make her eyes focus.

Mr Cox appeared at Stokeham's side.

'What do you mean, "taken"?'

'It is no longer under our control, Endlessness.'

'How can that be? Who has taken it?'

The harka dipped its snout. 'We do not know.'

Delphine felt a rush of jittery excitement. Mr Garforth had made it past the guards. Stokeham rounded on Propp.

'What's going on?' said Cox. 'What have you done?'

Propp was kneeling, his eyes closed. He said nothing.

Loosley hit him. The liquid black toecap of the beast's polished boot drove into Propp's stomach again and again and Propp doubled-up, retching.

'Right.' Cox and Stokeham snapped their right hands into fists. Cox addressed the harka wielding Delphine's sawn-off. Its fierce gaze never left the beakmask. 'Take a cohort. Seize the channel and kill everyone responsible. Mr Loosley – you go with them. Ensure my will is performed.'

Loosley ran a claw through the patchy fur on his scalp and gave a snort that passed for assent. He chitter-clicked something in the vesperi tongue and a dozen vesperi left the main force to join him. The silent bullman fell in behind him.

The cohort marched out. Stokeham began to pace, boots clomping on hardwood floor, overcoat whipping out with each abrupt about-face. The white beak pointed downward.

Delphine felt the rope biting her wrists. She itched to rip free and rush at Stokeham. Mother was making a face at her again. Delphine could not tell if it was intended to convey worry or support.

The beakmask tilted up, towards the clock on the fireplace. Stokeham produced a pocket watch, flipped it open.

'It's about time I executed my first prisoner,' said Cox. He leant over Propp, who lay on his side, coughing. 'Quite sure you haven't had a change of heart?'

Propp shook his blood-smeared head. 'Look. See what you have become.'

'Oh, spare me. You've murdered more than two dozen of my staff this evening. Where was your pity then? Where was your mercy?' Cox turned to the guests. 'Now . . . which of you shall it be? How about . . . ' His forefinger moved up and down the line of prisoners. 'You.' It came to rest on Delphine.

'Don't. You. Dare,' said Mother. 'Shoot me, you horrible little man. Shoot me in cold blood. Go on!' She shunted her stool towards Stokeham. The legs growled against the wooden floor. 'Do it. You're a bully and a coward. Without your thugs, you're nothing. Take them away and I'd slit your belly like a pig's.'

Mr Cox flashed her a bored glance. He beckoned the harka with the rifle.

Mother spat. 'Look me in the eye!' She dragged her stool forward another couple of inches and vesperi moved to intercept her. 'Take off that ridiculous cow-skull and *show your face*!'

'Right.' Cox's fists rose to his ears. He pointed to Delphine. 'Shoot her.' His finger swung to Mother. 'Then her.'

The harka lifted its rifle, pressing the brass cheekplate to its square jaw.

'Stop!' said Delphine. 'I'll tell you! All right, I'll tell you!'

The rifle muzzle dipped.

'Speak quickly,' said Cox.

Delphine closed her eyes. 'She's . . . she is in the stables.'

'Impossible. We checked there.' Cox turned to the bullman. 'Kill her. She's wasting my time.'

'No!' Delphine had no idea what she was saying, just knew it had to convince. 'She's in a secret room. Under the floor.'

'Nonsense,' said Cox, a note of uncertainty entering his voice. 'I oversaw the design of every concealed passage, door and annex on the estate. There's nothing under the stables but mud and rock.'

Propp raised his head to look at Delphine. 'Do not lie. You will only anger.'

'The room is new.' She turned to Propp. 'There's no point resisting him. I'm sorry.'

Propp's face flickered with confusion. Delphine widened her eyes, nodding. Propp stared at her. His expression changed.

'No!' he said. 'You fool! Once they have her, they kill us all!'

Cox turned to the vesperi, swatting hair out of his eyes. 'Two. Stables. Now.' The pair nearest him performed a fist salute and began marching from the room. 'If this proves to be some asinine ruse, I will execute you and three others immediately.'

Delphine glanced at the swarm of vesperi still remaining, the gigantic bullman at Stokeham's side.

'Wait,' said Delphine. 'She's not alone.'

'What.'

'You didn't think we'd leave her unprotected, did you?' She made herself stare into the mask's dead lenses. 'She has two armed body-guards.'

Cox's eyes thinned. 'What are their names?'

'Mr Enfield and Mr Vickers. They've got trench guns.'

Mr Propp feigned an anguished gasp.

Stokeham studied the fire for a moment. Cox closed his eyes. He nodded.

'Very well.' He addressed the harka. 'The stables are the outbuilding on your left as you leave the house. Lead a cohort inside. Search the building *thoroughly*. If the child is present, recapture her by any means necessary. If she is not, return here immediately, where you may kill this one in whichever fashion you please.' He pointed at Delphine.

'By your will, Endlessness.' The harka spoke in deep, accented English. It bowed to Stokeham, before leading a dozen vesperi out the door.

Mr Cox cast a worried glance over the remaining troops. There were almost as many guests as vesperi. He peered at Delphine.

'Pray that he does not return empty-handed.'

Delphine had no idea what to do next. Her bluff had bought them ten minutes, at best. She might have evened the numbers, but her fellow guests were tied and unarmed, most of them in no condition to fight. She glanced at Propp, hoping he had a plan, but he did not meet her gaze. Professor Carmichael sat beside Mrs Hagstrom, his arms bound, stubbly chin against his chest. His eyes were closed. He was squirming and grinding his teeth.

She watched Stokeham standing at the hearth. The masked figure was so unlike the pale, meek man she had seen in the portrait. The Silent Earl was supposed to have been shy and kindly. How could a person live so long? Who on earth was the child Stokeham wanted? Delphine had never seen another girl at the Hall in all the months she had lived there. What could she bargain with?

Miss DeGroot's legs twitched. Her palm slapped the floor like a landed trout.

'Ah,' said Cox. 'She's coming round.' He strolled to her side. 'Now you will be privileged to witness a truly rare event: the birth of a peer.' He went down on one knee and, with obvious distaste, slipped a palm under Miss DeGroot's brow. 'I regret the vulgarity of using my herald as midwife, but Mr Loosley is engaged in other business.' He rolled her onto her back. She was pallid. Her eyes were closed. Her throat was swollen and purple. 'Death is a judgement upon the unworthy.' She began convulsing silently in his arms. 'Most are unworthy.'

Miss DeGroot spluttered and hacked. She opened her eyes.

She whispered something to Cox. He let out a trickling chuckle. 'No,' he said. 'Not quite.'

'I feel . . . ' Miss DeGroot frowned at the ceiling. 'Unbalanced.'

'As you should.' He slid his palm from beneath her head. 'You are an abomination, madam. You exist in defiance of natural law. Your every breath is a howl of naked rebellion against the Creator.'

Miss DeGroot smiled, rocking the back of her skull against the hardwood.

'Abomination. I like that.' She bucked and clutched the swelling in her throat. 'Oh, oh. It hurts.'

'Try to savour it,' said Cox, rising. 'It may be the last true pain you experience.'

'Oh, oh.'

While Miss DeGroot moaned to herself, Stokeham stood at the

hearth, leather-gauntleted hands clasped behind back, the fingers of one hand encircling the wrist of the other. The skirts of the heavy, dark coat came almost to the floor. In profile, Stokeham's silhouette was a black scythe.

At last, Miss DeGroot was still. She lay with her back arched, breathing.

Cox offered his hand. 'Allow me to help you up.'

She swatted it away. 'Don't touch me.'

'As you wish.' Cox stepped back, massaging his knuckles with a thumb.

Miss DeGroot started to get up, using the wall for support. Her blond hair was damp with perspiration. She tested her balance, hesitated. She stroked the wallpaper.

'My fingers are numb.'

'The honours manifest in different ways,' said Cox. 'The full effects may take time to . . . emerge.'

'And my tumour . . . '

'Gone. Arising purges the body of impurities. But your elevation is not complete until you anoint your first handmaiden.' Mr Cox closed his eyes as he spoke, folding his fingers round the hem of his jacket. 'Those in your service are blessed with bearing the discomforts of the flesh on your behalf. They enhance your noble talents while freeing you from petty suffering. Only then may you truly rise above the mundane and the vulgar and turn your mind towards eternity.'

Miss DeGroot took a couple of tentative steps, her face full of wonder.

'So, I'm . . . alive? For ever?'

'You are perpetual.'

She examined her hands with an infant's curiosity. 'I cannot die.'

The corner of Cox's mouth went up. 'Unless you decide to crawl into a furnace or bathe in acid, yes. This is a gift of the honours.'

'And my . . . helpers . . . will they live forever too?'

Cox shrugged. 'If you look after them, certainly. The ravages of age will not touch them, but unlike a genuine peer they are suscep-tible to frailties of the flesh – destruction, poison, disease.' Delphine thought she detected a twitch in Cox's eye. 'The honours confer a hardy constitution upon footmen and handmaidens, but make no mistake – their gifts are in no way comparable to ours.'

'But still . . . I'd be granting them immortality.' She did not look at Stokeham as she said this. 'I'd be saving them.'

'To serve is a great privilege.'

'Mmm.' Miss DeGroot sniffed; her snub nose wrinkled. 'And if I prefer to remain . . . independent?'

'Then you prefer to remain a frail travesty of a peer. Your talents will burn dimly. Your ability to survive injury will be greatly arrested. Your enemies will seize upon your weakness, and rightly so. The agonies that may be inflicted upon a perpetual body are . . . substantial.'

'Yes, yes, all right. Don't milk it.' The colour had not yet returned to her cheeks, but the bulge in her neck was darkening. She pressed a palm to the ripe, soft flesh. 'Oh my. I think I'm ready.'

Delphine felt a queasy mix of panic and revulsion. In a few minutes the search party would return empty-handed, and if she had not thought of an escape plan she would die. She cast about the room for inspiration, for a useful object or means of escape, but there were just hard walls and armed vesperi and Stokeham, arms folded, Mr Cox wearing a cruel, smug leer that was surely duplicated beneath the mask.

Miss DeGroot began walking the line of tethered guests, her soles patting against the hardwood floor. She seemed unsure of what to do with her face – her expression kept switching between a show of intense dispassionate scrutiny, half-hearted smiles, and a sort of blanching distaste.

She lingered in front of Alice the maid, looking the girl up and down, cocking her head. Pink streaks broke up Alice's face. Her hair was undone, spilling forward like hanks of wool. She was shivering.

Miss DeGroot frowned and continued down the line. She stopped in front of Mrs Hagstrom.

'Miss.' Mrs Hagstrom's face was flushed. She raised her chin defiantly. 'The only service I'd care to render you is ripping your head clean from your shoulders.'

Miss DeGroot blinked and moved on.

She stopped in front of Delphine.

'Hello,' she said. Her blond hair was clumped in wild spikes. A smudge of cold cream glistened on her earlobe.

Delphine felt her head filling with anger and fear and a strange, needling pity. She could smell Miss DeGroot's citrusy perfume, and it made her think of the treehouse. She had unrolled the rope ladder. She had told Miss DeGroot everything. In fact . . .

Delphine felt breathless. She had given Miss DeGroot Kung's notes. Not a week later, Miss DeGroot had taken the grey book from Daddy's studio. Might Delphine have caused all this?

She tried to speak, but her jaw was shaking. She dug her nails into her palms.

'You must save us,' she said.

Miss DeGroot dropped her gaze. Her reply was almost too quiet to hear.

'I'm trying.'

Up close, the bulge in her throat was formed of little fluid-filled bumps, each one capped with a livid blotch. She swallowed, and they rippled.

Miss DeGroot called to Stokeham: 'I've chosen.'

Delphine felt her gorge rising. It was over. She had fought and resisted but it had not been enough. She shut her eyes.

'This one.'

Delphine looked. Miss DeGroot was pointing at the underkeeper, Reg Gillow.

Reg's arms were tied behind his back. The collar of his tan shirt was dark with sweat. He did not look at her when she walked over to him; he seemed barely conscious.

'I've watched him working around the estate.' She reached out and touched his temple. He twitched. 'He's young and resourceful.'

Cox raised his eyebrows. 'It is traditional for a woman to pick female attendants.'

'Is it.'

'It is.'

Over to Delphine's left, Alice began to sob. 'Don't you touch my Reggie!'

'Reggie? Oh.' Miss DeGroot clenched at the growth on her throat. 'Oh God . . . I think something's . . . oh . . . ' Her eyes rolled back in her head. A wet smacking sound began to insinuate itself in the nook of Delphine's ears. The vesperi averted their eyes. Cox relit his pipe.

Delphine watched as Miss DeGroot tightened her small white fingers over the blueing flesh in her throat. Buboes burst with a soft *paf*. The popped boils began extruding shining, tooth-coloured tubes. Miss DeGroot squeezed her boils. As the white tubes pattered to the floor Delphine saw what they were: a harvest of sticky, puckered grubs.

Miss DeGroot squeezed again and more grubs oozed out onto her hand. She held her hand to the light, the grubs turning translucent. The loose flesh of her throat hung honeycombed and shredded.

She moved the hand towards Reg. He snapped from his stupor and jerked his head away, kicking the floor.

'Don't touch me! Ali! Help me!'

Miss DeGroot hesitated.

Cox nodded at the vesperi either side of her. 'Hold him down.'

Two vesperi clambered onto the leather arms of the chair, pumping their wings for balance. They grabbed his head with eager, fine-furred hands, forcing his mouth open, wedging a dagger between his teeth. He howled, struggling in their grip, as Miss DeGroot brought her grub-covered hand closer, closer.

Her teeth were clenched. She was weeping.

'Don't fret, Reggie,' she said. 'Be an angel.'

Reg screwed his eyes shut. Miss DeGroot's fingers cast a lengthening shadow across his face. Delphine stared, her tummy churning, unable to watch, unable to turn away, unsure which was the greater betrayal.

Miss DeGroot smeared her hand across his face. She anointed him.

'Stop it!' yelled Delphine. 'Get off him!'

Reg bit down on the knife blade. Blood trickled from the corners of his mouth. Grubs were on his nose and lips. The vesperi twisted the dagger and his mouth opened. Grubs dropped onto his tongue. He was hollering, retching, tongue working uselessly.

'Please!' Delphine almost rocked forward onto her feet. She was ready to charge, chair still tied to her back, but there were at least half a dozen vesperi between her and Miss DeGroot.

Mr Cox smoked his pipe blandly.

Miss DeGroot stepped away, red-eyed, shaking.

Reggie's howls subsided. There were pale wet shapes all round his mouth. He inhaled, snorted hard several times; a grub dropped from his nose and stuck to his knee. The vesperi slid the blade from his mouth and released their grip.

Reg spat a grot of brownish phlegm onto the rug. He spat again and again. Grubs came out in his spit.

He opened his mouth and brown water gushed over his chest and crotch. His head dropped to one side and he stopped moving. One of his eyes was open. Something twitched beneath the upper lid.

Stokeham turned towards the door. Cox sighed a slow tide of smoke.

'Now,' he said, 'where are those troops with my daughter?'

CHAPTER 34

MR GARFORTH SEES IT THROUGH

The Little Gentlemen rigged explosives around the spots Henry had marked. They set the charges then sealed spun aluminium washing-up bowls over the top to help direct the blast. They ran a fuse back to the centre of the room. Henry watched their complicated fingers working and felt overwhelmed with sadness and love.

They had not asked for this. He had promised to protect them, and here he was, dragging them into yet another war they had not started. Well, it would end here. One way or another, it would end tonight.

He found himself thinking of Abigail, the warm round loaf of her body in the bed beside him, of walking Molly down by the dunes through the long evenings of an Indian summer, of his father handing him his first taste of soapy ale in a chipped mug, of the shelduck chicks he once rescued from a tomcat, Christmas cake, the sun through mist. He thought of all these things and he was afraid, because he realised he was saying goodbye.

No. Not yet. Come on, you stupid bugger.

He heard the *thwip* of a tripwire, the gasp of a vesperi being immolated. They were getting closer. The Little Gentlemen stood watching the entrance. He swept the torchbeam across their polished shells.

'Hide yourselves,' he said. Slowly, they turned to look at him.

It was the eyes. If he lived to be a hundred and fifty, he would never get used to the eyes. Blue pupils floated in pools of brilliant white. And now, they rested on him.

'I'll be fine,' he said. 'I'll make a bargain. It'll all end in peace.'

And now, the eyes were on his gun.

'Go,' he said. 'Make yourselves shadows.'

The Little Gentlemen blurred and scattered.

Henry wedged the gunstock between his ribs and bicep. Freezing pain lanced through his knees. It was so acute he barely noticed it. It was funny what you got used to. No, not funny. Sad.

A harka stepped out of the tunnel with Delphine's sawn-off in its big hands. Before it knew he was there, Henry shot it in the head.

While he was reloading, an ornate metal flask bounced *tink tink* out of the tunnel, coming to rest beside the body of the harka. It began pouring thick blond smoke. The entrance disappeared. Henry moved to grab it, and as he bent a blow struck him sharp across the brow and he fell onto his backside.

He lay dazed. A beast stepped from the fog in a blue velveteen coachman's jacket and square-buckled boots. A blunderbuss pistol hung at its right thigh, a duelling pistol at its left, and its shrivelled right hand gripped a cudgel. Two vesperi emerged at its flanks, armed with daggers, beating at the smoke with their wings.

Henry reached into his pocket for a cartridge. He had fallen badly on his hand and when he tried to make a fist round the shell, his fingers spasmed with pain.

The valet watched, polishing its little yellow teeth with the hem of its jacket. It took the blunderbuss pistol from its belt and aimed at Henry.

Something dropped from the roof and struck the gun. The blunderbuss discharged into the floor and shots ricocheted around the chamber; a vesperi fell shrieking, clutching its ankle. The valet tossed its pistol aside and advanced. Lying on the ground was a segmented ball of maroon armour. The valet stood over it. Henry tried to slot the cartridge into the breech but his hand slipped and the shell went skittering across the floor. He tried to rise and his spine erupted in cramps.

The monstrous valet lifted its boot and stamped. Henry cried out. The beast stamped again and the ball ruptured. Black fluid oozed from the cracks. The beast stamped again and again. Henry fumbled for another cartridge but he was too late. The ball was reduced to a pulped mosaic of shell and guts, one snapped leg ticking like a Morse key. The valet stepped over the mess. It lifted the cudgel and bore down on Henry, grinning.

CHAPTER 35

A FAREWELL TO ARMS

At a quarter to ten, Miss DeGroot's arm began to melt. The flesh had taken on the clammy, corrugated pearlescence of raw steak on the turn. When she lifted her hand, her middle and ring fingers had fused together.

'Peter.' Her face was a study in composure. 'Is this normal?'

Stokeham was staring out the window.

'The honours manifest in different ways,' said Cox.

She pinched the skin under her forearm. When she let go, it held the imprint of her thumb like clay, leaving a sallow fleshy pouch.

'Oh dear,' she said. 'I feel rather queer.'

Behind her, the fireplace danced and crackled.

Mother kept making a face at Delphine. It was very distracting. At last, Delphine mouthed: *What?*

Mother glanced about, then she leaned forward on the piano stool and mouthed something like: *Char him.*

Delphine frowned. She mouthed back: *Char who?*

Mother shook her head emphatically. *Char him.* She glanced at the guards – who were preoccupied with the deterioration of Miss DeGroot – then nodded at her armpit. *Char him.*

Char him?

Cham *him.*

Cham him?

*CHAM **TIM***. The tip of her tongue flicked out from behind her front teeth.

Cham tim? And then she got it.

Mother was saying 'jam tin'.

Waiting till no one was watching, Delphine mouthed: *Jam tin?*

Mother nodded frantically, then jerked her chin towards her armpit. She was holding her arm at a peculiar angle, as if she had something wedged beneath it.

Delphine mouthed a swearword.

The door burst open and a vesperi skitter-scrambled in.

Stokeham turned.

'Report,' said Cox.

The creature spat a volley of ticks and chirrups. It was clearly agitated.

Stokeham turned to Mr Propp, hunched and silent in the centre of the room.

'The first floor is on fire,' said Mr Cox. He held out his palm and a vesperi placed a flintlock pistol in it. 'Ivan, you are more trouble than you are worth and now I am going to kill you.'

Miss DeGroot let out a throttled mewl. The fingers of her right hand were elongating like warm wax. The vesperi nearest to her began backing away. She tried to make a fist, gasping with the effort, but her fingers swayed limply.

'Peter! What's happening to me?' She glared at her hand, straining to turn it palm upwards. She gritted her teeth. Slowly, slowly, her long, creamy digits began to retract, like lengths of saliva drawn back into the mouth. Miss DeGroot's cheeks coloured. Her hand was almost restored.

She grunted. Her arm fell and burst on the hearth rug.

Miss DeGroot stood staring at the mess of pink-white fluid. It ran from the stump of her shoulder, dripping down the skirts of her evening gown and spread in a feathering mane across the hearth. She vomited down her front. She looked at Stokeham helplessly, her chin glistening.

Delphine heard a clatter from off to her right. She glanced across and Mother had let the jam tin drop to the foot of the piano stool.

Mother kicked the improvised grenade and it slid towards Delphine like a puck. It caught a nick in the floor and flipped onto its side, rolling under Delphine's chair.

Stokeham had been approaching the fireplace and wheeled round at the noise.

'What was that?' said Cox.

The remaining sixteen or so vesperi drew their daggers. Delphine slid her ankles together, trying to hide the grenade, but the action drew Stokeham's attention. Cox set down his pipe and advanced on her.

'What have you got there?'

'Don't let him have it!' said Mother.

'Stop her!' said Cox. 'Bring whatever it is to me.'

Four vesperi converged on her. Delphine rocked forward onto her feet, lifting the chair off the floor. One vesperi grabbed the sleeve of her cardigan. A second reached for the jam tin. Mr Cox was bearing down on her. She twisted, catching the second vesperi in the forehead with the leg of the chair, then toe-punted the jam tin at the fireplace. The old condensed milk can rolled, bootlace fuse whipping round and round like the leg of a clockwork spider. Miss DeGroot blinked dumbly as it spun past. Calmly crouching by the fire, Stokeham reached out to stop it. The tin clipped the lip of the hearth. It bounced over Stokeham's waiting glove and into the flames.

A vesperi tackled Delphine's knees and she let herself fall, yelling: 'Everyone down!'

Out of the corner of her eye, she saw Stokeham stooped over the fireplace, thrusting a leather gauntlet into the glow. Cox screamed.

Everything went white.

In the underground chamber, Henry lay bleeding from the mouth. The bat-monster pressed a bony knee into his chest and raised the cudgel for the coup de grace.

Its gristly face crumpled. It dropped the cudgel. It clutched its gut. Henry grabbed the unloaded shotgun and drove it up into the valet's fangs with the heel of his palm. A crack echoed off the dripping stalactites and the beast staggered back, slobbering blood.

Henry grabbed a cartridge from the floor and slid it into his shotgun. Before he could close the breech, the lone remaining vesperi was retreating. He traced it with the gun as it scrambled for the exit, let it go. The valet was doubled over, spitting out teeth. Henry planted the gun stock on the floor and rose unsteadily, grunting. His kneecaps felt as if someone had driven steel pegs through them.

He brought the muzzle to bear on his opponent.

'A word about the terms of your surrender.'

From the balcony of the Great Hall, Gideon watched as the front doors opened and the Devil strode in. His curving horns were unmistakable. A dozen angels marched behind Old Nick in perfect lockstep.

It was just like Arthur had promised.

The bowstring was taut beneath Gideon's fingers, the firebombs snug against his belly. He had recovered the righteous weapon, and now Satan stood in the courtyard waiting to be absolved. The chequered floor marked out the distance in neat, stark squares. Black and white. Death and rebirth. An end to all pain. A beginning.

Gideon stepped from cover and let fly.

Delphine heard the windows shatter. A moment later she felt the force of the blast against her closed eyelids.

She tried to look up but the grenade must have blown the fire out and toppled the lamps because the banqueting hall was black. She thought she saw the crystal pendants of the dead chandelier, scintillating like sardines in the darkness, then a vesperi was on top of her, pressing the flat of its dagger to her windpipe. Its dark brown eyes scanned her face, pink bootlace tongue whipping over the grey stumps of fangs. It lifted its head; its nose-leaf flared as it called: *Rrrrrik-ik-ik-ik. Rrrrrik-ik-ik-ik.*

Across the room, calls bubbled in reply. A clawed toe dug into her ribs. A necklace of twine hung from the skinwing's throat, threaded with pink shells that brushed her chin as it breathed. Its breath smelt of burning hair. The fallen chair creaked beneath their combined weight.

She heard the scuffling of taloned vesperi feet converging on the hearth. Delphine concentrated on a white fleck of foam in the corner of the vesperi's mouth. It reminded her of the foam in Mr Kung's eyes on the beach. He had died in a hospital bed, alone and very far from home. Delphine knew she might die now, and the thought of Mother, sitting or lying a few yards away, was comforting. The vesperi's face became blurry, and she had to blink to make it clear.

An unearthly calm had settled over the room. This was what soldiers meant by the dread when the Hun's artillery went quiet. You expected it to feel like a relief, but then you began to wonder: why has it stopped? What are they planning? And you listened for clues but your ears were ringing from the noise and there was nothing but the sense of something terrible and lethal and huge, silently preparing to administer the masterstroke.

The creature kept grimacing, drilling a finger in its earholes. The noise of the explosion seemed to have affected its hearing. It looked back over its shoulder. Downy white hairs filled the hollow of its ear.

She thought about trying to roll out from beneath it while it was distracted. The blade was still at her windpipe, not cutting – restraining. The vesperi on top of her pip-pipped something. A reply echoed back through the darkness, but the creature didn't seem to hear. It returned its attention to Delphine.

Something cracked against its skull. The skinwing hit the floor and skidded a couple of feet on its jowl.

'Now!' Professor Carmichael stood over her, grasping the huge ceremonial warhammer. He had ripped it from its wall mounts – a steel bracket swung from the gemmed handle as he turned to face the room. 'Everybody! Fight!' He knelt at Delphine's side. 'Hold still. I'll cut you loose.' He picked up the vesperi's dropped dagger. He turned left and slashed: 'Ungh.' She heard the knife rasp through fabric and flesh. A body clattered to the floor and the Professor stabbed it once, *pfft*, the creature expiring with a sigh.

He leant over her and began sawing at the rope.

'Where's Peter?' said Delphine.

'You mean that bastard in the mask? Dead.'

'And Cox?'

'I don't know.'

She could hear footsteps, chairs scraping, cries. She heard a male exclamation, a thump, a scream. The Professor's knife dug into the trench between her wrists, chewing through the ropes. Her bonds slackened then sloughed off. She slapped her palms to the floor and sprang to her feet just in time to see three javelin-wielding vesperi surrounding her and the Professor. Standoffs were taking place all round the room. Her eyes were adjusting. She saw shifting outlines, havoc.

The Professor pressed Delphine's crab hook into her palm.

'Give the buggers Hell.'

He lifted the great silver warhammer above his head like some figure from Norse legend. The three vesperi spread out, attempting a flanking manoeuvre. One was whistling – a tremulous, intermittent tone, like someone tuning a wireless.

'Stick close to me. Yah!' He stamped and all three vesperi recoiled, furling their wings and hopping out of range. Delphine brandished her hook and tried to look menacing. The creature nearest her seemed to sense her reluctance; it advanced, spreading its wings till it was wide as it was tall. She backed away. The creature closed in.

'Grrrah!' The Professor swung the hammer in a broad arc, missing all three vesperi but driving them back. The weight of the huge gemmed head pulled him off-balance and he stumbled. Seeing its chance, one of the creatures drove at his exposed flank with its javelin raised, but the stumble was a feint and he brought the hammer's pommel nut crashing back into the skinwing's temple. As the creature went down its neighbour jabbed at the Professor's thigh; he parried with the hammer shaft then brought his knee up under the javelin, cracking his opponent's jaw. The creature squawked and he laid it flat with a forehand stroke. The final vesperi, the one which had been cornering Delphine, hesitated. The Professor roared. It fled.

He looked at Delphine. He was panting.

'In one piece?'

She nodded.

'It seems,' he said, 'today . . . you are to put . . . some of your theories . . . on warfare . . . into practice.'

Across the room, the remaining vesperi had surrounded Alice, Mrs Hagstrom and another male guest. The hostages stood marooned on the sofa, arms tied behind their backs. Mrs Hagstrom was kicking and snorting. A vesperi slashed at her and she gasped. The Professor wiped his mouth on his sleeve and charged.

Before she knew what she was doing, Delphine had joined him. The creatures turned round, click-shrieking. She raised her crab hook. The vesperi raised their curved daggers in response. Professor Carmichael bellowed. At the edge of the pack, a skinwing flinched. It bolted. Delphine screamed. The other vesperi glanced from their knives to each another. They held. The Professor raised the warhammer to strike, his tawny hair sticking out in peaks of clotting blood.

The vesperi scattered.

Delphine watched them go. She ran to where Mother lay face down.

'Delphine?' Mother had a bruise under her eye the size of a mandarin segment.

'Hold on. You're nearly free.' Delphine sawed through the ropes binding Mother's wrists. She offered Mother her hand. Mother looked at it, disorientated. She closed her long cold fingers around Delphine's palm. Delphine helped her up.

Delphine's eyes were adjusting. Her head felt swimmy. She could make out Stokeham's crumpled body in front of the blown-out fire. It looked as if the masked figure was sleeping, then Delphine tilted her head and moonlight caught the ruptured sternum, the glistering mush. A leather-gauntleted hand lay open, grasping nothing.

A few yards away, Mr Cox lay prone, chestnut locks spreading from his scalp in a starburst, legs splayed beneath his brilliant blue rump. It seemed the servant could not survive without the master.

Delphine and Mother joined the group led by Professor Carmichael. Mr Wightman stepped aside to reveal Mrs Hagstrom lying on her flank, clutching a long deep slit in her arm. Dark blood bubbled up between her fingers. Her skin was tight and marbled.

'Come on now, my dear.' The Professor rested a hand on her

shoulder. 'Up you get. It's closing time.' With Mother's help he lifted Mrs Hagstrom to a sitting position.

Mrs Hagstrom looked at Delphine. One of her eyes was flooded with red.

'Sorry I didn't believe you,' she said.

Through the ringing in her ears, Delphine thought she heard a noise. It solidified into a word:

'*Wait.*'

The voice was dry, tremulous. It was coming from the middle of the room. Delphine turned.

Miss DeGroot was trying to stand. Her burst arm had hardened into thick strands, stretching from her shoulder to the floor in a fleshy cobweb. Ropes of tendon and scar tissue tightened as she rose, dragging up sections of rug.

'Wait,' she said. Steam twisted from a chunk of horseshoe lodged in her eye socket. She focused on the ruin of her arm. Parts of it had fused with the floor. The sinews went taut. She exhaled and they fell slack.

Reg Gillow started coming round. He moaned, went rigid in the armchair. Professor Carmichael ran over and slit his bonds. One of his arms hung by his side. His other hand went to his eye. He doubled-up, howling.

'Reggie!' Alice dashed across the banqueting hall and hugged him. Reggie was gibbering, shrieking and clutching his face. 'What's wrong? What happened to you? Reggie, tell me, please!'

'No, no, no.' Mr Wightman was dazedly making his way towards the doors. 'I've had enough of this madness.'

Delphine looked from Reggie, to Miss DeGroot, to the door. The vesperi should have returned by now.

'We must go.' The speaker was Propp. He had managed to stand. His wrists were still tied behind his back. His waistcoat was torn, face fruiting with bruises.

'Wait!' Miss DeGroot tried to walk towards them but the remnants of her arm tethered her in place. She tugged and twisted but only succeeded in rucking the hearth rug. She swore. She was weeping from her remaining eye.

Miss DeGroot spun to face Delphine.

'Please,' she said, reaching out with her human hand. 'Don't leave me.'

Small fires guttered around Gideon and the Devil.

They faced each other on the great chessboard. The angels were dead. The Devil stood with His horns low, two arrow shafts sticking from the hump of muscle behind His neck. He breathed in wounded snorts. He could not raise His head.

Gideon held a curved angel dagger, serrated on its inner edge. He pressed the pommel to his crashing heart.

The Devil charged.

Delphine fought against her shuddering hands and the sickness rising in her throat, and forced herself to meet Miss DeGroot's gaze.

Miss DeGroot took a long breath.

'I don't . . . feel anything.' She looked back at the flesh trailing from her shoulder and seemed to experience a kind of vertigo. 'I can feel the *shape* of it, but . . . there's no pain.' She squinted the raw cauterised flesh of her eye around the shrapnel.

'Mmm.' Propp stepped forward. He nodded towards Reggie, who moaned as Alice cradled his head and wept. 'He feels your pain now. It cannot be undone.'

Miss DeGroot swivelled to face him, melted arm plaiting round on itself. 'This is your fault.'

'Please, noble friend . . . '

Miss DeGroot closed her eyes and shook her head.

'No, Ivan. No more of this . . . of this Mr Ghandi schtick. I can't bear it.' She sighed and massaged her hairline with her fingertips. She glanced at Delphine. 'Please. I need some help.'

Delphine stared at her.

'Look,' said Miss DeGroot, 'I never meant for Titus to get hurt. I was just trying to reunite a daughter with her father.' She took a step towards Delphine and the wet ropes tensed, jerking her shoulder back. 'The cancer was eating me alive. Ivan wouldn't tell us how to beat it. Don't you see? I had. No. Choice.'

There was a flurry of footsteps and a bang from the double doors. Delphine turned. A quick inventory of the room revealed that Mr Wightman had made his escape.

'Hey!' Miss DeGroot cast about. 'Who was that? What are you doing?'

Professor Carmichael cupped his hands to his mouth. 'Everyone – *run!*'

Delphine froze, unsure of which way to turn.

'Please!' Miss DeGroot's face passed through confusion and fury, before settling on desperation. She grasped for Delphine with her normal hand, her bare feet slipping on the hardwood. 'Don't leave me!' Her fingers opened and closed on air.

Delphine glanced around for Mother, saw her tugging at Alice's elbow, trying to get the girl to stand. Alice made a small, choked sound. She had Reggie's blood and vomit down her dress.

Delphine looked back at Miss DeGroot. She was kicking and straining against the tendrils binding her to the floor, but they were thick as oak roots. A vein stood out on Miss DeGroot's forehead. She turned to Delphine, her single pupil shrunken with fear.

'Wait,' she said.

Everyone else was moving towards the east doors. Delphine hesitated.

'Wait!' said Miss DeGroot. She swallowed. She clutched at the air between them. 'Why won't you wait for me?'

Delphine took an involuntary step back.

Cables of skin and muscle stretched taut, elongating as Miss DeGroot pulled against them. Reggie screamed. Where they met the floor, they had begun to secrete a black, oily fluid. She had blood on her teeth. She reached for Delphine. 'Come . . . here . . . '

Delphine could not move. She was paralysed by the motion of Miss DeGroot's clammy human fingers. The air was full of a warm stink like brewer's yeast. Miss DeGroot grimaced, bracing her knees.

'Miss Venner!' Professor Carmichael was calling.

Delphine looked away.

'No!' The ragged strands radiating from Miss DeGroot's shoulder began singing with mounting tension. They were puddled in tarry liquid. It smouldered. 'Come . . . ' She swiped at Delphine with her good hand. 'Here . . . '

Delphine began backing away. Miss DeGroot's face fell. 'Please. Don't leave me here.' She grunted and gasped, advancing her trembling fingers an inch, half an inch.

The yeasty stink grew stronger. Delphine took another step back and her heel slipped in something black and viscous. Dark fluid was pooling around her. It seemed to be bubbling up through the floor.

'Delphine!' said Mother.

Miss DeGroot cried *hnnngh* and jerked backwards. Around Delphine's feet, shapes started rising from the fluid. She tried to run and something whip-thin coiled round her ankle. Delphine yelled and grabbed at it. A wet, knuckled appendage lunged from the black water and snared her wrist. More were rising – sticky, half-formed tendrils, grasping for her, clutching.

She twisted to look at Miss DeGroot and saw her crouched, her shoulder almost to the floor, raw, living flesh flowing into the smoky dark pool beside the hearth.

Delphine felt a tendril oozing round her throat and tried to claw it loose with the crab hook. A second, thicker limb slid round her rib cage. Above her spread the lunar mandala, a shining diadem.

'Let go!' she said, but she barely had the breath. The ringing in her ears grew deafening.

She heard footsteps. 'Delphine!'

'Everybody stop!' Miss DeGroot lay on her side. Her panting echoed through the banqueting hall. 'Nobody take . . . another . . . step.' Slowly, slowly, she clambered to her feet. Pale tissue trailed from her shoulder into the steaming pool beside her. She took a breath. She glanced at Mother, Professor Carmichael. 'If you move, I will hurt her.' The thicket of limbs binding Delphine squeezed. 'I'm not a bad person. I just . . . ' She gripped her brow with her human hand. 'Just give me a moment to think.'

CHAPTER 36

MERE OBLIVION

Martin Wightman emerged in the Great Hall, panting. His breaths echoed in the cavernous space. What were those idiots playing at, staying behind?

Well, he supposed it didn't matter. This was clearly a nightmare.

The full moon shone through the portico windows. He allowed himself to admire the play of silverblue light, marvelling at the complexity of the delusion. He could smell smoke. There were bodies all over the floor, mostly winged fiends. They were black and sticky, as if scorched. He wiped a palm across the ridged scar on his scalp. The sweat on his fingers felt warm and slick. Incredible.

The body of a minotaur lay in the centre of the chequered floor. Funny – it had two arrows sticking out of its wide back. They were the same type the Society used for archery practice – he recognised the red fletching. His mind had obviously taken elements of the real world and reused them for his dream. He walked over and tapped the shafts with the back of his finger. Lodged in the creature's withers, they shivered.

There was something queer about the minotaur's head. He peered at it, frowning.

A noise from the top of the stairs. Despite his certainty that all he saw and felt was no more than a nasty hallucination – and it was, of course it was, what sort of pillock believed in goblins – his belly cramped. He would very much like the dream to end now.

A man stepped onto the staircase, clutching a bow. He was wearing some sort of sling.

Mr Wightman squinted.

'Mr Venner?' His paunch dipped over his belt as he exhaled. 'I thought you were another monster.'

Mr Venner said nothing. His teeth gleamed in the moonlight. Mr Wightman could not see his eyes.

Mr Venner reached into his sling. Very slowly, he withdrew two long, pointed objects. Mr Wightman took a moment to realise they were horns.

He glanced at the dead minotaur. Protruding from its flat brown skull were two rough nubs.

'What in Hell's name?' said Mr Wightman.

Mr Venner's chuckle echoed through the bloody hall. He lifted the horns to his temples.

'Moo.'

Henry kept the shotgun trained on the grimacing bat-monster and tried to forget about the pain in his legs.

'Surrender,' he told the hunched beast, his voice echoing through the low, rocky chamber. 'Tell your master the fight can't be won. This chamber's rigged with explosives – look for yourself.' He gestured with the gun but the valet, shuddering, did not look up. 'In fifteen minutes I'm going to detonate the charges and if you and your forces haven't retreated through it you'll be cut off from your homeland for all time.'

He wasn't sure if the creature had heard. It was barely conscious, sprawled in the middle of the room, beside the swirling black pool. Perhaps an old battle wound had opened up during their fight. Perhaps it had taken a blow to the head earlier on which was only just taking effect. Still, if it couldn't get back to its master, the plan was ruined. Stokeham needed to order a retreat – needed to believe Henry was prepared to blow up the chamber and strand the troops in England. Of course, if Henry really did detonate the charges, then yes, Stokeham would have no way of getting home, but the remaining troops would fight with the tenacity of cornered rats. Henry was gambling that Stokeham would not call his bluff – that, as someone who had lived for more than a century, Stokeham was prideful but patient, and would sooner withdraw than die in a glorious last stand.

But to order a retreat, Stokeham had to know the battle was lost. Henry was not sure the creature before him was capable of climbing a flight of stairs, never mind running back to the Hall to deliver terms of surrender.

'Do you understand me?' said Henry.

The beast grunted, spat blood.

'Don't test me. *Do you understand?*'

It nodded.

'Good. And do you agree to tell your master my terms?'

The valet pressed a claw to its stomach. It nodded.

'That's what I like to hear. Now, off you go.'

Blood foamed over the creature's lips. It mouthed something.

'What?' said Henry. He hadn't thought the beast could talk.

A tendon stood out in its neck as it strained to lift itself upright. Its shrivelled wings pumped. It spat more blood. Its lips worked through the same motions.

Henry could not make out words. He leant forward.

'Don't toy with me.'

The valet exhaled, spluttered. With its good hand, it steadied itself against the raised edge of the pool. It tried again.

Henry watched the movement of its thin, furred lips. He felt he almost had the words, but for whatever reason the creature was unable to aspirate them.

'I've no time for this. Whatever you've got to say, I don't want to hear it. Go. Tell your master. You've now got fourteen minutes.'

The valet dropped to one knee, gasped with agony, clawing at its gut. Blood stippled its lapels. Still, it mouthed through the pain.

Henry watched its lips.

You must . . .

He leaned in nearer. 'What? I must what?'

The creature's jaw was taut. The capillaries in its eyes had burst. It inhaled in three jagged stages, wiped the blood from its lips.

You must . . .

It collapsed into wheezing.

'What?' Henry was at the pool edge. He could make out the hiss in the thing's throat, could hear it trying to speak.

Be . . . ware . . .

The valet thumped a fist against its heart.

'Beware? Beware of what?' He could almost hear the words.

Be . . . ware . . .

'Of what?'

Be . . . ware . . .

'Why?'

The claw flashed up from under the valet's velveteen jacket and connected with Henry's jaw. The force of the blow lifted him up onto his heels, enough time for the creature to swat the shotgun from his grip then climb onto the lip of the pool, swinging round behind him to put him in a chokehold. Henry grasped at air; the weight of the valet dragged him backwards.

In the shadows, he caught a glow of huge eyes: one of the Little Gentlemen watching. If this creature killed him, they would be next. Henry felt a blow to his temple and his vision pulsed with sparks. He tried to reach behind his head but he was losing strength. He had one last move in him before he passed out. His heels were pressed against the raised edge of the pool, the yeasty smell building in his nostrils. He made his decision.

Henry grasped the arm around his throat and dug his fingers in. He shut his eyes. He kicked his heels against the wet stone floor and pushed himself backwards into the pool. The valet realised too late what was happening and tried to let go, but with the last of an old man's dogged, bloodyminded tenacity, Henry dragged the monster in with him.

The black liquid plopped like a peat bog. Henry felt it close over his head, oozing into his nostrils, pushing past ceramic dentures into his throat. He pressed his tongue against the upper plate and felt it crumble like mint cake. The crackling in his ears dropped to a rumble. He was numb. His eyelids tingled as the fluid melted them, ate into his corneas. He bit down, and his tongue had dissolved. The rumbling grew louder than his thoughts.

He broke apart on the tides.

CHAPTER 37

SHE WHO FIGHTS MONSTERS

'Put her down, Patience.'

It was Mother who spoke. She stood five yards or so from Miss DeGroot.

'I said give me a moment!' Miss DeGroot bunched a clump of hair in her fist and took some deep breaths.

Delphine struggled but she was held fast. She glanced down at the tendril wrapped round her wrist. It was fat and translucent, sweating like melted cheese.

'Is this what you want to be?' Mother stood with her hands on her hips. 'Really? A bully?'

'What I *want*, Anne, is justice.'

'Then let my daughter go. She's not your enemy.'

Delphine felt the grip on her throat slacken.

'I couldn't help it,' said Miss DeGroot. 'I didn't mean to. Ivan . . . he forced me into this. Look at me. Look what he's done.'

Mother licked her dry lips and took a breath. Delphine could see the fatigue flickering at the edges of her eyes.

'You're right to be angry. It's wrong to exploit the innocent to satisfy one's own needs. So now you must make a choice. Are you someone like that . . . ' Mother took a step forward. 'Or are you someone who helps?'

Delphine shunted with her elbows, trying to ease the pressure on her lungs. Miss DeGroot's grip loosened a little further. Delphine inhaled, her nostrils filling with the peaty, beery smell.

'I can't go back now,' she said. 'You heard Ivan. It can't be undone. I've chosen.'

Mother's gaze shifted to Delphine. Her expression softened.

'Nonsense, Patience. We are always choosing.' She glanced at the body slumped in the fireplace. 'I don't suppose *he* can ask any more of you. You're free. Now. Who do you want to be?'

Miss DeGroot's eyelid trembled. She looked to Delphine, then down at the waxy cables hanging from her shoulder.

'I want to be human,' she said quietly.

'Then choose accordingly.'

Miss DeGroot stared at the floor for a long time.

Delphine felt the tendrils binding her sag. They fell away, sliding back into the black puddles. Delphine staggered, found her feet.

She glanced up. Miss DeGroot spat a purple-blue mist. Something small and hard was sticking out of her windpipe. Reggie spluttered.

Miss DeGroot twisted to the left. An arrow was protruding from her neck.

Delphine turned. Daddy stood in the doorway, soaked in blood.

'Giddy?'

'Daddy!'

Miss DeGroot made a strangling noise.

Delphine began running towards her father. Daddy was alive. Her whole body tingled with relief and joy and the need to get him and Mother to safety. Soot smutted his face and his hair swung in tangles. He nocked a second arrow, raised it at Miss DeGroot. His jaw worked as he closed one eye.

Delphine's elation turned to panic.

'Don't shoot! We were talking to her!'

Daddy calmly relaxed his fingers. The arrow flew: *kwip*. Reggie arched his back and yelled, but when Delphine turned she saw Miss DeGroot had parried the shot, the shaft embedded in the pulsing meat of her transformed arm. The flesh had reknitted into a thick club head. Purple juice ran from the wound.

'Stop it!' The cry came from Alice. 'You're hurting Reggie. Every time you hurt her, it hurts Reggie.'

Daddy did not seem to hear. Delphine had almost reached him when someone spoke.

'Stay where you are.'

The voice did not belong to Miss DeGroot.

Delphine turned and saw Mr Cox brushing dust off his silk waist-coat. Behind him, midriff lacerated with greasy scar tissue, stood Stokeham. A gauntleted hand went up, adjusted the mask. The beak had a hole in it the size of a ha'penny, cracks spidering out. Through it, Delphine could make out white flesh, the dark slash of a mouth.

'Don't trust them, Patience,' said Cox. 'They will flatter and deceive but, in the end, they are rats. I see they have kept you suffi-ciently distracted to let Ivan make good his escape.'

Delphine glanced around with a start. Mr Propp was gone.

Cox unhooked the flintlock pistol from his belt. 'We must defend ourselves.' He hesitated. He blinked at the doorway. 'Who on earth is that?'

'Even inner God,' said Daddy. Something smoked in his fist. A milk bottle. He swept his arm back.

Alice ran at him. 'No!'

He threw.

The bottle arced to the right and smashed against the quatrefoil-patterned wallpaper. Ginger-white flames flowed down the wall and across the floor, along spreading channels of turpentine. Delphine had to shield her eyes. As they adjusted she saw the silhouette of Miss DeGroot shielding her face with her huge, engorged limb. She did not seem to be fully in control of it; she staggered under its weight, flailing. The arm swung out, crashing through a rosewood teapoy with Stokeham's little lacquered pine cabinet on top. The cabinet fell open and the stop-pered jar inside burst against the floor, spraying chips of glass.

Something black and irredescent zigzagged from the wreckage.

Delphine staggered to her feet. She heard screams. A guest lunged at Miss DeGroot and she pancaked him into the wall with a horrible crunch of bone.

Daddy did not spot Alice until it was too late. She had picked up a knife. Delphine saw the dull flash as Alice lunged.

'You're hurting him!'

'Daddy, look out!'

Daddy tried to spin aside and the blade glanced his thigh. Delphine screamed, reaching uselessly.

Daddy staggered back into the hallway. Alice stood, shivering. The knife slipped from her palm.

'Run!' said the Professor. 'Now. Everyone.'

Delphine sprinted for the open doors. The Professor was ahead of her. He threw a huge arm round the stunned Alice and dragged her along with him.

Delphine heard a pistol report and a chunk of door frame splintered. When she glanced back Miss DeGroot was backlit by flames, a nest of black snakes. Tentacles slipped under Reggie and plucked him from his chair.

Delphine ran into the hallway, heading south. Daddy was nowhere to be seen. The corridor was dark after the glare of the fire. Greats from Ancient Greece lay beheaded and cloven.

Her shoes crunched on broken glass. Mother was with her. Mrs Hagstrom and the one surviving guest hobbled behind.

She followed the Professor as he lumbered down the corridor.

'Wait!' she said.

He glanced back, panting. He seemed to get bigger every time she looked at him.

Delphine felt a hand pushing her, driving her onwards.

'Keep going,' said Mother, lips almost touching her ear.

'What about Reggie?'

'We can't,' said Mother. She inhaled sharply, clenched her teeth as she ran. 'We can't.'

The Great Hall's domed ceiling had disappeared behind roiling grey smoke. A glow came from the corridors beyond the landing. The crump and crickle of combustion.

There were corpses everywhere. Mrs Hagstrom staggered towards the entrance, grimacing with each step, clutching her sodden blouse in her fist, yanking at it.

'I'm not leaving without Daddy,' said Delphine.

Professor Carmichael let Alice slump against the door frame. 'Miss Venner, *please*. You can't risk your life on – '

'There!' Delphine pointed at the top of the staircase. 'The bow he was carrying.'

'I'm going with you,' said Mother.

Delphine did not have the strength to argue. She nodded.

'Algernon – get them all to safety,' said Mother.

The Professor dipped his huge head. 'Yes, Mrs Venner.'

Delphine was turning towards the stairs when she saw Mr Wightman asleep against the bannister, grey flesh pooling around his chin.

She stepped towards him. 'Hello?'

He did not reply. She moved closer.

He had his bottom lip pushed out, as if sulking.

'Delphine . . . '

'Shh.' Delphine held her hand up to silence Mother. 'Mr Wightman? Can you hear me?'

An oval shadow spread from his chins across his paunch. But the light was coming from the windows . . .

She saw.

His throat was slit. The shadow was a bib of black blood that had hardened and corrugated on his shirt. His cheeks were the colour of suet.

Mother was on the stair. She put a hand to her mouth: 'Ah.'

Mr Wightman's dented head sagged to one side. Delphine stepped back and the Hall spun and she heard her yells echoing off the walls, then she was trapped, arms pinned to her side, and Mother was gripping her from behind, whispering into her ear: 'Suck it down. Suck it deep, deep inside you. That's it. You'll have time for upset later, but for now, you must find a strongroom down in your belly and lock it all away.'

Delphine took a long breath and held it.

'Good,' said Mother. She let go and began vigorously rubbing

Delphine's arm. 'Stand tall. You're even stronger than you think.'

Delphine nodded, felt her jaw shake as she exhaled. She could not stop staring at Mr Wightman. On the step beside him was a severed horn, the tip tacky with blood.

CHAPTER 38

SAY, FATHER, SAY

February 5th 1935 / September 12th 1935

B ack in February, someone set Delphine's school on fire. There were three suspects.

Agnes Trevanion was a fourth-former who smoked imported cigarettes on school grounds, sneaked out late to meet surly boys with borrowed motorcycles and factory jobs, and once punched Mr Fitzwilliam when he patted her thigh in the Classics room at lunchtime. People said she had only escaped expulsion because her father was very rich, or her father was something to do with the Cosa Nostra. She stood ramrod straight with black hair that fell piratically across her left eye. Delphine was hungrily in love with her.

Meredith Roylance was a doughy grey girl in the year above with a tubercular cough and weeping pink eyes. Sunlight picked out long scintillating whiskers on her upper lip and chin. She had no friends. She moved from room to room like a baleful fog. At night, noises came from her bed that might have been eating or sobbing. A popular rumour held that she drank her own menstrual blood and called it 'Communion'.

The third suspect was Delphine – a girl middling in all respects, whose watchful silences, once taken for shyness, would soon be diagnosed as the brooding, icy rage of the moral defective, whose inoffensive demeanour was reimagined as reptilian cunning, whose few minor transgressions against the patience of her teachers were recast as the first crackling pebbles that presaged a great landslide of infamy. In their minds, she had always planned to visit destruction upon St Eustace's, ever since she had stood in the hall on her first day, straw hat clutched to her chest, palm raised towards the headmaster as she recited the school pledge.

After all, it was in her blood.

On the night of the fire at St Eustace's, minutes after she had left Eleanor Wethercroft tied up in the boiler room, Delphine sneaked back across the shadow-drenched quadrangle to free her. She would march down the stairs smiling, saying it was all a joke, ha ha. What a fun game we played together, ha ha. Eleanor Wethercroft would go along with the pretence to save face. Revenge would come later.

Delphine was halfway through the solid black of the Sacred Arch when she realised there was someone in there with her. She held her breath and waited for the axe to fall.

'Delphine Venner.'

The millstone grate was unmistakable. Mrs Leddington: pinheaded bruiser, silhouette like the ace of spades. She stepped from the murk. Her thin eyes were initials carved in a desk.

'Delphine Venner, 2H.' She said 2H like coordinates, like she was about to sink Delphine's battleship. 'What are you doing out of your bed so late?'

Delphine pressed her shoulder blades to the wall, running her palms over cold stone. Any answer she gave would be wrong.

'I forgot something, miss.'

'It is forbidden for girls to walk the school grounds after lights out.' Mrs Leddington invested the words of the School Code with atavistic gravity, breathing wetly, moistening her lips with her tongue. All the rules began that way: 'It is forbidden' or 'All girls are expected', never admitting by whom or why.

Mrs Leddington leant in close to Delphine. Her voice dropped to a murmur.

'Are you all right?'

Delphine recognised the trap. Mrs Leddington wanted her to lower her guard, incriminate herself. She focused on the boil that split Mrs Leddington's left eyebrow into two ovals of coarse black hair.

'I'm sorry, miss. I'll go back to bed straight away, miss.'

She turned to leave. Mrs Leddington's palm shot out and slapped the wall, blocking Delphine's path. Skin bulged either side of a thick gold ring.

'The last few weeks must have been very hard for you,' said Mrs Leddington. Something on the side of Delphine's head caught her attention. She leaned forward, squinting. 'Delphine . . . ' Her breath smelt of medicine. She drew back. 'How long has your hair been grey?'

Delphine felt her face getting hot.

'Since I was little, miss.'

Mrs Leddington closed her eyes and nodded. When she opened them they glistened with a terrible, burrowing charity.

'I had a word with your friends. Prue and Eleanor and Jacqueline. To explain what happened.' She coughed. 'Regarding your father.'

'Miss, that's none of their business.'

'In times of hardship, a young woman needs the compassion of her peers. They were very understanding and agreed to support you.'

'I don't want their support.'

'I know it's hard to – '

'You shouldn't have told them.'

'Miss Venner, please do not raise your voice. May I remind you – '

'It's none of their business.'

'Miss Venner!' The gold ring clacked as the palm struck stonework. 'Regardless of your circumstances I will not countenance disrespect. You will report to me tomorrow morning before breakfast. Return quickly and quietly to your dormitory.'

Delphine pressed her lips together. She inhaled through her nostrils till her lungs were tight, held it.

'Yes, miss.'

Often, in the months that followed, she wondered what would have happened if she had never encountered Mrs Leddington beneath the Sacred Arch, if she had not been forced on that long trudge back across the gloomy quadrangle. Perhaps she would have freed Eleanor Wethercroft without drama. Perhaps no one would have thought to blame plain, average Delphine Venner, troubled father notwithstanding.

And if they had not blamed her, she would not have been expelled. If she had not been expelled, she would not have come to Alderberen Hall with her family. And if she had not come Alderberen Hall, who could say? Perhaps the air above the woods would never have blackened with needle-gobbed skinwings. Perhaps Dr Lansley would have sat in the drawing room, fiddling with his deaf-aid battery and scowling, heedless of the lack of a hole in his skull. Perhaps Mrs Hagstrom would have trimmed the lid of a mutton pie before dropping the soft rind into her mouth, while Alice did wicked, continental things to Reg Gillow in the broken shifting moonlight of the orchard. Perhaps the bleak inferno of Daddy's madness would have guttered and died.

Perhaps Delphine was the critical geartooth in a dire and intricate machine.

As she lay in her bed on the night of the fire – before anyone *knew* it was the night of the fire – she began a ritual that sustained her for months, becoming so automatic she forgot anything had come before.

She closed her eyes, and from the darkness behind her eyelids swam the stricken catfish leer of Mrs Leddington.

She gazed upon the face and her gut tightened. Then: the hate.

Delphine lay unable to sleep. The dorm was freezing. The window was left open even in February, on account of Judith Shenk's asthma.

She had pulled the blanket up to her nose. Each time she inhaled, her nostrils stung with cold. Most nights, the ceiling's tea-coloured water stains looked like a treasure map. Tonight, they were burning houses.

Morag Gethin-Spence was snoring – a steady, rolling purr. Outside, bats chirruped as they swooped between the eaves. Delphine smelt motor oil, toast.

She sat up sharply. She sniffed.

The scent was distinct and familiar. The room seemed to roll astern. She grabbed the mattress to steady herself. She felt sick. It couldn't be.

Delphine dropped from her bed and tiptoed to the window. Even through thick woollen socks, the floor felt icy. She slipped behind the long curtains.

A wheezy voice murmured: 'Hey . . . don't close . . . the window . . .'

Delphine leant over the sill, gazing out across the quad, the bell tower, the sloped black roof of Koblenz wing, the changing huts, and the playing fields beyond. Above the boiler room, the windows of the Domestic Science rooms pulsed with a faint amber light.

Her cheeks smarted in the cold. The smell was crisp and clear and undeniable.

Fire.

The sour tang thickened in her nostrils as she ran down the corridor. The air grew gauzy; lavish portraits of school patrons past and present faded behind grey mist. She was out of breath. Her eyes stung.

Eleanor Wethercroft might be burning alive. Smoke might be churning about her ankles as she screamed for help, her throat ragged, her hair hanging in lank, oily ropes.

In the darkness, the school felt papery and slight. She felt like a ghost haunting her old life. She glanced out of a window and saw only her reflection: a bright staring girl, floating in black.

The rules were superstition. She had foresworn their protective magics long ago. She was going to get expelled whatever she did.

Delphine hit the alarm and pushed –

– on through Alderberen Hall's smoke-filled corridors, dark clouds thickening overhead.

'Daddy!' A picture frame cracked under her heel.

'Giddy!' said Mother.

Delphine grasped a door knob then pulled her hand away with a cry. The metal was searingly hot.

Mother kicked it.

'Giddy? Are you there?' She kicked again and the door swung inward, a blast of heat and black –

– opaque smoke on the other side of the frosted glass, surging like ink in water. Her route to the boiler room was blocked. Delphine felt a breeze on the nape of her neck as the fire drank air; a wall display of sixth-form still-life sketches began applauding. The doors to Domestic Science juddered in their frames. Paint bubbled and oozed. The fire alarm was a distant ache.

She would have to go round the long way, see if she could break in through the back doors.

She ran back down the corridor, her head a blizzard of slander: the lunatic's daughter, the murderess. She had done this deliberately, they would say – *revenge*, Prue Dunbar and Jacqueline Finks-Hanley would attest, shaking their heads solemnly, *we were only teasing, miss, it was just a joke, but she threw a **fit** . . . and the eyes, miss* – and here Prue Dunbar would gasp into her hankie – *I was so afraid of her . . . of what she might do.*

She passed the school trophy cabinet, caught a flash of movement – no, it was just her reflection in the glass. She was almost at the door. After that it was a long jog round the outside of the block. She flicked hair out of her face then an arm clamped around her throat –

– and she whirled round, slamming her back into the wall; the vesperi released its grip and fell. Mother moved in, dagger raised.

All around, antique furniture roasted, black skeletons on white flames. The vesperi folded its wings over its head, cowering.

Mother hesitated.

'Kill it!' Delphine screamed; the words were a reflex, a trigger-pull.

Mother waited. The beige wings were spidered with capillaries; wrapped over one another, they looked like the panels of a complicated kite. Delphine's skin tingled in the heat. Breathing was making her thirsty. Dust sheets peeled away, shedding black flakes edged with molten orange that floated up drunkenly. The windows were open. Outside, it was raining.

Mother stepped back, gesturing for Delphine to do the same.

'Go,' she said.

The crumpled vesperi did not move.

'Go now,' said Mother, louder. 'I don't want to harm you.'

One of the wings rucked, exposing a single bluegrey eye. The eye peered at Mother.

She took another step back.

The vesperi shut its wings and stood. Delphine saw now it had blood crusted around its muzzle. One of its arms hung limp. Its pupils were pinpricks.

The vesperi stared into her eyes for a long instant.

It turned, running into the chaos of the burning room. A drop-leaf table collapsed in a shower of cinders; the vesperi jumped, its wings spreading, slapping the air. Smoke wafted in loose parentheses, fanned back; flames flared; the vesperi jumped again, beat its wings. It was going to hit the wall. It jumped a third time; its wings met in a steep V, pumped; it tucked its legs in and swished over the sill, out the open window, into the night.

A hand on Delphine's shoulder.

'Come on.'

Mother shook her. Delphine could not stop staring at the window.

'Delphine!' Mother yanked Delphine's –

– arm pinned to the floor under a knee as Eleanor Wethercroft clouted her in the nose. Delphine's eyes watered; she clutched at Eleanor's throat, felt her fingers close around the cold, sharp crucifix that hung from Eleanor's necklace.

'I'll kill you, I'll kill you, I'll kill you.' Eleanor chanted the words with breathless momentum until they slurred into nonsense: 'you I'll kill you I'll kill you'll kill you'll kill you'll killyul killyulk ill yulk illyuk'.

Delphine tugged and felt the delicate silver chain snap. Eleanor shrieked, clawing at Delphine's face – the cross was a keepsake from her dead grandmother.* Nails broke the skin. Delphine swatted with her free hand – her pinned arm was going numb.

---

* 'I'll let you look at Nana Florence's cross' was a common bargaining ploy of Eleanor's. Its counterpart – 'I swear on Nana Florence's cross' – was used as collateral when auditioning for custody of prized confidences. Eleanor had never explained why Nana Florence's cross was due the sort of veneration usually reserved for the remains of an apostle – as far as she was concerned, its status as a storied relic was self-evident.

She tried to roll but Eleanor's knees had her trapped. Eleanor spat on her and punched her in the eye and clamped her hands round her neck. Eleanor was a good half a stone heavier. Delphine walloped her arm and she did not flinch. Rage had made her implacable.

Delphine had the crucifix bunched in her fist. She could not breathe. Eleanor had lost her reason. She was going to throttle Delphine. Delphine let one of the crucifix's wicked little trefoil heads slip out between her third and forth knuckles and prayed to Nana Florence for absolution. She lunged and raked it down Eleanor Wethercroft's exposed arm.

It snagged sickeningly. Blood welled in a deep trench. Eleanor's eyes bulged; she gripped her tricep and immediately her palm slipped in blood. She squeezed and fat red droplets like cherries oozed over the webbing of her fingers.

Delphine flung the cross across the corridor; it jangled off the wall, gleaming. Eleanor watched its trajectory and in the instant of distraction Delphine grabbed her earlobe and pulled, hard.

Eleanor Wethercroft –

– screeched, its wingtips smouldering. The straggling vesperi dropped its javelin and fled.

Delphine and Mother picked their way down the corridor, heading west, towards the long library. Smoke was thick now, and they had to drop to a crouch. Delphine pulled her cardigan over her mouth.

'Daddy!'

The corridor was a detritus of vesperi corpses, some battered or stabbed, several charred, still smoking, as if the creatures had dragged themselves from the fire before dying.

'It's no good!' said Mother. Delphine ignored her and pressed on. The heat and the noise thickened and Delphine's crouch became a crawl. She was heading into the heart of the inferno. 'He can't be here!'

'He must be!'

'Delphine!' Mother snatched at her wrist. 'We have . . . ' Mother stopped to hack and splutter. 'You must stop this!'

Delphine could not draw a breath to reply but her answer was clear. She was not going back. She knew Daddy was up ahead. She could still find him. She could still save him.

She glanced back and the smoke was too thick and Mother was gone.

Don't follow me, she thought. Mother had spent her whole life sacrificing. It was time to let someone else take their turn.

Delphine crawled into a black and endless tunnel. Her bare skin brushed metal, blistering.

'Daddy!' She could not get low enough beneath the smoke. Her burns stung fiercely. '*Daddy!*'

She thought she heard something off to her left, muffled.

'Daddy?'

'Go away!'

'*Daddy!*'

The door was ajar. Delphine levered it open with her crab hook and found herself back –

– in the brawny clutches of Mrs Leddington. Delphine knew better than to struggle.

Eleanor Wethercroft sat on the floor, panting. Clotting blood banded her arms. She turned Nana Florence's crucifix over and over in her palm.

'She ambushed me, miss,' said Eleanor. 'I heard the alarm and I ran down to see if I could save anybody and – '

'Shut up, Eleanor,' said Mrs Leddington.

'But – '

'The building is *on fire*. Stand.'

Eleanor hung her head. She made a show of wincing as she got to her feet. Mrs Leddington grabbed Eleanor by the wrist. She began dragging the girls towards the exit.

Eleanor Wethercroft whimpered and gasped. At last, she said: 'But she tied me up in the boiler room, miss.'

'And you wriggled out like Houdini.'

'The knots came loose. She's a rotten knot-tier, miss.'

Delphine resisted the urge to swing for her.

'Is she?' said Mrs Leddington. 'I thought you ran down because of the alarm.'

'No. Well . . . I only said that because I didn't want to get her expelled. She tied me up.'

Delphine kept her eyes on the floor. 'It's true. I did.'

'Oh, don't insult my intelligence,' said Mrs Leddington. 'You're a pernicious little bully, Miss Wethercroft. You think you're above justice. Well, justice today.'

Eleanor Wethercroft muttered: 'My father shall hear of this. At least he's not a – '

Delphine was on her before she could say the word again. Mrs Leddington was caught off-guard and the girls tumbled to –

– the floor on her hands and knees. She had reached her bedroom. The collapsed wardrobe was burning. Smoke frothed low.

Daddy lay against the wall beneath the window, his face filthy. His shirt was open. He was clutching a ball of paper.

Delphine dragged herself towards him. Her lungs felt as if they had been creosoted. She hacked and spat.

'Daddy.'

He did not answer. A familiar dullness coated his eyes.

'Daddy, we have to go.'

He groaned. His mouth hung open.

'Daddy. It's Delphine.'

'Delphy?' He blinked once, twice. 'Where are you?'

'The house is on fire,' she said. She took his hand. 'Follow me.'

Daddy snatched his hand away. 'Can't.'

'We'll crawl,' said Delphine. She coughed in her palm. 'I'll help you.'

Daddy shut his eyes. 'I'm not leaving without Arthur.'

'Come on!' She yanked his collar. 'We have to go. There isn't any time.'

'Arthur!' Tears had washed away the soot either side of his nose, leaving canals of clear wet skin. 'Dear God, man, where are you? Arthur!'

'Daddy, please. You're not well.' She grabbed the front of his shirt and a button tore off. The heat in the room was tremendous. 'Arthur died years ago.'

Daddy tipped his head back against the wall, rolling it from side to side. He coughed and spluttered.

'No, no, no. You don't understand. You don't understand at all.'

'Don't argue. Just come.'

'Arthur! I'm in here!'

'Please, Daddy. I can't carry you any more. I'm not strong enough.'

Daddy shut his eyes. He had blood on his teeth. How would Mother handle this?

'Gideon.' Delphine fought down the tremor in her voice. 'Now, listen here. Don't be obstinate. Everyone's waiting for you, you silly man. If you want to die, you can die tomorrow.'

Daddy's eyes remained closed. He frowned.

'Arthur?'

Delphine fanned smoke away from her mouth.

'Yes,' she said. 'It's me. Now, come on.'

'Oh, Arty!' Daddy gazed into the descending smoke. 'Oh God, I . . . ' He clutched his throat, made a retching noise. 'I knew you'd come. It's been black without you. I . . . ' coughing, ' . . . I couldn't see a damn thing.'

'You must follow me.'

'Sit a moment.' He patted the floor beside him. 'Abide.'

'There isn't time! We have to – '

'I kept it from all of them, old man.' Daddy grinned tightly. 'I think . . . I think Anne knew, perhaps. Perhaps she guessed.'

Sweat fell from Delphine's chin onto the hot floor. 'Guessed what?'

'Ah!' He held up a forefinger. 'Ah ha ha! Nope, you won't . . . you won't trick me that easily. We made a pact, and I never . . . argh, Christ.' He spat something black. 'Look, they've . . . I took a knock in that last barrage. My leg's done in.'

'Then crawl! Come on!' Delphine grabbed his arm and pulled.

'I want you to take a message to my daughter.'

Delphine let go. 'What's the message?'

Daddy's breath heaved in and out.

'Tell her . . . ' He broke off to cough. 'I read her note.' He relaxed his fingers and the crumpled paper spread its petals. She could see the 'F' of 'FATHER', scrunched back on itself so it looked like an 'M'. 'Tell her . . . to listen to her mother.'

'Are you quite finished?'

'Utterly.'

She wiped sweat from her eyes. 'You have to follow me.'

'You go, dear. I'll rest here a while.'

In the midst of the flames, cold panic swamped her chest. He wasn't going to listen to her. She slapped him in the stomach.

'No! Come now,' she said. He did not move. 'Venner! I am giving you an order!'

Daddy massaged his brow with his fingertips. He squeezed the bridge of his nose. His fingers left smutty trails.

'All right, sir.' He blew out slowly. 'All right.'

Delphine cradled his head. He let her help him onto his hands and knees. The air was so hot she had to breathe through clenched teeth and still it scalded her tongue. She pushed her face to the rug, where the smoke was thinner.

'Follow me!' she shouted. She began crawling towards the door. The glass in the window burst. She felt a sudden scorching breeze, flames sucking at the new fuel source. It hurt to keep her eyes open. She pressed on blind, feeling ahead with the crab hook. 'This way!' Daddy did not reply. 'Gideon? Are you there? Daddy?' She inhaled a great lungful of smoke and started spluttering. She tried to draw in fresh air but she could not stop coughing. She kept crawling. She could not feel her hands. Her scalp was burning.

She opened her eyes and saw only smoke. She could not see the door. She could not breathe.

'Daddy!'

What if she was going the wrong way? What if she had lost him?

Her legs felt so heavy. She swished the crab hook back and forth, hoping to catch a wall. The heat was all round her now. She was so tired.

She thought she might go to sleep for a while, till all the fuss was over.

* * *

Strong arms gripped her waist and she was rising. Pain – a sharp blow to the ribs – heat and sweat and fingers digging into her guts.

The temperature rose till it was unbearable, till she must be on fire. Maybe this was dying.

She blacked out.

CHAPTER 39

ARISE

Delphine felt drizzle against her cheeks. When she opened her eyes, she was looking up at Professor Carmichael.

The lawn was wet and cool and lit by the blazing Hall. The Professor knelt at her side, in the lee of the ha-ha. His jumper had a fist-sized hole scorched in the shoulder. The skin beneath was covered in greasy blisters like the white of a fried egg.

'You're alive,' he croaked.

Delphine tried to speak but her tongue was burnt. She coughed and it was a kick in the chest.

'Steady,' said the Professor, wincing with the effort. He looked back towards the house. 'They're coming.'

Delphine sat up slowly, the Professor supporting her. Across the grass, limping in silhouette, came Mother, supporting a ragged and delirious Daddy. Flamelight turned their outlines golden.

Rain fell in wafting layers. A few yards away, Mrs Hagstrom sat with Alice's head in her lap, running fingers through her hair and murmuring to her. Alice's chest rose and fell fitfully. Mrs Hagstrom's shoulder had been clumsily bandaged with a stocking. Droplets ran down her hollow cheeks. Somewhere she had lost a shoe. The male guest whose name Delphine still did not know sat quietly beside her, hugging his jacket to his shoulders.

Delphine leant an arm against the wet stone of the ha-ha and stood. There was something hard in the sleeve of her cardigan. She shook it out and the crab hook dropped into her palm. The metal was hot to the touch.

She looked back at the Hall – fire was raging in the west wing. Blue smoke haemorrhaged through a collapsed section of roof, underlit, looming. Great orange flakes rose into the rain and withered. The long library was gone.

Mother's dress hung in charred streamers round her waist. She had draped a throw rug over her shoulders. Vapour spilled from Daddy's lips. He was shivering. As they moved into the lee of the ha-ha, Mother waited to see if he could support himself. She stepped away.

'Do up your shirt, dear.'

Daddy started fastening the bottom button. His fingers were clumsy and slow. Professor Carmichael watched him warily.

'Mrs Hagstrom needs a doctor,' said the Professor. He glanced at the bloody slit in Daddy's trousers. 'We all do.'

'His Lordship's car was out the front of the house,' said Mrs Hagstrom. 'Reggie . . . uh, that is . . . it was due a wash. If it's still there . . . I think I can manage the drive.'

'Right,' said the Professor. 'I'll head to Pigg and telephone for the police. They've a phone in the Brown Bull. Delphine, you go with Muriel. Get the car.'

The Professor stood.

Delphine hacked up a brown gobbet of phlegm.

'I've got to help Mr Garforth.'

'Mr Garforth?' said Mother.

'Henry.' Everyone looked at Delphine blankly. 'The head keeper. I'm afraid something's happened to him.'

'Delphine, this isn't the time.'

'If it wasn't for him we'd all be dead!' Delphine's chest cramped and she paused to cough. 'He made sure no more monsters can cross the channel.'

Professor Carmichael raised a blackened eyebrow. 'You mean . . . they're French?'

'No. I don't . . . Never mind. Mr Garforth knows about it but he might need our help.'

'Right. Fine.' The Professor slapped a huge palm against his chest. 'I'll go and look for him. You stay with your mother.'

'You don't know your way through the woods. I'm going with you.'

'You are not, Delphine.' Mother grasped Delphine by the scruff of her cardigan. 'You need to see a doctor.' On top of the Hall, more tiles caved in with an almighty woof of sparks. Mother did not flinch. 'I have given you tremendous latitude this evening and you have almost died and I won't stand for it any more because I love you.'

'Listen to your mother,' said Daddy. 'Ow!'

He slapped his neck.

Daddy examined his hand. Something like a smear of boot polish gleamed in the fluctuating light of the fire. Delphine stepped closer.

'Giddy?' said Mother.

Daddy held out his palm. Across his fingers were the turquoise-magenta wings and smashed carapace of a hornet.

'I think I've been stung.'

At the far end of the west wing, the music room window blew out. Mr Cox, immaculate in riding coat and blue breeches, stepped out of the window. Behind him was Stokeham. Cox dropped down onto the gravel. He turned, reaching up to accept the leather gauntlet of his superior.

'Get down,' hissed the Professor. Everybody dropped behind the ha-ha.

Delphine and the Professor peered over the lip of the stone wall, back towards the house.

Rain dripped from Stokeham's bone-white beakmask. Cox raked his fingers through his shining chestnut hair. From the shattered window clambered Reggie. Delphine could not make out his eyes. Sluggishly, he reached through the frame, reached into thickening smoke, and lifted out Miss DeGroot.

'What on earth's he doing?' muttered the Professor.

Miss DeGroot staggered as her feet touched the gravel. Her arm was wrapped in a singed curtain. It dragged as she took a few uncertain steps forward.

Cox unhooked a flintlock pistol from his belt. He said something to Miss DeGroot. She did not appear to answer. Stokeham gazed across the estate. Cox began walking towards the ha-ha.

'What do we do now?' said Mrs Hagstrom.

Professor Carmichael ducked back behind the ha-ha.

'We can't stay here,' he whispered.

'Alice can't move,' said Mrs Hagstrom. Alice whimpered and Mrs Hagstrom stroked her brow, shushing her.

'Giddy?' said Mother. She nudged Daddy, who was lying on his back. 'Come on, now.' She looked up. 'He's passed out.'

'We have to go *now*,' said the Professor.

Delphine glanced over the lip of the wall and saw Cox walking a few yards ahead of Stokeham, one palm sheltering his pistol from the rain. Miss DeGroot and Reggie were following, her club arm flattening the wet grass. Miss DeGroot's eyes were half-lidded. Cox was scanning the darkness. Unless he changed direction, he would be upon them in less than a minute.

Delphine turned to Mother.

'Keep everyone safe,' she said.

'What? Delphine, no!'

Delphine ran east in a low crouch along the ha-ha. She waited until she was a clear thirty yards from Mother, Daddy and the others, then broke cover. Slippery grass squeaked beneath her soles. She glanced back at Cox.

He had not spotted her. He was continuing towards the group's hiding place. He seemed totally unaware. By blind luck he was about to stumble on everyone. Delphine almost called out, but that would make it too obvious a diversion. He had to believe she did not want to be seen.

She began backing away. Cox was not even looking in her direction.

A familiar ticking came from overhead. Delphine glanced up to see a vesperi swooping towards her, the drizzle bouncing off the outline of its wings. It called out to its masters. Stokeham whirled round.

Cox's eyes widened.

'There!'

Delphine turned and ran.

A crack rang out. A breeze whipped past her ear. She felt a paralysing dread. She sucked the feelings down and focused on the woods. She just had to draw them away from Mother and Daddy and Alice and the Professor and Mrs Hagstrom. Her legs felt like bags of wet sand. Perhaps she should stop, turn and face them. She could spread her arms, close her eyes and wait for it all to be over.

But what about Mr Garforth? He might need her. She couldn't give up, not till she'd found him.

The ground sloped down towards dark, close-packed trees. Any other night, the woods would have looked foreboding, but now the liquid black promised acres of precious cover.

'Deeeeellphine!' Cox's hallooing voice bounced off the trees. 'Come back! We only want to talk to you!'

Fear spurred Delphine on. She was drawing them away from Mother and Daddy and the Professor, and that was all that mattered. If she could just make them chase her into the woods, everyone else would be safe.

Stokeham was alive. A homemade grenade to the stomach and somehow Stokeham was alive.

Another crack – a branch on the tree ahead shattered with a crazy ricocheting sound.

'We don't want to hurt you!'

She was into the woods. Roots tore at her ankles and she fell and scrambled and she was into the bushes and away, dirt stinging her cuts and burns, soaked, breathless.

CHAPTER 40

YOU WILL DIE, BROTHER, IF YOU GO TO IT LONG ENOUGH

Delphine lay on her belly, hidden amongst a splash of gipsy-wort in the dried-up riverbed. She listened to voles threading through brittle undergrowth, the thin eerie note of an owl. She was cold and wet. She waited for Stokeham and Cox to find her, the pistol to the temple, the white light.

If she stayed where she was she could survive till daybreak. Perhaps, by then, they would have given up searching for her. Perhaps they had already given up.

On the other hand, moving would be safest under cover of darkness. There was no sign of Stokeham's troops withdrawing, nor Mr Garforth, which meant that the plan had almost certainly failed.

But why hadn't Mr Loosley returned? Had Mr Garforth stopped him somehow?

As soon as Stokeham, Cox and Miss DeGroot gave up, they would head for the burial vault. They needed reinforcements.

If Mr Garforth was alive, he was in terrible danger.

Delphine thought of Dr Lansley and Mr Wightman and the male guest killed in the banqueting hall. She wondered if they were in Heaven now, or some black unplace of non-existence. She did not want to join them. If she hid here, and kept very still, the danger might pass. She might escape and keep on living for years and years.

She might learn to forgive herself the cowardice – but if she got caught, these few minutes would be her last on earth.

She understood now, the soldier's need for a talisman. She muttered in her head *please God, please God, please God,* but she knew too well that she was just one amongst hundreds of scurrying wretched creatures in the woods that night. She had no special claim on living. She was no more entitled to it than the anonymous guest who had died on the banqueting hall floor, or the dozens of vesperi shot, roasted or bludgeoned.

If Stokeham succeeded in seizing the channel, all England would be in peril. She might run a hundred miles and still die in the resultant war. Mr Wightman had died trying to flee. If death wanted you, escape was impossible.

She pictured Professor Carmichael, swinging his warhammer, colossal in his frenzy. She pictured Mother, squaring off against Miss DeGroot, her eyes hard, brilliant. She pictured dear Mr Garforth, warming milk for her in a saucepan, standing over it and stirring, so it didn't get a skin.

She listened. The entire wood seemed to hold its breath. The loudest sound was her heartbeat. Pressing her palms to the damp soil, she rose.

People had passed this way. Footprints trailed through the muddy earth, beside a long, shallow gouge, as if one of the party had been dragging a heavy object.

Delphine stuck to the shadows, creeping parallel to the trail, knowing with a sickening clarity where it would lead.

When she reached the edge of the clearing, she saw. The footprints and the drag mark led into the open tomb.

So they had made it inside. She heard a snap, threw herself flat. She held her breath, listening, praying.

A minute passed. No one came.

It was no good letting Stokeham hunt her. She had to find a weapon and fight back. If Mr Garforth was still alive, he needed her. She was a better shot than Cox. More to the point, his flintlock pistol was archaic and almost certainly waterlogged – a stupid affectation, just like everything else about him. She wouldn't let them terrorise her any more. She would force them to retreat, and if they wouldn't retreat . . .

No one was invincible. Somehow, Stokeham would die.

The anger gave her energy. And she knew exactly where to look for a gun.

Hidden amongst wind-hunched oaks was a cottage.

The door was open. The horseshoe over the lintel had fallen to the ground.

She ran inside without thinking. Embers winked in the hearth. The table had been upended and crockery lay shattered across the tiles. She ran into the bedroom.

Propp's sister was gone.

Even as the hollow feeling spread through her belly, Delphine realised she had expected this.

In the back room she rummaged through packing crates and heaped bric-a-brac looking for something to even the odds. It was all junk. She found a box of fishing weights – could she drop some into a pillow case to use as a cosh? Mr Garforth had taken all the gins. There was a bottle of Young's Draw Game and some other, more sinister-looking concoctions. Delphine was sliding a small, brown glass vial of rat poison from the back of the box when she heard footsteps.

She pressed her back to the wall and held her breath. Her heart-beats seemed to shake her whole body. She listened.

The front door croaked on its hinges. It might have been the wind.

A snap. Perhaps a knuckle of wet twig popping in the fire.

She tipped her head back till her scalp touched the wall, listened for someone listening for her. She gripped the crab hook. It was not much, but better than nothing. The metal shaft could parry a knife and the curved part might work for gouging an eye. She was not sure she could really drive a hook into someone's eyeball. Then she thought of Mr Wightman's ruptured throat, and her fingers tightened.

She heard a breath. She had definitely heard a man's breath. A box next to her slipped an inch. The entire contents of the shelf came crashing down.

'Who goes there? Show yourself.'

Delphine stepped out from behind the door. 'God. Professor.'

'Delphine?'

'I nearly hooked your eye out.'

Professor Carmichael touched a finger to the ridge of his cheekbone. 'Listen. You have to come. Your Mother thought she'd lost you.'

Delphine took a step back. 'Mr Garforth needs me. If I don't help him they'll bring more monsters, hundreds more – the whole country will be in danger.'

The Professor sighed with his entire body. 'Now, you listen to me. You barely got out of that house with your life.'

'Thank you, Professor.'

He swatted the air. 'Stop it. You may be feeling very cocksure but you're just a child. You can't do anything to stop them. None of us can. This is a job for the army. We've enough witnesses that they'll have to believe us. We must get as far away as possible. After you left, your father collapsed. He had a funny reaction to a sting.'

A squat shadow appeared in the doorway. Axle squealing, Lord Alderberen rolled into the cottage.

The lower half of his face was puckered and shrunken as a peach stone, thick mauve lips pouting while his good eye ticked from Delphine to the Professor, back again.

'Hello,' said the Professor.

Lord Alderberen nodded: *yes, yes, yes*. A few fine golden hairs floated above his bluish, pitted scalp. His shirt and grey flannel trousers hung in loose folds. He looked strangely childlike.

He reached into his lap. His arm was shaking. When he lifted it, he was holding a pistol.

'Don't think I won't fire, because I will.' His tongue slopped over empty gums. 'Any silly nonsense and I shall kill you both.'

'Lazarus, really . . . ' Professor Carmichael raised his hands.

'Don't you speak to me as if you know me!' Alderberen's voice was shrill and lisping. 'Just shut up and do as I say or God forgive me I shall end you both in this room.'

'But we're on your side! We're not going to hurt you.'

'I said shut up!' Lord Alderberen jabbed the pistol, a little black broomhandle Mauser, towards the Professor's belly. 'Wightman thought I was bluffing too. I told him to stop where he was and he laughed. He actually laughed. A bloody dogsbody who spends his days patching drainpipes, and he laughs at *me*? He would've told the papers – he would've undone generations of hard work for his twenty pieces of silver. So I did for him. I shot him then I slit his fat throat as if he were an antelope. Now you, both of you,' he gestured at Delphine with the gun, 'you come with me. I want you to walk five paces ahead of me, side by side. No more, no less. Remember, I shall be behind you. I can wheel this thing with one hand.' The Mauser wobbled in his grip. He frowned at the Professor. 'If you try to run I shall shoot the girl first.'

'But why? What have we done? We – '

Alderberen swung his arm to the right and fired once – *BLAM!* – into the fireplace. A gout of orange sparks went up and Delphine nearly fell.

'Last warning.'

Alderberen pointed to the door with the pistol. Delphine looked at Professor Carmichael, who nodded.

She was halfway to the door when she heard a noise. She turned and the Professor was already on top of Alderberen, grappling for his throat. Alderberen made a noise – *gnuh* – and his face tightened, soft jaw retracting into his upper skull like the wet flesh of a limpet. Professor Carmichael stepped away. He had his back to Delphine.

'Oh,' said the Professor. 'Oh. Oh. Oh.'

He sat down heavily. He put his hands on his stomach. Sticking from his jumper was the handle of a letter-knife.

'I warned you!' said Alderberen.

'Oh,' said the Professor. He closed his fingers round the knife. There was blood on his fingers. He doubled-up.

'Now,' said Lord Alderberen, aiming the pistol at Delphine. 'Move.'

She hesitated. Professor Carmichael lay on his side on the tiles, gritting his teeth.

Alderberen narrowed his eyes. He pointed the gun at the Professor's head.

'I'll shoot him like a lame horse.'

Slowly, Delphine turned and walked out of the door. The wind swiped at her hair, blowing so hard that she didn't catch Lord Alderberen's next instruction until the third time he said it.

'To the ice house.'

CHAPTER 41

WHAT SHE STRIVES TO SHUN

Mist rolled across the lake. Alderberen Hall was a skull lit from within.

Delphine paused at the top of the hill.

'Why are you doing this?'

Hunched in his wheelchair, Lord Alderberen scowled beneath a caul of rainwater.

'None of your bloody business.' Droplets clung to the Mauser's long black barrel. 'Inside.'

Rain burst against the roof of the ice house in little white explosions, running down the low dark walls into boggy grass. The half-rotten door had been torn from its hinges.

Delphine rested a hand on the doorway. She took a deep breath, then turned.

'Why does your father hate you so much?'

She expected him to pull the trigger. She watched the muzzle, waiting for the gun to kick. Rainwater streamed down his greyblue cheeks. He inhaled, a long stuttering motion. His bad eye closed.

'My father is dead.'

As he slurred the final syllable, his chin twisted into his chest and he began to convulse. He clutched the arm of his wheelchair. His pistol hand cramped.

Delphine feinted left then sidestepped right. Alderberen swung the Mauser towards her but she parried the barrel with her hook. The gun barked. A shot ricocheted off the ice house.

'Why, you . . . ' Alderberen lunged for the hook. Delphine twisted her wrist, wrenching the pistol from his grasp. It dropped between his legs and landed on the grass. He clasped the shaft of the crab hook, reaching for the gun with his other hand. His face puckered with effort. 'Bloody . . . damn . . . ' His fingers flexed and closed a clear foot above the gun. 'Christ's sweet tree!'

With indecent ease, Delphine tore the hook from his grip and drove the blunt pommel into his chest.

The force of the blow knocked him upright, shoulders slapping the back of the wheelchair. He stared at her, wide-eyed. The chair began to roll backwards.

He swung for her, but his hands clipped his rising knees as the chair clattered down the steep hill, accelerating. Behind him the lake spread black and huge and silent.

The squeak of the axle built to an urgent trill. He tried to glance back. The chair hit a patch of reeds. The wheels jammed and the chair tipped.

From the top of the hill, Delphine heard the splash.

She waited for him to surface. Ripples radiated from the handles of the wheelchair. She almost ran to help him.

Then she remembered Mr Garforth.

Delphine took the Mauser from the wet grass and flipped up the safety lever with her thumb. She stepped over splinters of wood and ducked inside the ice house.

Rain drummed on the domed roof. The interior stunk of wet cement. Why on earth had Lord Alderberen wanted to take her here?

She squinted against the gloom. The hairs on the back of her neck prickled. She was on the precipice of a deep conical pit. Perhaps thirty feet across and built of brick, its sloping sides narrowed to a funnel. She could not see the bottom. Rainwater drooled from the ceiling, finding channels in the brickwork so the pit seemed to ripple and flow.

She remembered following Propp here. What was all the fuss about? It was just a hole.

And then, she heard voices.

She could not make them out – the dimensions of the ice house turned every sound into a strange, keening echo – but when she closed her eyes and concentrated, it sounded like a woman crying.

Delphine pulled back the bolt on the Mauser and checked the box magazine. A cartridge sat in the chamber and there were more beneath. Lord Alderberen had fired twice, and once more when he shot Wightman. Assuming he had started with a full magazine and hadn't reloaded in between, she had seven rounds left.

Delphine sat down on the cusp of the pit. She slid her legs over the side. The walls were steep, but not sheer. Parts of the brickwork had crumbled, forming toeholds. She wedged the head of the crab hook into the mortar between two stone floor slabs, then turned and began lowering herself into the pit. She dug her foot into a crack, tested putting her weight on it. The brick held. Slowly, she descended, towards the voices.

Sections of brickwork were slimy with rainwater. She picked her way around them. Near the bottom the gradient flattened out, till she could turn onto her backside and shuffle the final few feet. In the floor's centre was an opening the size of a wishing well. Two rusted hooks were set into its perimeter. She held her breath. The pit seemed to close in around her. She glanced up at the distant roof. How would she get back out?

The voices were clearer; she was sure she heard Propp's sister crying. One of the others had the fruity, grating cadences of Mr Cox. And then, unmistakable, deep and lulling:

'I forgive you both.'

Cox's sigh echoed through the chamber below.

'Do you know, from the very first time we met, I knew you were a fraud. But like all habitual, inveterate liars, you have spent so long at your poisonous arts that you have deceived yourself. Even now, you act as if you are the injured party.'

In a series of small, cautious movements, Delphine lay on her belly and peered over the lip of the hole.

She saw a cave, illuminated by what looked like lamplight. The drop to the ground was at least twelve feet. A long shadow stretched into her line of sight, gesticulating.

'It's over,' said Mr Cox. 'You will return with us and be tried in public. Then you will be executed.'

'I am glad to hear justice will be done,' said Propp.

'Oh, cling to your sarcasm if it comforts you. Dozens of my loyal staff were murdered today. They came without guns, intent only on ensuring the safe return of my daughter. You slaughtered them wholesale.'

Delphine dug her toes into the brickwork behind her and leant forward a little more. She could see the horned silhouette of a harka – no, wait, it was just a statue – but Propp and Stokeham were still out of view. Where was Mr Garforth?

'Why did you do it, Ivan?' said Miss DeGroot. 'What did you want?'

'Same thing as any dancer.'

'What's that?'

Propp made a short, throaty sound that might have been a grunt or a pained laugh. 'Balance.'

Delphine leant forward a little more. She felt her foot pop loose from its toehold. She threw an arm out to steady herself and slid forward on her tummy, knocking a nugget of mortar *click-clack* echoing to the floor below. Blood rushed to her head. The cave swung above her and she flailed at the edges of the hole, dropping the crab hook, grasping wet stone as she fell. She lurched rightways up before falling. She landed on her backside so hard that she saw white and her eyes watered.

Over three seconds Delphine saw and heard and thought this:

She was sitting in the middle of a cavern. There were six stone statues of harka, vesperi and humans. Mr Cox was standing to her left. He had taken his jacket off and the silk of his dirty gold waistcoat scintillated in the light of an oil lamp burning on the floor behind him. Miss DeGroot was to her right, thick arm swaddled in crimson fabric, cowlick bobbing over the knuckle of shrapnel lodged in her eye socket. Reggie sat beside her, milk-white under his short red hair, hollow-eyed, twitching. Propp was on his knees, his wrists bound – maybe he had never managed to untie them? – directly in front of her. Lying on her back in the centre of the chamber, next to a black and twisting pool – the channel, surely – was the old lady, Propp's sister. She was pawing at the air, clenching and unclenching her delicate fingers. Between Propp and his sister, statuesque in a long black overcoat, stood Stokeham. A crack ran across the beak-mask, twisting its dour, aloof frown into a sneer.

She saw no child. Delphine felt the broomhandle grip of the Mauser in her palm. Miss DeGroot said 'Hey!' then her arm burst its wrapping, sprouting wet pink cords that whipped towards Delphine.

Delphine raised the pistol and pulled the trigger.

Nothing happened.

She had left the safety on.

A tendril wrapped round her arm.

'You little rat!' Cox was charging at her.

Delphine thumbed the safety down and fired once, twice. She hit Miss DeGroot in the torso and chin. Reggie grunted and collapsed. The impact of the second shot twisted Miss DeGroot's head back; the cord round Delphine's wrist sagged, melting into stringy mulch. Delphine yanked her arm free, brought the gun round and shot Cox in the gut. He pivoted with the shot, his momentum carrying him into her. Delphine was thrown flat against the floor. Cox stank of tobacco and cologne and something chemical.

Propp was up on one foot. He stood with a gasp, grey eyes bulging. Stokeham did not react for a moment, then the mask swivelled, owl-like, to regard him.

Delphine's gun arm was trapped under Cox. He was heavier than he looked.

Stokeham marched at Propp. Propp let out a small, mournful sound, 'Ah,' then Stokeham's leather gauntlets were round his throat.

Delphine rolled. Cox groaned above her. She tugged at the gun. Her hand slipped free. The splattered puce remains of Miss DeGroot's arm coalesced on the wet stone, knitting themselves into a single grasping limb. Even though Cox had been shot in the stomach, he raised a fist to pound Delphine.

Delphine rested her temple against the ground and closed one eye.

She shot Stokeham twice in the shoulder, feeling Cox buck with the impact. She tilted the muzzle up and blew a hole in the beak-mask's right lens. A spritz of juice and bone splinters left the back of Stokeham's skull. Stokeham toppled and performed a little jig on the ground.

Freed from Stokeham's grip, Propp staggered towards the pool. Miss DeGroot made a blustering sound – 'Pwah aw pah!' – and her half-reconstructed arm reared up like a giant python. Propp had an arm round the old lady's shawl-wrapped shoulder.

He smiled.

'Adieu.'

Miss DeGroot's big crude claw of a hand lunged at his throat. He tipped backwards into the pool, pulling the old lady with him. Delphine heard a slop, like a rock dropping into a swamp. The long liquid limb dived after him.

It surfaced clutching a triangle of shawl.

'No. No!'

Miss DeGroot staggered across the cavern, ranting, swearing. She paused at the threshold of the pool. Her arm retracted and solidi-fied, fingers pushing out of the undifferentiated stump, lengthening and separating. She made a fist, shaking with the effort, then unfurled her fingers one at a time. She was marinating in sweat, glorious. For a moment, she looked almost human.

She glanced back. Lamplight glinted in her eye.

'Come on, Reggie.' She held out her other, human, hand. Reggie stood and walked to her.

'Reggie, wait!'

Delphine tried to drag herself out from under Mr Cox. She felt a sharp pain in her hip. His coils of chestnut hair brushed her throat and it was this, of all things, that made her gag.

Reggie did not look back. He took Miss DeGroot's hand. They looked at their reflections in the pool. Miss DeGroot nodded.

Together, they fell.

Mr Cox caught hold of Delphine's wrists. She was trapped. A beaked silhouette appeared in the corner of her vision.

'Well,' panted Cox, one eye screwed shut, 'this *is* disappointing.'

CHAPTER 42

THE FIRST BLAST OF THE TRUMPET

Mr Cox released her.

As he stood, he kicked away the Mauser and it skidded to the foot of a vesperi statue. Now she had time to examine the figure, it looked like Mr Loosley – stocky shoulders, small, bunched wings. A white streak of lime bisected its left eye and ran down over its chin, where water had dripped from the ceiling.

Mr Cox slipped his hand inside his tawny waistcoat and poked a finger through the hole in the stomach. The finger wriggled, like a white worm breaking the surface of a molehill. He removed the waistcoat. Underneath, leather straps held a black metal cuirass plate to his sternum. He pressed his thumb into a shining dent at its centre, gasped with pain.

When he had got his breath back, he slipped his waistcoat back on. He glanced at Delphine.

'Get up.'

Perhaps the sedative had finally worn off, because Delphine found it hard to breathe. She looked around the chamber. She saw vesperi corpses, a fallen harka at the foot of the stairs, her sawn-off beside the mound of its corpse. Attached to the south wall, obscured by shadow, was a cluster of aluminium washing-up bowls. So Mr Garforth *had* been here.

'You've lost,' she said, trying to ignore the catch in her throat.

Mr Cox tilted his head back and looked at her. He and Stokeham made a swatting gesture.

'Yes, all right, then,' said Cox, the trace of a smile playing on his lips, 'stare at the herald. I suppose you've earned the privilege.'

He plucked at a loose thread trailing from the hole in his waistcoat. Delphine glanced at Stokeham. They seemed in no hurry to kill her. She could not understand it, and that made her heart race because it meant they knew something she didn't.

'How *did* you find us, by the way?' said Cox, without looking up.

Delphine shot a glance at Stokeham. Cracks radiated out from the beakmask's shattered lens. The eye beneath was in shadow.

'Your son brought me here.'

'Really?' Cox began dabbing at the tacky blood with a handkerchief. 'What happened to him?'

'I . . . I pushed him into the lake.'

Cox and Stokeham exchanged a glance. It was the first time Delphine had seen them acknowledge one another's existence directly, and she felt the frisson of a weird taboo snapping.

Mr Cox looked back down at his stomach. He sniffed, nodded. He began to chuckle. He patted his belly, threw his head back and laughed.

'It's not funny. He might be dead.'

'No, Delphine, no.' Cox wagged a bloody finger at her head. 'That is *precisely* why it is funny. The father dies in a fire, and his son, some eighty-one years later, *drowns* on the same estate! The Stokeham Curse strikes again.'

'But you didn't die, did you?'

Again, Cox shot a glance at Stokeham, who appeared to return it.

'No,' said Cox. 'I did not. Do you know you're an incredibly re*source*ful young lady, getting this far? How old are you, fifteen?'

'Thirteen,' said Delphine, a little proudly.

'Thirteen.' Cox whistled. He supported his elbow with one hand and tapped his chin with another.

She gritted her teeth against the cold weight in her chest. 'Are you going to kill me, then?'

Cox rolled his eyes. 'No. I am not going to kill you.'

She looked at Stokeham, whose arms were folded. To Stokeham, she said: 'But I helped Mr Propp escape.'

'Is that what you think you did?' Cox strode to the pool in the centre of the chamber. He ran his fingers along the low, flat wall surrounding it. 'What, you think that waiting for him on the other threshold is a lovely party with plum cake and macaroons and a dancing bear? The soldiers you saw tonight were just a bridgehead, a forlorn hope, uh . . . *les enfants perdus*. Back in Avalonia, I command an army. The false prophet has merely handed himself – and my daughter – into their custody.'

'What do you mean, your daughter?'

'I mean the child who was here but minutes ago.' Stokeham gestured at the pool.

'She wasn't a *child*.'

The beakmask tilted. 'You don't understand a thing, do you?'

Delphine made herself focus on Stokeham, struggling to formulate a plan while she kept her expression meek and engaged. She mustn't give up now. Mother said there was always a way.

'Teach me,' she said.

'Very well.' Cox appeared shocked at the words leaving his mouth. He turned to Stokeham, aghast. 'But, Endlessness, you can't . . . ' At this, Stokeham's body stiffened. Cox dropped to one knee and bowed, colouring. 'Forgive me, Endlessness. I forget myself. Naturally, you can do anything.' A long auburn forelock swung before his eyes. 'If my words implied disrespect, I am *mort*ified, Endlessness, I only intended to advise, ah . . . that is, to *clar*ify . . . ' He took a deep breath. His eyes rose slyly. 'Endlessness – are you sure?'

Stokeham did not answer. A gloved hand signalled for Delphine to rise. This time, she did not resist. If she got the opportunity to run, it would be easier from a standing start. Her whole body ached and stung.

Still bowing, Cox said: 'We are of one mind, you and I.'

Delphine glanced towards the exit.

'By all means, run. I shall not stop you. Unlike my enemies, I would not murder a child in cold blood. I have achieved my aims for the time being. You can cause no more mischief. Go, if you wish.' Stokeham held up a palm. 'Or, if you prefer, you may hear me out.'

Delphine breathed through clenched teeth. 'What do you want?'

'You have impressed me, young lady, with your insolence and enterprise. Therefore, I propose an experiment: I shall tell you the truth. Then, you must make a choice.'

The leather gauntlets rose behind Stokeham's head. Delphine heard the click of a buckle being unfastened. The great curved beak sagged. In one smart movement, the gloves gripped the sides of the mask and tossed it to the floor, where it lay, rocking.

'Hello,' said its owner.

She was beautiful.

CHAPTER 43

OUR POISON'D CHALICE

From behind one of the statues Mr Cox produced a satchel containing a gemmed flask and four ivory cups. The flask was a stylised turret constructed from hundreds of tiny silver bricks, its battlements lined with cannon. Cox unscrewed a crenelated lid studded with sapphires and poured a treacly, bruise-coloured substance into three of the cups. He grimaced as he handed a cup to the woman, and touched two fingers to his stomach. He offered a cup to Delphine.

She took it. Incised around the sides of the cup were hanging cadavers, all harka.

'Drink.'

The woman's voice was dry and quavering but her face was young and supple, her skin the soft pink of rose quartz. Her large eyes gleamed. She sat on the ridge surrounding the pool, lifting the skirts of her overcoat so they did not drag on the damp ground. She looked Delphine up and down. Her yellow-white hair was swept from left to right and fastened behind her ear with an ivory clasp. A sheen of perspiration stood out on her brow. She smiled.

Delphine looked at the cup uncertainly. The liquid had a heavy, nettley musk. She tilted the cup; its contents oozed towards the rim.

'I don't like speaking,' said the woman. 'Mr Cox helps me. He, uh . . . ' She screwed her eyes shut. '*Interprets.*' Mr Cox bowed modestly. 'But he adds things. I want to speak to you. Just me. My name is Anwen.' She raised her cup.

'Where's Sir Peter?' Delphine said.

'Dead.'

Delphine stared down into her drink.

'Why did you pretend to be Lord Alderberen's father?'

'I didn't.'

'But you said he was your son.'

'He is.'

Delphine frowned. 'Then . . . you're Peter Stokeham's wife?'

'Widow.'

'You died in a fire. He went mad with grief.'

The corner's of Anwen's mouth creased. 'Not quite.'

Delphine could not tell if she was smiling.

Mr Cox stepped forward. Anwen held up a hand. 'No, thank you.' She waved him away. 'I would like to explain myself.'

Cox nodded, a taut smile on his face as he stepped back. Delphine heard the hiss of air leaving his nostrils. From his pocket he took a clay pipe and tobacco pouch.

'When I married Peter,' said Anwen, 'I didn't know about the family secret.' Her voice was almost inaudible. Between each sentence, she took a sharp breath. 'He told me on our wedding night. The Stokehams had found a way to live for ever.

'For generations, when people in his family got old, they did not die. Instead they travelled to the new world, where they could live, with their servants, and their servants' families, for all time.

'I thought he was mocking me. Then I thought he was mad. I asked for proof. So he brought me here.'

She lifted her arms and gestured at the chamber. 'He showed me the threshold. We couldn't use it ourselves, of course, but when the first visitor emerged I knew he had been telling me the truth.'

'What about the fire?' said Delphine.

'I was very young. I didn't realise at first that my husband was . . . misguided.'

'He was weak and naïve,' said Mr Cox.

'Yes, thank you, Cox,' said Anwen, sharply.

'Apologies, Endlessness.' He returned to filling his pipe.

'He . . . ' Anwen sighed. She rubbed her eyes with thumb and forefinger. 'He wanted to break the covenant. He wanted to open up our paradise to everybody. He hadn't thought of how he would protect Avalonia from people who might destroy it. He was ready to expose the new world to all the villains and thieves who spoilt the old one. I thought he was wrong. But I was young and with child, and I said nothing.

'Conscience is not so easily denied. I was troubled. This did not go unnoticed.' With a slight inclination of her head, she indicated Mr Cox. 'I confided in him. He shared my concerns.'

'We were *of a mind*, Endlessness.'

Anwen rolled her eyes. 'He was only the first footman, but I was alone in the Hall. For the first time, I felt I had met someone who *understands*. Together, we came up with a plan to save the new world.'

Cox straightened up, wearing a broad smile. He produced a matchbook, lit his pipe, and performed a few leisurely puffs until the shag took. He slipped the matchbook back into the fob pocket of his waistcoat.

'One night,' Anwen said, 'the under-butler was off-duty, so Mr Cox took supper to his master. After this meal, my husband fell ill and died. He often stayed in his chambers for days. The servants knew never to disturb him. To hide his death for a short time was not so very hard. Two days later, an ambassador arrived from across the channel. I explained what I had done, and why. I explained my husband's plans to break the centuries-old covenant and reveal Avalonia's existence to the rest of the world.'

'But you *killed* him,' said Delphine. 'They ought to have hanged you.'

'The covenant was Avalonia's most sacred law,' said Cox. 'It kept the new world safe from plunderers. He would have blackened the Stokeham name. His ancestors would have been excommunicated. We spared him that.'

'The ambassador was impressed. I received the honours in my husband's place.'

'Her Ladyship and I,' said Mr Cox, almost sighing the honorific, 'embarked on a little *folie à deux*, as I believe they call it these days.'

'I'm sure you can guess the rest,' said Anwen. 'We started a fire, then pretended I had died and grief had turned my husband into a recluse. I had builders construct tunnels and secret passages so I could come and go as I pleased. Whenever I left the house, my face was covered. Servants knew better than to speak to me. We let senior staff go, of course – hired people who had not known the Earl before his, ah . . . hibernation. On the rare occasion someone absolutely had to talk to "Sir Peter", Mr Cox accepted the role with aplomb.' Cox acknowledged this with a nod. 'We would insist they spoke to him through a door, or, in the final years, over the telephone.'

'You're idiots,' said Delphine. 'You should have just said your husband died in the fire. Then you could have been yourself.'

'That would have been easier, certainly, but there were a number of political and legal obstacles that only the 3rd Earl of Alderberen could surmount. My husband's failure to enter the perpetuum would have caused . . . unrest. The ambassador proposed that, in the interests of stability, we delay news of Peter Stokeham's passing until we had cemented some alliances.

'I still remember the moment I announced the truth. Bechstein looked like he'd swallowed a cricket ball. But he couldn't stop me. None of them could. It was too late.' She let out a laugh that was more like a sneeze. 'Some of them still can't accept it. But that's the thing about, uh . . . ' She snapped her fingers.

'Vacillating, hidebound cowards, Endlessness?'

'Mmm. They'll do anything to avoid admitting that the worlds are changing. We can use that. To this day, some of them refuse to believe I'm not Peter. They think all *this*,' she indicated her face and torso, 'is just a product of my arising.'

'The honours manifest in different ways,' said Cox.

'What about your son?' said Delphine.

Anwen's smile withered. 'What about him?'

'Didn't he notice you weren't his father?'

'He was six weeks old. He didn't notice anything. I sent him off to India, out of the way. Later, after we had decided it was time for the Silent Earl to, ah . . . '

'To pass beyond the veil,' said Cox, with a sweep of his palm.

'To die,' said Anwen, 'and Lazarus inherited the Hall, we made contact, and revealed to him the truth.'

'The revelation is a test in itself,' said Cox. 'He did not pass.'

Delphine transferred the cup to her left hand. She looked up, squinting into the shadows behind the two human statues at the back of the chamber.

'Did you have these made?' she said, pointing.

Anwen and Cox turned to look.

'No,' said Anwen. 'Before my time.' She turned back to Delphine. 'Why are you interested in statues all of a sudden?'

Delphine shrugged.

'Well, then.' Anwen lifted her cup to her lips. 'Let us drink.'

'Wait,' said Delphine. 'How do I know it isn't poisoned?'

'Why use poison when I could have you bludgeoned to death?'

'Aesthetics?' said Cox.

'Enough,' said Anwen. She glanced at Delphine, who made a show of peering into her drink doubtfully. 'Oh, very well. Mr Cox, swap cups with her.'

'As you wish. In the interests of diplomacy.' He held his cup out for Delphine to take. Trying to hide her shaking hand, Delphine accepted it and gave him hers.

'Now,' said Anwen, 'this is nectar. Our national drink.' She raised her cup. 'To new alliances.'

'And the death of old ones,' said Cox.

Delphine drank. Nectar coated her tongue. She felt it filling the gaps between her teeth and cheeks, thick and cool and intensely bitter. It tasted like engine oil. Her jaw clenched. She swallowed.

When she opened her eyes, Anwen was wiping her lips with the back of her sleeve. Mr Cox dabbed at the corner of his mouth with a fresh handkerchief.

'I know you must think badly of me,' said Anwen. 'I did not want this violence. Ivan Propp kidnapped my daughter. She's just a baby. So you see, I had to act.'

'Why does everyone keep calling her that? Baby. Girl. "The child." She's an old lady.'

Anwen laughed and touched two fingers to her mouth. Her smile melted into a look of astonishment.

'You really don't know, do you? All this time and no one explained to you how it works.'

Delphine smeared a palm across her cheeks. The nectar had left a slimy film that she could not wipe away.

'Delphine, I want you to join me.'

Delphine's hand halted in its passage across her mouth.

'It's not without precedent. When I first met Mr Loosley he tried to rob me,' said Anwen, setting her cup down on the edge of the pool. 'He had a, uh . . . '

'A certain *contempt* for death,' said Cox.

'Exactly. He was brave. I could've had him tortured and executed. Instead, I recruited him.' She smiled at Delphine – a hard smile, full of threat. 'I'm not intimidated by strength. If we punish rebellion and kill our most powerful, what are we left with?'

'An island of sheep,' said Cox.

'I no longer feel the weight of Mr Loosley. He may be unconscious, he may be dead. Either way, he has failed me.' Anwen stood. 'Of course, you are far too young to cross the channel as a human. I shall have to anoint you here.'

She reached up and peeled back her stiff high collar, exposing a fist-sized tumour.

'This is another reason why living unmasked after the fire would have been . . . problematic.' The tumour flexed as she spoke. 'You will live eternally. You will hear my thoughts. You will feel my pain as if it were your own.'

'Together,' said Mr Cox, 'we will unite continents: Mr Cox as the Tongue of God, you as Her Fist.' He spread his arms. 'This – *announces her Ladyship stirringly* – is your final test. Will you serve House Dellapeste, and bring civilisation to the worlds?'

Delphine took a step back. 'What if I say no?'

'Then you may go,' said Anwen. 'I make you the same offer I made Loosley. If you join me out of fear, your choice means nothing.

Walk out, if that is your will.' She swung a palm towards the stairs. 'But know this. I will not fail in my quest to rescue this once great nation from the hands of scoundrels.'

'Great Britain?' said Mr Cox. 'Not any more – *her Ladyship exclaims ruefully* – my agents have brought me the papers. Soldiers begging on the streets. Spies in every hamlet.' His voice grew full and lusty. 'Honest farmers robbed by bailiffs. Knighthoods sold to the highest bidder. Politicians frittering away the Empire. Landless financiers fomenting war to line their pockets. Bolsheviks,' he spat the word, 'plotting high treason.'

'In Avalonia we have something better,' said Anwen.

'Something pure,' said Cox.

'What are you going to do?' said Delphine.

'What else? I will set Britain free.'

'But you said Avalonia had to be kept secret! You said it's your most sacred law.'

'*Was* our most sacred law,' said Anwen. 'And its purpose is to protect us. It is no longer sufficient. War is coming. We must move first.'

Delphine straightened her chin, hoping to disguise the tremble in her jaw. 'The army will stop you. We have the greatest army in the world.'

Anwen and Cox shared a special, confidential look.

'Many – such as yourself – will see the wisdom in following me,' said Anwen. 'For those that remain . . . I have a weapon that will prove their equal.'

'Avalonia is one of many countries beyond the threshold. It is a land of great opportunity, but also great danger,' said Cox. 'If Britain does not make itself strong, there are . . . factions far less interested in justice than us.'

'A good heart is useless without power,' said Anwen. 'If you cannot protect those who deserve your protection, your love is no better to them than callous disregard.'

Delphine nodded slowly. Her mouth was dry. The nectar had left a metallic aftertaste.

'May I have a moment to think?' she said.

'Please.' Anwen popped her collar back up over the growth on her neck. 'You may consider my offer for as long as you wish.'

'Ah.' Cox held up an index finger. Delphine watched as he walked across the chamber, kneeling at the corpse of the harka to retrieve the sawn-off shotgun. He walked back to the pool and tossed the gun into the churning depths. 'Just in case you haven't learned your lesson. Not that I fear pain, you understand . . . but I should like to return to Avalonia with at least some of my garments intact.' He flicked at the hole in his waistcoat, smiling sardonically.

'You forgot one,' said Anwen.

Cox picked up the Mauser from the foot of the statue.

'Quite so.' He pulled back the bolt and checked the magazine. By Delphine's reckoning there was one round left. 'Hmm. I consider this rather handsome. I may, ah . . . retain it while the young lady remains in our custody.'

Delphine began pacing the room, her hands clasped behind her back. She scanned the floor for anything useful, preferably a box of matches. She had left her only box in the slip pocket of her bando-lier. She noted the length of safety fuse running away from the charges. It coiled across the stone floor. How many seconds per foot had Mr Garforth said it burned at – twenty? He wouldn't have left himself less than three minutes' grace – enough time for an old man to hobble back up the steps and clear of the blast.

Was it possible Cox and Anwen hadn't noticed the charges? Or did they not realise what they were?

Delphine paced. She could walk away. Anwen had said she could just walk away. Perhaps they were lying, perhaps they would shoot her in the back, but then, they had honoured their agreement with Miss DeGroot, hadn't they?

What about their plans to conquer Britain? A whole army waiting on the other side of the channel, and some terrible weapon. If she walked away now, if she didn't try to stop them, how many people would die?

Delphine twisted the hem of her cardigan round her fingers and tried to keep her expression neutral. She could leave and never look back and she and Mother and Daddy could escape to America.

Perhaps Anwen was bluffing, anyway. Perhaps she didn't really have the troops to mount an invasion. What could she possibly have that would stand a chance against machine guns and tanks and planes and hundreds of thousands of British soldiers?

Of course, there was another option.

What if Delphine joined her? Immortality. A journey to another world. Delphine felt a sick pain in her belly. She didn't want to leave England. She didn't want to leave her parents.

Maybe, if she cooperated, she could convince them to call off their attack. Maybe she could make them choose peace.

Except it was too late for that. She was already committed.

'Stop that.'

Delphine froze.

'Endlessness?' said Cox.

'Stop tapping your foot.'

Cox glanced down at his boot. 'I beg your pardon. I was not aware I – '

'Yes, yes. Shh. Let the girl think.' She flashed a faint smile at Delphine.

Delphine glanced at Cox. He had two fingers hooked into the collar of his shirt and was grinding his teeth. Sweat painted his neck.

She had to make a decision. She had to come up with a plan. In a couple of minutes, it would be too late.

But she was sick of having to decide things. She was sick of the responsibility. She shouldn't have to be strong. She ought to have people looking after her.

A noise from the passageway.

'Who goes there?' Cox squawked the challenge. 'Show yourself! Damn you, I'll, uh, uh . . . ' He wagged the pistol towards the noise.

'Mr Cox, control yourself!' Anwen rose and stomped the rock. 'You're skittish as a maiden aunt. What on earth's got into you?'

Out of the gloom of the tunnel trudged four vesperi. One was supporting its comrade, whose snapped wing dragged along the ground. The creature's arm was crudely splinted with a branch and strips of cloth. Its nose-leaf was clogged with clotted blood. The front two vesperi glanced from Delphine, to Cox, to Anwen. On seeing their leader, unmasked, they dropped to their knees, shielding their eyes.

'How dare you enter unannounced?' Cox's rage snapped off the walls of the cavern. 'How dare you lay your worthless eyes on – '

'Rutherford!' Anwen dealt him a backhanded slap across the face. Cox reeled, blinked, looked at her. 'I will not tell you a third time.'

Mr Cox was shivering, chewing at the air. He closed his eyes, nodded.

'Y-yes, Endlessness.'

Anwen turned to the vesperi. 'Please, girls.' She swept a hand towards the pool. 'Go. Be comforted. And thank you for your service.'

Their brown eyes fixed on the floor, the four creatures filed up to the edge of the channel. Delphine watched as they lowered their injured comrade into the liquid. The beast laid its head back, sinking with a dry rasp. The other three climbed in one at a time, closing their eyes as the thick black water oozed into the hollows of their ears, closed over the thistledown that covered their scalps.

Anwen shook her head. 'They have lost greatly today. See how they adore me, Delphine. I am the only family these poor children have ever known.'

'They're not children.'

'Oh?' Anwen looked at Delphine pityingly. 'A vesperi can't fly after her fourteenth year. She grows too big. You saw Mr Loosley.'

'But . . . but . . . '

'Oh, so *now* you feel regret? Did you think just because they looked different to you, they were monsters?'

'No, I . . . '

'So you see it's all very well to call *me* a beast, Delphine. I only wanted my daughter back. You and your associates have killed dozens of children.'

'No!' Delphine felt the familiar pull of the stammer, fattening her tongue. 'Wuh . . . wuh . . . ' She took a breath. 'We were duh . . . ' Another breath. 'We were defending ourselves.'

'As you should have.' Anwen pressed both hands to her breastbone. 'As was I. Don't you see, child? We're the same, you and I. We hold the same things dear. The world will call you wicked for what you've done, but *I understand*. Armchair moralists never have to face the consequences of their actions, of their inaction. The country we love will perish without our help.'

Anwen shook her head. 'Fallen cherub, to be weak is miserable.'

She moved quickly towards Delphine, wrenching down the collar of her heavy overcoat. 'Enough waiting. Join me.'

'Eh-Eh-Endlessness . . . '

Anwen rounded on Cox. 'What did I just tell you?'

'Eh-Endlessness . . . please . . . '

Cox jerked his head back, grimacing. The Mauser twitched in his grip.

Footsteps approached through the tunnel.

'More stragglers,' said Anwen, cupping the swollen sac of grubs on her neck. Delphine turned to look, her heart thundering. She had to act now. This was her last chance.

Out of the darkness stepped a lean man with silvery hair, stripped to the waist.

'Who are you?' said Anwen.

Daddy swayed, the air around him buckling.

'Oh my God,' said Anwen. Her hand dropped to her side. 'He's one of us.'

CHAPTER 44

WHILE MEN SLEEP

Daddy took a step forward. His bare foot hit a puddle and the water frothed, evaporating. Steam rose from the surrounding rock, droplets forming on his chest hair. His eyes were pink.

'He's been stung,' said Anwen. 'He's a peer. But I . . . I don't . . . '

'A pr-pretender!' said Cox. 'I'll . . . k-kill you!' He dropped the pistol and held his arm straight, palm up. 'D-d-damnation!' He opened his mouth in a snarl then apparently found himself unable to close it. He glanced from his shaking arm to Anwen and began emitting a low whine.

'What's wrong?' said Anwen.

Daddy took another lurching step. Water hissed and vanished.

'Daddy!' said Delphine.

He blinked, swung his head blindly.

Anwen was staring at Mr Cox. 'Rutherford? Speak, damn you. Oh God, you really *did* poison her drink, didn't you?'

Cox arched his back and cawed. His teeth clacked shut. Sweat beaded along his jawline.

'He didn't,' said Delphine. 'I did.'

She let the bottle of rat poison she had found in Mr Garforth's back room roll from her sleeve, into her palm. It was empty.

She flung it at Anwen's face. Anwen threw her arms up. Delphine ran at Cox.

He saw her coming and pivoted with his whole torso, trying to slap her with his rigid arm. She ducked, driving her shoulder into his ribs. She hit him hard. Cox twisted, tripping over his feet. As he fell, he clipped his head on a harka statue.

Delphine leapt on him. He writhed and kicked under her, hands stiffening into claws. She thrust her fingers into his waistcoat's fob pocket, hunting for the matchbook. The pocket was empty. She reached for the other one. Cox gargled. He was weeping. The silk was hot and smooth beneath her fingertips. Her nails found the ridge of the matchbook then strong hands gripped her shoulders and she was surging upwards.

'Get *off* him!' Anwen rattled Delphine back and forth. Delphine kicked. She felt her foot connect with Anwen's stomach. Below, Cox grunted. Anwen turned and hurled Delphine. Cold air rushed over Delphine's ears then a flash of white –

A great carpet of heat prickled her flesh and pressed like a weight. She came round on her back. A droplet of water fell from the ceiling and struck her – *tap* – in the centre of the forehead.

It was warm.

'Rutherford?' The voice made her sit up. In guttering lamplight, Anwen Stokeham stood over the body of Mr Cox. He lay at the base of the stern harka statue, legs splayed clownishly, one arm twisted over his face. 'Rutherford?' Anwen put out a hand, but it froze, as if encountering glass. She clutched her temple. 'Rutherford? I can't hear you! Rutherford!' She was shouting. Her blue eyes were fixed on a patch of floor. 'Rutherford. Rutherford. Rutherford.'

Another almighty gasp of heat broke against Delphine. Shielding her eyes, she turned towards it.

Daddy's pale body flickered in the heatwarp.

With each crackling step, water vaporised. Steam condensed on the ceiling. Droplets fell and exploded *pfff ahhhhh pfff* on his head and shoulders. Rills of white vapour coiled and shifted around the contours of his body. Flame broke out near his collarbone; flesh blistered, cauterising; the flame extinguished. He swung his head, grinding his teeth.

'Daddy!'

She tried to get up. A stabbing pain lanced behind her right kneecap. Her skull throbbed.

Anwen was down on one knee, clutching at Mr Cox's lapels. Water dripped onto her yellow-white hair.

'Rutherford, please. Rutherford. Don't leave me.'

She pressed her face into the breast of his jacket. His limp body shook as she held him.

'Daddy? It's Delphine.'

Daddy had the blind stare of a sleepwalker. The jacket of the dead skinwing at his feet bloomed into flame. He inhaled and the air round him billowed.

'We were going to walk the universe,' said Anwen. She lifted her head; her face was streaked with tears.

Her eyes found Delphine. 'You.'

'Daddy!' She took a step towards him but the heat forced her back, stinging exposed skin. 'Daddy, you have to go back!'

Anwen picked up the pistol. She aimed it at Delphine's head.

Her index finger slid from the trigger guard. She rotated the broomhandle grip till the muzzle pointed back at her. She held the gun out.

'Kill me.'

Delphine did not move. Anwen marched at her.

'Kill me!'

Delphine backed away.

'Arthur?' Daddy spun to face her, ruddy-eyed, groping at braids of vapour. Fires were breaking out all over his body. 'Arthur, where are you?'

'Here! I'm here!'

Delphine's shoulder blades bumped into the moist rock of the chamber wall.

'Do it!' Anwen thrust the pistol at her. 'Do it, you bloody coward!' She grabbed Delphine's wrist and tried to force the Mauser into her hand. The ivory clasp had fallen from Anwen's hair; wild strands raked her face. Sweat streamed down her. Her breath reeked of petrol. 'Finish what you started!'

'Daddy! Help me!'

'Arthur!' Daddy let out a frothing howl. Black smoke streamed from his throat. He slapped at flames rising from a wound in his gut. The gash sizzled shut, flesh bubbling under his fingers. His forearm kindled; flames chewed through regenerating skin. He gargled, staggered. His steel-grey hair blackened, regrew. He was burning, healing, burning.

One of Daddy's eyes began smoking. He arched his back, gasping. Delphine heard the eyeball burst with a soft *potch*.

'Daddy!' Delphine tried to run for him, but Anwen shoved her back against the wall.

'You could help him,' said Anwen, pushing her face close to Delphine's. 'You could take away his suffering.'

Delphine saw translucent blisters swelling on Daddy's throat. Grubs waiting to hatch. His regrown eyeball popped.

'He has no handmaiden,' said Anwen. 'Without servants a peer feels all the pain of the honours himself. Agony without end.'

'Daddy! I'm here!'

'Arthur!' In his blindness, he groped for her, raw pink arms trailing steam.

'It's your daughter! It's Delphy!' Even at this distance, the heat was incredible. It stung her face, making her squint.

Daddy lowered his arms. Charred flesh on his neck crackled sickeningly as he turned towards her.

'Delphy?'

'Daddy. You're hurt, but you're going to be all right.' She inhaled through her nostrils and smelt the coppery, bilious stink of roasting flesh.

Anwen's breaths were quick gusts against her cheek.

'You could lift his burden,' said Anwen. 'Or are you too proud?'

Delphine felt strangely calm.

'Daddy,' said Delphine. 'Stay still. Let me come to you. I will take your pain.'

Anwen stepped back.

'Stay where you are, Daddy. I'm coming to you.'

She moved towards him. The heat was like a wall.

'Stop!' Daddy held up a palm.

Delphine kept walking.

'Delphy! No!' He clenched his hands into fists and slammed them to his temples. The air whistled and flexed.

All over his body, gouts of flame extinguished. The temperature dropped.

He staggered.

She ran to him, caught him. His skin was dry and warm, but not scalding.

'It's all right,' she said. 'It's all right. I've got you.'

'I know.'

'Oh God. I thought you'd burn for ever.'

'Delphy.' He clutched the neck of her cardigan and dragged her till his lips were at her ear. 'I can feel it inside of me. I'm holding it in but it wants to come back. I can't . . . I can't stop it.'

She looked into his eyes. He looked back. He could see her. It was him.

'I will take your pain for you,' she said, her voice breaking. 'You won't hurt any more. We can be together forever.'

Daddy took a deep breath. He touched a hand to the fluid-filled growths on his throat. He smiled.

'This is my burden.'

He began to back away.

'No!' Delphine tried to run after him but an arm caught her round the neck.

'So this is your daughter?' said Anwen.

Daddy halted. 'Please, let her go.'

'Joining the perpetuum is not a gift. It is a duty.' Anwen brandished the Mauser in her right hand. Her voice shuddered with malice. 'Duty requires sacrifice. She can be your payment. You must learn what it means to live as others die. I'll take her from you as she took from me.'

Anwen stepped away and turned the gun on Delphine.

'No!' Daddy stepped forward. His heel fell on the length of black safety fuse snaking across the floor. Nothing happened, then –

An angry hiss came from under the arch of his foot. The fuse began burning in both directions, fierce orange flames with white hearts. Daddy grunted; coils of smoke twisted from his fingertips. Tendons stood out on his neck as he made a fist, *squeezing* the smoke in his hand till it extinguished.

Anwen glanced at the burning fuse. Delphine shoved her. Anwen stumbled. Delphine twisted out of her grip and ran for the fizzing fuse. She had to cut it, somehow. Daddy cried out. Delphine glanced back, saw Anwen aiming the Mauser.

There was nowhere to hide.

She closed her eyes.

A blast of flame.

CHAPTER 45

DON'T LOOK BACK

S he opened her eyes. Daddy bowled into Anwen, blazing. The heat forced Delphine back. She threw her arms up.

Seconds later, she was rising.

Daddy had her by the scruff of her vest. His other hand was planted beneath her armpit.

'I've got you.'

She dropped her arms. He was standing on the cusp of the channel, using the low wall as a step. As she watched, heatwarp made the stone flutter. Delphine felt herself lurch. She was sweating. Black waters boiled below. Overhead was the hole she had dropped through.

'Go,' said Daddy. 'I can't . . . hold it back . . . any longer.' Behind his words, she heard the safety fuse, hissing.

Delphine swung for the lip of the hole with her crab hook. It was too far away. Daddy strained to hoist her higher. His temperature was rising. His palm was a branding iron pressed into the small of her back. He reached up, up.

'Go,' he said.

'Don't leave me!' She tried to look back over her shoulder.

She heard Daddy inhale.

'We'll meet again.'

Delphine twisted to look. She saw Daddy, then Anwen rearing

up behind him, the shattered beakmask pressed to her raw and smouldering face.

'You . . . are not . . . *leaving*!'

Trembling yellow blisters the size of walnuts stood out on her skin. The paint on the beak bubbled and smoked. Anwen clawed at Daddy's eye. Delphine turned towards the gap in the ceiling and lunged with the crab hook; Anwen howled; Daddy slipped.

Delphine felt metal bite metal.

She pulled for all she was worth. The crab hook had snagged one of the iron hooks in the opening. Pain made little suns burst round the edges of her vision.

Daddy let go.

The heat was blinding. Delphine opened her mouth to cry out but the air was sucked from her lungs. She sank, refused to submit.

No, no.

She pulled and struggled and raked the slimy rock with her fingernails, dragged at it, fought for it. Beneath her, a groan, a splash, a roaring hiss. She heaved her knee up into the bottom of the ice house well and pulled her other leg clear of the cavern.

'Daddy!' she called, but there was no answer, and even as the word rang off stone she was turning and scrabbling up the steep wet sides of the pit, digging the crab hook into cracks, smashing out chunks of mortar. She slipped, hit her head against the brickwork, swore, kept climbing. *God please. God please. God please.*

Her toecaps scraped on brick. The black damp ice house echoed with her breaths.

As she approached the top, she was choking, weeping. She didn't have the strength. She felt her knees buckling, her fingers refusing to grip. She clutched at stone. They would not obey. She could not muster energy that was not there. She slipped backwards.

A shape solidified in the darkness.

A hand gripped the cuff of her cardigan and pulled.

Delphine kicked and flailed the final few feet, into the waiting arms of Mother.

Together, they stumbled towards the ice house doorway: a rectangle of blue night, the smell of grass.

They were in cold air, the hill rushing up. She heard the rumble a second before she hit the earth. The impact walloped the air out of her. The ground buzzed. Something struck her forehead.

She came to on her back on the wet hillside. Smoke hung in creepers. Mother lay beside her, not moving. Delphine moved her arm – a freezing pain. Her wrist was broken.

She gazed into the night sky. Flakes of ash fell in pale drifts.

How lovely, she thought as she slipped back into unconsciousness. *It's snowing.*

INTERLUDE 3

He is choking on his teeth.

As Henry wakes, they catch in his throat and he coughs and clenches and vomits and cannot breathe. The ceramic dentures slip onto his tongue like an oily fish and he spits them out. They ooze down his cheek. He is on his back. His hot breath condenses on his face. He opens his eyes. He cannot see.

Some sort of material covers his face. Is he in a sack? Is he dead? Not dead. His skull hurts.

He thinks he hears breathing. His hearing is exceptionally sharp. Best not to make any sudden movements, in case someone is watching him.

From the sound of it, he is in some kind of stone chamber. He relaxes his knees just a little.

No pain. The floor seems to tip and spin. Tears come to his eyes. Has it worked? Has it really worked?

He bites down. Full sets of upper and lower molars lock together, rooted, solid. He runs his tongue over the smooth backs of his incisors.

Everything they told him is true.

But what about Delphine? She needs him. He has to get back.

He sits up. In doing so, he realises two things.

First: he is not inside a sack, but his own clothes. As his head emerges from his waxed jacket, he sees his shirt sleeves sagging emptily, his trousers puddled on the floor.

Second: he is not alone.

The giant of tarnished brass breathes. Its steaming armoured body rises, sinks. Behind the visor-slit shine familiar blue pupils.

The first blow catches him in the forehead. He sees white.

He is lying on his stomach. A crushing pain behind his eyeball makes him gasp. He smells vomit.

Instinctively, idiotically, he tries to get up. A shadow closes over him.

He braces for the second blow.

A gauntlet sweeps beneath his sternum. Plated fingers dig into his ribs. They lift.

He slams down over an armoured shoulder, spine-first. He is hanging upside-down, the gauntlet pinning him in place. The air is warm against his hairless legs as the giant turns.

He sees the cavern inverted. He sees Stokeham's valet slumped against the wall, boots pointed inward, one eye open, the other a stoved-in crater. He smells the hops-and-petrol stink of the threshold. He hears the distant slap of gunfire.

As the giant begins to carry him away, Henry realises, with absolute certainty, he will never see home again. The cavern sways, shrinks. Vanishes.

This is the second blow.

EPILOGUE

December 1935

Delphine woke screaming from a dream of teeth and guts and eyes.

She sat up. The bedroom was black. A mauve wedge of moonlight picked out the brass handles of her wardrobe, the varnished shell of her carved tortoise.

It always took her a moment to remember where she was. Her old room. The Pastures. Home.

She swung her legs out of bed, her heart racing. She tucked her feet into her slippers, padded over to the wardrobe and took out her dressing gown. Her pyjamas clung to her sweaty skin as she fastened the two halves of the belt in a Flemish bend. It took her a couple of attempts. By the time the knot was secure, her breathing had returned to something near normal.

Delphine walked to the window. The world was brilliant with frost. She gazed, stunned by fields of flat deep white. Down in the garden, encircled by what looked like twelve large round stones, shone a single candle.

She went downstairs, closing her eyes, feeling the cool bannister beneath her palm. She smelt pipesmoke. It grew stronger as she entered the hall. She opened the door to the sitting room. Stockings hung around a rippling fire – fifteen in all, the longest on either end, a dozen little ones between. In the corner by the window stood a

Christmas tree. Delphine left the door ajar and dropped into an armchair.

'I was hungry,' she said.

Professor Carmichael looked at her over a hardback the same deep russet as his sweater. His pipe dipped.

'I had some reading to do.'

Delphine nodded. Some nights, she was the first to wake up. She had got good at building fires. She rose from the armchair and took a log from the big wicker basket. As she knelt in the hearth, a shriek came from upstairs. She balanced the log on top of the others and blew. The heat made her cheeks glow.

She sat in the armchair and watched firelight play across the curtains. Footsteps rattled down the stairs. The door creaked open. Delphine and the Professor looked up.

'Thought I'd make a start on the stuffing,' said Mother.

The Professor tapped the cover of his hardback. 'Reading.'

'Hungry,' said Delphine.

Mother smiled wanly. She had dark purple smudges beneath her eyes. From the kitchen came the clatter of the catflap.

'Here come the apostles,' said the Professor. Mother stood in the doorway, looking out into the corridor.

The first entered clutching the stub of a candle in a jam jar. The flame's reflection wavered in the pearlescent globes of his eyes. The others followed in solemn procession. Delphine still found it hard to tell them apart. At Mother's prompting, they had each chosen a name: Immanuel, Timothy, Martha, Abel, Ezra, Gabriel, Naomi, Matthew, Thomas, Isaiah, Joel, Esther. 'Little Gentlemen' no longer felt appropriate, especially now two of their number (Naomi and Martha) were pregnant. Professor Carmichael had proposed they be known as the Keepers.*

The candle-bearer – she thought perhaps Ezra – walked up to

---

* The Professor was particularly proud of this bit of etymology: 'From "Kheper" or "Khepri", the scarab-headed God of Ancient Egypt, d'you see? But they're the keepers of the Thresholds. And they worked for Henry as under-keepers. Do you follow?' Delphine had nodded, and the Professor had closed his eyes, basking in the satisfaction of a well-done sum.

the hearth and set the jar down before the fire. He retreated, then turned to face his companions. The group bowed to Mother, the Professor and Delphine in turn.

'Well,' said Mother, clapping, 'since we're all here, shall we have the Christmas?'

'And it came to pass, as the angels were gone away from them into heaven, the shepherds said one to another, Let us now go even unto Bethlehem, and see this thing which is come to pass, which the Lord hath made known unto us.'

Wine-red armour gleamed in the firelight as Professor Carmichael read in a steady, droning voice from the book of Luke. Keepers sat round dishes of warm sugar water, three to a dish, dabbling their proboscises as they listened. Mother lay back on the long settee, sipping at a cup of cocoa and occasionally massaging her shoulder. It had set badly and Delphine knew that the rheumatism was worse than she let on.

Delphine drifted in and out of awareness. She breathed in the scent of woodsmoke and pine needles. In her doze she was running through the crowded streets of Bethlehem, hunting for an inn. She pushed into an alleyway. He was there. Backed against a wall. His eyes –

She woke with a gasp. She was in the living room. The Professor continued to read. The fire crackled pleasantly.

Later, they opened presents. The Professor gave Mother an electric vacuum cleaner.

'It beats as it sweeps as it cleans!' he said.

Mother regarded the contraption with bemused tolerance. 'Yes.'

Esther cracked a monkey nut in her mandibles and tossed it to the Professor. Mother showed everyone how to skin a tangerine so it all came off in one long spiral. Delphine and the Keepers tried to copy her and soon the sitting room was perky with spritzing citrus. Mother and the Professor had a glass of sherry each and Delphine showed the Keepers how to play Pelmanism with her new pack of picture cards. Next, she taught Martha and Thomas how to play Snap. Since they couldn't shout 'snap' – or not, at least, in a manner that she, as official adjudicator, could apprehend consistently – she fetched them a bell each from the tree, which they had to ring if they saw a pair. After a slow start, the game soon attracted a rapt audience. Martha and Thomas took it extremely seriously, crouching like sprinters as they laid down Dog, Plum Cake, Soldier.

Professor Carmichael sat at the piano and everyone gathered round for 'Once In Royal David's City' and 'Away In A Manger' and 'Silent Night'. The Keepers did not sing, simply lowering their smooth crimson heads. What the Professor lacked in precision he made up for in gusto, flourishing his big hands between chords, closing his eyes as he romped into the chorus. When he was done, he let out a big sigh and sat back on the piano stool.

'Why don't you play us one, Delphine?' said Mother.

'Mo*ther*.'

'Oh, go on. It'll be good practice.'

Delphine rolled her eyes, but Professor Carmichael made way for her. The velveteen cushion was still hot from his backside as she sat and flipped through the sheet music.

She played 'O Tannenbaum', and this time, nobody sang. At first, she felt a little awkward, as if everyone was humouring her, but as she went on her playing grew less stilted; she let phrases flow with her breathing; she even began to mimic the Professor's hearty pedalling and attack. When she had finished, she closed the lid and swivelled to face her audience, biting her lip.

The Professor was dabbing at his eyes with his handkerchief. Mother had her head cocked to one side. Her smile was wide. Her cheeks gleamed.

'Perfect.'

'It's lovely,' said Mother, holding up a loose-weave woollen scarf in regal purple. 'How thoughtful of you. Thank you, Algernon. You really are a man of hidden talents.'

Professor Carmichael raised his pipe in acknowledgement. In all the turmoil that had followed the razing of Alderberen Hall, the biggest shock had been discovering the Professor's knitting habit. When Delphine first walked in to see needles in those apelike hands, clattering out a tea cosy as he listened to the news, she felt like she had interrupted him on the lavatory. Now, he gave lessons to the Keepers, who were naturals. He had tried teaching Delphine, but in his words: 'Knitting is the Way of the Farmer, Miss Venner. Yours, I'm afraid, is the Way of the Warrior.'

Delphine handed her Mother a crisp brown paper parcel. She watched anxiously as Mother began to unwrap it, cutting along the seam with a pair of scissors so the paper could be folded and reused. Since they no longer had domestics,[*] Mother had adopted waste-not, want-not as a holy regimen.

'It's probably stupid,' said Delphine. 'I can get you something else.'

'Don't be silly,' said Mother, 'I'm sure it will . . . oh.'

Mother let the paper fall away. In her hands were three leather-bound volumes with gold-leaf embossed spines: *Civilisation And Its Discontents*, *Beyond The Pleasure Principle*, and *Introduction To Psychoanalysis*, all by an 'S Freud'.

'I'm sorry,' said Delphine.

Mother turned the books over and over in her hands. 'Why did you get me these?'

'I don't know.' Delphine picked at a loose thread on the hem of her dressing gown. 'I haven't read them, I just heard . . . ' She glanced up. 'Sometimes people get lost. I thought you could help guide them home.'

Something strange happened to Mother's eyes. She looked at the books for a very long time. At last, she nodded.

'I shall read these.' She looked at her daughter. 'Thank you.'

Delphine scratched her head and looked away.

'Here.' The Professor thrust a parcel into her lap.

'Oh,' said Delphine. She tore it open in two strokes.

The book was plain, with no title. The cover was a dismal

---

[*] When Mother had announced they would do without servants, Delphine had said, 'Like Bolsheviks?'
Mother had given a strained smile. 'I don't think Bolsheviks buy their companion sets from Fortnum's.'

grey-brown. There was a hole in the middle, the width of a drillbit.

The book slipped from her fingers and hit the floor with a *whap* that made Immanuel lose at spillikins. Delphine looked up at the Professor.

'What is this? Where did you get it?'

Professor Carmichael peered over his reading spectacles. 'You know what it is. Patience dropped it after we came out the scullery. I thought it might be important and stuck it up my jumper. Turns out it was bloody important. Saved my bacon.'

Delphine picked up the book and let it fall open. Whole sections were stuck together; corrugated red poppies bloomed from the puncture wound at the centre of every page.

She slammed it shut.

'I don't want this.' She turned to Mother. 'I don't want this.'

The Professor and Mother exchanged a glance.

'It's not for reading now,' said Mother. 'Not today. But someday.'

'Even if we can't tell other people what we saw,' said the Professor, 'it's no use lying to ourselves. What you heard Mr Propp say was right, you know. War is coming.'

'I don't care. I don't want to think about it.'

'But you *do* think about it,' said Mother. 'We all do.'

'Why don't we go straight to the Prime Minister, then? Why don't you take Matthew and Martha and Joel and Gabriel and all the others and say: "Look, Mr Baldwin – now will you take us seriously?"'

The Professor regarded her gravely.

'Because they asked us not to. Because they deserve to live their lives in peace. Because we promised.'

Delphine hung her head. 'I just want it all to go away.'

Mother made a noise out the side of her mouth.

'Demons love appeasers.'

'Look,' said the Professor, 'I don't know if that book will be much help. It's a little, ah . . . soiled. But we've got excellent research assistants.' He gestured at the Keepers. 'And I found the late Mr Kung's research notes tucked into the back pages. We can't very well just ignore it, now can we?'

Delphine rested her chin in the soft nook beneath her shoulder. Every undistracted moment, she thought about Daddy and Mr Garforth. Were they still alive, somewhere? Would she ever find them? And what of Propp?

What of Anwen?

Delphine set the book down on the arm of the chair.

'Fine. But not today.'

'Not today.' Mother walked to the door. 'Now – who's going to help me with the turkey?'

The floorboards rippled with footsteps.

Delphine entered the garage through a sidedoor from the main house. It was freezing. She began dancing furiously. From the hutch in the corner came shuffling.

'Brrr! Merry Christmas, boys! You didn't think I'd forget you, did you?'

Maxim and Lewis burst from their newspaper nests and grappled at the bars with white-pink forepaws. She flipped the door catch and let them run up her arms. They stank. She dangled a blob of raw turkey giblets and Lewis champed it out of the air. She fed some more to Maxim and the two ferrets wriggled and revelled and lapped at her greasy fingers.

She gazed into their bright black eyes. She felt a sudden terror that she might lose control and hurt them.

She put the ferrets back in their cage. Her tears fell and darkened the cement floor.

She sobbed and sobbed. Lewis and Maxim watched her cry. They were beautiful, and so sickeningly fragile.

She knew the solution to Mr Garforth's riddle. Of course she did. She had known it all along.

The answer was humanity.

ACKNOWLEDGEMENTS

Firstly, big thanks to my beta readers, Steven Rayner, Andy Bennett and Robin Mueller, who painstakingly read through early, not very good versions of the novel and gave solid advice. Thank you to Molly Naylor, Chelsey Flood and Iain Ross, who offered feedback on early extracts. Thank you to Laura Dockrill, who discussed ideas with me and helped me build up the courage to start writing. Thanks also to Luke Kennard, who generously allowed me to blather at him for an hour over the phone about plot anxieties with almost no context. It really did help.

Particular thanks to Nathan Filer and Joe Dunthorne, for their kind words and support throughout the book's journey.

I'm indebted to Chris Gribble and the brilliant team at Writers Centre Norwich for their ongoing support. From initial inspiration in Australia, to the fiction workshop with Henry Sutton where I found my direction, to the final work of shaping and editing, they have provided crucial help through the whole creative process. Thank you also to the Arts Council, whose support gave me that all-important crack at a focused period of writing.

Heartfelt thanks to my agent Sophie Lambert, whose boundless enthusiasm, articulate and honest feedback, intimidating work ethic and professional acumen have been a constant inspiration.

I'm very grateful to my brilliant editor Jo Dingley, who believed the story could be better, and helped me make it so. The best bits in the book are there because of her.

Thank you to the tireless team at Canongate for the huge amounts of energy they have channelled into the book, and to Peter Adlington for designing such a badass cover.

The love and reassurance of my parents has kept me going through some difficult years, as has the continued tolerance of the rest of my family, Nan, Ben and Megan Clare. Sincere thanks to them. This book is dedicated to my grandmother, Omi, who was tough and kind.

Finally, thank you to my incredible wife, Lisa Horton, who puts up with a husband only half in this world, listens with patient encouragement to interminable monologues on obscure historical curiosities, and has, in the years since I met her, quietly made my life miraculous.